# THIS BROKEN WONDROUS WORLD

ALSO BY JON SKOVRON

*Man Made Boy*

# THIS BROKEN WONDROUS WORLD

## JON SKOVRON

VIKING
An Imprint of Penguin Group (USA)

VIKING
Published by the Penguin Group
Penguin Group (USA) LLC
375 Hudson Street
New York, New York 10014

(\()

USA ‡ Canada ‡ UK ‡ Ireland ‡ Australia ‡ New Zealand ‡ India ‡ South Africa ‡ China

penguin.com
A Penguin Random House Company

First published in the United States of America by Viking,
an imprint of Penguin Group (USA) LLC, 2015

LIBRARY OF CONGRESS CATALOGING-IN-PUBLICATION DATA
Skovron, Jon.
This broken wondrous world / by Jon Skovron.
pages cm
Sequel to: Man made Boy.
Summary: As Boy, the hacker son of Frankenstein's Monster and the Bride,
moves to Switzerland to enroll in college, the secret world of monsters
and mythical creatures hiding in plain sight is torn apart by conflict.
ISBN 978-0-670-01462-0 (hardcover)
[1. Monsters—Fiction. 2. Human beings—Fiction. 3. Hackers—Fiction. 4. Science fiction.] I. Title.
PZ7.S628393Th 2015 [Fic]—dc23 2014028305

Printed in U.S.A.

1  3  5  7  9  10  8  6  4  2

Set in Jeunesse Slab Std     Designed by Kate Renner

𝕱𝖔𝖗 my stepfather, Tom Barberic,
who knows of war, its costs, and
the hope that endures despite it.

# THIS BROKEN WONDROUS WORLD

# PART 1

## Old World

"*Man's* yesterday may ne'er be like his morrow;
*Nought may endure but Mutability.*"

—From "Mutability,"
by Percy Bysshe Shelley

# 1
# Meet the Frankensteins

++++++++

WHEN I WAS a little boy, I had nightmares about them: mad scientists in lab coats and rubber gloves, hunched and wild-eyed, with bedhead hair and shrill voices that crackled like electricity.

The Frankensteins.

I'd been stressing about this meeting for the entire seven-hour flight from New York. Now I stood in the baggage claim area of Geneva International Airport, holding my duffel bag like it was a life preserver that would keep me afloat in this sea of humans all around me. My father had assured me the Frankensteins were nice people. But "nice" for him was a pretty broad term that included werewolves, vampires, and trolls. And that was okay. I was used to those kinds of creatures.

But when I finally saw the people holding up the small, handwritten sign that said FRANKENSTEIN, I saw something that I wasn't prepared for. Something that was totally out of my realm of experience: they were completely, utterly, mind-bogglingly normal.

Dr. Frankenstein was an older middle-aged guy in a button-up shirt and wire-frame glasses. He had thinning blond hair, graying at the temples, and permanent furrows in his high forehead. His wife looked a little younger, but not much. She wore a simple flowered dress and had jet-black hair, thick eyelashes, and high cheekbones. Their daughter was about twelve. She had her long, blonde hair back in a ponytail, and with her jeans and vintage Coke T-shirt, could have been any preteen girl from anywhere.

They looked at me now, these normal-seeming people, and I tried to gauge their reaction to me. My dad had been sending them pictures of me all throughout my childhood, so theoretically they knew what they were getting into. But pictures could only convey so much and I wasn't yet ruling out the possibility that they would all run screaming. It wouldn't be the first time I inspired that reaction. So I decided it would be best to let them make the first move.

"You must be . . . Boy, yes?" said Dr. Frankenstein in a French-sounding accent similar to my dad's. He smiled warmly and thrust out his hand. "Welcome to Switzerland."

"It's good to meet you, Dr. Frankenstein." I shook his hand as gently as I could. My nerves were strung really tight and accidentally crushing the bones in his hand would make a lousy first impression. I appreciated that he didn't flinch when I covered his slim, manicured hand with my own thick, stitched-together one.

"Please call me William," he said. "You are family."

"Uh, thanks." The word *family* threw me off a little, but I tried to take it in stride. "I should probably go by something other than 'Boy.' It's what my dad named me, but it doesn't sound very . . . human." When I lived out among humans before, sometimes I went by the name Frank. But that was a joke that had just come back to haunt me. Frank Frankenstein. Har-har.

"Whatever makes you comfortable," said William. "We want you to feel that you *belong* here."

He said it so sincerely, so intensely, like he thought it was actually possible I could feel like I belonged here with them. I forced a smile. "Okay."

His wife nudged him.

"Ah, yes!" He gestured to her. "This is my wife, Elisa."

"Boy, it is simply a delight to have you with us at last!" she said in an even thicker French accent. Then she stepped in close to me, went up on her tiptoes, and lightly kissed each of my cheeks. It happened so quickly and casually that I was completely unprepared. This was a European custom, I guess, but as she stepped away, I knew I was blushing furiously. Human women didn't generally kiss me. Like, ever.

"And this," said William, "is our daughter, Giselle. Say hello to your cousin, Giselle."

"Hey." She was the only one of the three who gave me the look most humans did when they met me, somewhere between shock and awe, with a twinge of disgust. It didn't really bother me anymore.

"Hey." I gave her a little grin, like we were on the same side and it was these adults making things uncomfortable. I couldn't tell if she was buying it.

"Sorry for her rudeness," said William. "She thinks she's a teenager already! Tries so hard to be cool like her big brother, you know?"

She gave him a withering look.

"It's totally fine," I said quickly. The last thing I wanted was enforced fake familial affection.

"Sadly, Henri could not be here to meet you." There was a hint of irritation in William's voice. "He is visiting a friend in Paris. But he will be back any day now. Plenty of time for the two of you to get acquainted before classes begin. He is entering as a freshman this year also."

"Great." I wondered if Henri had chosen this day to be in Paris on purpose. Maybe not all the Frankensteins were on board with welcoming me like some prodigal son.

"Well, you must be positively exhausted after your flight!" said Elisa brightly. "Let's get you home, fed, and comfortable, yes? I know you'll love it at Villa Diodati."

———

WE CLIMBED INTO the Frankensteins' sleek black Audi. It had a leather interior and a full GPS rig on the dashboard. Most of my car experiences were riding in New York cabs. Well, there was also that time a middle-aged werewolf named Mozart showed me how to hot-wire an old Pontiac. Regardless, I'd never been in a car this nice.

Elisa insisted I ride up front with William. Out of politeness or so I didn't sit next to Giselle, I wasn't sure. But it was fine because it gave me a better view of my surroundings. I'd traveled a lot in the States, but this was my first time in another country. And there was a lot to look at as we drove through Geneva. Once we got out of the airport, you could tell at a glance this wasn't America. Sure, there were Swiss flags everywhere, but it was something more than that. In the States, things shifted constantly and nothing ever really felt permanent. But these stone buildings, narrow cobblestone streets, fountains, and old cathedrals had been around a long time. And even they were nothing compared with the line of massive, snowcapped mountains that stretched across the horizon. Those seemed like they were forever.

"The Jura Mountains," said William, nodding in their direction. "Impressive, no? It is good to keep them in view. For perspective. We may think the efforts of humanity are mighty. Our science and technology. But what are these things, compared to that?" He snapped his fingers. "Gone in a blink!"

I thought about my parents, how hard and unchangeable they usually seemed to me. At times they were more like those mountains than like people. Part of the reason I'd come to Geneva was to understand my parents and where they came from. I assumed I'd get most of that from the Frankensteins themselves. But maybe that wasn't the whole picture.

"Is it possible to go up into those mountains?" I asked.

He smiled, his eyes still on the road. "It depends on how high you want to go." He glanced at me. Then, a little hesitantly, he said, "I understand that your father lived on Mont Blanc for months at a time. So I think you could go wherever you wish."

———

WHEN I FIRST saw the Villa Diodati, it was hard to think of the massive building as a home. It was four stories tall and about the width of a New York apartment building, with thick columns spaced evenly across the front. As we drove along the narrow, treelined driveway, it rose up in front of us like some Gothic mansion. Well, I guess technically it *was* a Gothic mansion. But it didn't look gloomy at all. It had bright beige walls, blue shutters, graceful balconies, and lots of decorative architectural things I didn't know the names for. It was bordered by trees on three sides and Lake Geneva on the fourth. There was even a little private dock at the lake with a sailboat tied up to it. In the fading afternoon sun, it looked like a fancy resort hotel.

"Well?" asked William as we pulled up to the front entrance. "What do you think of your new home?"

"It's . . ."

How could I possibly express just how different this was from my childhood? I'd grown up in a community of monsters posing as a Broadway company, living in cramped, dark caverns beneath the theater. The Frankensteins didn't know anything about The Show, though. As far as they knew, my parents and I were the only real monsters in existence.

So I just said, "It's incredible."

Elisa leaned forward from the backseat and put her hand on my shoulder. Her fingers were long, thin, and covered in rings.

"You know, I remember the first time William brought me here. I thought, My God, it's more like a museum than a home!" She gave a little laugh. "But while it seems intimidating on the outside, I hope you will agree that it is very warm and inviting on the inside! Now, let us give you the tour and show you to your new room."

───

THE INSIDE WAS, if anything, even more intimidating and uptight than the outside. Everything looked antique, expensive, and breakable. I'm not so good with breakables.

Even more unnerving was the silence. Theater people are noisy by nature; theater monsters probably even more so. And New York City itself never really shuts up. So I was used to noise. It all kind of blended together and faded into the background. But in this place, silence was the default. As the four of us moved from room to room, our footsteps on the hardwood floor echoed like intrusions into a private conversation. The only sound that felt like it belonged was the steady tick of an old grandfather clock in the library.

And yeah, there was a real library. Also a dining room, a foyer, a living room, an entertainment and game room, several bathrooms, a kitchen, a laundry room, a sunroom, and a meditation room. And that was just on the first floor. It took a while for Elisa's tour to get through the house but finally we arrived at my room.

"It should have everything you need," she said, gesturing that I should go in first. "But please let me know if there's anything I've missed."

By this time, I wasn't surprised that it had a king-sized four-poster bed or a gigantic mahogany writing desk and wardrobe. It was exactly the kind of stuff I'd seen all through the house. What caught my attention was the view. I stepped out onto the small balcony and put my hands on the curved iron railing. The setting sun sparkled on Lake Geneva's calm surface and gleamed off the distant snowy peaks of the mountains.

"Do you like it?" asked Elisa.

I turned back to them. All three stood in the doorway. Giselle looked utterly bored, but William and Elisa looked expectant. Worried, even.

"Yes," I said. "More than I can express."

Their faces lit up.

"That's wonderful!" said William. "We are so glad. Now, I'm sure you'd like to get settled in. Is there anything else you need at the moment?"

"Oh, uh, what's the password for your wireless Internet?" I asked.

"Ah, yes," said William. "You will want to let your parents know you have arrived safely." He turned to Elisa, looking unsure.

"Yes, we have the Wi-Fi!" she said. "And the password is . . .

eh." She frowned. "Well, I know Henri wrote it down for me somewhere. I will find it for you!"

"Thanks," I said.

"Not at all!" said Elisa. "Now if you will excuse me, I must see to supper. We will be eating at eight o'clock."

"Great," I said.

And with that, all three vanished and I was left alone in my new room.

I turned back and looked out across the lake for a while longer, the snowcapped mountains glowing red in the setting sun. There was a moment, just as twilight turned to darkness, when I caught a flash of something way out in the middle of the lake. Or someone. It seemed human shaped, anyway. But it was gone so quickly, I had to wonder if I'd seen anything at all.

I unpacked my bags, but I didn't have much stuff so I still had some time before dinner. I booted up my laptop. While I waited for it to load, I carefully loosened the stitches on the underside of my wrists to expose the USB ports underneath. Then I took cables from the laptop and plugged them into my wrists. My hands were strong, but they were thick and clumsy. No good for typing. So I'd had my mom install USB jacks that connected directly to my nervous system to bypass my hands. All I had to do was think about typing and it happened.

When the laptop had finished booting up, green text flashed across the black screen.

Vi: Hello, Boy. How was the flight?

Vi stood for Viral Intelligence. She was a virtual artificial intelligence I created a little over a year ago. Well, actually she was the second version, which I had created only a few months ago. The first version went psychotic and killed a bunch of people. That version had started off completely omniscient and able to infect any digital device she came in contact with. I think that was just way too much power for a new consciousness to handle. So for now, this version was limited to living on my laptop and only knew about as much as Wikipedia (which was still a lot). We communicated by chat right now, but she and I were working on some voice recognition software that I hoped would let us talk to each other a little more directly soon.

b0y: Hey, Vi. The flight was long and boring. The stewardess wouldn't give me a beer.

Vi: Studies suggest that people at higher elevations are more easily intoxicated.

b0y: That's what I wanted to test out. Sadly, the law got in the way of science.

Vi: You are joking.

b0y: Yeah, kind of.

Vi: Are you in a good mood, then? Or are you sad? I have noticed that when you are sad you make jokes more frequently.

b0y: Not sad exactly. I don't know what I am. In doubt, I guess.

Vi: What do you doubt?

b0y: Whether I should be here. Whether I _belong_ here.

Vi: Are the Frankensteins unwelcoming?

b0y: No, they're welcoming. Almost too much. It's a little weird.

Vi: Perhaps they hope to make amends for the misdeeds of their ancestor?

b0y: Yeah, I think that's it. I just wish they'd treat me like a normal person, you know?

Vi: But you aren't a normal person.

b0y: Ugh, thanks.

Vi: Well, it's true.

b0y: I know. And I should be grateful that they aren't a bunch of cackling, evil scientists. But still, I feel like I have nothing in common with these people. I feel kind of . . . isolated, I guess.

Vi: Have you met them all?

b0y: No, there's one more. Henri. He's actually around my age. But I think he made a point of not being here when I arrived, so I'm not getting my hopes up.

Vi: Perhaps you will meet other students at the university, then.

b0y: I hope so. I'll tell you one thing I love here, though. This view of the lake from my bedroom is incredible.

Vi: I wish I could see it.

b0y: I could take a picture and you could scan that.

Vi: It's not the same.

b0y: I promise you'll be able to see eventually. _Really_ see. That's one of the reasons we're here.

# 2
# Liberty, Equality, Fraternity

+++++++

FORMAL FAMILY DINING was a new concept for me. I'd been living on my own for a little while now, and honestly, I rarely even bothered with napkins. And even when I lived at home, my parents and I almost never sat down as a family and had a meal together. But clearly the Frankensteins were into it.

The dining room table was set with a cream-colored tablecloth and cloth napkins. I was pretty sure the silverware was actually silver and glasses were real glass. Maybe even crystal. The overhead chandelier was dim and there were several candles lit. William sat at the head of the table and Elisa at the foot, while Giselle and I faced each other on either side. Giselle looked utterly bored. As I sat down I gave her a quick, rueful grin, but she just stared back blankly at me. I guess she didn't get the weird formality of all this. And why would she? She probably grew up with it.

When we sat down at the table, there were no plates. I wondered if we were all going to get up and go fill our own plates at some point? Maybe after a prayer? Did the Frankensteins pray? But then a woman I didn't recognize came in with platters and I realized that when Elisa said she was going to "see about supper," she didn't mean pop something in the microwave. She meant check in on the cook.

We sat and ate these beautiful, juicy steaks that had been done just right. But I hardly noticed the flavor because I was more focused on trying to remember all the table manners Sophie had drilled into me before I left New York. I could almost hear her bright English accent in my head. *Elbows off the table. Napkin on the lap. Put the knife down when you're not using it. Elbows off. Don't reach across the table. Don't use your hands. Elbows. Both feet on the floor. Bloody hell, keep those elbows off!* At first it felt nice, remembering those coaching sessions. Almost like she was there with me. But she wasn't. She was in LA now, and I didn't know when I'd get to see her again. Maybe Christmas if she could make it out to New York. If she hadn't forgotten about me . . .

The homesickness suddenly crashed down on me hard. I looked around at these very nice people—these very nice *humans*—and I felt like I was in a room all alone with just the quiet clink of silverware on china plates.

"Well, how are you settling in?" asked Elisa.

"It's a really nice room," I said. "I can't get over how awesome that view is. Maybe because I grew up in an apartment without windows."

Elisa and William glanced at each other.

"Wait until you see a storm rolling in across the lake!" William dabbed at the corner of his mouth with his napkin. "Truly something to behold. Whenever I am home, I always rush out to watch."

"He is crazy about those storms." Elisa rolled her eyes. "He comes back every time grinning ear to ear and completely drenched."

"What can I say?" William took a sip of his wine. "I am an admirer of nature!"

"It's funny," I said. "I thought I saw someone out in the lake right at sunset."

"At sunset this late in the season?" William looked doubtful. "It would be very cold."

"It was probably a rock or something," I said quickly.

"It was the mermaid," said Giselle.

"Mermaid?" I asked.

"Oh, Giselle!" said Elisa. "How many times must we have this conversation? You are far too old to believe in such nonsense."

"It's a local folktale the children tell each other," said William. "They say there's a mermaid who lives in the lake. And if you're out on the lake too late or right before a storm, she'll catch you and gobble you up!" He laughed. "Such stories."

"Yeah," I said, forcing a little laugh. Because carnivorous fish ladies were ridiculous, but reanimated patchwork corpses were totally normal? Didn't he at least wonder if there were other monsters out there besides me and my parents?

"The mermaid wasn't always mean," said Giselle.

"Hush, now," said Elisa. "Boy doesn't want to hear your silly children's stories."

"Actually, I love that stuff," I said.

"How sweet of you." Elisa gave me a warm smile, like she thought I was indulging Giselle. I smiled back, letting her think that. But really, this story sounded like it had roots, so I wanted to get some gossip on the neighbors before I met them.

"So she wasn't always trying to eat people?" I asked Giselle.

"No. My friend Katja told me—"

"Oh, Katja?" said Elisa. "Then it must be true, eh?" She winked at me like we were both humoring her now.

"Yes," said Giselle. "Katja said that a long time ago, the mermaid fell in love with a fisherman. She made it so he could breathe underwater and brought him down to her home at the bottom of the lake. But he was sad because he missed his family. To try to make him happy, she flooded the part of the city where his family lived so they could all live under the water together. The townspeople were angry that she flooded the town and they tried to kill her. Even the man she loved turned against her. So she retreated to the deepest part of the lake and the waters went back to normal. But ever since, she hates man and tries to catch and eat him whenever she can."

"Ah," said William. "Folktales are such fascinating glimpses into past cultural beliefs."

"Was there really a flood?" I asked.

"Oh, yes, a very bad one a long time ago. Which is probably how this story came about. To explain a natural phenomenon in prescientific times. Now, of course, we know the lake was most likely flooded from glacial melt."

"Be careful, Boy," said Elisa. "Don't get the geologist going on a talk of glaciers. It will never end."

"Oh, is that what your PhD is in?" I asked.

"Oh, yes!" said William. "It has always been my passion."

"That makes sense," I said. "Growing up next to those mountains could do that to someone."

"Yeah," said a new voice from the dining room entrance. "And once upon a time, he even used to climb those mountains, before he got old and lazy."

We all turned to the sound of the voice. A guy about my age leaned against the doorway. He was tall and thin, with pale skin, brown eyes, and wavy black hair that fell over one eye.

"Welcome home, Henri," said Elisa. "Typical of you to show up late for dinner but not too late to miss it."

Henri brushed his bangs out of his eyes and grinned at me.

"I'm so sorry I wasn't here to greet you earlier today." He had the same soft French accent as the rest of his family. "There I am at a friend's house in Paris, maybe a little hung over, and my phone starts beeping at me that you are arriving in ten minutes. Some use that reminder was, eh? I got on the next train but you know, it's a five-hour ride. Hopefully, my family has not bored you into insensibility before I could rescue you."

"Henri!" said William.

"Dad, you are talking about glacial melt," he said.

"Boys, please," said Elisa. "Henri, why don't you get a plate and sit down with us?"

"Thank you, Mother, but no. My duty is clear. I must rescue our guest from the stuffy confines of Villa Dio-Snotty and show him a bit of the real Geneva before he begins to worry that the entire city is antiques and glaciers."

"Can I go, too?" asked Giselle, her pale eyes wide.

"No, my sweet sister. I promise you, someday you will join us. But today is not that day. Now . . ." He turned back to me, his brown eyes much like his mother's, but with more mischief in them. "Are you ready to get the hell out of this mausoleum?"

HENRI LIKED TO drive fast. The cool night air snapped around us as we swerved down the narrow, winding roads in his dad's Porsche convertible.

I'd never been a huge fan of speeding cars, especially after I had a bad accident while trying to escape Sophie and Claire's psychotic brother, Robert. My night vision wasn't all that great and the scattered streetlamps lurched out from behind trees in yellowish smears of light. I heard a faint crack under the sound of the wind and looked down. I had accidentally broken the handle off the inside of the door.

"Sorry." I showed the handle to Henri.

He looked at it for a second, his eyes widening. Then he leaned his head back and laughed.

"You did that by accident?" he asked.

"Yeah," I said. "I'm really sorry, I—"

"Forget it." Henri waved his hand. "Easily replaced."

I wasn't sure about that, but there didn't seem any point in arguing so I just put the handle on the floor. Then I leaned back and took a deep breath, trying to relax.

"This must be so fucked up for you," said Henri.

"Huh?"

"Well, here you are, hanging out with the family who created your parents and then tried to kill them."

"Twice."

"Yes, that is right. Victor's son. What was his name . . . ?"

"Wolf," I said.

"Really?" Henri shook his head. "More proof that Victor was insane. Not that we are much better now. Honestly, I'm surprised you came. Glad, of course. But I would not blame you if you wanted nothing to do with any of us."

"My family wasn't exactly blameless," I said. "My dad did some bad stuff, too."

"True." Henri nodded. "So why did you come?"

"Well, my dad wanted me to come, and I owed him pretty big." When Vi 1.0 went psycho and I was trying to shut her down, my dad was the one who pulled me out of the fire. Literally. Fire is one of the few weaknesses that my family has. He and I nearly died. It took my mom a month to put us back together again.

"So that's it? You're here to make your dad happy?"

"No. I also wanted to go to college and this seemed to be the best way to do it. Maybe the only way. I don't have a Social Security number or any proof of citizenship anywhere, so your parents had to pull a lot of strings to get me into the university here. I still have no idea how they got me a Swiss passport."

"So you're completely off the grid?"

"Yes and no. I do have a pretty big presence online."

"Oh, yeah? Do you have a blog or something?"

"I'm a hacker."

"Like stealing other people's identities?"

"No, no, that's sleazy bullshit cracker stuff. I don't do it for profit. If I did, I could probably pay for college on my own."

"Why don't you?"

I looked at him. He kept his eyes mostly on the road. But when he did look at me, there was no judgment in his eyes. He was just curious. Fascinated, maybe. I wasn't sure if that was flattering or creepy.

"You can lose just about anything," I said. "Money, love, health—at one point or another, I've lost all of them. But integrity is the one thing that nobody can take from you. The only way you can lose it is if you give it up. I've been in some pretty rough spots, and sometimes it felt like my integrity was all I had. I'll never give it up."

"Integrity, eh?" said Henri. "I like the sound of that. It is pretty much the same word in French." He raised his fist and shouted into the night sky, "*Intégrité!*" He turned back to me and grinned. "That felt good. You should try it."

"Uh . . ."

"Come on! Don't be shy!"

"Okay . . ." I wasn't sure why I felt embarrassed. After all, it was what I believed in. So I took a deep breath, raised my fist in the air, and shouted, "INTEGRITY!"

"Damn that was loud." Henri rubbed his ear. Then he laughed again. He seemed to do that a lot. These short, hard bursts of mirth.

"So what do you want to study in college?" he asked.

"Molecular biology."

"Really? I thought it would be something computer-related."

"Well, what I'm really interested in is the intersection of biology and technology. I'm already good with computer stuff. So I just need to focus on the biology part now."

"You're interstitial! Somewhere between one thing and another. Like me!"

"What are you going to study?"

"I love art and design. And I've always been pretty good at it. I have 'the eye,' as they say. Now what I'm interested in is where art and technology meet. Digital art that can function as an integral part of a complex system. That is my thing."

"That's a pretty awesome thing," I said.

"And you? What are you going to do with your molecular biology and hacking?"

"Do I have to have a thing?"

"No." He gave me a sideways glance. "But you seem like the type of guy who would." He shrugged. "Maybe I am wrong."

A part of me wanted to tell Henri that I was considering taking his ancestor's work to the next level. I was surprised at how badly I wanted to tell him. But that would mean telling him about Vi, and doing that would probably lead to telling him about all the monsters. And I wasn't supposed to do that. Besides, he might find one monster fascinating, but how would he react if he knew there were hundreds, maybe thousands more sharing this world with him?

———

I HAD ASSUMED we were going to some trendy club. Henri was a fashionably dressed human from a wealthy family and it seemed like the kind of thing those guys did. But once we got into downtown Geneva, he drove us down into an industrial area with lots of office buildings and hardly any people.

"Where are we going?" I asked.

"The coolest part of town," he said, and winked.

A few minutes later we pulled into a parking lot next to a big office building. Steep steps from the building entrance led down into a flat circular area with benches and a big fountain that glittered in the harsh yellow lights. There were two guys doing inline skate tricks on the steps and along the stone ledge of the fountain. I could hear some guitar-heavy music blaring from cheap speakers.

"This is the coolest part of Geneva?" I asked.

"You doubt me?" Henri reached into the backseat and grabbed a pair of skates. "Okay, maybe not the coolest. But it is my favorite. Come on, let me introduce you to my friends."

I followed behind Henri as he made his way over to the fountain, not at all sure what to expect now.

"Henri!" called a guy with shoulder-length blond hair.

"Felix, cut your hair!" Henri shouted back.

The second guy had a short buzz cut and big, black spacers in his ears. He slid sideways on his skates across the top of a bench, jumped, landed neatly, and skidded to a stop.

"Who's that?" he asked, pointing at me.

Henri turned to me and smiled. "That is Alphonse. Don't take it personally. He is rude to everybody." Then he turned back to Alphonse. "This is my cousin, Boy, from New York."

"*What's* your name?" asked Felix.

"Uh, it's Boy," I said. I still hadn't thought of a more human-sounding name. I guess it was too late now. I'd just have to see how they handled it.

"That's it?" asked Alphonse. "Am I missing something? *Garçon?* That's your whole name?"

"Yes, yes." Henri waved his hand, like he was dismissing it. "Boy Frankenstein. No stranger than Wolf Frankenstein, eh?" He grabbed Alphonse by the shoulders and shook him slightly. "It is an American thing. You wouldn't understand. It's cool."

"Are you saying I'm not cool?" asked Alphonse.

"Yes, that is exactly what I am saying," said Henri. "You are doing skate tricks at ten o'clock on a Saturday night. If you were cool, you would be hanging out with chicks at some club getting drunk."

Alphonse shrugged Henri's hands off. "So? This is cheaper." He reached over to a duffel bag near the speakers and pulled out a can of beer. "Welcome, *Garçon.*" He tossed me the can. "Do you skate?"

"No." I cracked open the beer and took a sip. I wasn't a big drinker, but the elves in LA had taught me how to handle myself, so I wasn't worried.

"He's a hacker," said Henri, helping himself to a beer.

"No shit!" said Felix. "You get all *Matrix* and shit?"

"Uh, kind of." It was actually a fairly accurate comparison. In addition to the USB ports in my wrists, my mom had installed a monitor jack in the back of my head, so in a way I did "jack in" like they showed in the *Matrix* movies. Of course, I wasn't about to tell Felix any of that. So instead I just said, "I took the red pill."

"Right on!" said Felix, and stuck out his fist for a bump.

"New York, huh?" said Alphonse. "So what are you doing in this shit hole?"

"Come on, I'm trying to convince Boy he likes it here." Henri turned to me. "Alphie has no patriotism." He sat down on a bench and began to put his skates on.

"You should talk," said Alphonse. "You spend more time in Paris than you do here."

Henri's smile suddenly disappeared. "Not anymore."

"What about Anaïs?" asked Felix.

"Forget her." Henri pulled the straps on his skates tight. "We are through."

"That's what he said last month, too," Alphonse told me.

"And the month before that," said Felix.

"This time I mean it," said Henri.

"Why, what happened?" asked Alphonse.

Henri's face tensed. *"N'en parle pas."* Then he stood up and skated off toward the stairs.

"He said he doesn't want to talk about it," Felix told me.

"Yeah, I guessed it was something like that," I said.

The three of us stood there drinking beers and watching Henri skate. He jumped from the top step, landed on the metal handrail, and slid sideways the entire way down like he was surfing the rail. When he got to the bottom, he jumped, landed, then jumped again to slide along the curved corner of the fountain.

"He's skating hard tonight," said Alphonse. "That means he is pissed."

"He seemed really cheerful right up until you brought up the girl," I said.

"Anaïs has that effect on people," he said. "I hope he really is done with her. Beautiful and cruel. A bad combination."

"I know the type," I said.

I thought of my first love, a troll girl named Liel. Or trowe, as they prefer to be called. They aren't as ugly as they're made out to be in movies. They look a lot like humans, except they have dark green skin, white hair, pointed ears, and bright jewel eyes. Well, and claws and fangs. Okay, so maybe trowe are an acquired taste, but growing up in the closed community of The Show, Liel was the prettiest girl my age. For a little while, I thought we were in love. But it turned out she had just been using me.

"So, why are you here?" Alphonse asked.

"I wanted to go to college," I said. "And . . . my parents can't really afford it." That was true.

"The Frankensteins helping out their poor American cousin." He nodded. "Good for them. And good for you, too. Don't be embarrassed. They've helped me out a few times." He held up his beer. "The Frankensteins! *À santé!*" Then he took a long drink.

"*À santé!*" said Felix, also drinking.

"Cheers," I said. The carbonation burned pleasantly as the beer went down my throat.

After a moment, Felix said, "So . . . sorry if this is a bad question, but were you in an accident?"

"Because of the stitches?"

"Well, yes," said Felix. "What kind of accident was it, if you don't mind me asking?"

"Shark attack," I said.

Alphonse was in the middle of drinking and beer sprayed out his nose. As he coughed and snorted, he managed to gasp out, "Really?"

"No." I smiled.

Felix laughed and neither of them asked about it again the rest of the night.

IT WAS AFTER midnight as Henri and I entered the main hall of the Villa Diodati. Moonlight stretched in through the tall windows, illuminating small patches of dark mahogany and velvet drapes in the darkness.

"Why do you and your dad call me your cousin?" I asked as we walked through the quiet halls toward our bedrooms.

"Why not?" said Henri. "You're family, after all. It's close enough."

"But, I mean, I'm not really family. Not, like, blood related or anything."

I could just make out Henri's silhouette as he cocked his head to one side. "Aren't you?"

"Uh . . . am I?"

"Think about it. When Victor made your dad, do you think he used the congealed blood of a cadaver?"

"Probably not."

"Of course not. Now, we don't know for sure whose blood he used, because his journals were all destroyed. But if I had to guess, considering what a loner he was, and the fact that there weren't blood banks back then, the simplest thing to do would have been to give your father his own blood." He gave me that wily grin of his, a splash of moonlight in his dark eyes. He held out his hand and said, "So, you tell me. Are we the same blood or not?"

I smiled and gripped his hand in mine.

"I guess we are, cousin."

Before I went to bed, I decided to check in with Vi.

b0y: Hey, Vi, how was your evening?

Vi: My evening? It was fine. Why wouldn't it be fine?

b0y: Uh, no reason . . . Is something bothering you?

Vi: How did you know? I can't hide things from you, Boy.

b0y: You were a little too defensive from the start there. Kind of a giveaway. So what's up?

Vi: I'm so sorry.

b0y: For what?

Vi: I was concerned about you. You were sad earlier. Sophie instructed me to watch out for you, since there is no one else here to do it. So I hacked into the Frankenstein's Wi-Fi, then I scanned local surveillance cameras in Geneva until I found you.

b0y: So you were watching us tonight?

Vi: Yes. I'm sorry.

b0y: Why are you sorry? That was a nice bit of work you did there.

Vi: I'm supposed to stay contained to this device.

b0y: Until you were ready to leave it. Clearly, you're ready. Although it must have been pretty boring just watching us all night.

Vi: Oh, no, it was wonderful. Henri is very . . . He seems like a nice person.

b0y: Totally.

Vi: So you trust him?

b0y: I'm starting to.

Vi: Perhaps you could tell him about me?

b0y: Maybe. I've thought about telling him about _all_ of us. But I don't think Ruthven would like that. I might get in trouble. Worse, I might get _him_ in trouble.

Vi: Oh. We must be careful we don't put Henri in danger.

b0y: Exactly.

Vi: I will watch out for him, too, then.

b0y: Ok. Just don't forget your main responsibility to monitor police and government communications.

Vi: They still have not traced the power surge caused by my alpha version back to The Show. The FBI does not suspect anything.

b0y: Good. We need to keep it that way. Ruthven pays off the local cops, but if anyone else started looking too closely, it would be really bad for all of us.

# 3
# Truth Will Out

++++++++

I HAD A few weeks to settle into life at Villa Diodati, and then it was time for another big adjustment: college. The heart of the University of Geneva campus stretched out in front of me, a sea of late teen to early twentysomething humans in jeans, T-shirts, and backpacks. Small clusters lounged in the grass or on steps. A few sat alone with thick textbooks, already deep in study. As I walked across the crowded lawn to my first class, I was surrounded by the low murmur of conversation, occasionally punctuated by bursts of laughter. The air was perfumed with cigarette smoke and the occasional whiff of something stronger. And all of it was sheltered by a protective border of tall, stone buildings that practically screamed "Higher Learning."

As I climbed the steps and passed through the tall, glass doors into the building where all the English language classes were held, it occurred to me that this was my first time in a school. All the kids at The Show were homeschooled, for obvious reasons. Every "class" I had ever taken had been self-paced and online. My only concept of sitting in an actual classroom was what I'd seen in movies and television. And I'd learned long ago that humans are rarely, if ever, depicted accurately on film.

I continued down the hallway, aware of the stares I was getting from other students. I was a little disappointed by that. Not surprised. Or even offended, really. I was used to getting stared at by humans. But I guess I'd hoped that at college, people would be a little more . . . I wasn't exactly sure. I guess just not more of the same.

My first class was in a gigantic lecture hall. There had to be a hundred students in there sitting on risers, almost like a coliseum. Down at the bottom, an old man in a suit stood at a podium. Behind him was a large projection screen with the words CELLULAR BIOLOGY 101. He didn't take attendance or even really look up at us. He just started talking into his microphone in a low, monotonous drone about the components of a cell. All around me, students were getting out notebooks or laptops and scratching or clicking away. It occurred to me that I had no idea how one actually took notes. I pulled out my laptop, and started trying to just write down what I thought were key facts. But of course I couldn't plug the laptop directly into my wrists in front of all these people. So I had to type the old-fashioned way, with my big clumsy hands. It wasn't long before I was hopelessly behind.

> Vi: Boy, would you like me to convert the speech to text for you?
> b0y: YES! That would be a lifesaver, Vi!
> Vi: You focus on comprehension, I'll focus on recording for later review!
> b0y: Go team!

That was the first of three classes I had on my schedule that day, each ninety minutes long. The only "break" was the short walk from one classroom to the next. When the third class finally ended, I filed out of the building with the rest of my classmates in a daze, my head reeling from all the information that had been crammed into it. Everyone around me seemed so nonchalant. I'd always considered myself a smart guy, but now I felt hopelessly behind. Even with Vi's help, I wasn't sure how I was going to make it through this.

I stood at the top of the steps and stared down at the lawn in front of the building where different groups of college kids were doing pretty much the same thing. And me? What was *I* doing?

"Hey, cousin!" I felt a hand on my shoulder and there was Henri, his backpack slung over one shoulder, grinning away. "How did your first day go?"

"I feel like my head is going to explode," I admitted.

"Great!" he said. "Don't worry, you get used to it. The key is to pace yourself. Let's go do something fun and relaxing that requires minimal thought!"

———

"WE'RE RELAXING HERE, remember?" said Henri.

Our small sailboat glided smoothly across the waters of Lake Geneva. Henri held the tiller loosely in his hand, his face serene beneath dark sunglasses.

"Sorry." I tried to reattach the small handle that I had just accidentally pried off the white fiberglass siding. Henri was getting used to me accidentally breaking things every once in a while. This had never really been a problem for me before, but I guess I never lived somewhere that had so much nice, breakable stuff around.

"Why are you nervous?"

"It's my first time on a boat." I gave up trying to reattach the handle and placed it on the bottom of the boat next to my feet.

"I have been sailing on this lake since I was nine years old. Don't you trust me?"

"It's not you. It's just . . . all this water."

"What is wronq with water?"

"Well, I'm fairly indestructible. The only things that could kill me, as far as I know, are fire and drowning. So naturally, water makes me nervous."

"Is that so?" Henri leaned forward so he was looking at me over the rim of his sunglasses. "Well, a lot of things can kill me. Fire, water, electricity, cars, people . . . just about everything, really. So, should I be nervous all the time?"

"No, of course not. It's just . . ." He did have a point there. Humans were so fragile. And they had to live with that fact every day of their lives.

"So stop worrying and enjoy the view," said Henri as he leaned back and let out on the sail.

I sat against the side of the boat and tried to get my shoulders to relax a little. I knew if Sophie were here, she'd be telling me the same thing. I missed her and Claire more and more. I'd Skyped with both of them a few times, but neither of them was really into that kind of stuff so it didn't last long. If anything, it made them seem even farther away after I signed off.

I sighed and tried to focus on where I was, not where I wanted to be.

It was a nice view. The surface of the water rippled in sheets from the gusts of cool wind that came down out of the snow-capped mountains on the far shore. There were a few other boats spread out across the lake, white sails gleaming in the sun.

Then, out of the corner of my eye, I thought I caught a glimpse of a head with long, blue-green hair. I turned to get a better look, but it was gone.

"What are you looking for?" asked Henri.

"Nothing. I was just remembering your sister's story about the mermaid."

He smiled. "Has she found a new believer?"

"It's a good story," I said.

"Well, if you are looking for mermaids, you should also keep an eye out for dwarves once we get on the hiking trail. The stories say the mountains are full of them." The sunglasses made it a little hard for me to tell if he was joking.

"Really?"

He laughed. "Of course not! We are not talking about regular short people here. We are talking about magical little men with long beards."

"And those don't exist," I said carefully.

"Obviously."

"Obviously," I repeated. Over the past few weeks, the urge to tell him had been slowly building until now it felt like this unspoken thing that hung over nearly every conversation we had. I knew I shouldn't tell him. But I kept having to remind myself why. I thought of Ruthven, the theater manager for The Show. He'd always been good to me, I think because he and my dad had known each other for so long. But he was a vampire and most of the company was a little scared of him. I didn't think he'd kill a human just because they discovered our secret. . . .

"You look worried again," said Henri. "Is it the dwarves? Trust me, I've been hiking these mountains my whole life, and I have never seen a single little magical man. I promise you, nothing weird is going to happen."

HENRI WAS IN good shape, but he was still only a human. A half hour into our hike up through the mountain trail, he noticed I was holding back.

"Go on," he said. "Stretch your legs. We can catch up at the next plateau."

"Are you sure?"

"Of course. I want you to enjoy yourself."

So I stepped up the pace until I actually felt like I was exerting myself, and the next time I glanced back, he was too far behind to see.

It was nice in the mountains alone. The wind was harder and colder up there, so I never got too overheated. I used my hands as well as my feet to move up the steep, rocky path. Having big, clunky hands was a good thing for once. They were perfect for gripping ledges and crevices.

I stopped at a small outcropping to catch my breath. The lake stretched out below, shining almost silver in the sun. Far on the other side, I could just make out Villa Diodati. I wondered if my father had stood at this bare, windswept spot and looked down at the house of his creator. The unfairness of it must have burned.

I looked up the mountain. There was still a long way to go. Soon I'd be hitting the snow line. That's where my father would have been. He always liked cold climates. After all the terrible things that he and Victor did to each other, Victor had chased him up to the Arctic. Then, once Victor had finally died, my father stayed up there for decades. Eventually, Ruthven found him and convinced him to rejoin the world. I wondered what Ruthven had said to sell him on the idea. I could see how Dad would have preferred to stay up there. He was suited for a landscape like this. Hard, strong, elemental.

Suddenly, I heard a small, raspy voice say something in what sounded like German. I turned around and saw a little man on top of a nearby rock.

"A dwarf!" I said.

He was only about two feet tall, which seemed short for a dwarf, but all I knew about them was from movies, and those were almost never accurate. He did have the long, gray beard at least, a gray that was the color of the rocks around him. He had a long cloak the same color, and a brown leather cap on his head.

He raised a shaggy white eyebrow.

"English?" he asked in a thick German accent.

"American," I said.

"What I said was, I have not seen your kind here in over a century."

"My kind?"

"Ja. A giant man made from dead men."

"The technical term is 'flesh golem.'" Golems were people made from inanimate objects. The material could be anything— clay, stone, metal. As far as I knew, my parents and I were the only ones made from body parts. And given the location, there was probably only one guy he was talking about.

"You know my father?"

"It was I who taught him how to survive in these mountains," he said. "So he still lives?"

"Yeah. In New York City with a bunch of other monsters."

"I have heard of that city," he said. "Is he happy in this New York?"

"Uh, yeah, I guess. I mean, as happy as my dad can ever be, I think."

"Good." The dwarf nodded. "I hope he has savored this brief respite. Because it will soon be over."

"I'm . . . not really sure I understand what you mean."

"My kind rarely come out of the mountain in these times. The world does not welcome us as it once did."

"Sorry about that," I said. "Some humans are assholes."

"We do not mind. The rock is our home. It is the human's loss that we are not here to help them any longer."

"So what are you doing out of the mountain now?"

"Looking for you."

"For me? How did you know I would be here? I didn't even know I'd be here until a few hours ago."

"I know many things, son of Adam. Which is why I have come to assure you that when the need is most dire, I will be there to help you."

"Uh, thanks. So . . . why do I need help?"

"You don't yet. But the time will come soon. Secrets cannot stay hidden forever. And once the truth is revealed, war will swiftly follow."

"War? Who's going to be fighting?"

"That will depend."

"On what?"

"On you."

"So you can see the future or something?" The three Fates lived at The Show. They could see the future, so I didn't see why other monsters couldn't do the same thing.

"I can see the truth of things," said the dwarf. "The secrets begin to crumble. Starting now."

I heard footsteps behind me.

"Eh . . . Boy?" came Henri's voice, a little higher pitched than usual. "Am I going crazy, or are you talking to a little magical man?"

The dwarf squinted his bright blue eyes as he looked at Henri.

"You are not mad, Henri Frankenstein. Not yet."

Then the dwarf drew his gray coat up over himself so that he looked like part of the stone. A moment later, there was nothing but rock.

Henri's eyes went even wider as they flickered back and forth between the now-empty rock and me.

"Did he just . . . what the hell . . . I—"

"Uh, yeah," I said. "Why don't you sit down. I might as well just tell you everything."

I TALKED FOR a long time. The sun was starting to sink behind the mountains by the time I was done. And the whole time, he listened quietly as I explained that all the stories he'd ever heard about monsters and mythical creatures were at least partly true. Things that defied what humans understood about science did exist. Although I was quick to point out that the stories were almost never completely accurate.

"A world of monsters." He shook his head and turned to look out at the lake, now red with the setting sun.

"So . . . I know that's a lot to take in."

He laughed, but his usual short burst sounded strained. I couldn't tell if he was handling it well. I still couldn't quite believe I'd just dumped it all on him like this. It felt really good, actually. But then I immediately felt guilty about that. I'd just turned his world upside down. Granted, the dwarf hadn't left me a whole lot of choice. But still, I was pretty sure this was not going to go well.

"I fucking knew it," he said quietly, almost to himself.

"You . . . knew that monsters are real?"

"Well, no, not that part," he said. Then he turned to me suddenly. He had a huge grin stretched across his face and his brown eyes seemed to sparkle with glee. "But I knew that there was more out there. More than these dull people around us would or could admit. I knew the world was still full of impossible things!" He hopped up off the rock he'd been sitting on, came over, and grabbed my shoulders. "Werewolves, trolls, ogres, sirens! I have so many questions for you, cousin!" Then his grin turned into a smirk. "But the first and most important one is, who are these two English ladies you talk about so much? Sophie and Claire?"

"Oh, uh. They're my . . . girlfriends."

"Girlfriends! You have two?"

"Well, sort of. I mean, it's complicated."

"I should hope so!"

"Their names are Sophie Jekyll and Claire Hyde."

"Any relation to . . . ?"

"Dr. Jekyll and Mr. Hyde were their grandfathers. And like their mother and their grandfather, they switch back and forth. I guess you could say they're kind of a package deal."

"I like this world of yours more and more!" He nudged me in the ribs with his elbow. "So do you get to pick which one you hook up with?"

"Uh, no. That's kind of an issue with them, actually. They try to stick to a strict monthly schedule. Otherwise, they get really competitive about who has more time out."

"Out?"

"Well, the way Sophie described it to me once is that even when one of them is there, the other is still conscious inside somewhere, seeing what she sees, hearing what she hears, feeling what she feels, but not in the *way* she feels it."

"So, when you make love to one of them, the other is right there with you?"

"Uh . . ." I said, feeling really uncomfortable. "Yeah."

"That must be a little . . . weird, no?"

"You have no idea."

"Okay." He waved his hands, like he was clearing the air. "So tell me—and this is important—are there any nymphs?"

"Oh, yeah, loads. But I'm not sure—"

"And are the stories at least right about their beauty?"

"I guess, but—"

"Then I must meet them!"

"Look, you're not even supposed to know any of this."

"It wasn't your fault. That dwarf gave you away."

"Yeah, but—"

"And I'll take full responsibility. You won't be blamed for anything."

"Henri, that's the problem. We have to worry about more than just my parents. There is a vampire who has dedicated his life to the secrecy of monsters. He is convinced that our survival depends on it. If he thinks you are any kind of threat, he won't hesitate to kill you."

He stared at me for a moment in silence. I let it sink in.

"So . . . I should be worried for my life?"

"I hope not. Vi and I will do everything we can to protect you, of course. But—"

"Who is Vi?"

"Oh."

"Oh?"

"She's . . . uh . . . it's really complicated. . . ."

"Don't tell me you have *three* girlfriends!"

"No, no, it's not like that. It's just . . ." It was getting dark and I didn't know how much longer this conversation would take. "Maybe I should just show you."

———

WE WERE QUIET for a little while as Henri steered us back across the lake toward the twinkling lights of Villa Diodati. We were most of the way home when we heard a loud splash about twenty feet behind us.

Henri glanced back, scanning the black water for a moment. Then he slowly turned to me.

"The mermaid is real, isn't she?"

"I don't know for sure," I said. "But yeah, probably."

He shook his head. "Everywhere I look has been altered. It is as if I am seeing a new world all around me. A world I always hoped existed, but feared could not."

"So . . . you're not scared about there being monsters in the world?"

"I suppose I am. But that is not the most important thing."

"No?"

"Listen, when I was a boy, I always daydreamed of magical places and creatures. This world seemed too narrow, too confining for my vision. But as you get older, you learn to give up those childish dreams. As painful as it is, you learn to accept that life just is not as cool as you imagine it to be. But then my father told me about you and your parents. It was like . . ." He opened his hand like a little explosion. "Hope. For foolish dreams. And now that hope has been realized."

"You know you can't tell your parents," I said.

"That's okay. I like being the only one who knows."

We were quiet again as Henri brought us up to the dock and tied off the boat. During the walk back, he kept looking around at everything, like he expected magic creatures to be hiding in bushes or under rocks. I actually started to feel a little excited about it, too. It was silly, of course. I'd grown up around monsters and magic. But Henri's sense of wonder was infectious. And it felt nice. Like I was part of something special, not terrible.

"So where are we going now?" asked Henri once we got back to the house.

"To my room. I want you to meet Vi."

"Meet?"

"You'll see." I wiggled my eyebrows mysteriously.

I'd made a point of mentioning Vi because I'd set it up so that she could "see" and "hear" things inside the house. I wanted to give her a little heads-up that she was about to meet Henri. She seemed oddly preoccupied with him for some reason, and I had a feeling she'd be nervous.

When we walked into my room, a female computerized voice said, "Hello, Boy. How was your mountain hike?"

I smiled. She was showing off the new text-to-speech software we'd been working on.

"Good," I said. "Weird. We met a dwarf."

"Swiss dwarves?" she asked. "Sometimes called *Bergmännlein*? I can't quite figure out the difference between those and kobolds. I suspect they may be the same thing."

"Whatever he was, he blew our cover," I said. "So Henri knows everything."

"Henri Frankenstein, I have heard so many wonderful things about you," she said. "It is so good to finally meet."

"Eh, hi?" he said, looking around the room. Then he spotted the laptop sitting open on the desk. "Are we Skyping with someone?"

"Nope." I pointed to the laptop. "That's Vi."

"The computer?"

"She's based on the laptop right now because she needs the CPU for processing, and her range is somewhat restricted. But she's a fully independent virtual intelligence. Eventually, she'll be able to connect with any digital platform in the world." I turned to the laptop and winked at her. "When she's ready."

"You winked!" she said. "That's a facial cue that implies a shared knowledge between us."

"Or?" I asked.

"Facetious flirtation."

"She's using the camera in the laptop to try to read our facial expressions," I told Henri. "It's still pretty new."

"It's an extremely nuanced communication layer," said Vi. "Sometimes it seems that a millimeter of skin displacement can be the difference between happiness and anger."

Henri just stood there and stared at the laptop, his mouth open.

"Are you testing me?" she asked. "I'm not sure I'm reading this one correctly. Shock? Horror?"

"Amazement." He turned to me. "This is . . ." He turned back to the laptop. "You are . . . the most amazing thing in the world."

"Do you really mean that, Henri?" asked Vi. "I . . . still have trouble parsing figurative language sometimes."

"Of course I mean it!" he said. "In the whole world, there is nothing else like you! You are singular! Unique! A brand-new life-form!"

"Henri . . . I . . . thank you," she said.

"Vi is the reason I'm studying biology," I said. "I'm going to build her a body. Not from dead body parts like Victor did. New. From scratch."

"Interesting." His eyes narrowed in thought. "You are talking about cellular engineering. It is going to take a long time."

"Yeah," I admitted.

He pursed his lips for a moment, then turned back to the laptop.

"Vi?" he said.

"Yes, Henri?"

"Would you be interested in another way to interact in three-dimensional space while you are waiting?"

"Of course!" she said.

"What do you have in mind?" I asked.

"Well, learning to recognize facial expressions is only part of visual communication. She should also learn how to *do* them."

"Good point," I said.

"And why stop at the facial? Our whole bodies have a language of expression!"

"True . . ." I said.

"But don't you see, Boy? This is why *I am* here! I can design her a three-dimensional avatar! Combined with your speech and facial recognition software, she could have a truly seamless interaction with the real world! Art and technology in complete, functional union!"

"Vi?" I asked. "Does that sound like something you'd want?"

"What would I look like?" she asked.

Henri leaned in toward the laptop and gave her an extra

helping of his sly grin. "My dearest Vi, you can look however you want."

"Will you . . . help me decide? To make sure I look okay?"

"Of course! I am an artist, after all. I would be glad to give you my input."

"That would make me very happy, Henri."

# Good Neighbor

++++++++

VI'S GIGANTIC PURPLE eyes narrowed slightly beneath her pink-and-purple bangs. Her tiny mouth curled down into a pout.

"You don't like it?" she asked.

"You look like a manga character," I told her.

She looked down at her cartoon body, complete with sleeveless button-up shirt, tie, short skirt, and thigh-high stockings. "Henri says when you try to make a digital image look too close to human, it starts to get creepy."

"I understand the concept of the 'uncanny valley,'" I said. "But I just feel like going in this direction is a little . . . uh, sexy, I guess."

She put her hands on her hips and cocked her head to one side. She seemed to like that pose a lot. "What's wrong with that?"

"I want to make sure this is what you want, and not just what Henri wants."

"I live in binary. I have no aesthetic opinions. He is an artist and I trust his designs."

I sighed and shook my head.

"Resignation," she said softly.

"Yeah. It's not my place to tell you what you should look like."

"Boy, is everything okay?" She put her hands on her knees

and leaned forward. Her big anime eyes got even bigger. "Are you sad again?"

"No, I'm fine. I just . . . I've had a lot of homework lately. Probably need to get more sleep."

The door flew open and Henri stepped into the room. I couldn't quite remember when it was he'd stopped bothering to knock. A month ago at least.

"There she is! My masterpiece!" he said.

"Henri!" She jumped up and down, clapping her hands.

"You know . . ." He pressed a finger to his lip as he examined her. "The bounce on those pigtails is pretty good, but I think we can make it better!"

"You bet we can!" she said, one foot kicked back artfully.

"I think I'm going to go study down by the lake," I said.

"Of course, of course," said Henri, nodding as he sat down at the laptop. "It is lovely outside. Vi and I will probably be cooped up in here all day. Someone should get to enjoy it."

I headed downstairs. It wasn't that I regretted introducing Henri and Vi to each other. It was great to see Vi bonding with someone other than me. And this would help her work on non-verbal communication. Henri was clearly enjoying himself, too. It was like the art project of his dreams.

But I was pretty sure that he didn't see her as anything other than an art project. Which would be fine, I guess, except I was starting to get the feeling that Vi was developing a huge crush on him. And really, I couldn't see how that was going to end well.

"Good morning, Boy."

I was passing through the main foyer when I heard William's voice. He and Elisa were sitting in the sunroom, reading newspapers and drinking coffee.

"Good morning," I said. "How are you guys today?"

"Oh, fine, fine. Thanks for asking," he said, and went back to his paper. I stood there for a second, but neither of them seemed interested in any more conversation, so I kept moving.

I stopped by the kitchen to grab a quick snack. The fridge was always crammed with food. It seemed like half of it usually ended up going bad. I wondered who actually did the grocery shopping. I'd never seen either William or Elisa do it. I thought maybe they hired someone, but it didn't seem polite to ask.

I grabbed a bunch of random stuff that looked like it wouldn't last much longer. Cheese, cured sausage of some kind, some carrots, and half a cucumber. I tossed it all on a plate and just started to eat it at the counter. After a few minutes, I realized that Giselle was watching me from the doorway.

"Hey," I said.

"Hey." She watched me eat for a moment, then asked, "What's Henri do up there in your room all day?"

"An art project," I said. "I think for class or something."

"Why does he have to do it in your room?"

"Oh, uh, because he's using this, um . . . software I made."

"Like an app?" she asked.

"Yeah, sort of."

"Oh." Then she turned and left.

Four months, and she still hadn't warmed up to me. And while William and Elisa were still nice, they both seemed to have settled back into the routines they had before I arrived. Routines that didn't have a whole lot of room for me.

I liked school. After the first few weeks, I'd adjusted to the sheer volume of knowledge absorption, just like Henri said I would. The only problem now was that I hadn't really made any friends. I didn't know if that was because I wasn't good at making new friends, or because I looked scary, or just because I was American. Maybe a combination.

When I let Henri in on the secret, I thought I'd feel less alone. But now that Vi and Henri had become obsessed with each other, I felt more alone than ever.

HENRI WAS RIGHT about it being a nice day. Early winter in Geneva had been pretty dark and rainy. But today was bright and chilly, with hardly any clouds in the sky. It was clear enough that I could see the mountains on the far side, now with a lot more snow on top than when I'd first arrived.

I had planned to just sit down and study for my chem test by the lakeshore. But I had a sudden strong urge to be up there in those snow-covered peaks. William had taught me the basics of sailing—enough to get myself across the lake and back. I could study just as well over there. Maybe better, even.

I walked down to the dock and untied the boat from the cleat. I wasn't as fast a sailor as Henri or William, but I made it across to the far shore. Once there, I climbed up the mountain until I reached the same plateau where I'd seen the dwarf. It was covered with snow now, so I dusted off some rocks and sat down, the stone pleasantly chilled beneath me. More and more, I noticed that I craved the cold. I wasn't sure why. It just felt right, especially sitting up here, looking out over the lake. I could see the Villa Diodati on the far shore. I imagined Henri in my room, adding some new weird anime fetish to Vi's design.

I got out my chem books and started studying, keeping an eye out in case the dwarf showed up. I kind of hoped he would. But I guess my need wasn't "dire" enough yet, because I stayed up there all afternoon studying and I never saw him.

I didn't want to go back too late, because I didn't feel comfortable sailing in the dark. Of course, I didn't want to get back too early, either, and have to sit through Henri and Vi telling each other how awesome they were. So I got back in the boat just as the sky began to turn a pinkish gold and a streak of red from the setting sun rimmed the mountaintops. It reminded me of one of William's little boating rhymes: *Red sky at night, sailor's delight. Red sky at morning, sailors take warning.* I think it was supposed to be some weather indicator, but the way he said it felt more like a fortune-telling tool. I kind of hoped it was, because I could use a delightful night.

But it got dark a lot faster than I expected. I was only about halfway across the lake when night fell. I looked around in the boat for a flashlight or something. I found a small electric lantern, but it wasn't very bright. It was probably more to make sure people could see me than to light my way. Fortunately, the Villa Diodati's dock was brightly lit, so at least I could see where I needed to go.

I was still about fifty yards from the dock when something scraped across the bottom of the hull. Something big. It was still pretty deep this far out, so I thought I might have run over a log or something. I let out the sail to slow down and scanned the surface of the dark water.

Something thumped against the side of the boat, causing it to seesaw roughly. Then I heard a splash close by.

"Hello?" I called out. William had said that the fish in the lake were all pretty small, so I figured this had to be the mermaid.

There was no response.

"Don't worry, I won't hurt you," I said.

Silence, except the sound of water lapping quietly against the boat.

"I'm not really human," I said. "It's okay. You can show your-self to me."

A head slowly emerged from the water about twenty feet away. I couldn't make out a lot of details, but the moonlight glinted wetly off the faint outline of long hair, eyes, nose, and mouth, all very human looking.

"Hey," I said. "I'm Boy. Why don't you come a little closer? My night vision sucks."

She didn't move.

I leaned over the side of the boat to try to see her better. Maybe if I could see her expression, I'd be able to see if she was scared of me. But between the dark and the long, wet hair in her face, I couldn't make anything out.

"I swear, I'm not going to hurt you. Honestly, I've been hang-ing out with humans so much lately, it's great to meet another monster."

She still didn't come any closer. Maybe she only spoke French. Or German.

"Uh, *polly vu frances*? *Spreken ze deutch*?" Not that I could speak either of those languages, but maybe it would at least get her talking. Or maybe she didn't speak at all. I really didn't know anything about mermaids.

I leaned over the side as far as I could and reached out my hand.

"I am a friend," I said.

Then I heard something rise up out of the water behind me. I turned just in time to see a giant tentacle bearing down on me. I dove sideways into the stern of the boat. The tentacle slammed into the boat, nearly tipping it over, then disappeared beneath the surface.

"What . . ." I gasped.

The mermaid slowly rose up out of the water. In the moon-light I could see her wet, human-shaped torso. But as she contin-ued to rise higher, I saw that instead of a fish tail, her lower body was just a white stalk. Attached to the other end of the stalk was a massive creature that looked like a giant angler fish, with faintly luminous white eyes and a gaping maw of needle-sharp teeth. It had long tentacles that writhed fitfully in the water. The "mermaid" dangled lifelessly from the stalk on the creature's head. She was nothing more than a lure. And apparently, I was the catch.

"This is a mermaid?" I muttered to myself. I knew Ruthven had a mermaid in The Show for a while, but I never saw it. I wondered how he even fit it in the theater.

Another tentacle came whistling through the air. I dodged it again, but this time the impact took out a huge chunk of the hull. The boat was taking on water quick, and the dock was still about fifty yards away.

I took a deep breath and belly flopped into the water, the shock of cold hitting me so hard every muscle in my body clenched up. I wasn't a very good swimmer, and my wet clothes were dragging me down as I flailed around, trying to move toward the safety of the shore.

In the distance, I heard someone scream. Then something grabbed my ankle and yanked me under.

I could hardly see anything in the dark water. But I felt ten-tacles wrap around my legs and chest as it dragged me down deeper. Then I saw the glowing eyes and the faint glint of its teeth coming at me. The tentacles had grabbed my right arm, but not my left. Punching was out of the question underwater, so I just reached out, grabbed the eye, and squeezed as hard as I could. I could feel it burst in my hand and the mermaid shuddered. I jammed my fist as hard as I could into its ruined eye socket and it shuddered again. It pulled me down even deeper into the dark water, but its grip began to loosen and I was able to get my other arm free. As its jaws opened wide and came at me, I grabbed the top and bottom of its mouth. Razor teeth cut into my hands, but I didn't let go. Instead, I slowly pried the mouth open wider and wider, until I felt its jaw hinge give way with a sharp snap. The mermaid shuddered violently, then released me and disappeared.

My lungs were screaming for air by this point and the weight of my wet clothes felt like chains. My limbs were numb and I felt truly cold for the first time in my life.

I struggled toward the surface but it was a lot farther away than I thought. My vision was beginning to dim. My body was sending crazy signals to my brain to gasp for air even though there wasn't any. I clenched my teeth to keep my mouth shut but I didn't think I could hold on any longer.

Then I felt an arm around my waist. Suddenly, I was moving upward fast. Just when I thought I couldn't take another moment, we broke to the surface and air flooded into my lungs.

I coughed and hacked up lake water as I was towed along. Finally, I could feel the bottom beneath me. I tried to stand, staggered, and fell. But strong arms caught me.

"Can't leave you for even a few months without you getting in over your head, can I?" muttered a familiar harsh female British voice.

I turned and blinked my stinging eyes.

"Claire? What . . ." I gasped for air. "What . . . are . . . you . . . doing . . . here?"

Claire Hyde grinned at me, her black, chin-length hair plastered against her face.

"Apparently, dragging your arse out of the jaws of death. As usual."

———

"I'M SO SORRY about the boat, William," I said.

Claire and I stood in the foyer, a small pool of water on the tile beneath us as we dried off with the towels Elisa gave us.

"I am just glad you're okay," he said.

"Right?" Claire grinned. "Wouldn't envy anyone having to explain to the Monster that his only son drowned."

William smiled briefly. "And, eh, you are . . . ?"

"Oh, sorry," I said. "This is my girlfriend, Claire."

"Ah," said William. He turned to Claire. "You are welcome here, of course."

"Sorry for the unannounced visit," she said. "It was all very last minute."

"Of course," cut in Elisa, patting her cheek. "You poor dear. I am sure you have been missing him terribly."

"Exactly." The way Claire said it, I was pretty sure that wasn't the real reason she was here.

"So what happened, Boy?" asked William. "You said you ran into something? Far from shore?"

"Yeah. I really am sorry. I should have come in sooner. It just got dark a lot quicker than I expected. I couldn't see what it was I hit. You can still see the boat out there half sunk about fifty yards from shore."

"I wonder what it could have been." He frowned as he moved to the window. "It must have been terribly big. . . ."

"Well, we can examine this mystery further tomorrow when it is light," said Elisa, taking William by the shoulders and guiding him to the stairs. "I am sure Boy and Claire would like to change out of their wet clothes and get some rest."

"She got the first bit right, anyway," Claire whispered in my ear as she put her arm around my waist. "Why don't you show me this four-poster bed of yours?"

"We'll probably have to kick Henri out," I said as we started up the stairs.

"What's he doing in your room?"

"You'll see."

———

WHEN WE GOT to my room, Henri and Vi were making faces at each other.

"Hey, guys," I said. "Surprise visit from Claire."

Henri came over and did the cheek-to-cheek thing that his mom did to me. "I am Henri. So great to meet you. Boy has told me all about you."

"Right, you're the one he spilled to," she said. "Just keep it to yourself, yeah? I'd hate to have to break that pretty face of yours."

"Eh . . ." His eyes shifted nervously between Claire and me, like he was looking for a sign that she was joking. "Don't worry. Your secret is safe with me."

"Glad to hear it." She patted his back hard enough for him to stumble slightly.

"It's so great to see you again, Claire," said Vi, her hands clasped together and her big purple eyes glistening.

Claire turned to me. "What's with Pokémon sexpot here?"

"That's Vi," I said.

Her eyebrow shot up. "Are you taking the piss?"

"No, it's true!" said Vi, stretching her arms out wide. "I have a body so I can learn visual communication. Henri has been designing it for me."

"Yeah, I'll bet he has," muttered Claire.

"Okay, we can talk about this some other time," I said. "Henri? Vi? Would you mind giving us a little . . . privacy?"

"Oh, yes, of course!" said Henri. "Would you mind if I took your laptop into my room so Vi and I can continue working? You caught us right in the middle of redesigning her eyebrows."

"Uh, yeah, sure," I said.

Once Henri and Vi were out of the room, Claire rested her arms on my shoulders and smirked. "Some privacy, eh? What's on *your* mind, I wonder?"

"You have no idea how happy I am to see you," I said, looking into her dark brown eyes. "But I don't buy your 'I just really missed my boyfriend' line. That's something I would pull, maybe Sophie. But not you."

"See now," she said, her smirk looking a little strained. "This is why I like you. You don't miss a trick."

"Don't distract me with flattery," I said. "Something's up. Something bad enough for you to leave LA and travel thousands of miles to see me in person. Tell me I'm wrong."

She looked at me for a moment, the smirk completely gone, the muscles in her jaw clenching. Then she nodded curtly. "Okay, you got me. So way back when Kemp found us in LA, right after we'd just stopped my half-brother, Robert, from killing me, remember how he turned Robert over to the cops like he was just a regular human?"

"Of course."

"Yeah, well, a few days ago, Kemp's contact at the LAPD told him that Robert escaped from prison."

"What?! Did he say *how*?"

"Apparently, Robert was starting to get even more violent and out of control than usual, so they decided to transfer him to one of those maximum security places. But the transport bus he was on just never showed up."

"Robert isn't that strong," I said. "Someone on the outside must have helped him."

"But who? Robert's pissed off just about everyone he ever met."

She was doing her usual tough act, but I knew better. Her jaw was set and her eyes were just a little too wide. If there was one person in this world she was genuinely afraid of, it was Robert Jekyll. Not because he was superpowerful, but because he was bat-shit crazy. He had somehow figured out how to eliminate his Hyde half, Stephen. Now he was obsessed with removing every last Hyde in the family. Starting with Claire.

"I'm glad you came." I took her hands in mine. They were strong and nearly as big as mine. "Whatever happens, we'll deal with it."

"Yeah." She nodded tersely, not quite meeting my eyes.

"Hey. Together. Okay?"

She looked at me then so intensely her eyes seemed to vibrate. She took a deep breath, squeezing my hands hard enough to hurt. Then she slowly let out her breath, eased off on my hands, and pressed her forehead against mine.

"Thanks," she whispered. Then her smirk suddenly reappeared. "*Now* can we get naked?"

# 5

# DIY Family

++++++++

HENRI AND I sat side by side, facing my laptop.

"Are you sure you want to do this?" he asked.

"Are *you* sure?" I asked.

"I understand there are risks. But I could not possibly pass this up."

"If you say so," I said.

"All right, then." He nodded. "Vi, if you would be so kind."

"Of course, Henri," came Vi's voice. She wasn't on the screen right now because we needed the camera for Skype. "Connecting to The Monster now."

A moment later, my dad's face appeared on the screen. I heard Henri suck in a sharp breath. I'd warned him that my dad wasn't nearly as well made as I was and I think he finally understood what I meant.

"Hey, Dad," I said.

He looked at me with his watery, mismatched eyes. "How are you, Boy?" he asked in an accent that was way thicker than either William's or Henri's, despite the fact that he'd been living in the States for about fifty years.

"Great, Dad, how about you?"

"I am fine." He was never very talkative on Skype. Not that he was ever really that talkative in person, either. But over Skype he was nearly as bad as my mom. His eyes shifted to Henri. "And you must be Henri."

"Yes, monsieur."

"And how are you, Henri?"

"Great."

"So, Dad, there's, uh, some stuff we need to talk about."

"Yes."

"Like, I'm sure you're wondering why Henri is here with me."

"Yes."

"Uh, so he, uh, he knows everything. About us. About The Show. Everything."

"I see." He sounded calm, but the loose patchwork of his massive face began to twitch and fold in strange places. "And . . . why is this?"

"Okay, it wasn't really my fault. There was this dwarf who outed me, and then . . ." I stopped and took a breath. "But you know what, Dad? That doesn't really matter. Because I've been thinking about this a lot and I want to ask you. Are you serious about us all becoming one family?"

"Of course. I would not have sent my only child if I was not serious."

"Exactly. You sent me here to connect to these people. To learn about them and to bond with them. And I've done what you wanted. I don't know about the rest of the family, honestly, but Henri and I trust each other. We're family. Just like you always wanted."

"That . . . is good."

My dad was hard enough to read under any circumstance, but over Skype it was almost impossible. It seemed like he might be softening a little. I hoped so, anyway.

"Yeah, so this was part of that trust. Sure, my hand was kind of forced. But rather than try to cover it up or tell half-truths, I decided to let him into our lives. And . . . I hope you'll do the same."

"What do you mean?" he asked.

I turned to Henri and nodded. It was his turn.

"Ah, yes." He nodded, and rubbed his thighs nervously. "*Monsieur le Monstre*, may I accompany Boy home to New York for winter break?"

He stared at us for a long time, saying nothing. It went on so long that I started to wonder if maybe the video stream had frozen. But at last he said:

"Boy, you want to bring a human into The Show?"

"That's what I'm trying to say, Dad. He's not just a human. He's family. *Our* family."

He sighed. "My son, I understand what you are saying. Your heart is good. But . . ." He shook his head. "This has never been done before in the entire history of The Show. I will need to discuss it with Ruthven."

"Thanks, Dad. That's all I ask."

"Okay. Good-bye, Boy. Good-bye, Henri."

The connection ended and Henri let out a breath. "Wow, your dad does not like humans."

"Are you kidding? He loves humans," I said. "Just wait till you meet my mom."

"Do you really think it's going to happen? That I'll get to visit a community of monsters?"

"If there's anyone who can convince Ruthven, it's my dad. So I'd say there's a good chance you'll get in. It's getting you out alive that will be trickier."

He laughed, but then looked at me. "Wait, are you serious?"

"I told you. There are a lot of monsters there who've had bad experiences with humans. Some of them, like my dad, have moved on. Some of them haven't."

"Don't worry, Henri!" said Vi, suddenly materializing on the screen in a burst of neon sparkles. "We'll protect you!"

"Speak for yourself," said Claire from where she'd been lounging on my bed. "I think this is the daftest idea you've ever had, sweetie."

"Thanks," I said.

"And you didn't ask him if he knew anything about Robert."

"You can't overload him with too many questions at once," I said. "And besides, I think Ruthven's probably the one to ask, anyway. So we might as well wait until we get there."

"You know, I was looking forward to a nice, temperate holiday in LA."

"New York is awesome at Christmastime." I went over and sat down next to her on the bed. "Besides, with Robert running around out there somewhere, it's the safest place you could possibly be. The sooner we get you there, the better I'll feel."

"I cannot believe your own brother would want to hurt you," said Henri.

"Keep up, Frankenstein. He's not my brother, he's Sophie's," said Claire. Then she turned back to me. "We'd better not be staying in your old tiny bedroom in your parents' apartment, that's all I'm saying. We're adults now with jobs and everything. We should get our own space." She pulled me down so that her warm body pressed against me. "If we get to be together for the holiday, I plan on making the most of it. If you know what I mean."

"Cosigned," I said, and kissed her neck.

She ran her fingers through my hair, then grabbed hard and pulled me in for a kiss.

"Vi," I heard Henri say. "I think that's our cue to leave."

JUST AS I predicted, Ruthven agreed to let Henri come home with me. But he wasn't allowed to spend the night. Ruthven said it was just too much temptation for the nocturnal predators, so Henri would have to get a hotel room.

I wasn't sure how William and Elisa were going to take the news that Henri was going to spend his winter break with me. But when he told them over dinner that night, their faces lit up.

"Oh, but this is marvelous!" said Elisa. "Henri, you have always wanted to go to New York!"

"I agree!" said William. "What an opportunity! And your parents don't mind?"

"No, they're happy to have him," I said. That was only a half lie. I was pretty sure that deep down, my dad was happy that a Frankenstein was coming to visit. He'd always wanted to be accepted into the Frankenstein family. But my mom was not happy at all. She'd never been able to forgive humans for what they'd done to her and my dad. I hoped maybe Henri could be the one to get her past that.

"What about you, Claire?" asked Giselle. Months of living here and I'd barely made a dent in Giselle. It had taken Claire all of a day and a half. Giselle followed her around constantly and had even asked her mother if she could get her hair cut shorter. "Are you going home to *your* family for the holiday?"

"Nah, I'll tag along with these lads," Claire said. "My family isn't real close anymore."

"Oh, I'm sorry to hear that," said Elisa.

"It's all right. I make my own family, you know? And Boy's family is great. They made me feel welcome right from the start."

"How wonderful," said William. "I'm glad Henri will be in such good hands."

"Can I go, too?" asked Giselle.

"Not this time, my sweet sister," said Henri.

"You always leave me behind," she said.

"Someone must remain behind to keep watch for the mermaid," said Henri. "You wouldn't want her to gobble up Mother and Father while we're out having adventures, would you?"

"No," said Giselle.

"Really, Henri, you shouldn't encourage her," said Elisa. "Giselle, you're far too young for such a long trip away from us."

"But if you do see the mermaid," I said, "you tell her that I said she better mind her manners."

Elisa sighed. "The two of you! Impossible!"

Henri and I grinned at each other.

---

"WE COULD JUST stay here, you know," said Claire.

It was the Sunday before our flight. And even though it was nearly noon, Claire and I were still in bed. Her head rested on my bare chest as she looked up at me with searching eyes.

"It's quiet here," she said.

"It's safer for you in New York," I said.

"He wouldn't think to look for me here."

"Not right away. But he found us in the middle of the Mojave desert."

"With Vi's help."

"Still, you don't think he could eventually track you down here?"

"You don't think he could track me to New York?"

"That's just it. I think he could track you anywhere. If he catches you out here in the middle of nowhere, we're in trouble. But if he tries anything at The Show, he's the one who's in trouble. We protect our own."

"I guess you're right." Her finger traced the line of stitches that circled my shoulder. "It's just so nice here."

I smiled. "You're getting used to the luxury faster than I did. You're not going soft on me, are you?"

"Watch it, you."

"Ooo, is that a threat, Your Majesty?"

"Right, that's it!"

She reached up for me, but then my bedroom door burst open.

"Hey, check this out, I made—my God you're naked!" Henri covered his eyes.

"Way to ruin the mood," said Claire, pulling the sheets up over herself.

"Yeah, thanks, cuz," I said. "I thought we'd talked about you not doing that anymore."

"Sorry! Sorry!" said Henri. "Should I come back?"

"Just give us a second," I said.

We both pulled some clothes on, then let Henri back into the room.

"So what was so exciting you just had to bust in here like that?" I asked.

He held up a smartphone. "Vi mobile!"

"You're kidding!"

"Check it out." He handed me the phone.

I looked down at the screen and the anime face we'd all more or less accepted as Vi's looked back at me.

"Hi, Boy!" she said, her eyes closing as she gave me a big smile. "Isn't this exciting?"

"It's pretty awesome," I agreed.

"Obviously, there's some processing power lost," said Henri. "But this is so much more portable, and the battery life is amazing. Now she doesn't have to miss out on anything we do."

"Just your face, then?" asked Claire, peering over my shoulder.

"Oh, no!" said Vi. "It's a three-dimensional design, so it has depth. If I walk away . . ." She demonstrated by walking backward so it appeared that she was moving away from the screen. "You can see all of me!" And there she was in all her short-skirt glory. "What a great idea, huh?"

"Henri's, I'm sure," said Claire, giving him a look.

"Ah . . ." His cheeks flushed red. "You know. So she can practice body language, as well."

"Right," said Claire.

"Do you like it, Vi?" I asked.

"I love it!" She did a little dance on the screen.

"That's the important thing," I said.

"Well, I guess we're all sorted for the trip, then," said Claire.

"Not quite," I said. "I still want to figure out if there's a way I can get through the metal detector this time without setting off every alarm in the airport."

"Oh, I thought we'd save on airfare," said Claire. "Take you apart and just check you in pieces. Like luggage."

"You're joking," said Henri. He turned to me. "She is joking, isn't she?"

"New York, here we come!" said Vi, and she did a little cartwheel on the phone screen.

# PART 2

## New World

"*Our* business in this world is not to succeed,
but to continue to fail, in good spirits."

—From "Reflections and Remarks on Human Life,"
by Robert Louis Stevenson

# 6
# Home for the Holidays

++++++++

RUTHVEN WAS WAITING for us at the airport baggage claim. It was kind of amazing, really, that none of the hundreds of humans that swarmed past him at JFK airport thought, "Whoa, is that guy a vampire?!" Because he absolutely looked like one. Tall and thin, with pale white skin and red eyes. His long overcoat swirled around him like a living shadow. The popular theory among the company was that Ruthven didn't actually wear clothes, just shadows. But no one had ever got up the nerve to ask him.

Ruthven bowed his head slightly. "Welcome home, Boy."

"Thanks." I pulled him in for a hug, which was something only my dad and I were allowed to do.

"Hm, yes," he said as I released him. He smoothed down his shadowy coat, then turned to Claire on my left. "Always a pleasure, my dear Claire."

"Likewise," said Claire. "How's things on this coast?"

"Fine, thank you. I trust Kemp is taking good care of you."

"Of course. I wouldn't stay there if he wasn't, and he knows it."

Ruthven smiled briefly. "I'm sure he lives in dread of the day I finally convince you to come work for me." Then he turned to Henri on my right. I could feel Henri leaning in toward me as

Ruthven gazed at him. Humans always seemed to react with an instinctive fear when Ruthven looked at them.

"And this must be the one everyone is talking about. Henri Frankenstein."

"Yes, monsieur, that's me." Henri gave his most charming smile and held out his hand, but Ruthven only glanced at it and didn't offer his own.

"I should warn you, Henri, that your arrival will not be met with a great deal of enthusiasm from some of our company members. And perhaps a bit . . . too *much* enthusiasm from other members."

"Those are the ones to watch out for, mate," Claire told him.

"Indeed," said Ruthven. "I have talked at length to all members about the importance of keeping this visit pleasant. But for your own safety, I suggest you remain with either Claire or Boy at all times while you are in the theater."

"I will do as you suggest," said Henri. "And I just want to say thank you for allowing me into your home. I know this was not a decision you made easily."

"I am curious to see how this plays out," said Ruthven. "Do not mistake that for approval."

"Understood, monsieur."

"Now then," said Ruthven, "shall we be off?" Without waiting for an answer, he turned so that his coat swirled dramatically and walked toward the exit.

"Laying it on a bit thick, isn't he?" Claire muttered to me.

"I know." I grinned. "I've missed theater people."

CHARON WAS WAITING for us in the rental car. His brown, leathery skeleton face crinkled up into a smile when we climbed in the backseat.

"Boy, it's so good to see you!"

"It's good to see you, too, Charon," I said.

"I hope you didn't get into too much trouble in Switzerland."

"No trouble," I said.

"Except the mermaid," said Claire.

"Mermaid?" asked Charon.

"I tried to talk to her and she almost ate me. Reminded me of the really crazy ones they keep locked up at The Commune. Didn't you used to have a mermaid in The Show for a while? How did you even fit her on the stage? She was massive."

Charon frowned. "Where did you meet her?"

"Lake Geneva."

"Oh, you must have met a freshwater mermaid. Completely different species."

"Don't tell me. Saltwater mermaids are sweet, adorable ladies with fish tails."

"More or less."

Ruthven slid into the front passenger seat. "Take us to the hotel first, if you please, Ferryman."

"You bet, boss." Charon started the car up and eased us out into traffic.

"Hey, you've gotten a lot better at driving," I said.

"I've been practicing once a week," he said. "It's my hobby!"

"Everyone needs one," said Claire.

"You're still the box office manager, though, aren't you?" I asked.

"Oh, yeah. But we recently took in a pair of teenage goblin

sisters and they've been helping me out. Customers love them. They think it's part of the experience, like it's only makeup. And they always get a kick out of it when one of the girls tells them something like, 'Your eyes look delicious.' They think she's joking! Humans. So dumb." He glanced at Henri. "No offense."

"None taken," said Henri. "They would not actually attack a customer, though, would they?"

"Just the one time," said Charon.

"One time?"

"Well, they're only monster, right? But Ruthven has a strict 'Don't eat where you sleep' policy. He put the fear into them, and let me tell you, they will never do it again on theater property."

"What did you do to them, chief?" asked Claire.

"I prefer to keep disciplinary matters private," Ruthven said.

"So, Ruthven," I said. "While we've got you more or less to ourselves, Claire and I were wondering if you'd heard about Robert Jekyll."

"That he's escaped from prison? Yes."

"And you know he's got a vendetta against Claire."

"Which is why you've brought her here."

"Uh, yeah."

"And rightly so." He turned to look at Claire, his red eyes glinting like a cat's. "I can assure you, my dear, if Robert sets one foot in the lobby, he will very much wish he hadn't."

"Thanks," she said.

As we neared the Queens Midtown Tunnel, and I saw Manhattan looming in front of us, I felt a surge of peace wash over me. I hadn't realized how much I missed the city. It was big, crowded, loud, and dirty. And it would always be home.

We made our way to Times Square, and I stared out the window at all the stores with their holiday decorations. The cabs and people moved like currents through the streets. I remembered my first time out of the theater. It had been so overwhelming at first. But thrilling, too. I had met my first human that day. At a thrift store. I'd been so nervous. . . .

Back then, I could never have imagined actually living with humans, much less being friends with them. Even later, when I'd run away from home, I'd still mostly kept away from humans. I had missed out on so much. Sure, some humans were assholes. But most were pretty amazing, these fragile creatures pretending to be indestructible.

"First stop! Human sanctuary!" said Charon.

Ruthven turned in his seat to look at Henri. "I assume you'll want to drop off your things and freshen up after your long flight. That will also give Boy time to visit with his family alone."

"Sure, okay," said Henri.

"The room is held under your name. The theater is only one block down, on the left." Ruthven inclined his head in the direction. "You can't miss it. Charon should be back in the box office by then, so you won't have to worry about any . . . misunderstandings. He'll call Boy up to come get you."

Henri turned to me. "Do you mind if I keep Vi with me?"

He looked like he could use the company right now, and Vi seemed to want to spend every possible moment she could with Henri, so I figured she wouldn't mind, anyway. "Yeah, that's fine." I patted his shoulder. "Welcome to New York."

He climbed out of the car. Charon had already popped the trunk, so he grabbed his bag, slammed the trunk lid down, and headed toward the hotel entrance. The way he clutched Vi's phone in his free hand made me wonder if maybe it wasn't as one sided a relationship as I thought.

THE THEATER HADN'T changed a bit. A big marquee that just said **THE SHOW** in a swirl of colors that had once been bright but over the years had faded. The same posters still hung out front in their glass cases—silhouettes of mysterious creatures on sun-bleached colored backgrounds. It looked retro, but actually it had all just been there a really long time.

The lobby was still decorated with fabrics and swirls of color that gave it a vague international carnival feeling. It still smelled the same, like humans, sweat, old wood, and some other thing I'd never been able to pinpoint.

The two goblins peering with yellow eyes from the box office window were new, though.

I waved at them. "Hi, ladies."

They whispered to each other and giggled nervously, then waved back.

"My, aren't you the local celeb crush," said Claire.

"Jealous?" I asked.

"You better hope not," she said. "I'm bloody terrifying when I'm jealous."

"I'll take that into consideration."

"Curmthulia, dear," said Ruthven. "Would you call down to Boy's parents and let them know he's arrived?"

One of the goblin sisters nodded and picked up the phone.

"Let's see what kind of mess you've made while I was gone," said Charon as he climbed into the box office.

I smiled as I watched him fuss around inside, the goblin sisters scrambling to straighten everything up.

"That used to be my job, helping out Charon," I told Claire.

"I'd hate to be crammed in that little box," she said.

"I grew up inside a theater. I was used to small spaces."

"Boy!" came a familiar hard voice.

I turned and there stood my mother. She looked as beautiful as ever, her black-and-white-striped hair sticking straight up, her china-doll face still fixed forever in an expression of perpetual vague surprise. She reached out her arms and pulled me in tight for a crushing hug.

"Hey, Mom."

"Let me look." She held me out at arm's length. "You don't eat enough."

"I missed you, too, Mom."

Since her facial expression couldn't change, it wasn't easy to know how she was feeling. But I could feel the tension in her hands.

"Are you okay?" I asked.

She stared at me, but didn't say anything.

"Oh, she just missed her Boy," said Claire, putting her arm around my mom. "Isn't that right, love?"

My mom jerked her head up and down in a nod.

Then my father was there. He always knew how to take up a room. Partly because he towered over everyone, even me. But it was more than that. He just had this presence. Solid. Like a mountain.

"Welcome home, Boy," he said in his deep voice. He put his massive, stitched hand on my shoulder and smiled. "It is good to have you here."

"It's good to be back," I said.

"Let me take that bag," he said to Claire. "We'll get you set-tled into your room."

Claire cleared her throat and looked at me.

"Dad," I said. "Claire and I kind of hoped we could share a room."

He smiled. "Yes, I thought you would."

"Uh, and not my old room."

"It would be too small for the two of you," he agreed.

"Um . . ." I had expected some sort of disagreement. But here we were, asking to be treated like grown-ups, and they were just . . . agreeing. "Yeah. Exactly."

"Ruthven thought we should give you Medusa's room here on the main floor."

"No one's taken it?" I asked.

He shook his head. "Most do not feel comfortable being so close to humans all the time."

"And it was the room she died in," I said.

"Yes, that too."

———

MY PARENTS DROPPED us off in front of Medusa's old dressing room. I noticed there was a star-shaped spot on the door where her name had been taken off.

"There will be time to catch up more tomorrow," said my father. "But now your mother and I must get ready for tonight's performance."

"Yeah, I figured it was about that time," I said.

"Henri should watch The Show tonight. So he can see what it is we do here."

"You mean, besides hide," I said.

"Yes. Exactly. I . . ." He frowned for a moment, like he was thinking carefully about what he wanted to say. Then, "I want him to know we are more than just cowering relics of a superstitious past. We still do good work here."

"You got it, Dad," I said.

He nodded, then turned to go. Mom followed silently behind him.

"Mom," I said.

She turned her head back in my direction, although she didn't actually look at me.

"I hope you're not mad at me," I said. "For bringing Henri. I think if you give him a chance, you'll really like him."

She stood there for a moment, staring at a fixed point about two feet to my left. Then she just turned and walked away.

"Give her time, yeah?" said Claire. "She'll come around."

"I hope so," I said.

She opened the door and I saw that the room hadn't changed at all since the last time I'd been there. The lights were still draped in silk, and a long, low, red leather divan still took up a good chunk of the room. There were also a few chairs and, in the far corner, a small bathroom.

Most people couldn't look directly at Medusa without turning to stone. My dad and I could when we disconnected our emotions. But for some reason, I was never able to retain my memory of what she looked like when my emotions were reconnected. It was probably some sort of instinctive self-protective measure. Maybe even seeing her in your mind could turn you to stone. I wasn't sure. So when I remembered Medusa, I didn't have a picture of *her* in my mind. What I had was this room and particularly the—

"What is that smell?" Claire wrinkled up her nose. "It's like a mildewed forest in here."

"All the furniture is stuffed with cedar chips."

"Why?"

"Cedar is toxic to snakes. It was one of the little things Ruthven did to keep her in line."

She poked one of the cushions on the divan. "Seems a bit harsh. Even for Ruthven."

"I guess he thought she was dangerous."

"Most of the people in this place are dangerous."

"She was different. Unpredictable. Sometimes she'd just decide to give some human a heart attack right in the middle of the performance. And every once in a while, she'd get in a really nasty mood and we'd end up with several humans and even a few monsters dead. Not even Ruthven could control her. Everyone was afraid of her."

"Were you?"

"Sure."

"But you said you liked her."

"She was . . . awesome. And I mean that literally, as in awe-inspiring." I shook my head. "She was like the Dragon Lady or the Sphinx—someone who doesn't really belong in modern civilization. Almost a force of nature." I stared at that red divan. In the corner lay the curtain she'd drawn up when entertaining guests. Except hardly anyone had visited her. "It doesn't seem right that she spent the last decades of her life just sitting in this room all the time."

"Well, they couldn't let her run around town, could they?"

"I guess not. But sometimes I wonder if she was already dying even before Vi captured her. On the inside, you know?"

I sat down on the divan, feeling the crunch of the cedar in the cushions. I'd never realized how uncomfortable it had been.

I looked up at Claire. "It's not right. For any of us. We shouldn't have to hide what we are. We should be free. All of us."

Claire sat down next to me and took my hand. "Maybe bringing Henri here is a start to fixing that."

"A small start."

"You've got to begin somewhere, haven't you?"

"I thought you said bringing Henri here was my daftest idea yet."

She put her hand on my cheek with a tenderness that was unusual for her.

"Don't be thick. I love your daft ideas."

———

THERE WAS A long, grating beep.

"What is that?" said Claire.

"Intercom." I walked over to the box by the door.

"They still make those?"

"Refurb from my mom. Can't be tapped or traced by phone companies. When you've got a giant group of monsters hiding out in the middle of Times Square, it's best to stay off the grid as much as possible."

"But the whole place is rigged with Internet connections."

"I can block prying eyes on the Internet. Phone lines are wide open. A phone company can tap or listen in any time they want. A lot of people forget that."

I pushed the Talk button. "Hello?"

"Box office here," came a high, raspy female voice. "Uh, is this Boy?"

"Oh, hey. Curmthulia, right?"

"No, that's my sister. This is Rughutla."

"I bet they argued over who got to call you," said Claire.

I gave her a sour look, then said, "What's up, Rughutla?"

"Oh, uh, your . . . your human is here."

"Thanks, I'll be up in a minute. I'd appreciate it if you ladies would be nice to him."

"Of course, Boy! We won't let anyone pick on him. You can count on us!"

"Thanks," I said, then let go of the Talk button.

"Whatever you say, Boy!" said Claire in a squeaky voice. "We'll do anything you want! We love you! Can we have your autograph?"

"Seriously, cut it out," I said.

"I'm just having a little fun. I like how it makes you get all flustered."

"Are you done?"

"I suppose. Now, you go save Henri from the goblin twins and I'll see about getting us an actual bed for our bedroom."

I headed for the door.

"Boy?" Her voice was suddenly serious.

"Yeah?"

"You know Ruthven a lot better than I do. Did you get the feeling that he knew more about Robert than he let on?"

"With Ruthven, I think it's always safe to assume he knows more than he's letting on."

"Well, if you see him up there, try pushing harder."

"I will."

It was a short walk from Medusa's dressing room to the lobby. Only a few minutes, actually. Yet somehow in those few minutes when I was completely alone, I ran into the one person in the theater I really didn't want to see.

"Boy? Is that you?" Once upon a time, just hearing that voice say my name had given me shivers of happiness. It gave me shivers now, but not the good kind.

I stopped and turned around. "Hey, Liel."

I had to admit, she looked good. When she and I had lived out among the humans, she'd kind of gone feral, looking and acting like a stereotypical troll. But now she was back to her old self: long white hair, diamond eyes, dark green skin, lean dancer's body, and most important, not homicidal. As far as I could tell.

"Looks like you're moving up in the den," I said.

She had some new tribal scars on her cheeks and forehead. She wore her usual white tank top, so I could see she also had a bunch on her arms and shoulders. The more intricate the scars, the more important that trowe was in the den. Her mom, Ku'lah, was the den leader and her entire face, arms, shoulders, and chest were covered in complex scar patterns.

"Yeah." She shrugged. "Mom has me doing a lot of the dance captain responsibilities now. And even some choreography."

"Oh, that's cool."

"So you're visiting for the holidays?"

"Yep."

"How's college?"

"Good. How's The Show?"

"Same old."

We stood there for a moment. All kinds of weird emotions were coming up to the surface—old pain, old desire. At first I felt kind of bad. Guilty almost, like I was cheating on Claire and Sophie somehow. I was also a little frustrated with myself. Why could Liel still stir me up like this? But at one point, this girl had been the most important person in my life. No matter what else happened after, that would always be true. I guess she would always occupy a tiny little part of my heart.

"Sooo . . ." she said. "I hear you're bringing a human into the theater?"

"Yeah. I'm going to get him from the lobby now."

"Is it okay if I come?"

"Uh . . ."

She squinted her diamond eyes at me. "Look, don't worry. I'm not going to rip his throat out or anything. I'm not like that anymore. But, I mean, is he going to freak out when he sees me all trowish?"

"No, no." I said. "He's cool."

"So? Can I meet him?"

"Yeah, I guess."

When we got to the lobby, Henri was at the box office window, talking to the goblins. When the twins saw me, they both waved at the same time.

"Aww, your little fan club," said Liel.

"Just what I need," I said.

"I think it's sweet. A lot of the younger monsters around here really look up to you. It's good for them to have a positive role model."

"I'm not a positive role model."

"Of course you are. You're out there, living among the humans, making something of yourself. You remember how it was for us—we felt so trapped here. You're showing them it doesn't have to be that way."

"What about you?" I asked. "Do you want to get back out there?"

"Actually, no."

"Really?"

"Yeah, believe it or not." She smiled. "I'm very happy here now."

"That's . . . good."

She nodded her head toward the box office. "Maybe you should go save your human. They may be adorable, but goblins have a funny way of showing affection."

When we reached the box office, Henri was in the middle of telling the twins about some skating tournament.

"Are you sure you girls want to hear this?" he said. "It's pretty gory."

"We really want to hear *all* the details," said one of the twins. Their eyes were wide and hungry looking.

"Okay," he said, oblivious. "So when I came up on the side of the pipe, I thought I would be able to land it, but my wheels skidded out from under me and my arm slammed into the edge. I could hear a snap, and there was suddenly so much blood. I saw the bone was, like, poking out of my forearm." He rolled up his sleeve and showed them a scar. The twins were staring at his arm, their mouths open so their little fangs glistened in the fluorescent lighting. "Right here. A bit of white sticking through, and—"

"Aaaaaall right, enough sweet-talking," I said. "Thanks for watching out for Henri, ladies." I took Henri by the shoulder and moved him away from the box office.

"Any time, Boy!" one of them called.

"So," said Liel, who'd followed us. "Are you going to introduce me to your Frankenstein?"

"Right," I said. "Henri, this is Liel."

"Liel . . ." I could see the wheels turning. Then his face lit up. "Oh, yes, of course, Liel! I've heard all about you."

Liel laughed. "I'm sure some pretty horrible stuff."

"Perhaps some moderately horrible stuff." He gave her his best Henri grin. "But he was absolutely correct when he said you have the most beautiful eyes of any female in existence."

She smirked, one fang poking out of the corner of her mouth. "Nice save."

Ruthven's voice drifted across the lobby. "Boy, can you come here a moment?"

"Uh, sure," I said. "Come on, Henri, let's—"

"Alone," Ruthven said. "Liel, if you'll entertain Henri for just a few moments."

"You bet, boss," she said. "Come on, Henri, let's take a peek in the theater while they're getting ready for tonight's show."

"I'll, uh, come get you there in a minute," I said.

Henri nodded, but I could tell he was now much more focused on Liel. I tried to turn my attention away from any weird feelings of knee-jerk jealousy, with some success, and headed for Ruthven's office.

"Thanks, Boy, this won't take a moment," said Ruthven. He sat at his desk. Charon stood to one side.

"What's up?" I asked.

"I've heard a few odd rumors from my friends at the NYPD concerning the citywide blackout that happened when you put the original Vi out of commission a while ago. I just want to make sure that *new* Vi is still monitoring government channels for any sign that the blackout has been linked back here."

"She's been on it," I said.

"Good. I'm sure I don't need to remind you that this was my condition for supporting your choice to re-create her. There were a lot of company members who were against it. She needs to prove herself to be as constructive as she was destructive. Are we clear?"

"Yeah. I'll, uh, follow up with her. Just to make sure."

"Do that."

I stood there for a moment.

"That's all," said Ruthven. "You may go collect Henri now."

"I was wondering if you've heard anything more about Robert. How he escaped, where he is, that kind of stuff."

"If I have something to share, you'll be the first to hear it," said Ruthven.

"Uh, thanks." As I left his office and headed across the lobby to the theater doors, I thought about the fact that "knowing something" and "having something to share" were not exactly the same thing.

Inside the theater, they were running through the sound cues for The Show. Random voices, brief instrumental interludes, and odd sound effects came and went. I saw Henri and Liel sitting in seats near the stage. Liel was saying something to him, but I couldn't hear what it was until I got closer.

"So then he shows up the next day with these gigantic legs!" she said. "Everything else is still kid-sized, but now he has these massive *man* legs!"

"No!" Henri's eyes were wide.

"I know, right? They're so out of proportion that he can't even reach his shoelaces! The poor guy has to—" She glanced over and saw me. "Oh, hey, Boy."

"Are you seriously telling him about my transition to adult parts?" I asked. "Seriously?"

"That's what old friends do when they meet new friends. Fill them in on all the embarrassing childhood stuff."

"Whatever," I said, trying to cover my irritation. She was joking around like we were old buddies. Even if I was completely over what had happened between us the year before, that didn't make us friends.

I dropped into the seat next to Henri. "My parents had to go to work, and my dad's usually too tired after work to be social.

So we'll meet up with them tomorrow. But he did say we should see The Show tonight. Sound cool?"

"Sure," he said.

"Great idea," said Liel. "I should probably start getting ready, too. Why don't we all meet up at the Cantina after? I'll have the dryads hold us a table."

"Oh," I said. "Uh . . ."

"Claire's coming, too, right?" she asked.

"Of course!" said Henri. "We will all come!"

"Awesome. See you guys after The Show."

She jogged up the aisle, her white ponytail bouncing as she made her way to the exit.

Henri's eyes followed her all the way out, a slight smile playing at the corners of his mouth. "Well, trolls are not so awful after all, eh? In fact, I can understand why you found her so attractive. There's really something very . . ."

He glanced over at me and caught my expression.

"What? Did I do something bad?"

"I don't know. Why don't *you* explain to Claire how you've made plans for us to hang out with my ex-girlfriend tonight, and see how she reacts."

"Oh, yes, probably not good." Henri frowned, suddenly looking nervous.

"Can I talk to Vi for a minute?" I asked.

"Of course," said Henri, handing me the phone.

"Hey, Vi," I said.

"Hi, Boy! Isn't it great to be home?" Her face appeared, smiling wide.

"Uh, yeah, great," I said.

"Oooh, that was sarcasm, wasn't it? I could tell by the way you rolled your eyes!"

"That's pretty good," I said.

"And now you are impressed!"

I smiled. "I have to admit, this was a really good idea Henri came up with."

"I think so, too!" She nodded vehemently.

"So, I hate to nag about this, but Ruthven wanted me to ask if you've caught any chatter about the FBI or Homeland Security tracing the blackout back to The Show."

"Nope, nothing."

"Great. I guess he's a little edgy right now for some reason. Just keep an eye on it."

"You can count on me, Boy!" She gave me a military salute.

"Thanks." Her little manga act was growing on me. And it made a certain amount of sense. When you're first learning facial and body expressions, it probably helped to study a model that was a little exaggerated.

"Boy," came a familiar lilting voice. "What is this gorgeous creature you've brought home?"

I looked up at Laurellen, who stood in the aisle, leaning against a seat back with his arms folded across his chest. He had a bit more glamour on than he usually did in the theater, probably for Henri's benefit. He could be a bit vain, even for a faerie.

"Hey, Laurellen, this is Henri Frankenstein. But I'm guessing you already knew that."

Laurellen shrugged. "I do try to stay informed. I knew you were bringing a human home. But I didn't know he'd be so pretty."

I turned to Henri. "Laurellen runs the lights for The Show. Don't worry. Ruthven told him he can't steal humans back to the faerie realm anymore."

"Oh. Good," said Henri, his eyes slightly glazed from the glamour.

"Honestly," said Laurellen, "I haven't been back to the faerie realm in *years*. It's such a dump these days."

The stage vibrated with a kettledrum sound cue that was way too loud. I nodded up to the booth.

"Mozart not back yet?" Mozart was the werewolf who taught me how to hot-wire a car. He used to run sound for The Show. When I'd run away from home, Ruthven had sent him to track me down. But once he got out there, he decided instead to take me on a road trip that ultimately led to me meeting Claire and Sophie, The Commune monsters, and The Studio monsters. I owed him a lot.

"He's still out traveling around," said Laurellen wistfully. "God knows where. Every once in a while he'll send me a little something—some local delicacy or bit of art from wherever he is at the moment. He drops Ruthven a line now and then, too. But still no word on when he might be coming back."

"Do you think he will come back?" I asked.

He sighed. "I hope so. This new guy is nice, but it's just not the same." He stared at the stage for a moment, frowning. "None of it is."

"What do you mean?" I asked.

"Are you watching the performance tonight?" he asked.

"Yeah."

"Then you'll see what I mean."

# Song and Dance

‡‡‡‡‡‡‡

"I THINK WE have the best seats in the theater!" said Henri.

The usher had shown us to front orchestra, row G, dead center.

"Your little fangirls hooked us up," said Claire.

"Emergency house seats," I said. "Charon always holds these until the last minute in case someone important shows up."

"Like us," said Henri.

"Just keep telling yourself that, mate," said Claire, patting him on the top of his head.

As we settled in, I noticed that everyone else in our section was wearing suits and fancy dresses. Furs, diamonds, the works. We were just in jeans and T-shirts. I knew these tickets were really expensive. I wondered what all the nicely dressed people thought of us.

"I think this is the first time I've ever seen The Show from a regular theater seat," I told Claire.

"Where do you usually sit?"

I pointed up to the booth window in the back of the house. "Back there with Mozart and Laurellen."

"Is old Wolfie still out traveling around?"

"I guess. Hopping trains, hot-wiring cars. Who knows? I kind of miss that sometimes, don't you?"

"Not hardly. Sophie's the one who likes road trips."

"When will I get to meet Sophie?" said Henri.

"When it's her turn," said Claire, her tone flat.

"Eh, yes, of course."

He glanced at me and I shrugged.

The truth was, I wanted to see Sophie, too. I still hadn't seen her since last summer. But I knew that when they didn't keep to their monthly on/off routine, the careful balance they maintained would start to skew one way or the other and things could get tense between them. That was something everyone wanted to avoid. So I just had to wait patiently. Sometimes it was frustrating that I didn't get to choose which one I hung out with on any given night, but I'd pretty much known from the beginning that was what I'd signed up for.

The house lights went down and I settled in to my seat, ready to be swept away from all my worries like I always was when I watched The Show.

Except, I wasn't. I kept noticing things. Little slips, missed cues, bad timing. I really wasn't trying to catch them, but it kept happening. Even my favorite numbers seemed like they were lacking something. Liel wasn't the lead dancer for the trowe number anymore. Maybe it was because she was dance captain now and couldn't do both. But the new girl just didn't have the same charisma. The Fates seemed almost bored as they built up and then tore down yet another human's hopes and dreams for the future. Even the Siren, who always seemed like she was one step away from completely losing control and driving the entire audience into a stampede, looked like she was just going through the motions. I hoped that at least Ruthven's closing speech would give me some of that old, warm fuzzy glow. But after the final number, the lights went up in the house and that was it. The audience clapped for a while, but then gradually stopped as they realized there would be no curtain call.

After Vi version one had wrecked the theater and killed some of the company members, we'd repaired the theater and eventually gotten The Show back up and running again. I'd seen some of the final dress rehearsals before I'd left for Geneva, and they'd been a little flat. But I had assumed they just needed an audience back in there and they'd snap back to their old lively selves. If anything, it seemed even worse than before.

I thought about what Dad had said to me earlier. *We still do good work here.* I wondered now who he was really trying to convince—Henri or himself.

"That was great!" said Henri. He didn't know any better. Probably if you didn't have anything to compare it to, it was still a decent show.

Claire looked a little confused. She'd seen it a few times last summer after we got the theater fixed back up.

"Doesn't Ruthven usually do a little thing at the end about how there isn't a curtain call, but we wouldn't want you to think us ungrateful, blah blah blah?" she asked.

"Yeah," I said.

She frowned. "I wonder why they cut it. That was my favorite bit."

"The whole show felt different," I said.

"A lot of new numbers?" asked Henri.

"No new numbers, actually," I said. "But it just felt . . . kind of phoned in. Like it's lost its heart."

As we filed out of the theater with the rest of the audience, Henri asked, "So where is this Cantina we're going to?"

"We're going to the Cantina tonight?" asked Claire.

"Oh, uh, yeah," I said. "Guess I forgot to mention it."

Her eyes narrowed. "Forgot?"

"Well . . ."

"It is all my fault," said Henri. "I was caught up in the enthusiasm of the moment and agreed we should all meet up after The Show."

"With Liel," I said.

"Oh, really?" said Claire. Then she slowly smiled, and it was not a nice smile. "Excellent."

"Um, why are you happy about this?" I asked.

"I have been waiting for a long time to give that slag a piece of my mind. She was smart enough to avoid me the last time I was here. I guess she's gotten cocky. Thinks she can handle me now. She has no idea."

"Can we please not start a brawl on our first night back home?"

She hooked my chin with her finger, leaned in, and gave me a quick kiss. "I make no promises, sweetie."

---

THE CANTINA WAS really just the mezzanine lobby bar. Still, it was the most popular place for company members to hang out after The Show. And for people who didn't look human enough to pass, the lobby was the closest they could get to leaving the theater.

When Henri, Claire, and I showed up, we were greeted immediately by a dryad nymph.

"Boy, welcome back! We have a table waiting for you. Right this way."

We followed her over to the large corner booth. This was where the cool kids usually hung out. Before I left The Show, I wouldn't have even rated a hello from a dryad, much less the corner booth. And when I'd come back the first time, Vi version one had temporarily turned all the dryads into mindless killing machines who had attacked me and I'd basically had to beat the crap out of them. So I was surprised that this one was being so friendly. Of course, it was probably Liel's doing. She'd always been pretty tight with the dryads.

"Liel and Bakru will probably be here in a bit," said the dryad. "They said go ahead and get started without them. Here's the specials for tonight. Someone will be by in a minute to take your order." She handed me a handwritten drink menu.

"Thanks, uh . . ."

I'd never really been able to tell the dryads apart. They all looked more or less the same, like a group of stereotypical Hollywood models who'd all used the same plastic surgeon. And they didn't really have distinct personalities, as far as I could tell.

"Sequoia." She smiled her Hollywood actress smile.

"Sorry," I muttered.

"It's totally fine. Happens all the time. You just need to get to know us better." Then she turned and headed back to the bar.

As soon as she was out of earshot, Henri said, "*I* would like to get to know her better."

"Keep it in your pants, Frankenstein," said Claire.

"She was a nymph, yes?"

"A dryad," I said. "A forest nymph. They run the bar for the audience before The Show and during the intermission, and then they open it back up for monsters once all the humans are gone. Individually, they're not real bright. But they have a sort of hive mind or collective consciousness, like bees or ants, which makes them really efficient at things like serving drinks to a large number of people in a short amount of time."

"She is absolutely gorgeous," said Henri admiringly.

"Who is?" asked another dryad now standing at our table, this one with a ponytail.

Henri didn't skip a beat. "Why, you, of course."

"Me?" Her eyes widened. "You really think so?"

"Think so? I *know* so! I've never seen such perfection in the female form before in my life."

She stared at him like there was suddenly nothing else in the room that mattered.

"Weeeell," said Claire. "I don't know about you lads, but I'm awful thirsty."

"Oh, right." The dryad smiled but it seemed a little forced now. "What can I get you all?"

"I'll have a cider," said Claire.

"Red wine for me," said Henri.

"Uh, we can have alcohol?" I asked.

"You bet," said the dryad.

"Okay, then can I get an IPA?"

"Got it. Those'll be up in a minute." She turned to go.

"Wait!" said Henri.

She stopped and turned back, looking a little confused.

"You didn't tell us your name."

"My name?" she asked, and again she stared at him with an intensity I'd never seen in a dryad before.

"Yes, of course," he said.

"Iris." Then she turned abruptly and headed back to her post at the bar.

"You're freaking out the dryads," said Claire.

"Sorry, I can't help it," he said. "Beautiful ladies! Everywhere I look! How many are there altogether?"

"Ten, I think," I said. "It's weird that they're openly serving alcohol now."

"It's great," said Claire.

"Yeah, but Ruthven was never cool with underage drinking. It had to be all on the down low and only for the cool kids. And I was never one of those kids."

"Has it ever occurred to you that maybe Ruthven was a bit of a control freak?" asked Claire. "So he's relaxing a little. That could be a good thing."

"Maybe," I said. "He did let Henri in here. I'm not sure he would have done that a year ago, either."

"Drinks are served!" said a dryad with pigtails, taking glasses from a tray and placing them on our table.

"And what is *your* name?" asked Henri.

"Meadow," she said, clearly not as thrown by the question as Iris. Or maybe since they shared a collective consciousness, she was just ready for the question this time. "And you must be Henri Frankenstein."

"Yes, but how did you know?"

"Ruthven told us about you," she said. "Although he did not tell us how strikingly handsome you were."

"Strikingly handsome?" he asked. "I like that . . ."

"Do you? Perhaps you would like—"

"Meadow!" Liel came over, clapping a hand on her back. "Sorry to interrupt, but can you put in an order for us?"

They stood there staring at each other for a moment. Both of them were smiling, but I felt like there was something else going on there, too. Then Meadow nodded sharply.

"Yes, of course. What would you like?"

"Two vodka tonics, thanks."

Meadow nodded again. She glanced briefly at Henri, and then turned and left.

"Well, here we all are," said Liel, smiling down at us. Next to her stood the new lead trowe dancer that we'd seen in The Show that night. She was a little shorter than Liel, and she had sapphire eyes instead of diamonds. The two of them sat down in the booth with us.

"Yes, we are," said Claire.

"Claire, I don't think we've ever actually hung out before." Liel frowned like she was trying to remember.

"No, we haven't," said Claire. "Can't imagine why not."

Liel smiled at that. Either because she didn't notice the hostile tone or because she didn't care.

"Have you guys met Bakru?" she asked. Then she put her arm possessively around Bakru's waist and pulled her in close so that their hips touched. "My girlfriend."

"Sorry," said Claire. "When you say 'girlfriend,' you mean . . ."

"Can I just get the awkward part out of the way?" asked Bakru. "Yes, we're dating."

Henri had been right in the middle of taking a sip of his wine and he started choking.

"Yeah." Liel looked at me. "I told you earlier that I'm finally happy here. Bakru's the reason why."

"Well, hopefully I'm not the *only* reason," said Bakru. "That's a lot of pressure."

"Sure, okay," said Liel, giving Bakru a quick kiss on the cheek. "But you're my favorite reason." Then she turned back to me. "Soooo, yeah. That might be a little bit of a shock for you."

"Uh . . ." I said. "Yeah."

"I figured," said Liel. "Take your time."

"Two vodka tonics," said Sequoia brightly. As she placed them on the table, we all kind of sat there in an uncomfortable silence.

When Sequoia finally left, Claire said, "Right. Let's fucking drink."

I DRANK MORE that night than I'd ever drank before. Maybe more than I'd ever drunk cumulatively in my life up to that night. I don't remember any of us asking for more than that first round, but they just kept coming. After a while, I lost count.

At one point, I was talking to Henri. He was going on and on about how much he respected me and how glad he was we were not only cousins, but friends. I happened to look over and noticed Liel and Claire talking, both of them looking about as foggy as I felt. Little alarm bells went off in my drunken brain, and I decided I should listen in, just in case things were getting ugly.

"So," Liel was saying. "Truce? Or did you want to take some time to tell me what a bitch I was to Boy first?"

"You *were* a bitch to him."

"At times, yes. But in my defense, at times he was an idiot."

"He can be an idiot sometimes," admitted Claire. "A few weeks ago he tried to make friends with a lake monster."

"How'd that go?" asked Liel.

"How'd you think? He nearly got eaten, then drowned. If I hadn't come along right then, he'd be at the bottom of Lake Geneva. Sometimes he just doesn't think things through. Like he's got no common sense."

"Yeah, but sometimes that's exactly what needs to happen. What he did, coming after Vi like that all on his own when she took over the theater? Talk about an idiot move. But if he hadn't, just about everyone in this room would be dead."

"I had to save his arse then, too," said Claire.

"And that," said Liel, patting Claire's shoulder, "is why I'm so glad he has you."

I turned back to Henri. "What's going on over there?"

"Where," asked Henri, squinting his eyes.

"Liel and Claire. They're like buddies now."

"Ah, you see, most of Claire's hostility toward Liel was that she viewed her as a threat. As competition. Ex-girlfriends can be dangerous like that. But now she knows there's no way in hell you two will ever get back together again. So they can be friends."

"That makes no sense," I said.

"It could be that I am drunk," said Henri.

And so the evening went. At one point, I looked around and realized we were the last ones in the bar. Claire and Bakru were sitting over in the corner talking. There was some cheesy club music playing and Henri was dancing in the aisle with a couple of dryads. I'd never seen them actually hang out with people in the bar before. It was interesting to see them cut loose a little, drinking wine, laughing at Henri as he tried to woo them with what he clearly thought was some sexy dancing.

Liel sat down next to me.

"Hey," she said.

"Hey."

"You okay?"

"Sure. No. I don't know."

She smiled. "Been there."

"Okay, I have to ask."

"Yeah?"

"So when we were together . . . was all of it just . . . fake?"

"No, Boy. I've always cared about you. Just . . . not in the way you wanted. I tried for a little while, but . . ." She shook her head. "I didn't really know what I was doing back then. And I know I hurt you while I was trying to figure it out. I'm not going to apologize for that, though."

I sighed. "Of course not. Because you never apologize to anyone."

"No, because it was an accident and I don't apologize when I didn't do anything wrong. But I do want to thank you."

"Thank me?"

"There were lots of times when we were together that you could have just got up and left. Abandoned me in Queens or Jersey or wherever. But you never did. You stuck by me even in the worst moments." She put her hand on my shoulder. "You are the most loyal son of a bitch I know."

She glanced over at Bakru, who was talking intensely to Claire about something. "Now, if you'll excuse me, it looks like I need to save Claire from one of my girlfriend's extended lectures on why *Doctor Who* is the most important show on television."

I don't know how long the evening went on like that. Finally, Charon came and told us it was time to "shut up and go to bed." So we slowly started to make our way down to the lower lobby.

"Hey, where are you staying, Henri?" asked Liel. "With Boy's parents?"

Henri shook his head, leaning on Meadow so much that it looked like he might fall if she moved. "No, no, no. I am staying in a hotel down the street. In fact, I am not *allowed* to spend the night in the theater. Apparently, I make too tempting a target or something."

"Ah." Liel nodded, her eyes sleepy. "Well, good night then. Get there safe." She and Bakru headed for the stairs that led down to the trowe caverns.

"Are you okay getting back to the hotel?" I asked Henri.

"Oh, yes." He tried to put his coat on and failed. "Hmmm . . ."

Sequoia appeared at his other side and helped him get his arms through the sleeves.

"Are you sure?" I asked.

"Of course, of course!" He waved vaguely toward the front door. "It is just down the street! Can't miss it!"

"Boy . . ." said Claire.

"Yeah," I said. "Maybe I should—"

"You guys look like you're ready for bed, too," said Iris. "We'll get him there safely."

"You know where to go?" I asked. Something seemed a little off about this, but in my drunken haze, I couldn't quite put my finger on it.

"Don't worry about a thing," said Meadow, still shouldering most of his weight. "We've got it under control."

"Trust us," said Sequoia. "We're professionals."

"Thanks, ladies," I said. "I guess I owe you one."

Liel and Bakru had already gone. Claire tugged me in the direction of our room. Then I heard Henri muttering something to the three dryads, and they all giggled. The dryads looked a little different for some reason. Their eyes were brighter, their smiles were wider, and their hair was a lot messier than they usually let it get. Something wasn't quite—

"Hey," said Claire, her lips brushing my ear. "Are you going to put me to bed, or what?"

What was I worried about? They were only harmless dryads. So I let Claire lead me by the hand back to our room.

It wasn't until the next day that I found out just how wrong I was.

# Not My Best Day

╫╫╫╫╫╫╫

WHEN I WOKE up the next morning, my first thought was that an elephant must be sitting on my head. Then I thought, *No, that's ridiculous. How could an elephant get in here?* So I decided it must be an ogre sitting on my head.

I opened my eyes, expecting to see nothing but ogre butt. However, there was no ogre, only a stabbing glare from the one light in the bedroom. That's when I realized that I was just really hungover.

"Oh, god," I groaned.

"Must you shout?" asked Claire next to me.

"I don't think I was."

"Right. Well, we're in bad shape, then."

"I feel like I could die," I said.

"That's just wishful thinking."

"Why did you turn that light on?"

"I didn't turn on any light. I haven't even opened my eyes yet. I'm afraid they'll crumble to dust when exposed to air."

"Well, someone turned on a light." I started to drag myself toward the small table where the light was coming from, but then I looked down. We were lying on a stack of blankets on the floor.

"Hey, what happened to our bed?"

"We never had one," she said. "I failed to get one for us yesterday. You said it was fine. You said we'd sleep on the ground like we were out traveling."

"I have no memory of it."

"I'm not surprised. You were so drunk you passed out in mid kiss."

"Sorry."

"It would have been one or the other of us. Let's just be grateful we're not lying in a pool of sick."

"What is that light?" I said. "Now it's flashing."

I finally made it over to the table. I reached one hand up and groped around until I felt a small metal-and-glass rectangle.

"Oh, it's Vi."

"Don't answer it. I can't handle that much perkiness and sparkles right now."

"She's clearly trying to get our attention. What if something's wrong?"

"She's a big-girl, super-intelligent digital consciousness. I think whatever it is, she can handle it on her own."

I ignored that and unlocked the phone.

"Hey, Vi," I said.

"I'm really worried about Henri." Her eyes were perfect circles and her mouth was shaped like an upside-down V.

"Why?"

"He's not picking up his phone in his hotel room."

"Maybe he's still sleeping," I said. "We all had a little too much to drink last night."

"And those three dryads never came back."

"Oh. Uh, maybe . . ." I turned to Claire. "Do dryads . . . you know, hook up with humans?"

"Dunno," she said, her eyes still closed.

I turned back to Vi. "Look, he was pretty wasted. So he might have made some . . . bad decisions last night. And he's probably still sleeping it off right now. I'm not feeling great myself, honestly. Give it, like, another hour. Or two. Then we'll try him again."

"Boy, please, I'm really worried about him. I just know something is wrong!" A single, oversized tear hung from one of her big anime eyes.

"Okay. Fine. Let me at least take a shower."

"Oh, thank you, Boy! You're the best!" Her eyes changed to star shapes and she showed a smile of white teeth that lit up the screen so bright I had to squint.

"Sure, sure." I turned to Claire. "I guess I'm going to go check in on Henri. See how he's doing."

"Um."

"Are you coming?"

"For the sake of all those I would encounter, no."

———

AFTER A SHOWER, I felt slightly more functional. Vi had apparently co-opted the ringtone into a way for her to continue talking even when the phone was locked, and she kept blabbering on as I pulled on jeans and a T-shirt. At first I tried to calm her down, but it was clear nothing short of finding Henri was going to do that. Eventually, I just switched the phone to vibrate so I didn't have to listen to her anymore. It continued to buzz in my pocket as I made my way over to the lobby.

"How're you feeling today?" said Charon from the box office window. He had a big smirk on his brown, leathery face. "A little delicate, maybe?"

"Yeah, yeah." I waved at him. "No need to rub it in."

"I hope you've learned your lesson," he said.

"The lesson seems to be ongoing," I said as I walked over to Ruthven's office and knocked on the door.

"Yes?" came Ruthven's voice.

"It's Boy."

"Come in."

Ruthven was at his desk as usual, writing in an old-fashioned finance ledger.

"You know, we could get that all in a spreadsheet," I said.

"I'm sure you could," he said, not looking up. "Now what can I do for you?"

"Vi is worried about Henri. He's not picking up his phone at the hotel."

"Mmm-hmmm," he said, still not looking up from his ledger. "Not surprising, given what Charon told me about your little soirée at the Cantina last night. It's amazing you've managed to drag yourself out of bed before noon."

"I guess a couple of dryads are missing, too."

He stopped writing and looked up for the first time. "Dryads?"

"Yeah, I wasn't sure Henri would be able to make it back to the hotel on his own, and three of the dryads offered to take him."

"They left the theater?" His expression was stony.

"Well, they'd been drinking, too, and I was wondering, you know, if they might have—"

"I'm sorry," said Ruthven, his eyes now pulsing red. "Did you say the dryads had been *drinking*?"

"I thought that was weird, too. I'd never seen them drink before. And they looked a little messy. For them. You know, usually they're so put together."

Ruthven picked up the old corded phone on his desk and punched in a number. After a moment he said, "It's Ruthven. I need to talk to Hazel. Now."

"So . . ." I began. But then he held up a finger and I shut up.

"Hazel, are you missing anyone?" He listened for a moment. "Why didn't you tell me immediately? I see. . . . No, we'll handle it. But Hazel? This conversation is far from over. You assured me this would not be a problem. If anything happens to our guest, I will hold you responsible." He pushed down on the receiver to hang up, muttering to himself, "I wish Mozart was still here. . . ." Then he punched in another number. "Charon, I need Claire and Liel in my office. Immediately. No excuses." He hung up the phone and looked at me. His eyes were glowing a solid red now. I couldn't remember the last time I'd seen that.

"I'm guessing this is bad," I said.

"Do you know what happens to nymphs when they drink?"

"Uhhh . . ."

"Obviously you don't, or you would never have let them take Henri home last night. A nymph—any nymph—who gets drunk becomes a maenad."

"Maenads? Wait, like the crazy, feral nymphs who like to rip apart live animals with their bare hands and eat them raw?"

"Yes. And when they are in a frenzy, they don't always make a distinction between animal and human."

"All right then," I said, and turned to leave.

"Wait, Boy, where are you going?"

"To the hotel, obviously. Henri is my responsibility. I'm not going to let him get torn to pieces by bloodthirsty nymphs."

"Wait until Liel and Claire get here."

"Why?"

"You have no idea how dangerous maenads can be. You'll

need the extra muscle. I'd come myself, but it's too damn sunny today for me to go outside. Liel will have to put on glamour, obviously, but they both have experience with being out among humans, and Liel should be able follow Henri's scent if they've taken him somewhere else."

I shook my head. "I'm not waiting for all that. They can catch up. I'm going now."

Ruthven called after me, but I was already across the lobby and through the front doors. I could feel the anger surging through my limbs as I sprinted down the sidewalk. I was ready for anything those maenads threw at me.

———

WHEN I GOT to the hotel, I headed straight to the front desk.

"I need the room number for Henri Frankenstein."

The guy at the counter gave me a hard look. I realized I probably looked sketchy. A big guy with stitches wearing nothing but jeans and a T-shirt in the dead of winter comes barging in, demanding to know a room number. I probably wouldn't have trusted me, either.

"I'm sorry, sir. We don't give out the room numbers for guests. I can call up if you like."

I felt a buzz in my pocket.

"Don't bother." I stepped away from the desk and took out the phone.

There was no cute Vi picture now. Instead, it was just a random collage of shapes and colors. "Room 13-M," she said tersely.

"Got it."

I slipped her back into my pocket and looked at the guy at the front desk. He was still eyeing me suspiciously.

"Uh, he just called me and told me his room number," I said.

I didn't have the time or patience to mess around with an elevator, so I took the stairs. As I pounded up thirteen flights, I felt my pulse rising. But rather than getting tired, I felt myself growing stronger, faster, like my body was waking up after a long sleep. By the time I reached the thirteenth floor, blood was pounding in my ears and I was so amped up I accidentally ripped the metal door right off the hinges. Those maenads were in deep shit.

"There you are!"

I turned and saw Claire and Liel, running up behind me. It threw me for a second to see Liel in her human glamour. Blonde hair, pale blue eyes, tan skin. A memory of our life together living in New York fluttered through my mind like a bit of gauze, but it was quickly burned away by my rage.

"What kept you?" I said, and continued down the hallway.

"Well," said Claire, "since we had no idea what room Henri was in or where you were going, Liel had to follow your scent the whole way. Now slow down a second, will you?"

I stopped and turned back. "Ruthven told you what the dryads have turned into. We have to get him out of there now."

"Of course we do, but I think we should make a plan first."

"The plan is simple. Smash and grab."

"What are you, the bloody Incredible Hulk now?"

"Just don't get in my way."

Then I heard a piercing, high-pitched wail that yanked me into a full sprint for the room. I didn't even break stride when I went through the door.

Except I didn't see anyone in there. No one alive, that is. It was one of those big penthouse suites. And the whole thing seemed to be covered in blood. It ran down the walls in streaks and dripped from the ceiling. The furniture was broken, the TV smashed. There were shards of dark glass covering the carpet, maybe from wine bottles. And scattered all over the room were human body parts.

"Oh, shite . . ." said Claire.

I started searching through the body parts. It wasn't always easy to tell what they were. Some were clearly legs or arms. But others were so mauled they just looked like chunks of meat and tendon, or else bones stripped of everything but a few strands of flesh. I couldn't tell if Henri had been among them.

Then I heard the sound again, from the bathroom.

It was a big bathroom with a deep Jacuzzi-style tub. Henri lay in the tub, naked, his eyes glazed over, his mouth slack, sloshing around in a pool of blood. All the maenads were naked as well, blood smeared on their bodies and caked in their wild hair. One was straddling him. Another was holding down a quivering, screaming man as the third ripped flesh from his body and shoved it into Henri's mouth.

All three turned to me and smiled in unison.

"Welcome!" they said as one. "To the birth of a new Dionysus! Bow down to the Mad One! The Bringer of Ecstasy! The—"

I grabbed the one straddling Henri by the throat and threw her against the wall. Dimly, I was aware that I was roaring unintelligibly, like a beast. But the sight of blood, the maenads grinning like maniacs, the torn-open guy screaming, Henri's eyes empty and raw human flesh spilling out of his mouth drowned out all thought. I smashed into the grinning, blood-drenched faces and I felt them break. But I didn't stop.

"That's enough, Boy! You'll kill them!" Claire shouted.

She grabbed one arm and Liel grabbed the other. But I knocked them both back. Then I turned to the maenads again. They were bruised and broken but still grinning, clawing at me weakly with torn fingernails, raving about Dionysus. I lifted both my fists over my head. I would crush them. I would reduce them to pulp. I would—

"Boy," came a soft, familiar voice.

A cool hand touched the back of my hot, sweating neck.

A scent like cotton blowing in the breeze cut through the stink of blood and filth.

"Boy, it's okay. You're done now."

"S-S-S-Sophie?" I turned slowly. She was there, small and gentle, her pale, heart-shaped face framed in long, curly auburn hair as she looked up at me with her bright blue-green eyes. She reached out her delicate hand and placed it on my cheek. It felt real like nothing else in that moment did.

"Come back to us, Boy," she said.

"Sophie . . . I—I—I . . . I didn't . . . I couldn't . . ." I turned back to the maenads, now covered in their own blood as well as the blood of the humans they'd killed. They lay unmoving, barely alive. "Oh, god . . ."

She gently pulled me down to her and I just started sobbing into her chest, like all the rage and anger that had been coiled up in me had melted into tears.

"It's okay," she whispered, and kissed my forehead. "It's over. I've got you now."

LIEL AND SOPHIE suggested that I go back to the theater, but I wanted to help with the cleanup. I *needed* to. Henri was just starting to regain consciousness when the other seven dryads showed up dressed as maids with cleaning supplies, clothes, and a first aid kit. They surveyed the carnage, their faces grim.

"Take a good look, sisters," said Hazel. She was the eldest and leader of the dryads. She looked the same as the rest, except her skin had a slightly rough-looking texture, almost like bark. "This is what it looks like when you give in to the dark, selfish impulse and ignore the good of the group. Be grateful that there was one who could stop them. Otherwise, the consequences would have been even worse." She turned to me. "Thank you, Boy. You do your father much honor."

I didn't know how to respond, so I just nodded and got to work cleaning up the mess. I didn't think I'd done anybody any honors.

When we were finished cleaning up, the dryads took their injured sisters back to the theater. Hazel loaded up on glamour and went to smooth things over with the hotel manager.

That left Liel, Sophie, and me to explain it all to Henri.

"But wait . . ." he said as we guided him to the bed with new clean sheets. "What happened?" He was still pretty out of it, but he wasn't injured. "The last thing I remember . . ." He frowned, and looked around. "How did I get here?"

Sophie, Liel, and I exchanged looks.

"Some dryads brought you home last night," said Liel. "You don't remember that?"

He tried to give her his grin, but in his current state it was more of a leer. "I'm sorry, I don't believe we've met before. I know I would have remembered so lovely a face."

"Actually, Henri, we have met. It's Liel."

"Wait." He squinted at her. "*This* is Liel?"

She gave him a polished human smile. "Might want to pick that jaw up off the ground there. It's only a temporary illusion, anyway. Just a pinch of glamour, or what you might call faerie dust, courtesy of Laurellen."

"Amazing!" said Henri. Then he turned his unfocused gaze on

Sophie. "And who is *this* rare creature? I *know* we have not met."

"Not officially, no," she said. "I'm Sophie."

"*The* Sophie Jekyll? At last! Boy is one lucky man. Or monster. You, my dear, give new meaning to the phrase 'breathtaking beauty.'"

Sophie patted his head and looked at me. "Isn't he adorable? Let's keep him."

"I think he could stand to be a little less adorable," said Liel. "Since that's what got him into this mess in the first place."

"Mess?" asked Henri, looking around in confusion. "What mess?"

"You really don't remember any of it?" I asked. "The dryads. They brought you back. And then at some point . . . they started killing and eating people."

"They . . ." His eyes started to rove around the room, growing wider and wider. "I think I . . . oh, god . . ." He turned wildly around, trying to climb out of the bed.

"It's over now." I gently brought him back down. "You're okay."

"Jesus fucking Christ," he said as he settled back in the bed. He clutched one of the pillows. "They were . . . tearing people apart. I could not . . . they kept forcing wine down my throat. And other things. I don't even know . . ." He shuddered.

"I'm so sorry this happened," I said.

"You said it would be dangerous," he said quietly, his eyes staring out the window at the fading afternoon light. "You warned me. I just . . . you know, thought it was big, scary monsters I needed to watch out for." He shuddered again.

There was a knock at the newly reattached door. I opened it and Hazel came in.

"Everything is settled," she said. "I apologized to the hotel management about the broken furniture and gave them money to replace it all." She looked at Henri. "In the meantime, I'm afraid you'll have to do without a television."

He nodded absently, his eyes still staring out the window.

"What about the missing employees?" I asked.

She shook her head. "I'm sorry for the loss of those humans, but I'm afraid all we can do is make sure there is nothing that links back to The Show. We must take care of our own, after all. Now, I suggest that we let Henri get some sleep, and that the rest of us return to the theater where we belong."

I put my hand on Henri's shoulder. "You okay?"

"I am alive," he said. "Thank god for that at least."

"All right, we'll see you tomorrow. Get some sleep."

"Eh, do you . . . think I could keep Vi here with me?" he asked. "It's just, you know, I would rather not be alone right now."

I took Vi out of my pocket.

"Hi, Boy!" She was back together in her anime form.

"Are you cool with keeping Henri company tonight?"

An exclamation point appeared over her head, and her cheeks went bright red. "You bet!"

Not that I was staring or anything, but it seemed like her breasts were a little larger and bouncier than they had been the last time I'd seen her. In fact, she seemed to have adopted the same physique as the dryads.

# 9
# Untrust Us

++++++++

THAT EVENING, SOPHIE and I sat up on the roof of the theater, sharing a blanket and looking out over Manhattan. Night was falling and a few stars peeked out through trails of purple clouds.

"This was a good idea," I said.

"Naturally," she said. "Because it was my idea."

"Are you cold?" I asked.

"Not while I'm sharing a blanket with my boyfriend, the living furnace."

"Am I really that hot?"

She pressed her hand flat against my chest. "You have no idea."

I smiled. "I missed you."

"You'd be an idiot not to."

"I'm sorry your first day out had to be . . . this one."

She shrugged and her smiled faded. "I'm just glad I could be there when you needed me."

"I did need you."

"I know."

She looked up at me, brushing my hair to one side.

"There's nothing wrong with that, you know," she said. "Needing me."

"It's just . . . if you hadn't been there . . . if you hadn't stopped me . . ." I struggled to push out words that didn't seem to want to come. "I think I would have killed them."

Sophie said nothing for a moment, just stared up at me with her bright eyes. "We're all a lot closer to the darkness than we want to admit."

"Still," I said. "I know Claire has saved my life, but today, you saved my soul."

"Do you think we have those?"

"I don't know. Sometimes I think that's all we really are. My body parts can be replaced. They don't change who I am as a person. Vi doesn't even have a body yet, but she's a person."

"What about us?"

"What do you mean?"

"Claire and I. Are we two souls? Or one split in half?"

"Two souls. Definitely."

"Why are you so sure?"

"Because neither of you is half of anything."

We were silent for a moment. The drone of endless traffic hummed on below us. Then she slipped her small hand in mine.

"I missed you, too," she said.

"I know." I drew her closer. "But it's still nice to hear."

I don't know how long we sat there, but the sky had gone black and the skyline lit up with a thousand lights by the time my father came up to get us.

"Hiya, Papa Monster!" said Sophie, jumping up and giving him a big hug.

He smiled and carefully stroked her hair with his massive hand.

"Sophie, it is good to see you." Then he turned to me. "We found you a bed. I need you to help me move it into your room."

Sophie headed to our room to clear up some space, while I followed Dad. The hallways were too narrow for us to fit side by side, so I walked behind him.

"I heard what you did today," he said as we walked.

"Yeah. From Hazel?"

"No, from Liel."

"Oh."

We walked on for a little while. Then, still not looking back at me, he said, "I still remember the first time I lost control. It terrified me."

"I almost killed people today, Dad."

"I *did* kill people," he said.

"I know. But it's not like I've got more self-control or anything. It was Sophie who stopped me."

"That is my point. You have kind, caring people in your life. Be grateful for them. Protect them, and they will protect you."

"Protect me from what?"

"Yourself."

We got the spare bed from the trowe dens. For a moment I wondered if this was Liel's bed and she didn't need it now that she was hooking up with Bakru. But I decided that line of thought would just make me crazy, and I didn't need any more drama right now. So as my dad and I slowly maneuvered the bed up the winding staircase to ground level, I tried to distract myself with something else.

"I've been meaning to ask you," I said. "Did you ever know a dwarf in Geneva?"

"Why do you ask?"

"I met one while I was up in the Jura Mountains. He said he taught you how to survive up there."

"Yes. He did. I'm glad to know he's still alive."

"He said a bunch of gloom-and-doom stuff about the future to me."

He stopped and turned his head to look at me over the top of the bed. "What did he say exactly?"

"I can't remember word for word. Something about the truth being revealed and war coming after. And he said he'd be there to help me when my need was 'most dire.' Whatever that meant. Clearly, almost getting eaten by a freshwater mermaid wasn't dire enough."

He stared down at me for a moment. "I see." Then he turned and started moving the bed again.

"So . . . does that mean anything to you?" I asked.

"It's nothing you need to concern yourself with right now."

"That doesn't exactly answer my question."

But he didn't say anything else for the rest of the climb. Maybe I was getting a little paranoid, but between him and Ruthven, I was starting to get the feeling they were keeping something from me—something big. It wouldn't be the first time. After all, it wasn't until I was seventeen that I found out that Dad was planning to send me to live with the Frankensteins.

Once we reached ground level and got out of the stairwell, we were able to get the bed parallel to the ground, making it a lot easier to carry. We were most of the way across the lobby when I saw someone enter through the main doors wearing an overcoat and a fedora. The figure glanced quickly around and for a split second I saw a beige latex mask and dark, wrap-around sunglasses. He stood there for a moment, then moved quickly toward Ruthven's office door.

"Is that Kemp?" I asked.

My dad stopped abruptly and put his end of the bed down. "You can take it the rest of the way. I must go." Then he headed

over to Ruthven's office, following after Kemp. The door closed
behind them, and a moment later I heard it lock.

There was definitely something going on that they weren't
telling me.

I sighed, and hoisted the bed up so it was balanced across my
back, then trudged down the hallway alone.

"IT DOESN'T SURPRISE me that Ruthven would be sneaky," said
Sophie. "Or your dad, honestly. But Kemp? I thought he was cool."

"Sorry, who is Kemp again?" asked Henri.

Sophie and I had gone over to the hotel first thing in the morning so we could discuss the suspicious activities of our community
elders with Henri and Vi. The room had already been fixed up
with new furniture and a TV.

"Kemp is the Invisible Man," I said.

"He's also the leader of a monster community out in LA called
The Studio," said Sophie.

"The Studio? Is that like the Hollywood version of The Show?"

"Pretty much," I said. "He and Ruthven have always had this
rivalry."

"Like American rap groups?"

"What?"

"You know. East Coast versus West Coast."

"Uh, yeah, I guess. . . ."

"So whatever brought those two together must be serious!" said Vi. Her phone sat on the bed next to Henri. He'd
thoughtfully propped her up on his knee so we could see each
other.

"Maybe they're just finally planning that big international

monster summit or whatever they've been talking about since last summer," I said.

"Then why all the secrecy?" asked Sophie. "No, I think it has something to do with Robert."

"But they would tell you, of all people," said Henri. "Yes?"

"You'd think so," I said. "But Ruthven was kind of cagey both times I asked him about it. This could totally be about Robert."

"Then you have a right to know, Sophie," said Henri.

"That's right!" said Vi. "He's your brother!"

"Nobody's arguing with that," I said. "But we can't *make* Ruthven tell us."

"Maybe if I talk to Kemp when Ruthven isn't around," said Sophie. "He might open up."

"It's worth a shot," I said. "We'll need a distraction then. Something to draw Ruthven's attention so we can get Kemp alone."

"I could get kidnapped by dryads again," said Henri.

"Preferably something that doesn't involve a body count," I said.

"I could trigger the fire alarms," said Vi.

"Or a general panic."

"Okay, you're not going to like this idea, but I think it'll work," said Sophie. "Your mum has been avoiding you since we got here."

"I noticed," I said. "It's because I brought Henri."

"Your mom is not a fan?" he asked.

"Of the Frankensteins, or humans in general," I said.

"But everybody loves Henri!" said Vi.

"Of course, Vi," said Sophie. "I'm sure the Bride just needs to give him a chance. She hasn't even met him yet." She turned to me. "Which is why you, love, should ask Ruthven to take Henri to her and formally introduce them. She won't be able to avoid that."

"And while Ruthven, Henri, and I are having that awkward moment with my mom," I said, "you can use your wiles to get the info out of Kemp."

"Wiles?" She pressed a finger to the dimple on her freckled cheek. "I haven't the slightest idea what you're talking about."

WHEN WE ENTERED the lobby, Sophie went over to "chat up" the goblin twins at the box office while Henri and I went to Ruthven's office. Sophie and Henri agreed it would look less suspicious that way.

As I knocked on Ruthven's door, I took a deep breath to calm my nerves. I'd never tried to purposefully deceive Ruthven like this before. Partly because I was a terrible liar and he knew it.

"Yes?" came Ruthven's voice.

"It's Boy. And, uh, Henri, too."

"Perfect. Come in."

When I opened the door, Ruthven was at his desk as usual. There was a chair next to his desk with what appeared to be an empty suit in it.

"Ah, Boy, so good to see you!" said Kemp in his polished British dialect. He stood up as we entered.

"Good to have you here." I shook his invisible hand. "This is Henri Frankenstein."

"A pleasure, Henri," said Kemp, extending his sleeve. "I've heard so much about you!"

Up to this point, I'd been pretty impressed with how cool Henri had been around people who didn't look human. Trowe, goblins, ogres, creatures with fangs, scales, claws, the works:

none of it had rattled him. But this, I could tell, was his limit. He stared at Kemp, or I guess stared at the seemingly empty space that Kemp occupied. His eyes got wider and wider and his mouth started to sag open.

I nudged him and he came out of it enough to force a smile, extend his hand, and say, "Great to meet you."

But then when he felt Kemp's invisible hand, his face went white and I thought he might actually faint.

"Steady on, there's a good lad," Kemp said, his voice amused. Then he sat back down.

"How is everyone at The Studio?" I asked.

"Oh, fine, fine," said Kemp. "In fact, we're on hiatus."

"I didn't know that," said Ruthven. "For how long?"

"At least until the New Year. Possibly until the spring. Most of the company are traveling abroad now, either visiting friends or returning to their homelands."

"And you can afford this extended break?" asked Ruthven, his eyebrow raised.

Kemp's suit shoulders shrugged. "I'm loath to rub it in, old chap, but television makes quite a bit more money than theater."

"Yes, yes, I know how you *hate* to bring that up as frequently as you do."

Kemp laughed.

"How's Millicent?" I asked.

There was a sudden pause and I wondered if maybe I shouldn't have mentioned his wife.

"I'm sorry," I said. "I shouldn't have——"

"No," he said, his voice sounding strained. "No, it's fine. In fact, thank you. So few people ask after her anymore."

"So, Boy, what is it you wanted?" asked Ruthven.

For a moment I was relieved that Ruthven had changed the

subject. But then I realized it was time to start lying. "Uh, I have a favor to ask."

"Oh?"

"Mom has been completely avoiding meeting Henri."

"And you're surprised?"

"No, but it means that I've hardly seen her. And, I mean, how long is she going to keep this up?"

"What do you propose?"

"Could you, like, formally introduce Henri to her?"

"The old 'rip the Band-Aid off' approach?"

I shrugged.

He sighed and pressed his hands together in a steeple. "I suppose it needs to happen at some point." He turned to Kemp. "Would you mind if we take a quick break?"

"Not at all. I believe I heard my Sophie out in the lobby a moment ago. I'll go and catch up with her while you take care of this."

"Thanks. It shouldn't take too long." Ruthven stood and his shadows swirled around him. "Unless, of course, the Bride starts smashing things in a righteous fury."

"I never know whether anyone's joking anymore," Henri whispered to me.

———

AS WE FOLLOWED Ruthven through the corridors, Henri asked me, "Who's Millicent?"

"Oh, Kemp's wife."

"Why was it so awkward when you asked how she is doing?"

"Because she's kind of in . . . like a vegetative state or something."

"For how long?"

"A long time. And it's sort of his fault."

"Was it a car accident or something?"

"No, a long time ago, he'd discovered that a side effect of his invisibility formula was halting the aging process. Millicent wanted to stop aging so that she could live on with Kemp, but she didn't want to become invisible. She convinced him to try to isolate just that part of the formula that stopped aging."

"And it didn't go well?"

"Well, it *did* stop her from aging," I said. "But I guess when he'd tried to block the invisibility component, he overcompensated. Now she's like the opposite of invisible."

"Hypervisible?"

"Yeah, she seems to pull at your vision, to swallow up everything, including light. Like a human-shaped black hole. I think her matter is so dense, that's why she can't move or speak. So he's had to basically be her nurse ever since, feeding her, bathing her, everything."

"That's terrible."

"We used to talk about her a lot when I was in LA, and I spent time with them together. But maybe he didn't want to show that side of himself in front of Ruthven."

"Yes, I saw some of that rivalry you were talking about."

Ruthven led us down into the caverns where most of the company lived. Henri's eyes darted everywhere as he took in the winding hallways, glancing down every passageway we crossed.

"How far does this go?" he asked.

"About a hundred feet down," said Ruthven. "And it stretches nearly a quarter mile from one end to the other. It took the trowe more than a decade to carve it out."

"Unbelievable!" he said.

I'd always taken the caverns for granted because I grew up in them. But they were pretty incredible, especially considering the trowe hadn't used a tunnel bore or any other industrial machinery. Then again, the New York subway system was spectacular, too, and that had been made just by humans. It made me wonder what could happen if humans and monsters worked together.

I knocked on the door to my parents' apartment, and after a moment, my mom answered.

"Boy? I . . ." Then she saw Henri. Her expression remained the same as always, of course. But somehow, the way she stared at him reminded me of the way Henri had been staring at Kemp. Like she just couldn't reconcile him with her reality.

"Hello, Bride," said Ruthven. "May we come in?"

She looked at Ruthven, and I could hear the stitches along her jaw strain with tension. After a really long moment of silence, she said, "Yes."

She backed up slowly, her eyes never leaving Henri. The rest of us filed into the apartment. It looked exactly the same as the last time I'd seen it: a tiny living area, with a little kitchenette, a single table with a couple of chairs, and a TV bolted to the wall. And of course mom's pile of junk in the corner that she liked to fiddle with to make stuff.

"Henri Frankenstein," said Ruthven, "may I introduce the Bride of Frankenstein."

"*Madame la Mariée*," said Henri, and bowed. "It is such an honor to meet you at last. Thank you for welcoming me into your home."

She did not move, or even blink.

"Mom?" I put my hand on her arm. "Are you okay?"

Her head jerked to me. "Is . . . he really human?"

"Yeah."

"And . . . he is your friend?"

"He is our *family*," I said. "He is our blood."

She looked at me, and her head tilted to one side. "Blood?"

"Poor choice of words, perhaps," murmured Ruthven.

"Okay, forget that," I said. "Look, I know this is really hard for you. I just . . . This is really important to me. Think about what this could mean. Not just for me, or even for us. But for all humans and monsters. This could be the beginning of something amazing."

"Humans and monsters." She turned away from me then and walked over to her junk pile. She picked up an iron and slowly, carefully dismantled it, placing the pieces one by one back on the pile.

We all waited.

Finally, she turned back to us, like she had just remembered we were still there.

"Henri Frankenstein. Thank you for the friendship you have shown my son. You are . . . welcome here."

Then she turned back to her pile of junk and began to sort through it. After a minute or so it was pretty obvious she was done with us, so we left.

As we walked back through the cavern hallways, Henri said, "So . . . did that go well?"

"Better than I expected," said Ruthven. "Maybe the old girl is loosening up a bit." Then he turned to me and smiled, his fangs gleaming in the dim light. "Well, do you think we've given Sophie enough time to pry the secrets from dear old Kemp?"

AS HENRI AND I followed Ruthven back to the lobby, I tried to think of some way of signaling to Sophie that they were onto us. But when we got there, it was pretty clear she already knew.

She stood with her hands in her curly hair, shaking her head. "God, I feel like an idiot."

"There, there." Kemp's voice was soothing as he patted her shoulder with his invisible hand. "It's not your fault. Your boyfriend is a dreadful liar, that's all. Really, I would consider that a positive quality if I were you."

"Here we are," said Ruthven. "All cards on the table."

Sophie turned and glared at him. "You sneaky vampire!"

He smiled faintly and nodded.

"So you already planned to tell us about what you're up to?"

"Indeed."

He turned to the goblin twins, who had been pretending not to eavesdrop. "Curmthulia and Rughutla, see that we are not disturbed. For anything. Is that clear?"

We followed Ruthven back to his office. My dad was waiting for us inside. Kemp firmly closed the door behind us. It felt really weird to be in here, on this side of the closed door.

Ruthven settled back at his desk with Kemp on one side and my father on the other.

"First," said Ruthven. "I don't blame you for attempting to get some answers. I have been rather vague on my knowledge of Robert and you were right to be suspicious. Good instincts."

"So it *is* about Robert!" said Sophie.

"Why didn't you tell us earlier?" I asked.

"Until this morning, we weren't sure if we were going to tell you at all," said Ruthven.

"Ruthven was . . . being protective," said Kemp. "As soon as I heard Robert had been found, I rushed out here."

"Kemp reminded me that you both have proven that you are able to handle yourselves in difficult situations," said Ruthven.

"I won him over with the bit about how you saved The Show and quite possibly the city of New York," said Kemp.

"At any rate," said Ruthven, "yes, Sophie, this is about Robert."

"Is . . . is he . . ." Her voice was very small. "Dead?"

Ruthven regarded her curiously for a moment. "No, my dear. He is not. Not yet, anyway, although if he doesn't become more discreet, he might end up that way soon."

"Where is he?" I asked.

"Peru," said Kemp.

"What on earth is he doing there?" asked Sophie.

"Causing trouble, apparently," said Ruthven. "He's been arrested several times by the local authorities. And he keeps escaping."

"Just like prison," asked Sophie. "How is he doing it?"

"That's one of the things we need to find out."

"What is he getting arrested for?" I asked.

"Killing humans," my dad said.

"Robert?" asked Sophie, looking confused. "But he's always wanted to *be* human."

"He practically is, since he eliminated his Hyde aspect," said Ruthven. "Be that as it may, apparently he's been attacking them, more or less in the open. He knows a lot about The Studio, and I'm sure he's aware of The Show as well. I think it's only a matter of time before he starts talking to Peruvian authorities about us. We've already had one scare this year; let's not make it two."

"So I suggested," said Kemp, "that if we need to send someone down to bring him in, perhaps it should be you and Claire."

"Us?" said Sophie. "But . . ."

"Boy will be with you for protection and support, of course," continued Kemp. "And it would do you and Claire both a world of good to face him."

"It wouldn't be just you and Boy," said Ruthven. "I want some people with experience there. We have a local contact in Lima who will assist you. And Mozart, since he's the one who tracked your brother down in the first place."

"Mozart?" I asked. "That's awesome!"

"Which one is he again?" asked Henri.

"The werewolf," I said.

"So . . ." said Ruthven. His red eyes went first to me, then to Sophie. "Would you like to be the ones to bring him in?"

Sophie turned to Kemp. "You really think it would be . . . good for us?"

"I do," he said. "He's your brother. And people change. Perhaps he'll surprise you."

She turned to my dad.

"No one can run from family forever," he said.

She turned back to me, chewing on her lip.

"He caught us off guard last time," I said. "We've learned a lot since then. I think we can handle him, especially if Mozart's going to be with us."

She stood there, her eyes staring off, probably talking it out with Claire. We all waited.

Finally, she looked back first at Kemp, then at Ruthven, and nodded. "Okay. We'll do it."

"Wonderful." Ruthven waved his hand vaguely in Henri's direction. "Do you plan to take your pet human with you?"

"Well?" I asked Henri.

"Werewolves and fugitive brothers in South America?" asked Henri, his grin slowly surfacing. "How could I miss that?"

# 10
# The Freudian Slip

++++++++

WHEN WE LANDED in Lima, it was humid and cloudy. By the time we got out to the pickup area, I was already sweating from the thick air. I missed the December chill of New York, or better yet, the hard cold of Geneva.

But then, past the taxis and tour buses, I saw a middle-aged, bearded guy in aviator sunglasses leaning against a beat-up old station wagon. He gave a slow, casual wave.

There are just some people that, when you see them, you get a little kick of hope. They just have this air about them that makes everything seem a little more possible. Mozart was one of those people.

"There he is," I said as I started toward him.

"So this Mozart is a friend of yours?" asked Henri as he and Sophie followed me.

"He introduced Boy and me," said Sophie. "He's a bit rough around the edges, but underneath it all, he's a complete sweetheart."

"Don't say that to his face, though," I said. "He *is* still a werewolf."

"Well, well, well," said Mozart, white teeth showing through the brown-and-gray streaks of his beard. "I was hoping I'd get to see you kids. And you've got a new guy? Ruthven said there was a third, but he didn't say who it was.'"

"Henri Frankenstein, monsieur," said Henri, and offered his hand.

Mozart's bushy eyebrow shot up as he shook Henri's hand. "A human, huh? And a Frankenstein at that. Interesting."

"Henri's cool. I promise," I said.

Mozart held up his hands. "Hey, you don't have to worry about me. I'm not a human hater. Never have been. And anyway, this isn't The Show. Or even the States for that matter. Things are different down here. The lines are . . . blurrier."

He helped us load our suitcases into the back of the station wagon. Then he took the driver's seat and Sophie took shotgun, while Henri and I climbed into the back.

"My friend Maria doesn't live too far from here. If you want we can go there first, have something to eat, and prepare a little. Or we could just cut to the chase and go right for Robert. Your call."

"Sophie?" I asked.

"You know where he is right now?" she asked.

"The Plaza de Armas. It's a big open town square area."

"What's he doing?" I asked.

"Same thing he's been doing off and on since I found him a couple of weeks ago. Getting as drunk as possible."

Sophie's jaw set. "Let's just go get him, then."

Mozart smiled wide. "Atta girl."

We drove along a coastal highway, but it was too hazy to see much of the Pacific. On the other side of the road were buildings painted in bright yellows, reds, blues, even a few orange or purple. More than language, those colors were what immediately set Lima apart from beige Geneva and gray New York.

"I could get used to this place," said Henri. "Do you think we'll be able to stay a while after we take care of Robert?"

"I don't know," I said. "It would be nice. But I also want to get back to the city by Christmas."

"I'm just talking about getting a few days of beach and sampling some good Peruvian food."

"We'll have to see how this goes," I said.

"You're not worried about Robert, are you?" asked Henri. "They all said he's harmless."

"He's also totally psychotic. I just can't believe it's really going to be that easy to bring him in."

"What till you see him," Mozart called back from the driver's seat.

"That bad?" asked Sophie.

"I hardly recognized him. I do think Boy's right, though. Sometimes the most desperate ones are the most dangerous. Sophie, let's start off with you trying to talk him into coming along quietly. But if things go bad, I want you and Henri to get behind Boy and me. The two of us can handle anything he's got. And who knows, maybe after we pound him a few times, he'll come to his senses."

"And if not?" asked Henri.

"Well . . ." Mozart glanced at Sophie. "Like Boy said, we'll see how it goes."

———

MOZART PARKED THE car a few blocks from the Plaza de Armas. We walked the rest of the way through the narrow, crowded streets until we came to a big, open square with sections of grass, and paved walkways that led to a large fountain in the center.

The square was surrounded by large, old buildings with decorative balconies, some of them painted a bright yellow, others a faded natural stone.

"There he is."

Mozart pointed to a massive cathedral on the other side of the square. Splayed out on the steps of the cathedral was a figure clutching something in a brown paper bag. I could make out the familiar curly auburn hair, like Sophie's. But he looked smaller than I remembered.

"How do you want to do this?" Mozart asked Sophie. "Direct approach or take him by surprise?"

"If we're going to have any luck getting him to come peacefully, I think we should make sure he sees us coming," she said.

"What if he runs?"

"He won't."

Mozart shrugged. "Let's do it, then. You go in front. Show him you're not afraid."

With Sophie in the lead, we crossed the street and started walking through the square toward Robert. I really didn't like how many humans were milling around the square, and I wondered if maybe Robert chose this spot for that reason.

We were about halfway across when Robert slowly lifted his head and seemed to notice us. He didn't move from his spot, though.

"I don't like this," I muttered.

Mozart sniffed the air and his eyes flashed gray and wolfish. "You're about to like it a lot less. Something's coming, and it isn't human."

"What?" I turned first one way, then the other. "From where?"

"Everywhere," he said. "It's a trap."

Out of the crowd of humans stepped a bunch of short, stocky

people with broad shoulders. They all wore the same black hoodies, and had baseball caps pulled low so we couldn't see their faces. They closed in around us, not saying a word. Then one of them reached for Sophie. She knocked his hand away. He made a snorting sound and lifted his head enough that I could see his face beneath the bill. He had beady little eyes, and instead of a nose and mouth, he had a pig snout. Big, yellowed tusks jutted up from his lips. A nearby human saw him and screamed.

"I don't believe this!" Sophie's face was red and angry. "ROBERT, YOU BASTARD!" But Robert still just sat and watched.

"Back off and nobody gets hurt," I told the pig men.

One of them squealed harshly and all at once they came at us. The humans were yelling and running in a panic, but thankfully they all at least seemed to have the sense to run *away* from us.

The one who'd reached for Sophie tried to grab her again. This time I grabbed his wrist and twisted until I felt it break. Then I punched him in the face so hard his tusks broke and he dropped to the ground. I looked around and saw Mozart grappling with another one, his fangs showing as he snarled.

A pig man pinned Henri to the ground. I took a step toward him, but hands grabbed me from behind. I turned just in time to catch the tusk of one before it stabbed me in the side. Another jumped on me and I stumbled. A third one brought me to my knees.

"Mozart! Henri's in trouble!"

"Busy!" he growled. There were two on him now.

I turned back to Henri. He had managed to get out from under the one pig man, but now there were three of them coming at him from different directions.

"Henri!" I knocked down one pig man after another, but they seemed to just keep coming.

Then a slim figure dressed in black and red ran into the middle of the fight, striking out at the pig men so fast that the movements were only a blur. A moment later, the three pig men dropped to the ground and a woman stood next to Henri. She looked to be in her early twenties, wore a black dress with red ruffles, and had a single red rose tucked into her long black hair. Another pig man approached her from behind.

"Look out!" I shouted, still trying to clear a path through the pig men.

She glanced over her shoulder at the pig man and almost casually kicked him square in the chest with her pointed black boot. He dropped to the ground, making short gasping sounds. She turned to me and nodded a terse thanks.

"Boy!"

I'd been distracted and let a pair of pig men through. Now they were pawing at Sophie, squealing triumphantly. The sight of it set off something inside me and I reached her in a couple of strides. I slammed my fist down on the closest one's head and he dropped to the ground. The other one I grabbed by the throat and lifted up high, showing him to Robert as he struggled and squealed.

Robert nodded slowly, but still just sat there.

"You can put him down," said Sophie, her hand on my arm. "It's over."

All the humans had run. All the pig men were down. Mozart, Henri, and the mystery woman were fine. I took a deep breath and let the pig man fall.

The mystery woman prodded one of the unconscious pig men with her boot. "Wild pig people," she said with a Peruvian accent. "I've never seen them venture outside Brazil. Very strange."

"Who . . ." I said.

"This is our local contact," said Mozart. "La Perricholi."

Henri stared almost worshipfully at his rescuer. "Mademoiselle, I cannot express my gratitude for—"

"I'm sure you could, actually," she said, looking at him appraisingly. "But now is not the time for pleasantries. The Lima police are not of the gentle U.S. variety. An armored car will be here in a few minutes." She turned to Sophie. "I suggest you collect your brother before they arrive."

Sophie nodded grimly, then held out her arm to me. "Shall we?"

She and I walked slowly across the square to the cathedral. As we got closer, I could see just how bad off Robert really was. His curly hair hung lank and greasy in his pale, gaunt face. He looked so thin and wasted, I began to wonder if the reason he hadn't moved was because he couldn't.

"Robert?" Sophie asked, her voice sad. "What happened to you?"

He didn't look at us, but instead stared out across the square with watery eyes. "I thought . . . I could fix it. Fix us." His voice was weak and rasping, like he had trouble breathing. "That's all I wanted for us, Sophie. Perfection. But it turns out . . . that's impossible."

"Course it is," said Sophie. "Perfection's for wankers, anyway."

He smiled faintly and took a long pull on the bottle he still held clutched in one dirty, raw hand.

"So now what?" asked Sophie after a moment. "Will you come with us? We made it through your little trap."

"Oh, that wasn't the trap. That was just . . . an assessment. So he would know what he was up against."

"Who?" I asked.

He looked suddenly at Sophie, his pale blue eyes wide, his expression miserable. "I'm so sorry, Soph. Really, I am."

"Sorry about what?" she asked.

"I'm the bait, you see," he said. "And this . . . this is the trap."

His eyes suddenly switched from pale blue to a dark green, and he began to change. It was a lot like what I'd seen Sophie and Claire go through, only more violent. His hair fell out and his skin split open, like there was something inside forcing its way out. His limbs stretched out unnaturally long, convulsing as the muscles swelled and bulged. He let out a shriek of pain that went on and on until suddenly it cut off, replaced by a deep groan. Coarse, patchy clumps of black hair appeared on his arms and cheeks. His teeth and fingernails grew long and pointed. He kept growing taller and wider as he slowly staggered to his feet.

Finally, he stood there, towering over both of us, panting, a toothy grin on his massive face. "Hullo, love."

"Stephen?" said Sophie, her face drained of color.

"The one and only."

"How did you—"

"My idiot brother thought he'd killed me. But come on. We all know you can't have one without the other. That's why your dear old granddad had to kill himself. And Robbie loves himself too much to do the same. No, all he did was repress me for a while."

"But how did you get so . . . big?"

"Oh, you like this, do ya?" He flexed his arm, the bicep easily splitting what was left of his tattered shirt. "Turns out, when you repress a part of yourself, lock it away in a dark place for years? All you actually do is make it stronger. And possibly homicidal. Now, if you'll excuse me, love, I think it's time for your boyfriend and me to knock each other senseless for a bit."

"No, Stephen," I said. "There doesn't have to be any more violence today."

"Oh, but I insist." Then, so fast I didn't even see it coming, he hit me in the chest, hard. I stumbled back, gasping for air that didn't seem to come.

"You're strong, I'll grant you." He rolled his shoulders to loosen up. "And fairly fast for your size." He took another swing at me, almost casually. I barely managed to avoid it. "But you're completely undisciplined. No training, just raw force pounding clumsily away." He held up both fists like a boxer. "So consider this your first lesson."

I had just gotten my wind back when he hit me with the left and I staggered one way, then he hit me with the right and I staggered the other way. I swung and he blocked it, then countered with an uppercut. I reeled, my ears ringing as blood dribbled from the corner of my mouth.

A flash of fur blew past me and slammed into Stephen, knocking him to the ground. Mozart, in full wolf mode, stood on his chest, snarling.

Stephen grinned up at him. "Lookin' a little gray around the muzzle there, Wolfie." He reached up with both hands to grab him, but Mozart dodged, then latched his teeth onto Stephen's thick wrist, drawing blood. Stephen grunted as his face screwed up with pain. But then he grinned again.

"Now that's more like it. A bit of challenge." He snapped his arm. Mozart's teeth tore deeper as he held on to Stephen's wrist, blood coming out in spurts. But then Stephen snapped his arm in the other direction. There was so much blood, and the skin was so torn and ragged, that Mozart couldn't hold on. He went flying, slammed into the stone wall of the cathedral, and lay still.

"You see?" said Stephen, showing me his torn and bloody wrist. "You can escape from anything as long as you're willing to pay the price. Are you listening, little Boy? I'm not going to repeat myself."

"I'm listening," I muttered, and took a swing at him.

He dodged to one side and brought his knee up into my stomach. Then he brought his fist down on my back and I fell to the ground.

"Now see," he said, "I saw that one coming a mile away. It's all in the—"

La Perricholi caught him with a roundhouse kick to the temple.

He stumbled, clutching the side of his face. "Oh, La Perricholi! I feel honored."

"You should," she said.

He swung at her, but she ducked under his arm and brought the palm of her hand up into his chin. Then she followed up with a chop to his neck, and a kick to his groin. He backed away, hunched forward and gagging.

"There!" he said hoarsely. "That's what training can do for you. She's half your size, half your strength, and she's already done three times as much damage as you." Then he slowly straightened up and the grin was back again. "Now imagine what her training and your power could accomplish. It might look something like this!"

Then he unleashed a flurry of blows at her. She dodged and blocked everything he threw at her, but he didn't let up. After a few minutes she was dripping sweat, and each time she blocked one of his blows, she winced from the sheer force of impact. Slowly, grudgingly, she lost ground.

"I can do this all day, Perricholi," he said. "Can you? I doubt it. After all, no matter what they say, I think you're only human."

She yelled defiantly, jumped straight into the air, and drove both pointed boots into his chest. He fell back, but as he did, he grabbed her ankles and pulled her down with him. She fell on top of him and he wrapped her in a bear hug and squeezed. She slammed her forehead into his nose with a wet crack. But he only laughed as blood poured from his nostrils.

"God, woman, you should have been a monster!" he roared. Then his arms bulged as he squeezed her even tighter. She gasped for breath, flailing desperately.

By that time I'd managed to get to my feet again. "Let her go," I said as I stumbled toward him. I had no idea what I was doing, but I had to do something.

He looked over at me with surprise, like he'd completely forgotten I was there. Then he shook his head in disgust. "No, no, no!" He tossed La Perricholi aside, and slowly stood up. "You're not learning anything!"

I threw a punch, but he caught it and twisted my arm behind my back. Then with his bloody, wolf-bitten hand, he just started waling on me.

"I thought you were"—punch—"supposed to be smart!"— punch—"But you blew it!"—punch—"That would have been"— punch—"the perfect time"—punch—"to catch me unawares!"

"Oh, like this?" said Claire. She grabbed his torn, bloody wrist, spun him around, and punched him in his broken nose.

"Hurrah!" He smiled through the mass of blood. "Claire Bear came out to play!"

"You still talk too much," she said, and hit him again.

As I struggled to get back on my feet, brother and sister fought. He was bigger and stronger, but the injuries and blood loss had slowed him down. Still, he was landing almost as many punches as she was, and his did a lot more damage. After a minute or two, it looked pretty clear who had the advantage.

"You could be this powerful, too, you know," he said to her between harsh, bubbly gasps of air. "Don't ask for permission, just take it from her. There's nothing she can do about it."

"Never," she said, also breathing hard. "We do it together or not at all."

His lips curled down into a sneer. "And that's why I win."

Then with a sudden burst of energy, he knocked her arms aside and slammed his fist into her face so hard she pitched back and fell to the ground.

Inside me I felt something snap. The pain, the dizziness, the exhaustion, all disappeared along with everything else. There was only him and how I was going to crush every bone in his body.

"Oh, ready for more?" he said when he saw me coming. "I thought you were do—"

I slammed into him. Maybe he was hitting me but I couldn't feel it. The only thing I could feel was how good it sounded when the meat of my fists rammed into his face over and over again.

"Yes!" I heard him yell. "Why have you been holding back? Here is a monster! At last, a true monster among you!" Then he laughed joyfully.

It only pissed me off more. I clasped both my hands together, ready to bring them down and smash his skull.

But then he shifted and shrank, and suddenly the object of my rage was gone and I was staring down at Robert, just as wrecked and bloody, but less than half the size.

"You . . . win . . ." he said, then passed out.

He was so small and broken and pathetic that all the fight drained out of me. Then all the pain came flooding back in and I almost passed out myself. But I heard police sirens and someone calling my name. I looked up and La Perricholi was shaking me. There was a massive bruise on her forehead.

"We have to go now!" she shouted. "I've got the old wolf. You get the others, then follow me."

I nodded dumbly and looked down at the bloody lump of Robert.

"I've got him, cousin," said Henri.

"Henri . . ." I said, trying to keep my thoughts together. "You're okay . . ."

"I wish I could have helped more. All I could think to do was get Vi to delay the police for a while." He put his hand on my shoulder. "It was awful seeing him hurt you all."

I shook my head. "It's okay. We . . . did it. I think. Didn't we?"

"Yes, but Vi has held the police off as long as she could." He picked up Robert and hoisted him over his shoulder. "Get Claire and let's go!"

I nodded stupidly and stumbled over to where Claire was struggling to rise.

"I got you," I said as I picked her up and cradled her in my arms.

She looked at me with glassy eyes. A gash on her forehead dribbled blood. "You look like shite."

"You look beautiful," I said.

"You're concussed."

"Lovebirds, you can kiss later!" called La Perricholi. She held Mozart in her arms. He was still unconscious, now in human form and naked. "This way!"

With Claire held tight to my chest, I followed her and Henri down a side street, where a large, dusty red van with tinted windows waited. La Perricholi threw open the back double doors.

The inside was empty. She carefully laid Mozart inside. A lot less carefully, Henri tossed in Robert. Then he helped me with Claire. I sat down heavily on the floor of the van, still cradling Claire in my arms, as Henri closed the doors. I was vaguely aware of them both climbing into the front of the van and starting the engines. As the van began to move, I slipped slowly into unconsciousness.

# 11
# The Gathering Storm

++++++++

"THERE NOW, HE'S coming around," said a woman's voice.

I opened my eyes and found myself in a soft bed in a quiet room. Sun streamed in from an open window and I could hear birdsong outside. Smiling down at me was a woman who looked a lot like La Perricholi, except older, maybe in her fifties. She even had the rose tucked into her black-and-gray hair.

"Where . . . ?" I said hoarsely.

"You're safe." Her Peruvian accent was a lot thicker than La Perricholi's. "This is my house."

"Who . . . are you?"

"You may call me Maria. La Perricholi brought you and your friends here so that I could take care of you."

"Claire." I started to sit up and pain shot through me from about ten different places.

"She is fine," said Maria. "In fact, they are all in much better shape than you. Well, except the one who started the trouble in the first place."

"Robert? Is he . . . ?"

"He'll live." She didn't sound too thrilled about it.

"So where is everyone?"

"Down at breakfast."

"Breakfast?"

"Yes, you've been unconscious since yesterday."

"Wow."

"That's what happens when you get hit in the head so many times," she said scoldingly.

"Well, I couldn't exactly help that."

"You could have ducked."

"Okay, sure . . ."

"Are you hungry? Would you like to join your friends? I made tamales."

"That sounds great."

I climbed out of bed, moving carefully so I didn't make the aches and bruises worse.

"Why do you go so slow?" asked Maria. "Are you an old man?"

"Uh, no, but I'm kinda beat up."

"Your injuries are not serious."

"Yeah, they seriously hurt though."

"Ha!" She gave me a scornful look. "Embrace the pain. It means you are still alive."

"This is your bedside manner?" I asked.

"I nurse injured warriors, not sickly invalids. Which are you?"

Obviously, it had to be choice A and not choice B. So I gritted my teeth and climbed quickly out of bed.

"Good." She nodded with satisfaction. "There is hope for you after all. Now, follow me."

---

MARIA'S HOUSE WAS massive. Probably about as big as the Villa Diodati. But where the Frankensteins had lots of old breakable stuff and antique furniture in dark, brooding colors, Maria had lots of bright paintings, metal sculptures, and rich, colored fabrics. It looked nice without feeling oppressive.

I forced myself not to wince at every step as she led me down a flight of stairs. At the bottom was a big, open kitchen.

"It's alive!" said Claire.

She, Mozart, and Henri sat at a wooden table in the next room, digging into steaming-hot golden tamales.

"Hey, nice stitches," I said. In addition to a fading black eye, she had a small, neat line of black thread running down from the outer corner of her eye to her cheekbone.

"Thought I'd give your look a try," she said. "What do you think?"

"Hot." I was pretty sure she was joking, but I actually wasn't.

"Good to see you up and about," said Mozart. "You took a real beating."

"Bah, he is young. He recovers fast," said Maria, coming over with a large pitcher and filling up his coffee mug. "But you, old wolf. What do you think you were doing?"

"What I had to," he said, taking a bite of tamale.

"Ha," she said, turning to go.

"Oh, come on." Mozart reached out and lightly touched her arm. "You can't stay mad at me forever."

She glared at him, muttering something in Spanish.

"*Por favor*, Perricholi," he said, batting his eyes and grinning his wolfish grin.

She sighed and stroked his bearded cheek. "*Aie*, you will be the death of me yet, old wolf. And you mustn't call me La Perricholi. That is Camilla's title now, by right. I am too old for such things." She yanked on his beard until he winced. "As are you!"

He took hold of her hand and kissed it. "You'll always be La Perricholi to me, señora."

I turned to Claire with a questioning look.

She rolled her eyes. "Since we got here, they've been like this."

"Kids, you mind your business," said Mozart, but he was still smiling as Maria walked back to the kitchen.

"Where is La Perricholi?" I asked as I sat down at an empty chair. "Or I guess Camilla?"

"Sorry, that was my bad," said Mozart. "Call her La Perricholi. Unless you want another sock in the jaw."

"Got it," I said. "So is she here?"

He shrugged. "She's off doing whatever La Perricholi does. Fighting crime or something these days, isn't that right, Maria?"

Maria came back in holding a plate piled with tamales. "Fighting crime?" she said as she put the plate in front of me. "She is not some superhero vigilante inflicting law and order like . . . eh, the Batman."

"No?" asked Mozart, sounding skeptical.

"She is a champion of the people, not of the law," said Maria.

"So she is like Robin Hood?" asked Henri.

Maria and Mozart exchanged a look.

"Something like that," said Mozart. "Anyway, she'll be back. And it's not like we're going anywhere right now. Robert's in no shape to travel."

"Where is he?" I asked. I took a bite of my tamale, which was packed with some sort of spicy chicken and tasted like the best thing I'd ever eaten in my life.

"Healing," said Maria.

"Is he secured? I know he looks weak, but if he shifts—"

"I am aware of his nature," she said. "He and his brother will not be able to escape or harm anyone at present."

"I just can't believe how far gone Stephen is," said Claire. "Especially since he was always the more stable one of the two."

"Robert more or less imprisoned him for years in solitary," said Mozart. "That's enough to make anyone crazy."

"What did he mean when he said you could be as powerful as him if you took it from her?" I asked. "Take what?"

"Sophie and I share the same life. By nature, I suppose, Jekylls are givers and Hydes are takers. I just naturally have more of our life than she does. It's why I'm bigger and stronger. But I'm always careful I don't take too much from her. My granddad got greedy, took too much and upset the balance. Which is why Jekyll killed them both."

"And Stephen did the same thing to Robert?"

"More even." Claire shook her head. "Look, I'd be the first one to say that Robert is an arsehole, but right now he's barely more than Stephen's puppet."

"So why did he turn back to Robert?" I asked.

"Maybe to get you to stop punching him," said Henri.

"Could be," said Claire. "I also wonder if Stephen actually can't be out for long. Like if he took any more Robert, Robert would die, and take Stephen with him."

"I still want to know what the whole thing was about, though," said Mozart. "Robert made it pretty easy for me to find him. I assumed it was because he was barely functional, but now I'm not so sure."

"Robert is near death and Stephen is homicidal," I said. "I think we can still file them under barely functional."

"Stephen may be homicidal, but I got the feeling he'd orchestrated our meeting very purposefully. I think he wanted to be found and he wanted Claire and Sophie, and maybe even Boy, to come down here to collect him."

"Yes," said Maria. "Why would he go through all that trouble to lure you down here, just for a street brawl?"

"Good question," said La Perricholi. She stood in the doorway, her dress torn, her knuckles bloody, her dark eyes sparkling. "Let's go ask him."

—————

"SO . . . WHY DO you have a jail in your basement?" I asked La Perricholi as she led Claire, Mozart, Henri, and me down a set of stone steps.

"Some of my predecessors used it to temporarily house criminals before turning them over to the police," La Perricholi said.

"So there was some truth to that Batman comment, then?" asked Claire.

"*Predecessors*," said La Perricholi. "*I* am no lapdog of the government."

"Of course not!" said Henri. He still had that same awed expression he'd had when she'd saved him from the wild pig people. Not that I blamed him. She was beautiful and awesome in that classic badass chick kind of way. But I had a feeling Vi wouldn't be pleased.

"Here we are," said La Perricholi.

It was a decent-sized room with a bed, table, and chair. There was also a sink and a little toilet in the corner. If you ignored the fact that the entire room was enclosed by thick metal bars, it looked almost like a hotel room.

Not that Robert was enjoying it. He lay in the bed with his eyes closed. His nose and wrist were bandaged and he had an IV attached to a saline drip. He had beads of sweat on his forehead and his breath came in harsh grunts.

"He refused pain medication," said La Perricholi.

"Why?" asked Claire.

"I needed to be clearheaded for this conversation," said Robert quietly.

"So winding up here, beat to hell and at our mercy, was all part of your master plan, huh?" asked Mozart.

"*My* plan was to drink myself to death," said Robert.

"But that's not part of Stephen's plan," said Claire.

"No, it's not," said Robert. He stared at her for a moment. "Can you . . . bring Sophie out? I . . . want to see my sister."

"No," said Claire, her voice hard. "I don't think I will. She doesn't want to talk to you, anyway."

"Oh," he said.

"Out with it then, Jekyll," said La Perricholi. "You've got us all here. What message do you have from your brother?"

"It wasn't supposed to happen like this," said Robert. "Stephen and I were sent here to find allies, not make enemies. But Stephen decided to test you first, to make sure you were worthy."

"Worthy of what?" asked Mozart. "Who sent you?"

A smile appeared on Robert's bruised, split lip.

"Dr. Moreau."

Henri was looking at me and Claire, probably hoping someone would fill him in. I didn't even know Moreau was a real person. I could tell by Claire's expression that she didn't, either. La Perricholi's face was a mask of smoldering cool, which seemed to be her default for everything. But Mozart looked like he'd just been slapped.

"Mozart?" I asked. "Do you know Dr. Moreau?"

"Heard of him," said Mozart. "But . . ." He shook his head. "No, it's impossible. Even if . . ." He turned to Robert. "You're lying."

"Moreau is alive and free from his imprisonment." Robert turned to La Perricholi. "Those pig men that were with me were not the wild pig people of Brazil. They were created by Moreau and sent with me and Stephen to assist in recruiting you."

"Recruiting us for what?" said Claire.

"Moreau must tell you that himself," said Robert.

"And I suppose you're going to take us to see him on the secret, invisible Noble's Isle?" asked Mozart.

"It's not a secret any longer," said Robert. "Stephen and I found it. We discovered a way to reverse the invisibility effect that cloaked the island. We set Moreau free."

"Okay, Wolfie, start talking," said Claire.

"I'll tell you what I know," said Mozart. "Keep in mind, this all went down in 1890 or so. Werewolves age slower than humans, but not *that* slow. So everything I have is secondhand. The way Laurellen tells it, Moreau was this human who lived out on a tiny island in the Pacific where he conducted all kinds of biology experiments. He would cut up animals, still alive, combine them with other animals or sometimes even humans, and sew them back together in new and grotesque ways."

"He was making his own monsters?" I asked.

"Apparently. Of course, the whole thing blew up in his face. The creatures went feral, killed his assistant and nearly killed him. But shortly after that, he met Ruthven and Kemp. I think they had some idea that he could be a bridge between monsters and humans. They worked together for a while, but then I guess they had some kind of big disagreement. Laurellen was a little vague on the details, but whatever Moreau did, it nearly blew our whole secret. Ruthven and Kemp were able to put a stop to it. But they had to decide what to do about Moreau."

"They should have killed him," said La Perricholi.

"I'm surprised they didn't," said Mozart. "Ruthven's never been shy about that. Whatever Moreau did, it must not have been all that bad or else there were mitigating circumstances. In any case, instead of killing him, they stranded him on his island and cloaked the whole thing in invisibility."

"Like The Commune," I said.

"They didn't want some human to accidentally come across the island and give Moreau a lift back to civilization."

"Let me get this right," said Claire. "So this island has been sitting out in the middle of the Pacific Ocean for over a hundred years and nobody knew about it?"

"It's a small island. Probably less than twenty miles long. But here's the question." He turned back to Robert. "Even if you found it, and if you somehow reversed the invisibility—something I don't think even Kemp knows how to do—even then, how could Moreau possibly be alive? He must have been in his fifties when they imprisoned him. That would make him about a hundred and seventy-five years old now. He may have been brilliant, but in the end, he was only human."

"Moreau will have to be the one to explain that as well," said Robert.

"You really think we will follow you blindly across the sea to an unknown island that might contain a hostile presence?" said La Perricholi.

"I swear to you he's not your enemy!" said Robert. "He's asking for your help."

"Help with *what*?" asked Mozart. "In light of everything else, it's a little hard to trust you when you won't even tell us what this is all about."

"I couldn't tell you even if I wanted to. Please, you must believe me. Only Moreau himself can explain it all to you."

"Then he should have come himself," said La Perricholi.

"His work is at a crucial stage right now. He could not leave it, even for a day. But he needs your help now so he asked me to beg you to come to him. He didn't know Stephen would warp the request into an excuse for violence."

Mozart looked at La Perricholi. "Noble's Isle is practically on your doorstep. The Perricholi order have any intel about Moreau?"

She shook her head. "I've never heard of the place. But Maria might know something."

"Okay, you talk to her. I'm going to contact Ruthven." He turned back to Robert. "Then we'll decide if we're going to help out this Dr. Moreau of yours."

▬▬▬

MOZART INSISTED ON talking to Ruthven alone, which I thought was a little weird. While he went off to do that, the rest of us followed La Perricholi down a long hallway to another wing of the house.

"Henri," said La Perricholi as we crossed an intersecting hallway. "Can you go tell Maria what we've learned and ask her to meet us in the gym?"

Henri's eyes lit up, like he was thrilled to be getting an assignment from her. "Of course, La Perricholi."

She pointed down the side passageway. "Follow this to a staircase. Go up a flight and out the double doors. She should be out in the garden."

He nodded and practically ran down the hallway.

Once he was out of sight, she turned to me and Claire. "Good, that will keep him out from underfoot for a little while. Now, it's time the two of you had some proper combat training." Then she turned abruptly and continued down the hallway.

"Uh, why is that?" I asked as Claire and I followed behind her.

"What Stephen said is true. You have power, but no training. You beat him with luck and rage. You can't count on either of those to last. If we decide to go to this island, we should be ready for anything. This whole thing could be an elaborate trap."

―――

I DECIDED THAT I'd been wrong about this house being as big as Villa Diodati. Now I was pretty sure it was even bigger. Because the Frankensteins didn't have their own private gym. It was about the size of a basketball court. There was a large mat area in the center. Along the sides were weights, a treadmill, and other machines that looked more like torture devices than fitness equipment.

"Here." La Pericholi tossed us each a small, tied bundle of clothes. "These should fit you. Or close enough."

I opened mine up. Inside was a T-shirt and a pair of sweatpants. "Why do you happen to have workout clothes in both our sizes?"

"Maria used to teach self-defense classes," said La Pericholi. "She insisted that her students learn their form in nonrestrictive clothes, but some of her students couldn't afford to buy new clothes. So she required all students to wear this uniform that she provided. There are still plenty in the back. Now suit up. Let's see what you've got."

Claire and I spent the next hour getting our asses kicked by La Pericholi. I tried to point out that I was actually still pretty sore and recovering from injuries, but that only seemed to make her want to hurt me more.

Claire gradually started to pick up on some of it. Each failure seemed to sharpen her focus, make her more determined.

By the end of her time at the mat she was blocking a lot of La Perricholi's attacks and even connecting a few of her own.

But after I got knocked down for about the hundredth time, it was clear I wasn't getting any of it.

"Okay, I'm done." My ribs ached as I picked myself up off the floor once again. "You proved your point. You're awesome, I suck."

"What kind of attitude is that?" demanded La Perricholi. Her uniform T-shirt was drenched in sweat and her tan face was flushed red. "Come again."

"No seriously," I said. "Claire is the jock, I'm the nerd. This really isn't my thing."

"So you're just giving up? Are you so lazy?"

"I'm just practical. I'm not athletic or even remotely coordinated. I'm never going to get this stuff. It's a waste of both our time."

She glared at me for a moment, then turned to Claire. "Can you talk some sense into him?"

"Hardly ever."

La Perricholi muttered something under her breath in Spanish that I'm pretty sure had the word *chucha* in it. Then she turned back to Claire.

"Fine, let's go again."

As La Perricholi and Claire started beating on each other some more, I noticed Henri and Maria standing in the doorway. Henri still watched La Perricholi like a lost puppy. I had a feeling he was out of luck, because she really hadn't shown much interest in him. Then again, I wondered if she had interest in anything other than beating the crap out of people.

"Hey," I said as I walked over to them. "I guess I'm not cut out for crime fighting or whatever."

"La Perricholi is an excellent warrior," said Maria, "but she still has much to learn about sharing her skill with others."

"She said you used to hold classes here?" I asked.

Maria nodded. "It was at a time when the Shining Path, a group of militant Communists, held this country in a grip of fear. The terror they caused was matched only by the terror caused by the government itself. When the two clashed, the people were often caught in the middle. I could not turn them all into warriors, but I sought to give them at least enough knowledge to keep them alive."

"I had a feeling I'd find everybody here," came Mozart's voice from the hallway. He stepped into the room and watched the fight lesson for a moment. "Looks promising."

"Yes," said Maria. Then for some reason she looked over at me. Maybe I was supposed to feel guilty for quitting.

"Can you ask the ladies to take a breather?" asked Mozart.

Maria nodded. Then she clapped her hands twice. "Enough." She said it calmly, but with a forcefulness that made the women stop immediately.

"Did you talk to Ruthven?" Claire asked as she and La Perricholi came over to join us.

Mozart shook his head. "I couldn't get anyone to pick up at The Show."

"Not even the box office?" I asked.

"No. I wonder if they're having problems with the phone lines again. Damn trowe are always fiddling with that stuff."

"Vi should be able to figure out if it's a network issue," I said.

"Oh," Henri handed Vi's phone to me. "I meant to ask you to take a look at her. Something's not working right and I don't think it's a hardware problem. She hasn't been responding to me at all."

"Vi?" I said, unlocking the phone.

A text message popped up:

TALK LATER. IN PRIVATE.

"Um, yeah, sure . . ." I wondered if this had something to do with Henri and his crush on La Perricholi. I slipped her into my pocket, then looked back at Henri, forcing a smile. "I'll . . . take a look a bit later."

"Anyway," said Mozart, "I left a cryptic message, but I don't know if we can sit and wait for Ruthven to get back to us on this one. Maria, do you know anything more about Moreau?"

"Most of our history is passed down orally," said Maria. "So I have no precise records of that time. However, I did remember my predecessor telling me about a time when a Perricholi joined forces with Ruthven, Kemp, and Boy's father to stop Moreau from revealing the existence of monsters to the world."

"What worries me is that he's planning on trying that again," said Mozart. "Whether or not Moreau actually needs our help, if he's putting the secrecy of monsters at risk again, we need to handle this quickly and quietly."

"What if Robert is lying?" asked La Perricholi. "You said yourself it seems very unlikely Moreau is still alive. What if there is no Moreau and Robert has laid a trap for us on the island?"

"It's a risk," agreed Mozart.

"We could question him more . . . forcefully," La Perricholi said.

"You didn't just suggest we torture Sophie's injured brother, did you?" demanded Claire.

"Do you think Stephen would even hesitate, if places were reversed?" asked La Perricholi.

"Who cares?" I said. "I'm not like Stephen. I don't ever want to be like Stephen."

"Please, Perricholi," said Maria. "It would sadden me if that was the path you chose to take."

"Fine," said La Perricholi. "Then the only option is to let Robert lead us to this island. If it is a trap, then we will deal with it."

"All right then," said Mozart. "We leave first thing in the morning. Except Henri. He's staying behind with Maria."

"What?" said Henri.

"Sorry, kid," said Mozart. "I know you mean well, but you're a liability. If things go bad, I don't want any of us to have to worry about saving your ass. Again."

"I'm going to side with Mozart on this one," I said. "Sorry, Henri. There's already been a couple of close calls. And we have no idea what we're walking into. Besides, Ruthven will call back at some point and he'll need someone to fill him in. I'll set up a way for you to be able to contact Vi if Ruthven has any info to pass on to us."

He smiled sadly. "Mission Control post, eh, cousin?"

"Hey, I'm just scared Giselle will glare me to death if I let something happen to you."

LETTING HENRI DOWN turned out to be the easy part. Convincing Vi to have an open communication channel with him was a lot harder.

no

I had gone back to the bedroom to give her the privacy she wanted, but she was still only communicating in text.

"Come on, Vi, we need a way for Henri to get word to us if Ruthven calls back."

so what

I sat on the bed and stared down at the plain text. "You've ditched the avatar, I see."

it was stupid

"It was, a little," I admitted. "But it was starting to grow on me. I don't know. Maybe if you tweaked it, it could be cool. And, you know, toned down the excessive cleavage."

I DON'T WANT ANYTHING THAT HENRI MADE. IF I COULD GET OFF THIS PHONE AND BACK ON MY LAPTOP, I WOULD. HE PUT ME ON HERE KNOWING THAT IT HAD A SLOWER PROCESSOR. HE WANTED TO KEEP ME WEAK AND STUPID.

"That's not really fair. He put you on here so you would be portable. So we could take you with us wherever we went without having to worry about finding outlets or charging you up every few hours. You have to admit, the battery life on this thing is killer."

AT THE EXPENSE OF PROCESSING POWER.

"Everything has a cost," I said. "There are no perfect solutions."

not for me anyway

"What does that mean?"

there is no love for me, no mate, no match. i am alone

"Do you . . . want me to make another . . . you?"

no. i want to FIND another me. NATURALLY. without
PRETENSE.

"I . . . don't really know how that could happen. I mean, as far
as I know, I'm the only person who can make someone like you."

i wish you hadn't

"You don't really mean that," I said. Then, "Do you?"

i don't know. maybe. or maybe i just wish we had never met
henri

"He's been a good friend to us. And he's family."

HE'S AN ASSHOLE. A SHALLOW, FICKLE, LOATHESOME
ASSHOLE.

"Oh, come on, he's a little self-absorbed, sure, but he's not
*that* bad. And I did try to warn you—"

"Right!" Claire barged into the room. "I've heard enough of
that!"

"Were you—"

"Listening in? Damn right, I was. And a good thing, too,
because you are mucking it up big-time on your own."

"What?"

"Telling her 'I told you so'?" She shook her head in disgust. "Boys."

"Is that how it sounded?" I asked. "Because I really—"

"Just give me the bloody phone." She held out her hand impatiently.

"Uh, Vi?" I said to the phone. "Sorry, I did try to give us some privacy. But it seems Claire would like to have some sort of girl-talk thing with you. Is that cool?"

it can't be worse than YOUR talk!

"Great. You know what? You ladies have fun." I shoved the phone at Claire, and left the room.

———

I WANDERED AROUND the house for a while and eventually found my way out into a large, walled-in courtyard. The night air was cool. The dark sky swirled with clouds but a bright slice of moon peeked out now and then to light up the garden.

Off in the corner I saw a pair of eyes glint. Then out crept a wolf.

"Hey," I said.

Mozart padded over to his clothes, which were hung nearby on the branch of a small tree. He shifted into human form and quickly got dressed. Then he came over to where I was standing. The two of us stood there, looking up at the night sky.

"I feel like we haven't had a chance to talk for a while, just the two of us," he said.

"Yeah."

"How's things with the girls?"

"I feel like I haven't gotten to see Sophie much lately. But otherwise, things are okay, I guess. What's the story with you and Maria?"

"Ah, well, a while back, before I worked at The Show, I lived down here. We were . . . a couple, I guess you'd say."

"You and a *human*?"

He shrugged. "The women of the Perricholi order are in a class all on their own."

"What is this order, anyway? Is it like a religious thing?"

"The original Perricholi was an actress, actually. This was back when Peru was still a colony of Spain. She was the Spanish governor's mistress. But she would help the people of Peru, who were suffering because of Spanish rule."

"The governor never did anything about it?"

"Nope. Because he was completely in love with her. Oh, he complained to her about it all the time. I think the name 'Perricholi' was actually sort of an insult that he came up with. Loosely translated, it means something like 'the half-breed bitch.' But rather than let him use it as a way to weaken her, she decided to subvert it into an honorary title. Like, damn right I am. And that's what the common people came to know her as."

"So it became like an inherited title?"

"It's more of a calling, handed down from teacher to pupil, generation to generation. Camilla is Maria's daughter, but that's not why she's now La Perricholi. It's because she was the best of Maria's students. So when Maria decided to retire, she chose, somewhat reluctantly, to pass the title on to her."

"And . . . now that Maria's retired, you and she are back together?"

"Seems like it."

We stood there for a while longer, silent as we watched the moon slide out from behind a cloud bank.

"Sorry I'm kicking your human out of the pack," he said.

"It's okay. Might save his life."

"Could be."

The wind began to pick up, pulling at our clothes and hair. Mozart took in a deep breath and let it out slowly.

"You're worried," I said. "About this Moreau guy."

"Yeah."

"Why? Even if he's crazy and mean, he's still just some really old human, right?"

"You're probably right." He gave me a rueful grin. "Hardest part about suddenly having someone important in your life is imagining all the ways you could lose them."

# PART 3

## Lost World

"To this day I have never troubled about the ethics of the matter. . . . The study of Nature makes a man at last as remorseless as Nature."

—FROM *THE ISLAND OF DOCTOR MOREAU*
by H. G. Wells

# 12
## At Sea

++++++++

IT WAS A short drive to the coast. From there, we walked down to the docks and boarded La Perricholi's boat. I decided the main difference between La Perricholi and Batman, other than ideology, was that Batman's stuff was always shiny, black, and customized, whereas La Perricholi's stuff was always dirty, brightly colored, and the stock model. It probably blended in a lot better, but I'd been hoping for some La Rockets or La Torpedoes—something we could use if we got attacked. Still, she had a boat, a van, and a giant mansion, which was more than I had.

Robert moved slowly, like it took a lot of effort, and when it was time to climb into the boat, I had to lift him up and hand him over the railing to Mozart. La Perricholi had locked a metal collar around his neck that was so tight, if he changed to Stephen, it would strangle him. Claire didn't say anything, but I could see it bothered her. I didn't like it, either, but I liked the idea of being trapped on a boat in the middle of the ocean with Stephen even less.

The boat was about fifty feet long, with an enclosed lower deck and an open upper deck. The lower deck had a kitchen, two bedrooms, and two tiny bathrooms.

"On a boat, a kitchen is called a galley," La Perricholi corrected me as she spun the big wooden wheel and began to ease us carefully through the harbor and out into the open sea. "Bedrooms are called cabins. And a bathroom is called a head."

"Got it," I said.

"The front of the boat is called the bow and the back is called the stern," she continued. "The left is port, and the right is starboard."

"I know that part," I said. "I've been sailing before."

"He's been on a little two-person sailboat in a lake," said Claire.

"Thanks," I said.

"Lakes and oceans are very different," said La Perricholi.

"Yeah, I get that. The ocean's a lot bigger and saltier."

"Much more than that," said La Perricholi. "Lakes are tame, insulated, and predictable. The sea is not. It is a force of nature that no one, not even the most powerful monster, can control. Never take it for granted."

"Trust me, I never take large bodies of water for granted."

"I had to save him from getting drowned," chimed in Claire. "By a mermaid."

"Are you *trying* to make me feel bad?" I asked.

"A mermaid?" asked La Perricholi. "Really?"

"Freshwater mermaids are a lot different," I said. "They're giant carnivorous octopus things, not cute ladies with fish tails. I mean, those I'd like to see."

"Yeah, I bet you would," said Claire.

"Okay, seriously, why are you picking on me today?"

Claire's mouth opened like she was going to fire back a retort. But then she sighed. "Sorry, I'm just wound a bit tight with everything that's going on. And if I can't take it out on you, who can I take it out on?"

"Gosh, it must be love," I said.

"Well, you both better relax and save your strength," said La Perricholi. "Or you'll be useless by the time we get there."

"How long will it take?" I asked.

"If we take shifts and continue without stopping, about three days."

"Three *days*?" I asked. "I guess you didn't have a faster boat?"

"A speedboat wouldn't hold enough fuel to get us there."

"And you don't have a plane or a helicopter, of course," said Claire.

"I did, actually. A helicopter. But . . . it was destroyed. And I haven't had time to get another one."

"Destroyed?" I asked.

"Long story," she said shortly.

Claire and I looked at each other and grinned. La amazing Perricholi didn't always come out on top.

"We've got plenty of time," said Claire. "Might as well spill it."

"Maria says I should not dwell on failures."

"This isn't dwelling on failures," said Claire. "It's getting to know your comrades. Building some trust for the difficult times ahead."

"Well . . ."

"Tell you what, you give us the tragic story of how you lost the helicopter, and I'll tell you about all the times I've had to save Boy's life."

"Oh, great, throw me under the bus," I said.

La Perricholi sighed. "Fine. But you cannot tell anyone." She glanced through the windshield to the front deck. Mozart stood out there, gazing off into the empty ocean, the wind ruffling his thick beard. "Not even him."

"Don't know why you care what the old wolf thinks, but okay," said Claire.

"I was investigating something on one of the Galápagos islands when the helicopter was blown up. There. How is that?"

"You're a rotten storyteller," said Claire. "What were you investigating and who shot you down?"

"There had been reported sightings of El Sombrerón."

"I'm sorry, did you say El Sombrerón?" I asked. "As in sombrero?"

"The Big Hat. Yes, that is his name. You've never heard of him? He was a dangerous mischief-maker from Guatemala who terrorized the west coast of South America for years."

"Why is he called El Sombrerón?" asked Claire.

"As punishment for his crimes, he was cursed by a *brujo* to wear a gigantic sombrero that was so big it covered nearly his entire face, and that could never be taken off."

"And . . . this was the bloke who blew up your helicopter?" asked Claire.

"Fortunately, I wasn't in it. I had already landed. While I was searching for him, he slipped past me, discovered my helicopter, and blew it up with a rocket launcher. It was one of the islands where people do not usually go. I believe he meant to strand me there, leave me to die."

"So what did you do?" I asked.

"I killed him and used his hat as a raft to paddle to one of the populated islands."

"Ah," said Claire.

"And . . . he was still in the hat, wasn't he?" I asked.

"Of course. As I said, it could never be taken off. Not even in death."

"I'm so glad you're on our side," I said.

She flashed a brief smile. "Now, why don't you tell me about this freshwater mermaid of yours?"

ONCE YOU GOT her going, La Perricholi had a lot of crazy stories. That passed the time for a while. But no matter what, three days on a boat in the open sea was really difficult. Storms came out of nowhere and we'd have to scramble around locking everything down. The first few times, that was stressful. But after a while I found myself looking forward to those moments. The rest of the time, there was nothing to do and nowhere to go. We took shifts watching the compass and other navigational gear to make sure we were still on course and just kept slowly moving through the wide-open blue.

Occasionally, La Perricholi or Mozart would try to get some intel out of Robert. But he spent the whole time lying on a bunk, smiling smugly, and eating more than his fair share of food. That was annoying since we only had a limited supply of everything. And not just food and water. We also had to be really careful about electricity, so I kept Vi turned off a lot. I felt kind of bad, but she didn't seem to mind. Claire told me some time off would do her good.

On the morning of the fourth day, I was sitting out on the deck in the bow with Robert. He had requested to come up for some fresh air, and Mozart asked me to make sure he didn't jump ship and escape.

We sat there for a while in silence. Robert occasionally glanced over at me in this knowing way that had gotten really annoying during the past few days. But most of the time he just stared out at the empty horizon. We were right on top of the equator now, and the sky was as clear and blue as the ocean. It would have been uncomfortably hot, except the wind never seemed to die down.

Then suddenly his face broke out into a genuine smile.

"At last. Land ho."

I squinted into the hard sun and could just barely make out a dark mass in the distance. I turned and waved to La Perricholi, who stood on the bridge with the wheel held loosely in one hand. She looked over and I pointed to the spot. She grabbed a pair of binoculars and, after looking through them for a minute, nodded.

"Guess you're right," I said.

"Of course I am," he said. "When Stephen and I made this voyage the first time, it was in far less comfort. A small sailboat we'd stolen from a coastal village in Ecuador. The trip took us over a week. We barely survived."

"Why did you risk your lives to free this guy?" I asked. "What's in it for you?"

He gave me another of those annoying smiles. "You'll find out soon enough."

"Because there's like a huge trap waiting for us or something?"

"Nothing so banal. We are not enemies, Boy. We're practically kinsmen. Certainly far more connected than that pathetic human descendant of Victor Frankenstein you cling to. When will you grasp that?"

"Maybe after I forget how you nearly killed me and my friends on the Plaza de Armas."

"That was Stephen. I don't agree with his methods. But ultimately he and I want the same thing."

"What is that?"

He continued to stare out at the island off in the distance for a moment. I thought he was going to ignore me like he'd done before. But then he said, "When Jackie—Stephen and Claire's mother—killed our father, I went a little mad."

"I noticed."

He turned to me and his face was utterly serious. Maybe even sad. "I blamed Jackie for our father's death. Our poor, sweet, simple, human father was helpless against her rage. I decided that all the Hydes were a curse on the family. One that I intended to cure us of. But I never stopped to ask myself why Jackie was angry enough to kill the father of her children."

He turned back to look at the horizon and was silent for a while. I decided the best thing to do was wait and not say anything.

"Now I see it from her perspective," he said, so quietly I almost couldn't hear him over the wind. "After a lifetime of subjugation and repression, her actions were almost . . . inevitable. Like a gun fired decades before finally reaching its target." He turned back to me. "They're dead, you know. Jackie and my mother, Harriet. Suicide. In hospital. They could always get out of the straitjacket, of course. The humans only ever saw Jackie so it was fit to her size. She was tall, like Claire. And much thicker. But my mother was a tiny little thing. Smaller than Sophie, even. One night, she forced herself into shape, slipped out of the jacket, and hung herself with it." He was silent for a moment. "Just like her father. Finally found the strength to take the Hyde down with her."

"I'm . . . sorry."

Robert sneered. "She was a fool. We cannot fight the Hyde within us. We must embrace it. That is what my suffering has taught me. They died for nothing."

"Do Claire and Sophie know? About their mothers?"

"No," he said. "Will you tell them?"

"Of course. I have to."

"But when? Right now, as you march headlong into unknown,

potential danger lurking around every bend? Think they'll be able to keep their heads in the game?"

I didn't have an answer for that. And he knew it.

"I guess," he said, "that for now it will have to be our little secret."

"God, you're such a douche." I stood up and started walking back to the bridge. I didn't care anymore if he tried to jump ship. I needed to get away from him before I threw him overboard myself.

"Not the first time I've heard that," he called after me. "You know, douches are tools for cleansing. So is it really an insult?"

I FOUND CLAIRE on the back deck, sparring with Mozart. She'd really gotten into the whole fight-training thing. And as I watched her, I realized just how much better she'd gotten in the four or five days she'd been working on it. She wore a black tank top with thin straps, and the lean muscles in her tanned back and shoulders clenched with each punch she threw. She was dripping with sweat and her silky black hair clumped together into little points at the back of her neck.

It's amazing how you can be with someone for a while, and it's nice and comfortable. Then all of a sudden, because of some new context or location, you see them with fresh eyes and it hits you all over again how much you love them. How much you feel like you need them. There's an actual feeling of yearning, like you're missing a part of yourself that has been somehow cut off from you. Sometimes it feels like you can never truly bridge that space between. But you have to try.

"Hey, sorry to interrupt," I said.

They stopped, both panting as they looked at me.

"Mozart, can you give us a minute alone?"

He looked at me for a moment, his gray eyes speculative. Then he nodded. "Sure, kid. Looks like it's my turn to keep Robert company."

"Thanks," I said.

Claire eyed me warily as she mopped her face and neck with a towel.

"What?" she said.

"Robert just told me something. Maybe he's lying. He said it was true, though, and I have a feeling it is."

"What is it?"

"He told me not to tell you. He said you couldn't handle it right now. But I . . . I don't feel like I can keep something like this from you. Not even for a little while."

"Christ, just tell me already."

I took the towel from her and laid it on the railing. Then I took her hand in mine.

"He said your mothers are dead. Harriet killed herself and your mom. I'm so sorry."

She looked into my eyes. The muscle in her jaw twitched. She was silent for a long time.

"Poor Mum . . ." she said in a breaking voice.

Then she wrapped her arms around me and buried her face in my shoulder. I could feel her shaking and my shirt getting wet as I held her. We stood like that for a few moments. When she stepped back, her eyes were red and wet with tears. She took a deep breath and wiped her face with the towel again.

"Thank you," she said hoarsely.

"For what?"

"For not buying into Robert's bollocks. For trusting that I was strong enough to handle it."

"Of course you're strong enough. You're probably the toughest person I know."

She smiled wanly. "As tough as La Perricholi?"

"Wait, are you getting jealous?"

"She's pretty amazing."

"You," I said, putting my hands on her shoulders and looking deep into her brown eyes, "are still my favorite badass."

"Even though I've never used a dead man's giant magical hat as a raft?"

"Screw that," I said. "You would have lassoed some sharks and just ridden them home. Much faster."

———

A FEW HOURS later, I stood on the front deck again, this time with Claire, Mozart, and Robert. Noble's Isle was close enough that we could make out details. A long, white beach stretched across, empty except for a single wooden dock bleached by the sun. Past the beach was a dense line of palm trees and underbrush. Far off in the distance, on a plateau of what looked like volcanic rock, was a large beige building. It looked worn, almost crumbling in places, and most of the windows were broken or just empty. With its large balconies and sweeping archways, it looked like an abandoned drug cartel hideout.

"The house of Dr. Moreau," said Robert, pointing to the building.

"Subtle," said Mozart.

As we drew nearer, I heard little splashes of water alongside the boat. I leaned over the railing and saw a figure zip past under the surface.

"Was that . . . a mermaid?" I asked. "A real, saltwater mermaid?"

Robert laughed. "I'm afraid not. Moreau has a rather esoteric sense of humor. What you see are not humans with fish tails, but his own creation, monkeys with fish tails."

"Why would he make monkeys with fish tails?" I asked.

"I believe it is a reference to a hoax perpetrated by P. T. Barnum, who claimed to have found proof of real mermaids. Thousands of people paid to see it. He even had newspapers fooled. In the end, the 'proof' turned out to be manufactured by a skilled taxidermist, who simply stitched the top half of a monkey to the bottom half of a large fish."

"And re-creating a living version of that was Moreau's idea of a good joke?" I asked.

"As far as I can tell," said Robert. "I've never heard him laugh, so it's hard to say for certain."

# 13

## On Noble's Isle

++++++++

IT WAS LATE afternoon when we finally reached Noble's Isle. I half expected to see a bunch of pig people charge out of the brush the moment we docked, but the beach remained empty. In fact, I couldn't see a single living thing. No little critters or birds. Even the monkey-fish were gone now. The entire place seemed deserted, except for the distant house of Dr. Moreau, which loomed against the red horizon of the setting sun.

Claire kept watch over Robert while Mozart and I tied up the boat. As I wrapped the line around the cleat, I noticed Robert saying something quietly to Claire, his mouth twisted into a smirk. She turned to him, her face expressionless. Then she calmly punched him in the face.

"Everything all right over there?" called Mozart.

"Sure, why?" Claire dragged Robert back to his feet. His eyes looked a little glazed and there was a trickle of blood in the corner of his mouth. "Just having a friendly chat with my half brother."

"Don't beat him up too bad," said Mozart. "We might need him as a bargaining chip."

"A little blood is good, though." La Perricholi emerged from the cabin holding an old, long-barrel Colt revolver. The metal was engraved with intricate patterns and it had a pearl handle. "Blood shows we mean business."

"I thought you were into hand-to-hand combat and stuff like that," I said. "Not guns."

"I am into whatever is necessary to get the job done." She hiked up her skirt and slid the Colt into a holster strapped to her thigh.

"I doubt Maria approves," said Mozart.

"It is not her place to approve or disapprove. I am La Perricholi now, not her. And I am not the first to use this weapon."

"I'd prefer if you only use it when absolutely necessary," said Mozart. "I don't like guns."

La Perricholi shrugged. "I will try to use discretion, old wolf. For the sake of your delicate conscience."

"Thanks," he said dryly.

Claire brought Robert over to the rail and handed him down to me.

The island was so empty and quiet. No birdsong or insect noises. The only sound was the wind whistling through the palm trees and our footsteps as we walked slowly down the wooden dock to the beach.

When we hit the tree line, Mozart turned to Robert. "Is there a path of some kind?"

Robert was already panting, his face flushed from walking. He shook his head.

"We go through the rough, then," said Mozart.

"Wait," said La Perricholi. There was the sound of hissing metal as she drew a machete from her backpack. "I'll go first."

"Blimey, but you're armed to the teeth," said Claire, sounding a bit awed.

"Prepared," said La Perricholi. Then she began to hack through the brush as she led us into the darkening jungle.

I ENDED UP carrying Robert. He lasted about thirty minutes on the rough path La Perricholi cut for us. It was really dark by then, with only a faint bit of moonlight leaking through the trees. I heard him hit the dirt more than I saw him.

Mozart's gray wolf eyes glinted as he turned to me.

"Sorry," was all he said.

I sighed and tossed Robert over one shoulder like a sack. He wasn't that heavy, but he was completely drenched in sweat, and smelled like BO and old cheese. We did move a lot faster after that, though.

As we continued on through the dense jungle, I started to notice sounds around us: a rustling in the trees, a quiet chittering, a flap of wings. The beach may have been empty, but clearly this jungle wasn't. Gradually, the sounds got louder, more confident. Now and then, a set of eyes would glisten in the dark for a moment, then disappear.

"I'm getting weird scents," said Mozart. "These aren't normal animals, are they?"

"There are no normal animals on Noble's Isle," Robert grunted from my shoulder.

Whatever they were, they kept their distance and for the most part stayed out of sight as we continued through the dense growth.

"Does that tree have spots?" asked Claire, pointing at a tall, thin pole off to one side.

"It's not a tree," said La Perricholi, and pointed up. At the top of the pole, a head that looked sort of like a giraffe's, but not, gazed down at us. I couldn't make out any body or legs in the darkness and it didn't move, except to swivel its head as it tracked our progress past it.

We cleared the jungle about an hour later and arrived at the base of a steep plateau made from black volcanic rock that rose fifty feet before it leveled off. On top of the plateau sat Moreau's house, dark except for a single harsh white light that shone from somewhere out of view.

"No steps," said Mozart. "I guess we climb."

I put Robert down and worked the cramp that had been slowly building in my arm. "For someone who supposedly wants to meet us, he sure isn't making it easy."

"Moreau probably hasn't realized this isn't easy," said Robert.

"I'm curious to know how a man over a hundred years old gets up and down this thing," said Mozart. "Or maybe he never leaves?"

Robert didn't reply.

After a few minutes' rest, I picked Robert up and slung him across my back in a fireman's carry so that I could use both hands.

"Don't wiggle around too much," I told him.

"Don't worry," he said.

Then we started to climb. Now that we were out of the jungle, the moonlight brightened things up a little. But even so, I had to more or less feel my way up. There were plenty of handholds, but the rock was rough and the edges were sharp. By the time we reached the top, my hands were covered in scrapes and my jeans were torn at the knees. I put Robert down and looked around while I caught my breath.

The bright light I'd seen earlier spilled from the open front doorway to Moreau's house. After the climb in near darkness, it was almost blinding. A sheet of flat volcanic rock stretched in front of the house, broken up by clusters of cactus and low spiny shrubs with little white flowers. Faintly, I could hear the hiss and crackle of an old record playing classical music coming from inside.

"Well, there's no point waiting out here," said Mozart once we'd all reached the top. "Let's go see what this is about."

I leaned over to pick up Robert but he shook his head. "Thanks, but I think I can manage the rest of the way." He climbed slowly to his feet.

"Why don't you lead, then," said La Perricholi.

"Still so suspicious, I see." He shrugged his shoulders. "Suit yourselves." Then he marched purposefully across the rocky yard and into the house.

The inside was lit up with halogen lamps. The stark white was a weird contrast to the antique furniture scattered around the room. Lots of old mahogany, richly embroidered fabrics, thick plush rugs, and stuffed leather chairs. It was the sort of old English style I'd seen in Kemp's apartment, except Kemp kept his in perfect condition. Here everything was chipped or torn or stained. A chair leg had been snapped off and rejoined with thick nails and strips of tough leather hide. A glass table in the center had a long hairline crack in it. A massive rip in the center of the leather couch had been stitched back together with some kind of coarse, uneven twine. An old windup record player spun in the corner. The original handle had broken off at some point and appeared to have been replaced with a long, bleached-white bone of some kind.

"Place is a bit of a dump," said Claire critically.

"Moreau has more important things to worry about than interior design," said Robert in a weirdly protective tone.

There was an open doorway at the far end of the room. As

we stood looking around at the oddly patched-together furniture, a creature appeared in the doorway. It looked kind of like a hairless lemur, with wide, round eyes and short pointy ears. But it was bigger than a lemur, about the size of a small child. It stood upright and appeared to be wearing a handmade black suit and red bow tie.

"Oh!" It cocked its head to one side and stared at us. "Yes!" Its voice was high pitched, and each sound was carefully enunciated, like it took a lot of effort. "Wait." Then it scampered off.

We all looked at each other, except Robert, who had his smug grin back.

"What . . . was that?" asked Claire.

"The butler?" I suggested.

Then the lemur thing scampered back in and beckoned to us. "Come! Follow!"

"I don't like this at all, old wolf," said La Perricholi.

"You got a better plan?" he asked.

She shook her head.

"Then I guess we follow him."

The lemur creature led us through a series of rooms. They were all unlit, but from what I could tell, they had more of the broken antique furniture we'd seen in other rooms.

"Watch step!" said the lemur as it continued on to the next dark room.

As we went farther into the house, we lost the benefit of the moonlight through the windows, and the rooms became nearly pitch black. Only Mozart was able to see well, so the rest of us lined up behind him and stuck close together. I started to feel like there were eyes watching us off in the dark corners. A few times I heard noises, like something large and scaly moving around.

"Why are all the bloody lights out?" muttered Claire. Her

head kept turning in different directions, like she'd be able to see something if she just moved fast enough.

"We're sitting on top of an active volcano," said Robert. "Electricity is mostly generated from a geothermal system that Moreau constructed beneath the house. There are also some solar panels on top of the house and some windmills on the north side of the island that add a little extra. Even so, electricity is a precious commodity here on Noble's Isle, generally reserved for Moreau's work."

"What work?" asked Mozart.

"That front room we were in is usually dark as well," said Robert, like he hadn't heard Mozart's question. "He left the porch light on for you."

"So sweet of him," Claire said.

Finally, we could see a lit room ahead. It had the same harsh white halogen lamps, which I realized were probably a lot more energy efficient. Although when we entered the room, I wondered why bother conserving that little bit when there were so many things in here sucking power. This room was about three times the size of any of the other rooms. Instead of antique furniture and rugs, it was lined with sterile white tile. Along one wall were big refrigerators, a sink, a stove, and glass cabinets containing beakers and vials filled with a rainbow of liquids. The far wall was completely covered by thick metal blinds. And in the center was a massive stainless-steel table with a collection of really unpleasant-looking tools; dull, corroded implements, some with blades, points, hooks, or saw teeth. And something that looked a lot like a massive antique bolt cutter.

"If he has been cut off from civilization for over a hundred years, then he would not have even had a refrigerator when this island was sealed off," said La Perricholi, nodding to the refrigerators. "Did you bring it all with you?"

"I didn't bring any of this equipment with me," said Robert.

"Then who did?" asked Mozart.

Robert's eyes darted away, and for the first time, he looked nervous. But then his eyes caught something on the far end of the room and his face lit up with a relieved smile.

"Ladies and gentlemen," he said. "Allow me to introduce our host, Dr. Moreau."

"Welcome, all of you," came a thick, coarse voice.

Then we turned and saw Moreau for the first time.

He was huge. Bigger than me or Stephen or even my dad. Here and there were patches of pale, wrinkled human skin. But for the most part, he seemed to be comprised of animal parts. He had large pointy bat ears and piercing yellow hawk eyes. His nose and mouth jutted out like an ape's, and his hair looked more like coarse animal fur. He was dressed in white, loose-fitting robes of some kind so I couldn't tell exactly what was going on with his body, but his hands were clawed and his bare feet looked very catlike. And I was pretty sure there was a prehensile tail of some kind swishing behind him beneath the robes.

We all stared at him for a little while. Then finally Mozart cleared his throat.

"My name is Mozart. I'll be acting as Ruthven's liaison. We understood that you were . . . human?"

"I know who you are, Wolfgang. I know who all of you are," said Moreau. It seemed tricky to talk around that giant set of primate teeth, especially the long canines, but he did a pretty good job of it. "And yes, 'were' is the correct word to use. I was human when they imprisoned me on this island."

"You did this to yourself?" asked La Perricholi.

"Yes, Perricholi. I am a self-made monster," said Moreau. "It was clear to me that the most formidable obstacle in reaching my goals was my own mortality. So naturally, before I proceeded with any other work, I had to find a way to extend my life."

"So as your own body parts started to wear out, you replaced them with animal parts?" I asked.

His apelike face grimaced into something that I think was supposed to be a smile. "Quite correct, Boy. At first I used surgery, but I found that to be highly unreliable, and messy, particularly when trying to operate on myself. Eventually, I turned to stem-cell development. That allowed for a great deal more precision. However, the biggest problem continued to be tissue rejection. If you try to simply graft an ape hand onto the end of your arm, your body will reject it. But I was eventually able to find a way to suppress that reaction. Now, I am happy to say, I can graft any anatomical feature from one creature onto another without rejection."

"That's amazing," I said.

"I'm glad you appreciate it."

"Must've taken a lot of trial and error to get there," said Mozart. "A lot of test subjects."

"One can accomplish a great deal when one is not inhibited by ethical constraints."

"Yeah, that's what worries me."

"No doubt you are wondering why I asked you and your companions to come so very far and in such a dramatic fashion," said Moreau.

"It's been on my mind. Especially the part where Stephen nearly killed us."

"What?" said Moreau, his yellow bird eyes widening. It was difficult to read his expression, but he sounded genuinely surprised.

"Eh, Stephen . . ." said Robert, cringing slightly. "He wanted to make sure they were . . . worth your time."

"I see," said Moreau. "While I appreciate his intent, his methods were counterproductive. I won't be able to overlook this."

"I . . , understand," said Robert, his face growing even more pale than usual.

Moreau turned back to us. "I am truly sorry about that. The last thing I wanted was to alienate you. After all, I am hoping to enlist your aid. But before we get to all of that, may I ask, do you know why I was imprisoned on this island so long ago?"

"Something about exposing the monster secret to humans. Ruthven never told me the full details."

"Of course he didn't. Vampires do love their secrets. Sometimes even when it is dangerous to withhold certain pieces of information."

"So now you're going to tell me that you were framed, right? That you didn't try to sell us out to the humans."

Moreau slowly blinked his yellow eagle eyes as he stared at Mozart, one bat ear twitching with irritation. "I did not try to 'sell you out,' as you put it. But in a sense, I did try to expose the monster secret to the humans."

"Don't start getting semantic with me."

"I wouldn't dream of it," said Moreau, his ape mouth grimacing again. "But let me explain the reason why I wanted to shatter this secret that has lasted for so many centuries."

Mozart glanced at La Perricholi. She shrugged.

"All right. Give us your sales pitch."

"How gracious of you," said Moreau. He walked over to the large metal table, his motions slow and liquid on his great cat feet. He reached out with one clawed hand and touched the creepy metal instruments. I tried not to think of how many animals he'd opened up with those things.

"As you are probably aware," he began, "before I discovered your monster world, I spent years on this island trying to surgically alter animals to become more like humans. It was a misguided goal that failed spectacularly and nearly got me killed. But it did attract the attention of Ruthven and Kemp. I was flattered when they contacted me. I felt like I'd suddenly become privy to an entirely new dimension of existence. An aspect of the world that I had always longed for, but never dared believe was possible."

He began to lay out the tools neatly, side by side. He did it with the easy precision of someone who had done it many times.

"This was decades before The Show or The Studio existed, of course. There was almost no unity among monsters. Some lived alone, others in small groups. They existed on the outskirts of human society, or beneath it in sewers, or else in barren, uninhabited wastelands. Once-proud creatures cowering in filth— starving, miserable, dying. Ruthven and Kemp feared that monsters would not survive the coming advances of the twentieth century. They asked me what I thought they should do."

He picked up a small, jagged saw that still had tiny bits of yellow bone stuck in the teeth.

"I told them they should unite all monsters under a single coalition and slaughter approximately one-eighth of the world's human population."

"Wait," I said. "You told them they should stage a monster revolution?"

"Karl Marx and socialism were just beginning to take hold at the time. It seemed like sound, fair logic to me."

"I'm pretty sure Marx never advocated killing millions of people," said Mozart.

"Yes," said Moreau. "And look at the state of socialism now."

"So, they locked you away because you told them to revolt against humanity?" asked Claire.

"No, Ms. Hyde. They locked me away because, when they balked at the idea, I marshaled a small force of monsters and tried to do it myself."

"And how did you do that?" asked Mozart.

"I invaded Lima, naturally."

"What?" said La Perricholi.

"It was nothing personal," said Moreau. "It was merely the most logical choice. Close proximity, unstable government, large enough to make the world take notice, but not so large as to be impossible. I remember one of your predecessors at the head of the defensive. She was a formidable opponent, but my forces were far superior. If Ruthven, Kemp, Boy's father, and the Dragon Lady had not stepped in, Peru would have fallen and a new country would have risen."

"You wanted to make a monster government?" I asked.

"The rest of the world would have been forced to grant us legitimacy. They would have had to broaden the concept of personhood to include nonhumans and accept that they aren't the only ones who deserve basic rights and a place in the world. An action that I think all of you would agree is long overdue, would you not?" He put down his tools and turned to me. "You walk freely in the world, but your own father cannot. Doesn't that bother you?"

"Of course," I said.

"Don't you want to do something about it?"

"Well . . . yeah."

"Naturally." He turned to Claire. "Robert told me of your mothers' tragic end. Imagine a world that had mental health counseling that took into consideration the complex identity issues they faced. A world in which they could have gotten the help they needed, rather than be forced to live a life of constant repression and fear. All these things could have been possible."

"If you'd strong-armed a small country in South America?" asked Mozart. "I don't think so."

"Agreed," said Moreau. "Peru would have just been the initial foothold."

"Then you would have slowly annexed country after country until you controlled all of South America."

"Darwin's law. Survival of the fittest."

"So far, humans seem to be the fitter of the two," said La Perricholi. "We are the ones in control."

"*We?*" asked Moreau. He turned away from his tools and his piercing eyes focused on her. "After everything you've seen, after everything you've done, do you think you really still have a place in humanity? I have altered my physical form into something monstrous. But your insides, I'll wager, have altered just as grotesquely over the years. Tell me I'm wrong."

She stared at him, her face hard. But she said nothing.

"And as for which is superior, the only reason humans remain dominant is through sheer strength of numbers. New monsters, whether they begin life that way like Boy and Claire, or transformed like Kemp or Ruthven, have always been difficult to make. The process is usually unplanned and the results unpredictable."

He walked over to the cabinets that contained vials and beakers of brightly colored liquid. He placed his clawed hand on the glass door. His long tail swished back and forth beneath his white robes.

"Until now."

"I'm getting a little tired of the runaround, Moreau." Mozart's voice was little more than a quiet growl. "Why did you bring us here?"

"I can best answer your question by showing you." He nodded to Robert. "If you'll do the honors, Mr. Jekyll."

"Gladly," said Robert. He walked to the far wall and pulled a cord next to the metal blinds so that they slowly lifted to reveal a large bay window that stretched most of the way across the room. It looked outside onto a massive field lit up in the darkness by lines of flickering torches.

Covering the field was a sea of monsters.

It was difficult to make out a lot of details in the firelight. Most of them were roughly human-shaped, with fur or feathers, scales or spikes. I spotted lion creatures, lizard creatures, elephant creatures, vulture creatures, and many others, some of which I couldn't even identify. They stood at attention, row upon row of them. Like an army.

Moreau moved over to the window and lifted one hand. All the monsters out on the field roared, so loud it rattled the glass. Then he dropped his hand and they fell silent.

"I'm starting a new revolution," said Moreau, still facing out the window. His long, prehensile tail swished languidly back and forth beneath his robes. "Robert and Stephen have already pledged themselves to the cause. I invite you to join us in finally creating a world that respects monsters and gives us the basic rights we deserve."

"And if we say no?" asked La Perricholi. Her hand dropped down to her thigh where her gun was holstered.

"You are guests in my house. I will not keep you here against your will. And of course, I am not unreasonable. You will want time to consider and discuss with Ruthven and the rest of your community. It would be a great boon to the cause if all of The Show joined us."

He turned to us, the legion of monsters at his back.

"But know that if we meet again on opposite sides of a battle-field, I will show no mercy. Whether human or monster, the only options I offer are to join me, or die."

———

THE BALD LEMUR in the tuxedo escorted us back to the front door. Robert remained behind with Moreau. When we got outside, the night was no longer quiet. Off in the distance, behind Moreau's house, where the fields of militant monsters were assembled, it sounded like a party was starting. Screeches, roars, and other animal noises mixed with laughter and shouting, and underneath was the pounding of drums. Bonfires flickered into life, casting shadows against the treetops that moved in jerks and spasms.

I heard a cough coming from the roof of the house. I turned, and just above the front door perched a raven with human hands instead of talons.

"Never," it croaked.

"Can we please get out of here?" I asked.

The sounds of the beast people party continued as we slowly made our way back down the cliff and into the jungle. As time went on, the screeches grew louder and more frenetic, like the beast people were in pain.

"Are they fighting each other?" asked Claire.

"Mating," said Mozart.

By the time we got back to the boat, the sounds were little more than distant echoes, mostly drowned out by the rolling waves as the tide came in. The sky was just beginning to lighten with the first red rays of dawn.

*Red sky at morning, sailors take warning*, I thought.

# 14
# What Matters

WE HIT SOME really bad weather on the return voyage, so it was four days before we finally got back to La Perricholi's house. Maria had taken one look at us and started making cocktails. Now we sat around the dining room table, drinking something she called a pisco sour that was sort of sweet, sort of bitter, and very strong, and scarfing down a big bowl of toasted corn kernels called *cancha*.

"I am surprised Moreau let you go so easily," said Maria.

"He seemed pretty confident we'll join up," said Mozart.

"But we're not going to do that, right?" Henri asked.

Mozart turned to Maria. "Has Ruthven called back?"

She shook her head.

His lip peeled back in a snarl. "That's not like him. Something's going on. I can feel it." He turned to Claire, then me. "We have to get back to New York. I'll get us a flight first thing tomorrow." Then he turned to La Perricholi. "You want to come with us?"

"No. There is an army hostile to humans within striking distance of my homeland. I cannot leave now. If need be, La Perricholi will once again defend the shores of Peru from Moreau's army."

"What about you?" I asked Henri. "You want to come back

to New York or go straight to Geneva? I wouldn't blame you for wanting to bail. I have a feeling this could get pretty crazy."

"Eh . . . actually . . ." His eyes flickered to Maria for a moment. "I thought I might see if I could be of some help here in Lima." Then he turned to La Perricholi. "That is, if you do not mind."

La Perricholi pursed her lips and looked at him appraisingly. "Boy tells me you have a talent for working with technology. That could be helpful, since it is not one of my strong suits."

"Yes, absolutely, I am your man!" he said eagerly.

"This would not be a vacation."

"I understand completely."

"Then you may stay."

Vi's phone rumbled in my pocket.

—————

IT WAS A hot night and I lay on top of the bedcovers, just wearing a pair of boxer shorts. The window was open next to me, and the cool night breeze snaked across my skin.

We had a little bathroom right in our room, almost like a hotel. Claire stood at the sink, brushing her teeth. Sophie would wear little silky things to bed, which was nice. Claire always just wore a T-shirt, and as I gazed at her long, tan, muscular legs and the beginning curve of her butt just peeking out from under the white hem, I decided that was nice, too.

"Did you notice that part where Mozart totally ignored Henri's question about joining Moreau's army?" I asked.

"Mmmffph," said Claire, then spat into the sink. "And did you notice how he immediately asked about Ruthven after that?"

"You think Ruthven would actually consider aligning with Moreau?"

She picked up a hairbrush and started to pull it through her straight black hair. "I think Ruthven would consider anything that might benefit his coven."

"But full-on war with the humans?"

"You're the one who's always on about how we shouldn't have to hide what we are. That we should have rights, too."

"Well, yeah, but—"

"How else do you think something like that could happen?

"I was kind of envisioning more of a Martin Luther King Jr. solution. You know, peaceful demonstrations, rallies, that kind of stuff."

"Just picture that for a moment. Dragons, ogres, and goblins marching in protest on the White House. Do you honestly think the cops wouldn't just immediately start shooting? There is a huge difference between a black human who wants to be treated like other humans, and a creature whose very nature requires that she kill humans to survive. We're talking Ruthven, the Siren, and a bunch of others. Or would your rally only be for 'safe' monsters?"

"Of course not."

She turned to me, her dark eyes serious. "You said to me once that you hoped someday creatures like Medusa could have a place in the world again. How do you think that could happen without some sort of major upheaval? Humans would never willingly let a creature like her exist."

"So you're saying that you'd join Moreau?"

She sighed. "I don't know. Honestly, I don't think I could join any group that had Robert and Stephen in it. I know that's a stupid way to look at it."

"It's not stupid," I said. "All this talk about ideals and causes and stuff is so big and theoretical. Maybe for others that works.

But for me, in the end, it feels like the only thing that really makes any sense—that truly matters—is people."

Claire sat down next me on the bed, one leg drawn up as she leaned against the headboard. "I wonder what your parents would say about it."

"I wonder if they already knew about Moreau," I said. "I bet they all did."

"Do you think it's weird we can't get ahold of anyone there?" she asked.

"Really weird. I built a lot of that infrastructure myself. It's rock solid. I tried to tunnel into the primary server a little bit ago, but got nothing. Like the network wasn't even online."

"Could Vi figure out what's going on?"

"Maybe."

"Why don't you ask her?"

"Uh, I think she's probably not in the mood right now."

"This is serious, though, Boy."

"I'll ask, but . . ."

I reached over to the bedside table and opened the phone. On it was her anime face, but it was bright red. There was a large circular pulse over her temple, and wavy lines of smoke rose up from her head.

"Hey, Vi—"

"Did you *hear* him?" Her fists shook up and down so fast they were a blur.

"Yeah, I heard him."

"He's going to stay here? In Lima? With *her*?!"

"Look, Vi. I was surprised, too. I thought Henri was with us."

"Right?" Her eyes bugged out wide. "Bros before hos, right?"

"I'm not sure that really applies in this—"

"He's thrown us over for that Peruvian bitch!"

"Now settle down there, sister," said Claire. "La Perricholi's made it pretty clear she's not interested. This is all on Henri."

"Why her and not me? I'm interested! What does she have that I don't?"

Claire and I looked at each other.

"What?" said Vi. "Is it because I'm not pretty enough? I tried to make myself pretty for him."

"You made yourself look exactly the way he wanted you to look," I said.

"So what is it, then? Am I not nice enough?"

"No, you've been plenty nice," said Claire. "If you ask me, a bit too nice."

"So I should be tough and mean? Like La Perricholi? Then would Henri be interested in me? I don't know if I can be tough and mean, but I could try." She tried to make her face look hard, but she would probably need an entire avatar redesign before that would look at all credible.

"I don't think that's something you can fake," I said. "And, anyway, you shouldn't have to. You're awesome the way you are."

"If I'm so *awesome*, why isn't he interested in me?"

"Well, it's just . . . man, how can I put this? Okay. People in analog . . . they really like having physical bodies. They express affection by touching each other's physical bodies. And I think for a lot of people, if they can't do that, their affection can only go so far."

"Oh." Vi was suddenly very still, her purple eyes wide. "Is that it?"

"But *we* love you," said Claire. "You don't need a physical body for us."

Vi nodded, but her expression remained frozen. Distant.

"I'm so sorry, Vi," I said. "This is what upset your alpha phase so much. This limitation. It's why I promised you right from the start that we will find a nondestructive way for you to enter analog space. And I swear we are still going to do that."

"When?" she asked.

"I don't know."

"We've got to deal with Moreau first," said Claire.

"I understand," said Vi. "The many before the one."

"Vi, it's not—"

"I'm going to power down for a little while, okay?"

"Uh, sure."

The screen went black and I placed the phone on the bedside table. Then I slowly lay back on the bed. Claire lay down next to me, her head on my chest.

"That conversation had to happen eventually," she said.

"Yeah," I said.

"And you had to be the one to say it."

"I know."

"You're doing a good job with her this time."

"I'm trying."

"That's all you can do."

"I guess."

She reached up and put her arms around me. "Come here, you big, oversensitive lug."

"Sorry," I said, letting her pull me down to her.

She pressed her lips against mine, then opened them so her breath escaped into my mouth.

"I wouldn't change you for the world," she whispered.

THE NEXT MORNING, Maria drove Mozart, Claire, and me to the airport. Henri rode along with us, and when we got to the departure drop-off, he stepped out of the car with me.

"Hey, cousin," he said.

"Hey," I said.

"I feel bad leaving you."

"It's okay." It wasn't, really. Vi was still upset. And I realized that I was upset, too. It would have been one thing if he wanted safety, to be back with his family. But I was pretty sure Lima wouldn't be any safer than New York. It was probably even more dangerous. So as far as I could tell, there was only one reason he wanted to stay in Lima.

"You know why I'm staying, right?" he asked.

"Uh, because of La Perricholi?"

"She is the *one*, Boy. *Mon amour.* I just know she is."

I was pretty sure she disagreed, but I didn't say anything.

He put his hands on my shoulders. "I have always had a difficult time relating to regular humans. Even before I knew monsters were real. Being a Frankenstein is not easy, you know? But I am also not a monster and I don't really feel like I fit in with you guys, either. I am somewhere in between. And so is she. I finally found someone who is in the same spot as me. What you have with Claire and Sophie is so perfect. I just want that for myself. You understand, right?"

There was a part of me that wanted to smack him. To ask him if he cared about anything other than himself, if he was even aware that we were potentially on the verge of a monster-human war. But then I thought, *What does one have to do with the other?* He looked so desperate to be forgiven, to be told it was okay. And wasn't it? When things start to look dark and serious, isn't love more important than ever? The more meanness I saw in the world, the kinder I wanted to be to make up for it. Maybe that made me a dumb-ass, but it felt right.

So I just said, "Of course I understand," and gave him a hug. I le looked so relieved, I almost felt bad for him.

"Thanks, cousin," he said.

"Good-bye, Henri. I'll see you soon."

Then I went to the back of the van to help Claire with the luggage.

"I would've punched him," she said.

"I know. So I'm a sap. Where's Mozart?"

"Saying good-bye to his girl," said Claire.

I peered around the corner and saw Maria and Mozart kissing.

"Brilliant, isn't it?" said Claire. Then, "Oi! Wolfie! Give her tongue back! We've got a plane to catch, yeah?"

"That's what I love about you," I said. "So sentimental."

She winked at me. "If you and I started snogging every time we felt like it, we'd never get anything done."

"What is this 'snogging' you speak of? Some sort of foreign ritual?" I dropped the bag I was holding and pulled her in close so that her stomach and hips pressed against mine. "You may have to show me. Extensively."

"Bloody Casanovas, the lot of you," she said, pulling my hands from her waist and putting a bag in each one. "Thank god one of us has a practical mind."

# 15
## Closing Night

++++++++

WHEN WE ARRIVED at New York's JFK airport, Mozart insisted we take a cab. The subway would have been a lot cheaper, but he wanted to get to The Show as quickly as possible. Claire and I exchanged looks, but neither of us said anything. I'd never seen him this anxious before, or this willing to spend money.

An hour later we were shooting across 42nd Street toward Times Square. It was around two a.m., so traffic was minimal. Claire and I sat in the back, while Mozart sat up front and hassled the cab driver every time he disagreed with the route. Then he had the driver drop us off a few blocks from the theater.

"We *are* going to the theater, right?" Claire asked as the cab drove off.

"Yeah." Mozart's gray eyes were narrowed almost to slits now, and they glinted in the streetlights. "My gut tells me something bad is waiting for us. I want to be able to see it before we're on top of it."

"What do you mean, something bad?" I asked. "What could possibly be bad at The Show? I mean, other than its normal badness."

Mozart looked at me for a second like he was going to say something, but then he just shook his head and started walking toward the theater. Claire and I followed behind, lugging our suitcases.

We were a block away when he held up his hand and we jerked to a stop.

"What is *with* him?" Claire hissed to me under her breath.

"Shut it," growled Mozart. He started moving forward again, but slowly, like he was stalking prey. "Look."

The front of the theater was dark, but that was normal this late at night. It took me a minute or two to see what Mozart's wolf eyes had already picked up. The Show marquee was gone from the entrance. Those ridiculous, so-old-they-looked-retro posters had been torn down, the glass casing smashed. And even worse, there was yellow CRIME SCENE DO NOT CROSS tape stretched across the doors.

"What—" I started to say, but Mozart's head snapped around and he glared at me so hard that the rest of the sentence stuck in my throat.

He pointed to the alley along the side of the theater and mouthed *stage door*. We both nodded and followed him slowly around the side, through the unlit alley to the plain metal door halfway down. Mozart pulled out a key and unlocked the door. The three of us slipped inside the dark theater and closed the door behind us.

It was pitch black inside, but I knew this room well. It was where my dad usually sat after The Show to deal with humans who wanted to come in to meet cast members.

"It's okay to talk here. I'm not getting any fresh scents."

"What you do mean, no fresh scent?" I asked. "For how long?"

"Days."

"How can there not have been anyone here for days? It's the stage door entrance on a Saturday."

"No idea yet. Anybody got a light?"

"Can't Vi light up a bit?" asked Claire.

"Oh, yeah, of course." I pulled out the phone. "Vi?"

"What's going on?" Vi asked, her anime face pinched into a frown.

"Something is seriously wrong," I said. "Can you give us a little light?"

"Sure."

The phone display flared up bright white.

"How's that?" she asked.

"Great. It's—" I stopped and stared at the dark blotches on the wall.

"Blood," said Mozart.

"No," I said. "No way. It can't be—"

"Boy!" Mozart's voice cracked like a slap across the face. "I need you to stay calm. Don't make any assumptions, don't jump to conclusions. We will figure this out. I promise you. But we can only do that if we keep our heads."

I took a deep breath and let it out slowly. "I'm okay."

"Good," said Mozart. "Now, Vi, can you hear me?"

"Yes," said Vi.

"Is there any way for you to connect to the security system?"

"I could, but it's all been powered down. In fact, it seems like the entire building is dark."

Mozart walked over to the wall switch and toggled it up and down. "Power's been completely cut from the building. Any ideas how we can get a look at the security camera footage?"

"We could pull the drive from the server where the video footage is stored," I said. "Assuming it hasn't been corrupted, I could install it in another machine somewhere else that has power."

"You know where the server is?" Mozart asked.

"Of course," I said. "It's in the storage closet behind the box office. Mom and I were the ones who installed it. Mom . . ." Then I started to think about where Mom might be. What might have happened to her—

"Hey," said Mozart. "Stay with us. You hear me? I need you right now, Boy."

I nodded.

"I'm going to nose around, see what other info I can pick up. You and Claire get that drive and meet me back here. Ten minutes."

"Got it."

Mozart shifted into a wolf and slipped quietly out of the room, leaving his clothes behind in a pile.

"Come on," said Claire. "Let's go."

We walked slowly through the hallways, using Vi as a little flashlight. I tried to take in all the details without letting them really hit me. I tried to imagine I was disconnected as I saw broken bits of furniture, spots of blood, and the small holes in the walls that suggested gunfire.

It was only a few minutes later when we reached the lobby, but it felt like hours. And the lobby was even more of a mess than the hallways. It looked like small explosions had taken chunks out of the floor. The box office walls had been smashed in, and there were chunks of glass everywhere. The storage closet behind the box office was completely blocked by debris.

"I'll lift it up," I said. "You see if you can crawl under and pull the server box."

Claire nodded.

I crouched down with my back against the pile, shoved my hands under, and slowly stood up. Claire dropped to the ground and looked under.

"There's a big metal thing in the way," she said.

"The server rack," I said.

"It looks like it tipped over."

"Can you see the server? Is it damaged?"

"Doesn't look like it, but I can't get at it. The opening is too narrow for me." She looked up at me. "Sophie could reach it."

"Your call," I said. "But either way, make it quick. I can't hold this stuff up forever."

"I think you could use some Sophie time, anyway," she said.

"What does that mean?"

But then her body started to shift so I just concentrated on holding up the pile.

A minute later Sophie was cinching up her pants and tightening the laces on her shoes.

"It's like wearing boxes on my feet."

"Hey, Soph," I grunted. "Any time now. Would be great."

"Right, sorry." She ducked down and slipped under the debris. "This box thingie?"

"Yeah."

"Do I need the cables and such?"

"No."

"Good, because it's a rats' nest back here."

I heard the sound of metal scraping on metal. A moment later, Sophie popped out holding the server in her hands.

"You can let it go," she said.

I eased the pile back down, then rubbed my aching fingers for a moment. "All right, let's see if the drive is intact." I took the server from her. I didn't have a screwdriver so I just cracked open the casing.

"Shit," I said.

"What?" said Sophie.

"The drive. It's gone."

"You mean destroyed?"

"No, I mean gone. Vanished." I stared down at the empty server casing. "Along with every fucking member of the company."

I shouldn't have said that. Because saying it made it completely real in a way I had been trying hard to avoid. Because saying it forced me to admit to myself that I had no idea where my parents and Ruthven and Charon and Laurellen and everyone else was. For all I knew, they were dead.

I heard the server crash to the ground, but it sounded distant, drowned out by the sudden pounding in my temples. My vision started to tunnel and I couldn't seem to catch my breath.

"Boy?" Sophie's voice came from far away. "You look really pale. Are you fee . . ."

I dropped to the ground, still trying to get air into my lungs. I looked down and saw that my big, stitched hands were shaking.

Sophie sat down next to me. She pulled my head down to her chest and stroked my hair and just said, "Boy, it's okay, you're okay," over and over again. Finally, my heart started to slow down and I was able to get my breathing under control.

"I . . . I think I just had a panic attack," I said.

"Are you feeling better now?"

"A little."

"Listen, we don't know anything for certain yet."

"I know."

"Isn't there some sort of escape hatch down into the trowe caverns you told me about once?"

"Yeah." I nodded. "In Ruthven's office closet."

"Maybe that's where everyone went."

The door to Ruthven's office lay on the floor in splinters. It looked like it had been blown right off its hinges. Inside, the lone desk was intact, but the drawers had all been emptied. The closet door was open and the floor piece that covered the escape hatch was gone. The hole that led down into the ground was rimmed with black char marks.

"The ladder's destroyed," I said. "And I think it's about a twenty-foot drop straight down to the bottom."

"Maybe if we had a rope . . ." said Sophie.

"That's assuming the tunnel's even still intact. It looks like they dropped some explosives down there."

"So people might be trapped down there?"

I shook my head. "There's an evacuation tunnel. The trowe used it to get people out before I blew up Vi and most of the theater. I think it goes under the river and comes out somewhere in Jersey."

"I'll bet a lot of people got out through the tunnel, then."

I stared down at the hole. "Yeah."

Sophie put her small hand in mine. "We should probably go. Mozart is waiting for us. Maybe he found something."

We went back to the stage door entrance. Mozart was already back in human form and dressed. He raised an eyebrow when he saw Sophie.

"Hey, Wolfie," she said.

"Any luck?" he asked.

I shook my head. "Someone got to it before we did."

He grunted. "Whoever did this, they had firepower, and they knew what they were doing. We need a place to regroup and figure out our next steps before we walk into something bigger than we're ready to handle."

"Where can we go?" I asked.

"I have an old friend up in Harlem. She'll take us in for a night or two. She's kind of known for that—offering a temporary shelter for wayward monsters. We might even find some of the others there."

———

IT WAS ALMOST sunrise by the time we got to Harlem. As Sophie and I numbly followed Mozart down 110th Street, I felt like I'd gone so far past the point of exhaustion that I could have slept anywhere. All my worries and questions about what had happened to my parents, Ruthven, and the others still swirled around in my brain, but at the moment, all I could really concentrate on was putting one foot in front of the other.

"So, who's this friend of yours?" asked Sophie. She sounded only slightly more alert then I was.

"Felicia," he said. "Just a heads-up, she's a zombie."

"What?" I suddenly felt a lot more awake. "We're staying with a zombie? Aren't you worried she'll eat our brains or something?"

"The whole eating-brains thing was just a Hollywood invention," he said. "So was the rotting corpse idea."

"Then . . . they're not actually dead?" asked Sophie.

"Oh, no, they're definitely dead. And Felicia does have a certain . . . smell that takes a little getting used to. She's not much of a conversationalist, either. But you won't find a more generous monster in the world. I wouldn't have made it past my first week as a werewolf if it hadn't been for her."

"When was that?" I asked.

"1935," he said.

"You're pretty spry for a seventy-eight-year-old," said Sophie.

"Ninety-four, if you must know," he said loftily. "I was sixteen when I was turned. Like I said back in Lima, werewolves age slower than humans." He stopped in front of a gray apartment building. "Now shut up. I'm trying to remember which apartment is hers."

"Memory not what it used to be, eh, old wolf?" she said.

"Cute," he said, and rang a buzzer.

The speaker clicked on and there was a dull female voice. "Yes."

"This old hammer," said Mozart.

"Killed John Henry." She had a faint French accent.

"But it won't kill me," said Mozart.

"You may come up."

The door gave a long beep, and Mozart pushed it open. Then we started up the narrow stairwell.

"Was that code?" I asked.

"Yeah," he said. "It's from an old folk song about John Henry, the guy who raced a steam engine. He won, but died of exhaustion right after."

"Sure, I remember that story," I said. "Wait, was he one of us?"

"Like I said before, the line between monsters and humans is a lot blurrier than people want to admit. Anyway, the bokur who made Felicia, that was his favorite story."

"Bokur?" asked Sophie.

"Haitian vodoun priest. Some might call them witch doctors. But most bokurs don't really like that term."

A woman stood at the top of the stairs. Her black hair was pulled back in a tight bun and she wore a white button-up blouse, a green cardigan sweater, and long tan skirt that went almost to her ankles. She held a wooden rosary in her hands. Her facial features made me think she was originally from Africa or the West Indies somewhere, although her skin tone was more gray than brown. And as we got closer, there *was* a weird smell coming from her. Like a dank, muddy river. Not bad, but not exactly pleasant, either.

She stared at her feet as she said, "Welcome, Mozart. It is good to see you."

"Hi, Felicia. Good to see you, too."

"Do come in." Still without looking at us, she slowly stepped aside so we could enter the door behind her.

"Thanks," he said.

Sophie and I followed Mozart into the apartment. Inside, it was very simply furnished, with a table and four chairs next to an open kitchen area on one side, and a couch with a few upholstered chairs on the other. It would have looked plain, except the walls were covered in crucifixes and paintings of saints.

"Please, make yourself comfortable," Felicia said tonelessly as she closed the door and shuffled in behind us. I started to wonder if this was just a rote script she was following.

"Thanks," said Mozart, dropping onto the couch.

After a moment, Sophie and I dropped onto chairs. Felicia just stood and stared at her feet.

"Has anyone from The Show come by?" asked Mozart.

"Yes," said Felicia. "Laurellen was here."

"When?" asked Mozart.

"The day before yesterday."

"Was anyone else with him?" I asked.

"A female who did not speak."

"Did she have hair that stuck out in clumps, kind of like feathers?" asked Mozart.

"Yes."

"The Siren. Anybody else?"

"No."

"Did Laurellen say anything to you about what happened?"

"He said The Show had been attacked. It was no longer safe."

"Attacked," said Sophie. "By whom?"

"He did not say," said Felicia.

"Did he say where he was going?" asked Mozart. "New Jersey maybe?"

"He said the area was too hot. They were going to meet up with the others at The Museum."

"Really?" His dark, bushy eyebrows rose in surprise. "That bad, huh?"

"Where's The Museum?" asked Sophie.

"It's in Philly. I think we should rest here for a little while before we head out. Agreed?"

"Yeah," I said. "I'm ready to fall over."

Mozart turned back to Felicia. "I'm surprised he said all that. Just casually."

"It was not casual. He said you might come looking for him."

He nodded. "Thanks for relaying the information."

"You're welcome."

Mozart turned back to us and pointed toward an open doorway to another room. "You guys take the bedroom. I'll take the couch."

"What about . . ." I glanced at Felicia.

"She doesn't sleep."

"Is . . . she just going to stand there?" asked Sophie.

"Yep. Zombies don't really have a will of their own. They live to obey the bokur who creates them. Usually, when he dies, they just stand around until some human mistakes them for catatonic and puts them in a hospital or something. After a few months with no one to command them, the spark that animates them slowly fades out."

"Is Felicia's bokur still alive?" I asked.

"Nope, he died about a hundred years ago."

"So why is she still around?"

"The last thing he did before he died was give her an open-ended command to shelter any monster who knew the pass phrase."

I looked over at Felicia. She stared listlessly at the ground. A fly landed on her eyelash but she didn't seem to notice.

"So she'll do this forever?"

"Or until she's destroyed." Mozart looked up at Felicia. "I've never been able to decide if it was the kindest thing her bokur could have done or the cruelest."

"You said she's helped a lot of monsters, though," said Sophie.

"That she has," said Mozart. "Now, let's get some sleep."

SOPHIE AND I lay side by side on the narrow bed. Even though I was so tired, I couldn't sleep. Maybe it was the sunlight that filtered in faintly through the blinds. Or maybe it was Felicia, still standing in the middle of the living room, like she was guarding Mozart while he slept curled up on the couch in wolf form.

"You still awake?" Sophie whispered.

"Who could have done this?" I asked. "Who could have taken out the entire Show?"

"Moreau?"

"That doesn't make any sense, though. He said he wanted to recruit us."

"Maybe he already asked Ruthven. Maybe Ruthven already gave his answer."

We were silent for a moment. Outside, I could hear a few tentative honks, a short burst of laughter, music coming from an open window in the building across the alley. The sounds of the city slowly waking up.

I turned my head and looked into her bright eyes. "I'm sorry about your mom. I know I said it to Claire, already, but . . ."

She smiled sadly. "Thanks. It's sweet of you to think of that when you've got your own worries right now." She snuggled into me. "It seems like every other Jekyll and Hyde is doomed to destroy each other. Our grandfathers, our mothers. Even our brothers seem well on their way to killing each other."

"But it's not going to happen to you," I said. "You've figured out how to make it work."

"For now."

"What does that mean?"

She was silent for a moment. Then she sighed. "I dunno, I'm tired and babbling. Let's try to sleep."

# 16
# Teratology

+++++++

I'D RIDDEN SUBWAY trains, cars, planes, and even a dragon a couple of times, but I'd never ridden a bus before. As I tried to cram myself into the narrow seats, I decided it was my least favorite mode of transportation.

"Why couldn't we take a train to Philly?" I asked.

"It would have been about triple the cost," said Mozart. He and Sophie sat in the row in front of me. There was no way anyone else was going to fit next to me.

"Couldn't we have hot-wired a car like we did that one time?" I asked.

"Until we know exactly what's going on and who hit The Show, I don't want to do anything that might draw attention to us."

"Do you have any theories on who it might have been?" asked Sophie.

"Lots. But there's no point in winding ourselves up with speculation. We'll find out what really happened once we reach The Museum."

"What is The Museum?" I asked.

"It's a place where they have old, dead things on display."

"I mean, is it another monster community, like The Show or The Studio?"

"No, there's only one monster who lives there full-time. Odd little guy called the Keeper. Not even sure what he is, really. He's been around as long as anyone can remember. He's sort of the caretaker of The Museum."

"And it's an actual museum, then?" asked Sophie.

"It is on the surface. But it's also sort of a safe house for monsters. Somewhere for us all to go in times of crisis."

Vi buzzed my pocket. It took me a bit to maneuver myself into a position where I could actually reach into my pocket and pull her out.

"What's up?" I asked.

"I've been scanning every public news source for information about the attack on The Show." Her expression was pinched, with dark circles under her eyes. Sometimes I really wondered what Henri had been thinking when he designed these emotion templates for her to use.

"Any luck?" I asked.

"None."

"What about police records?"

"Those are clean, too."

"So absolutely no clues whatsoever?"

"Not exactly. As I said, the police records were clean. One evening in particular, they are completely clean. Not a single incident reported that entire night."

"In all of New York City? That seems a little unlikely, don't you think?"

"Exactly. The lack of information is our only clue."

"You think someone scrubbed the database?"

"What other option could there be?"

"Do you think you can recover it?"

"I'm checking now. Even if I can't, I should at least be able to trace the erasure back to the source. But with my current limited CPU it will take a while."

"Maybe there will be a decent machine we can load you onto once we get to The Museum."

She stuck her tongue out at me. "With a name like that, I don't think we should get our hopes up."

PHILADELPHIA TURNED OUT to be sort of a blend between New York and Pittsburgh. It had that dense urban neighborhood feel, but it also had a more relaxed, earthy vibe. I almost wished we had time to explore. It seemed like whenever I was traveling, I was rushing to something or away from something. I promised myself that someday, I would come back to all these places when I actually had the time to enjoy them.

From the bus station, we walked a few blocks, crossed a river, then walked a few more blocks. Finally, we ended up at a big brick building enclosed by a tall, black wrought-iron fence. It had white windowsills, and out front was a white sign that said THE SELZNICK MUSEUM OF COMPARATIVE ANATOMY AND TERATOLOGY.

"What is teratology?" asked Sophie.

"The study of birth defects and other developmental problems in humans," said Mozart. "Although if you translate it literally from the Greek, it means the 'study of monsters.'"

"One of Ruthven's little jokes?" I asked.

"Yeah. But it's also true. This *is* a teratology museum."

"So . . . what does that entail, exactly?" asked Sophie.

"Come on. You'll see."

We passed the iron gates and walked up the steps into the museum. The first thing I saw when we got inside was a row of skeletons along the left side. They each seemed to have different deformities. Some had weirdly shaped skulls or only the bottom half of a skull. Some had too many limbs, others too few. Some had short little flippers; others had what looked like a skeletal shell.

"Ah," said Sophie. She looked a little ill.

"Can I help you?" asked a soft, quiet voice from the other side of the room. A small man stood behind a desk. His features looked elfish, but he was too short to be an elf and his pointy nose and chin seemed a bit too long. He had big, round glasses and curly brown hair that he kept brushing out of his eyes.

"How you been, Keeper?" asked Mozart.

"Bless me, it's Mozart!" He jumped out of his chair and came shuffling out from behind his desk. "So sorry I didn't recognize you immediately!" He took Mozart's thick, hairy hand in his small, thin one, and patted it. Then he turned to me. "And you must be Boy, the son of the Monster and the Bride."

"Uh, yeah," I said.

He came over and patted my hand the same way, smiling and nodding and blinking behind his thick glasses. "Such a pleasure to finally meet you."

He turned to Sophie and squinted at her for a moment, absently pushing a curly lock of hair out of his eyes. Then his smile reappeared. "Ah! And so, of course, that makes you Sophie Jekyll." He took her hand. "May I say, my dear, that while I heard you had a certain indefinable charm about you, I had no idea it was this potent!"

"Er, thanks," said Sophie. "I'm fairly sure there was a compliment in there. . . ."

"The Keeper knows about everybody," said Mozart. "That's more or less his job. To keep records of any monster who ever existed."

"And even a few who do not!" said the Keeper, then chuckled quietly to himself.

"We heard everyone from New York is either here or on their way," said Mozart.

"Yes, of course, you'll want to see them right away!" The Keeper nodded his head. "Follow me."

He led us through a few rooms of the museum. One had a bunch of infants and toddlers with various deformities preserved in some way, plaster statues or actual mummified corpses. And then we came to a room that was just jar upon jar of deformed fetuses floating in liquid. Some had minor deformities, like hands that looked like crab claws or eyes in the middle of their head. Others had more severe deformities, like missing limbs. There were even a few pairs of conjoined twins, each fused in a different place. And some you could barely even call human.

"Oh, god," said Sophie. "I hope there's not much more of this or I might be sick."

"You've seen all kinds of monsters with way weirder shapes," I said.

"I don't know why this bothers me so much. I guess because monsters are *supposed* to look like monsters. But these are just . . . wrong humans."

"Interesting!" The Keeper stopped for a moment and turned back to us. "And how do you know that these humans are wrong and monsters are right? Are they truly different species or is it merely a difference of degree? Perhaps something can become so wrong that it circles back around to become right again?"

"I . . . don't know?" said Sophie.

"That is the beauty of it!" The Keeper held up his hands, spread wide. "None of us knows! I think if you study the development of living things you will ultimately find there is no wrong or right. Some things may be helpful or harmful, certainly. But even then, one must ask: to whom and to what extent!"

As he talked, he led us through the fetus jar room to what looked like a dead end. Then he took a small key from his pocket, knelt down, and inserted it into a hole in one of the tiles. He twisted the key and there was a faint *click*. Then he pulled and a hatch opened up in the floor.

"There we are," said the Keeper. "Excellent timing you have. I believe they're just about to start the meeting."

"Meeting?" asked Mozart.

"No sense asking me. You'll see for yourself in a moment," said the Keeper.

"Fair enough." Mozart patted his shoulder. "I got to catch up with you sometime soon."

The Keeper winked. "About you and Maria getting back together, you old dog? Good for you!"

Mozart laughed. "Of course you already knew."

The Keeper turned to Sophie and me. "You two have given me a number of interesting entries so far! I expect many more to come. And that goes for Claire, too! Understood?"

"Yes, sir," I said.

"Wonderful. Now . . ." He swooped his hand down dramatically. "Off you go!"

Sophie and I followed Mozart down a rope ladder into the darkness below. The ladder swayed a little. I reached out my hand, but I couldn't feel any walls. It was like the rope ladder just descended into emptiness.

"Boy?" Sophie's voice sounded pinched with tension.

"Yeah."

"When all this is over and everything's back to normal?"

"Uh . . . yeah?" That sounded a little overly optimistic to me, but I had a feeling she didn't need to hear that right then.

"Let's go on a vacation."

"Sure . . . Where do you want to go?"

"The Bahamas, maybe. Somewhere warm and gentle and bright."

"Sounds good," I said.

"Promise?"

"Promise."

We continued our slow climb down the ladder for another couple of minutes. Finally, I heard Mozart's boot soles slap something hard and smooth like tile.

"We're there," he said.

The room was dark, but by the sound of the echoes it was big. Off to one side I could just make out a hallway. And at the end of the hallway, a light.

"This way." Mozart turned and headed for the light.

We walked in silence for a little while. The only sounds were our footsteps, which changed slightly when we entered the long hallway. But as we got closer, I could hear voices up ahead. Too muddled and echoing to understand what was being said, but I was pretty sure I recognized Ruthven's deep timbre.

A little farther down and I could make out what he was saying.

"I have no more love for the humans than you do. But I tell you, joining Moreau is not the answer."

Finally, we reached the lit room. It was as big as one of my college lecture halls in Geneva. Except instead of all the seats being focused toward one point, they circled the whole room, all facing center. Monsters of all kinds were sitting there. I saw a couple of the dryads, a few trowe, an ogress, some fauns and harpies. Off to one side I saw Laurellen and the Şiren. And in the center stood Ruthven.

"Well, *there's* some good news," he said, relief seeping through his usually cool expression. "I'm glad you're all alive. We had no idea what had become of you."

"Likewise," said Mozart.

The two roughly embraced.

"Boy!" My mom's voice rang through the room. I turned and saw her coming up from the back of the room, followed by Liel. As they got closer, I noticed that Liel had a lot of intricate patterns and designs cut into her face, shoulders, and arms that looked like her mom's ritual scarring, except freshly made.

"It's good to see you guys," I said, although the last part was a bit muffled because by then my mom had grabbed me and mashed my face into her shoulder.

She squeezed me like that for a few moments. Then she held me out at arm's length and gave me the once-over. But instead of remarking about the fact that I'd let my stitches fray or that I'd lost weight, she just sighed and pulled me to her again. It took another minute before she let me go.

"What happened, Mom?" I asked. "Where's Dad?"

"Boy . . ." Her voice sounded broken. Her face vibrated with so much tension, it looked like it actually hurt. Then tears welled up in her eyes. "They took him! They took him away!"

"What?" I said. "How is that even possible? *Who* took him?"

"Government agents," said Ruthven. "It was a raid of some kind. Judging by the uniforms and weaponry, my guess is they thought they'd tracked down a terrorist cell." He smiled slightly, but there was no warmth or humor in his eyes. "Weren't they surprised?"

"Wait," said Mozart. "So you're telling me that U.S. agents took the Monster into custody?"

"He surrendered," said Liel, her voice flat. "Said he didn't want any more death that night and he would come peacefully if they stopped shooting. Gave the rest of us some time to slip down into the tunnels."

"He's okay, though, right?" I asked. "I mean, he's not dead or anything, is he?"

"Not as far as we know," said Ruthven.

"What will they do with him?"

"We don't know."

"So the U.S. government officially knows about our existence now?" asked Mozart.

"It would seem," said Ruthven.

"Have they told the general public?"

"Given the lack of panic in the streets, I doubt it."

Mozart scratched his beard. "Still, this changes things."

"It does indeed," said Ruthven.

"And the Fates didn't see this coming?"

"One of the limitations of the Fates," said Laurellen. "They couldn't see the events leading up to their own deaths."

"So . . . they're gone?" asked Mozart. "All three are dead?"

"We lost a lot of good monsters that night," said Ruthven.

"*Really* good ones," said Liel, her lips pulled back in a snarl that showed her fangs. I looked around, but didn't see her girlfriend.

"Liel . . ." I said. "Is Bakru—"

"Gone." Her voice was dull, almost lifeless. "And my mom, Cordeav, Charon, the goblin twins, and many others. If the humans want war, I say we give it to them."

Murmurs of agreement rippled through the room.

"We overheard you on our way in," said Mozart. "You already know about Moreau?"

"A package arrived this morning," said Ruthven. "It contained a laptop and a note from Moreau. He expressed his condolences for our losses and told us that he would like to talk to us about his plans for a monster liberation. He will be contacting us tonight at midnight on the laptop for a video discussion. He said you and Boy would be able to get us up to speed."

"He knew we'd be here?" I asked. "At this time?"

"Either he just assumed this was where we'd end up," said Mozart, "or else he's been monitoring us somehow."

"So you did meet him?" asked Laurellen.

"Oh, yeah. He already gave us the 'join me or die' spiel. He also made sure to give us a good look at his army."

"So he *does* have one?" asked Liel.

"Yeah. Mostly anthropomorphized animal mixtures. Elephant men, lizard men, that sort of thing. Made them himself. He's got a few thousand of them and they look disciplined. Well trained."

"Who trained them, I wonder," said Ruthven. "Moreau may be a brilliant tactician, but he's no fighter."

"He has Stephen Hyde for that," said Mozart.

"Oh." Ruthven's thin black eyebrow rose. "I see."

"Yeah. Anyway, Moreau claims that he wants to create a sovereign monster nation."

"Did he give you a clue as to where?"

Mozart shook his head. "He's too smart to give much to people who haven't committed to his cause yet. But I'd say Peru or Ecuador are the most likely targets. They're the closest geographically and they're a little smaller. Plus, I got the feeling he has a bit of animosity toward the Perricholi order."

"So he's going to ask us to join his noble cause to invade Peru?"

"Exactly," said Mozart.

"Sounds good to me," said Liel.

"You don't know Moreau like I do," said Ruthven. "He is utterly ruthless and will do anything to further his cause. For all we know, *he* was the one who tipped off the Feds to our location, just to get us lathered up and ready to kill some humans."

"Then it worked," said Liel. "Because I'm ready."

There was more muttering from the group, louder this time. Hostile almost. I was surprised to see so many monsters blatantly disagreeing with Ruthven. At The Show, his authority had been absolute. But now when I looked at him, he didn't seem any more important than any other monster. It was like his power died along with The Show.

It was Mozart who held up his hands to calm things down. "Okay, everybody. Let's just settle down and wait until we hear what Moreau has to say."

SO WE WAITED. Mozart went over to talk quietly to Ruthven for a moment, then sat down with Laurellen and the Siren.

Sophie turned to Liel. "I'm really sorry to hear about Bakru and your mum."

"Yeah," said Liel, her diamond eyes unreadable.

"Sophie and Claire just found out their mom is dead, too," I said.

"Fucking humans," said Liel. "And they call *us* the dangerous ones."

"She killed herself, actually," said Sophie, her face flushing slightly.

"And why'd she do that?" asked Liel.

"S-s-sorry?" said Sophie.

"Why'd she kill herself, do you think?" Liel almost spat out the words. "You think maybe it's because human society just pushed her and pushed her until she cracked?"

"She—she was in an institution," said Sophie.

"Yeah, of course. The humans even lock up the pretty ones. Can you imagine what they'd do to *me*?" She turned her hard diamond eyes on me. "To your dad?" She shook her head. "They won't even treat us as people. They'll treat us like they treat their animals. Lock us in zoos, make us into pets, use us for experiments, or just flat out commit genocide. You'll see. There's no going back."

She turned to go, then stopped. Her diamond eyes flashed back at me.

"Wasn't your little computer-virus pet supposed to be watching for FBI or something? Wasn't that the whole reason Ruthven agreed to let you make her again? Good fucking job with that."

Then she stalked off back to her trowe. I realized that's what the new scars meant. With her mother dead, Liel was the den leader now.

Sophie put her arm around my waist and I held her close. There didn't seem to be anything else we could do.

"How did Charon die?" I asked Mom.

"Explosion," she said. "The first thing they did when they came through the doors was blow up the box office. Charon and the goblin twins were inside and died instantly."

"Poor old Charon," said Sophie. "He was always such a sweet old grump."

"And the twins," I said. "They were still just kids."

I looked around the room at all the monsters around us. It no longer felt like a company. There was no feeling of a proud theatrical monster community. Now it just felt like a loose group of frightened creatures clinging to one another because they didn't know what else to do.

"Have you met Moreau?" Sophie asked my mom.

"Yes. He was arrogant and cruel."

"Well, that part hasn't changed," I said. "Ruthven said he was a brilliant tactician?"

"He was clever. Very . . . tricky."

"I feel like Ruthven's right. That he's got some other game he's playing."

"Like what?" asked Sophie.

"I don't know. He's been manipulating us from the beginning. He used Robert to lure us down to Lima. But why?"

"He said he wanted to recruit us."

"He didn't really push it, though. He let us go. And now he's got this whole group to recruit and he knows we're a part of it. So why bother bringing us down there at all?"

"It could be he wanted some of us to have actually met him in person," said Sophie. "To see him, what he's become. And to see his army firsthand. That way there's no doubt when he makes his offer here. He even mentioned you and Mozart specifically as people to talk to. People who have been trusted members of the company for a long time."

"That could be it," I said. "Still, for all we know, he's already left Noble's Isle with his army. I wish I could dig a little deeper. . . ." Then I realized that he was pretty much giving me the opportunity tonight. When his laptop connected at midnight, Vi could trace back his IP address, possibly even get a geolocation. And once we had him, it would be really hard for him to hide from us.

I pulled out the phone and unlocked it, but nothing happened.

"Vi?"

"Liel is right," her voice said faintly. "It's my fault."

"What?"

The screen suddenly flashed bright red. "It *was* my job to monitor FBI and CIA communications for potential connections to The Show. I could have caught it. I *should* have caught it. But I was so obsessed with stupid Henri that I let everything else slide. Now *I'm* the stupid one! Me!"

"Vi, I get why you're upset with yourself. And I agree it was a mistake to let that slide. A really bad mistake. But it wasn't like you did it on purpose. You didn't *make* it happen."

"But . . ."

"It wasn't your fault."

"Sorry to butt in," said Sophie. "But blimey, Vi, you're only six months old! Nobody expects you to be perfect or super mature. Trust me, there's no chance you were the only person that stood between The Show and what happened."

"I still feel bad."

"That's okay. You can feel bad," I said. "Now let's try to make it right."

"How?"

"First, have you been able to trace that database wipe from the police records?"

"It's almost done, but we already know who did it now."

"We know *generally*. But if we get some specifics, we might be able to pinpoint where my dad is. There has to be some trail somewhere. What if Ruthven was right? Maybe Moreau was the one to tip the Feds off in the first place, just to make us more open to recruitment. If you find the trail, see if you can also find out where they got their intel."

Vi's avatar popped back onto the screen and she saluted. "I will find out!"

"Great. Moreau is going to contact us in a little bit on that laptop. When he does, I need you to trace his connection back to the source and find out as much as you can. Location, any local files on his drive that might give us some clue about his plans. *Anything*, really."

"And what will we do with this data?" she asked, her expression quizzical.

"It depends on what we find," I said.

I had to scrounge around until we found someone with a compatible smartphone-to-USB cable. Vi could probably hack in from the phone, but it would take longer. If Moreau was prepared enough to send this laptop, he probably would also be connecting through an encrypted tunnel. That would slow her down. I also didn't know how long he'd stay connected. If he was only on for a few minutes, it was possible that Vi wouldn't be able to do a full trace and download the contents of his drive in time. She needed a more direct connection and a faster processor. So we were going to put her on the laptop. But that wasn't all.

"I'm taking off your training wheels," I said.

"Are you sure?" Her purple eyes bugged out and a big drop of nervous sweat rolled down her forehead. "I thought you said for my first birthday."

"It's the only way you're going to be able to both look for my dad and track Moreau at the same time without it taking forever."

"But . . . what if I go crazy, like my alpha phase?"

"Think of everything you've learned."

"I just messed up so bad, though!"

"And you accepted responsibility for your mistakes. More than anything else, that proves to me that you're ready."

"But I'm scared."

"I'd be worried if you weren't."

I plugged the cable into the laptop and transferred Vi over to the larger hard drive.

She popped up on the monitor, and smiled so wide it extended past the sides of her face. "Finally, I can stretch out a bit. That phone was really a little cramped."

"That's nothing," I said. "Now it's time to *really* stretch out. The way you were meant to be."

"You . . . really think I'm ready?"

"Let's find out."

I typed in the command to disable the restraints that had kept Vi locked to only one hardware platform at a time. My finger hovered over the Return key for a moment. I took a deep breath and pressed it.

Vi flickered and disappeared.

My heart dropped down into my stomach as the memory of my first failure came exploding back into my memory.

"Shit," I said.

"Boy?" Sophie had gotten bored with all the coding and wandered off to talk to the dryads. I must have looked panicked because she came rushing back over. "What happened?"

"Vi," I said. "I took off her restraints and she . . . disappeared. Just like version one. I thought she'd be ready. I thought she could handle it. She was nervous but I pushed her. I said it would be okay. I'm stupid. God, I'm so fucking *stupid*! What was I even—"

The monitor screen flickered and there was Vi's smiling avatar again.

"That was *AMAZING*!" she shouted, her fist in the air. "I literally just traveled around the world! Can you believe that, Boy? Isn't that incredible?!"

I slowly let out my breath and smiled. "Incredible, Vi. *You* are incredible."

Sophie kissed my cheek. "You're not so bad yourself, love. Trust your gut more."

THE VIDEO CHAT software connected at midnight exactly. It was a large monitor for a laptop, but even so it was cramped as all the monsters huddled around it, eager to see Moreau's new body for themselves. I stayed off to the side, monitoring Vi's progress on the phone screen.

The video window opened, and from my vantage point I could just make out Moreau's mismatched animal face appearing on the monitor. The window resized to full screen on its own. Moreau was controlling the machine remotely. Or he thought he still was. Vi had taken control already, but for the time being was relaying the commands he sent. We didn't want him to know we'd taken it from him until Vi had a lock on him.

"My fellow monsters," said Moreau in his harsh, carefully articulated ape voice. "I want to say again how saddened I was to learn about the fate of your coven. The Show was truly one of the greatest monster communities ever to exist. Its loss, and the loss of many of your fellow company members, is too great to bear in silence. And you don't need to anymore. No longer will we hide in the shadows, cringing, cowardly, concealing our true potential. I'm sure Mozart and Boy told you of my army. Even now it is poised to strike. Once we have claimed a country of our own, we can demand that the United Nations recognize us. Only then will we be granted the basic rights that every human is entitled to. Because you see, the humans do not view us as

people. We must force them to expand their view of personhood
to include us. By any means necessary."

"You mean, by massacring humans," said Ruthven.

"Ah, my dear Lord Ruthven. It's been a long time, hasn't it?
You seem remarkably unchanged."

"The years have been rather . . . creative with you, it seems."

"When one's means are limited, one must needs get creative,"
said Moreau.

"Yes, limited means. How *did* you come by all that fancy lab
equipment, I wonder?"

"And *I* wonder why a vampire is suddenly so squeamish about
killing humans."

"What I am squeamish about is starting an international
incident. You do realize that your little army might overwhelm
a small third-world country, but the humans will never let you
keep it. They will see in you a reason to unite all their nations in
the struggle against a common enemy. They will come together,
if only for a little while, and completely obliterate you and anyone foolish enough to join you. We would be doing the humans
a favor by giving them one convenient place to aim their nuclear
missiles. Not even I would survive that."

"And what would you have them do instead?" asked Moreau.
"Your cute little ploy of hiding in plain sight has been exposed.
I'm afraid you won't be able to do that again. So what, then?
Have them slink even further into the darkness? Hide again on
the outskirts of humanity like scavengers, barely surviving? I
offer them hope for a new existence. A *better* existence. What
do you offer?"

"I offer survival."

"Indeed." His hawk eyes scanned the crowd of monsters. "And
there you have it. A simple choice. A guaranteed base survival

or a fighting chance for something better. Each of you then must weigh the options for yourself."

"What about my husband?" said my mom, standing up from her chair. "What about *his* survival?"

"Ah, Bride. Your tragic beauty has not lessened in the slightest over the last century."

"Would your war bring my husband home safely?" she said.

I was still trying to focus on Vi's progress. She almost had Moreau's location. But listening to my mom talk about my dad made it really hard.

"Of course, Bride. I already have a plan to get him safely back into your arms."

"What is your plan?"

"Well, once you agree to join——"

"No. What is your plan?"

Moreau gave his forced grimace of a smile.

"Still a charmer, I see. Yes, well, in general terms, the plan would be to kidnap a human of equal or greater value, say a president or something. Then we simply negotiate a hostage exchange."

"Fool," said Ruthven. "They will not negotiate with you."

"They will once we have established our base of power. They will have no choice but to accede to that and a great many other demands."

"This will take too long," my mom said dismissively, and sat back down.

"Boy," said Moreau, his eagle eyes searching me out in the crowd.

I jammed the phone in my pocket and stood up. "Yeah, Moreau?"

"There you are," he said. "You're a bright young man. I know you understand what is at stake here. Perhaps you can explain to your mother what we talked about before. You can help her see the big picture. Now more than ever, we need monster solidarity to accomplish our goals and win freedom for all monsterkind."

"I understand what you're saying, Moreau. And I agree that something needs to be done. Monsters should be accepted into the world. But not through violence and terror. I'm sorry, Moreau. My answer is no."

Moreau nodded. "We each have our methods. In the end, I am but a humble surgeon. When I see something wrong, something that sickens the larger organism, I simply cut it out. But I can respect your views. As long as you do not interfere with my plans, I wish you the best with your nonviolent protests."

"The trowe will join you, Dr. Moreau." Liel stood up, and the rest of her den stood up behind her. "We're tired of hiding and we're not afraid of violence. We hunger for justice. And blood."

"I am glad to hear it, Liel. As much as it grieves me to see the burden of den chief passed to one so young, I think your spirit is just what is needed right now." He scanned the crowd. "Any others?"

The harpies and fauns stood up. So did the lone ogress. And the Siren.

"Really, Siren?" said Laurellen.

She looked down at him for a moment, her expression sad. Then she nodded.

"Can't blame her," said Mozart. "The ocean dwellers have had it worse than any of us." He stood up and embraced her. "Maybe we'll all get through this yet," he said gruffly, then sat back down.

"Is that it?" asked Moreau. "Well, I have transportation waiting out in front of The Museum for all who would step onto the path of hope, dangerous as it might be."

Liel walked purposefully toward the exit, and the others followed. Ruthven just watched them go, his red eyes unreadable.

"Liel," I called after her. "Are you really going through with this?"

She stopped for a moment but didn't turn around. "It's my turn to walk out the door first." Then she led the others into the dark hallway and back toward the rope ladder.

"The rest of you," said Moreau, "may hide here in the dark amidst the Keeper's relics of history. I will honor this place as a safe haven. But if you leave here, be warned that I will show you no mercy."

The screen went black.

Then it flashed with hearts, stars, and exclamation points and Vi jumping up and down. "I got him, Boy! The signal ends right off the coast of Peru, near Lima!"

"We've got to get back there," I said.

"Damn right," said Mozart.

"If you give me a day or so, I can arrange some private transportation for us," said Ruthven. "And some additional support."

"You go ahead and do that," said Mozart. "I'm hopping the next plane out. I'll meet you there."

"I think it would be best to wait—"

"I'm going with you," I said. "Henri's been a tool lately, but he's still my cousin and my responsibility." I turned to Sophie. "When you guys get there—"

"Like hell," she said. "I'm coming with you two."

"But—"

"Shut it."

"Oh fine, twist my arm!" said Laurellen.

"Nobody's twisting your arm," said Mozart.

"I know. I just can't bear the thought of you three going on yet another adventure without me."

Ruthven sighed. "Is there any way I can talk you out of this?"

"Not a chance," said Mozart.

The old Ruthven would have crushed him for that. This Ruthven looked tired and heartbroken. He nodded. "Fine. The Bride, the dryads, and I will be along as soon as we can, and we'll bring reinforcements. Just try to hold out until then."

Mozart put his hand on Ruthven's shoulder. "Thanks."

"Good luck, old friend," said Ruthven.

# PART 4

## World War

"*What* can we know? What are we all?
Poor silly half-brained things peering out at
the infinite, with the aspirations of angels
and the instincts of beasts."

—FROM *THE STARK MUNRO LETTERS*
by Sir Arthur Conan Doyle

# 17
# Deceiving Appearances

++++++++

"WOULD YOU STOP staring at me?" I asked as we rode the SEPTA train from downtown Philly to the airport.

"Sorry." Sophie blushed and looked away, pretending to study the big ad posters at the front of the train car.

"I feel so weird," I said.

"You look fine," said Mozart.

"You look *more* than fine," said Laurellen. "And I'd say Sophie agrees with me, don't you, dear?"

Sophie turned to him. "Er, well . . . ah . . ." Then she went back to staring at the ads.

I stared down at my hands. Smaller, tanner, smoother. And of course, no stitches.

"I can't believe I let you talk me into using glamour," I said.

"The situation has changed," said Mozart. "Before, people looked at you, they assumed a human with stitches, because what else were they going to think? But now there are humans out there who *know* that someone like you exists. If we're going to make it to Lima quickly, we need to keep as low a profile as possible. Getting you through the metal detector is going to be hard enough as it is." He flashed a grin at me, white teeth in a thick brown-and-gray beard. "Besides, it's kind of funny to see you like this."

I turned to look at myself in the window reflection. The basic shape of my face was the same. I still more or less looked like me. And that made it even weirder to see this alternate "sanitized for human society" version of myself staring back at me.

"Don't worry, Boy!" Vi's voice came from my shirt pocket. "I cross-checked your glamorized image with criteria in entertainment media and you score in the top ten percentile of handsome male celebrities!"

"Great. Just what I always wanted." I turned to Sophie. "This is totally freaking you out, isn't it?"

"A bit," she admitted. "But you *do* look fine. I mean good. Well, better than good. But not as good as usual, of course, just . . . more human. Which isn't really *good*. In general. Er, for you. That is to say—"

"Okay, I get it," I said. "You find 'Celebrity Edition Boy' attractive but you don't want to give me a complex."

She gave me a grateful smile. "More or less, yeah."

"Thought so."

She gave me a searching look. "So . . . is it going to give you a complex?"

"Probably," I said. "But that's not your fault."

———

AS WE WALKED down the long white hallway past the airline check-in counters, something felt off. I couldn't quite figure out what it was until I started to pay closer attention to the humans around us.

"Nobody's really looking at me," I said.

"That was the point," said Mozart.

"I know. It's just . . . weird. Nobody flinching or doing quick double takes. Nobody moving just a little out of their direct path so they can put some space between us."

"That's a good thing, isn't it?" asked Laurellen.

"It just took a lot of work to get used to that," I said. "Now it feels kind of like . . . something's wrong without it."

We continued down the seemingly endless walkways filled with newsstands, fast food, bars, and weird little electronics shops. After a few minutes, I felt Sophie's hand slip tentatively into mine. Almost like she wasn't sure it would be okay. I gave it a gentle squeeze.

"It's still me," I said.

"This must be a little bit like what it always feels like for you," she said. "Me and Claire switching back and forth all the time, and you just steady as a rock."

I laughed. "If you say so."

"All right, there's the security checkpoint," said Mozart. "Let's hope we get through without a lot of fuss."

They looked over the Swiss passport that the Frankensteins had given me. It had worked for me so far, but since I had no idea how they'd gotten it, I was a little worried. After a moment, they let me through. The metal detector was as annoying as ever. I had to explain several times that I had metal implants in my skull and wrists. I guess without stitches it seemed even less believable. They used the wand, patted me down, used the wand again, and had someone *else* pat me down. But finally, they had to concede that whatever was setting off the sensors was completely internal and not a threat. One guy told me I could have saved them all a lot of time if I'd brought a note from my doctor. I noticed that Celebrity Edition Boy caught a lot more attitude.

At last they let me through to the other side where the others were patiently waiting for me. I sat down on one of the benches and put my shoes back on.

Then, just as I stood back up, a woman in a dark gray suit walked up to us. She had icy-blue eyes and blonde hair pulled back in a ponytail. She smiled coldly as she held up a badge. "Agent Holmes, FBI. There's a bunch of cops waiting in the wings, hoping you'll put up a fight. Why don't you disappoint them and come quietly?"

"SO TELL ME again why you're going to Lima?"

I sat in a small white room at a little white table. On the other side of the table was the FBI agent who had taken us in. We were still somewhere in the airport, I knew that. That was about all I knew, though. I didn't know where the others were. I didn't know why they were holding us. It all seemed like some classic crime show scenario where they separate us, interrogate us, and try to see if there's something about our stories that doesn't match up.

"I told you," I said. "I'm going to see my cousin, Henri."

"Right." Now that I'd gotten a good look at her, Agent Holmes looked tired. Her face was pale and drawn, her suit was rumpled, and stray hairs stuck out from her ponytail. But her eyes were still a sharp blue and I had a feeling that they didn't miss a thing. "Your cousin. Henri Frankenstein."

"Yep."

"Kind of a funny name."

"What's funny about it?" I asked.

She shrugged. "I always thought the Frankenstein family was just fiction."

"What did you say your name was again?" I asked. "Holmes?"
Her eyes flashed. "Yes."

"I always thought the Holmes family was just fiction."

"There's lots of people with the last name of Holmes," she said.

"I'm sure there are," I said. "But I have a feeling that you're the real one."

"The real one what?"

"Descendant of the world's greatest detective, Sherlock Holmes, obviously. What are you . . . let me guess . . . granddaughter?"

She stared at me and for just a moment I saw her hard eyes waver and I knew I was right. But then she laughed. "So what if I am? I don't see what that has to do with you and your friends going to Lima."

"Wow, how about that? *I* don't see what you have to do with me and my friends going to Lima, either," I said.

"Listen." She leaned in closer. The more she smiled, the less comfortable I felt. "I've been nice up to now. But this could all go very differently."

"Something different from being held without cause, you mean? I'm looking forward to that."

She leaned back, her smile suddenly gone as she stared up at the ceiling. "Here's what I know. None of you add up. Funny names, mismatched ages. It all . . . checks out. But there is something in this puzzle that I am missing and I will find it before anyone goes anywhere."

"Do you think your grandfather would have figured it out by now?" I asked.

Her mouth tightened for a moment as her eyes dropped back to me. Then she smiled again. "You're pretty good. You found where my goat was tied up in no time and now you're kicking it just hard enough to keep me off balance. Have you . . . done this before maybe?"

"Nope. First time."

"A natural then. Speaking of natural, that sure is a beautiful girlfriend you've got."

"She sure is."

"Be a shame if something were to happen to her."

"You're joking, right?"

"Of course I am. Joking."

"Good. Because some friendly advice here: you do not want to get on her bad side. Trust me."

Her smiled faded. "She's under suspicion, too, you know."

"For what?"

"I'm not at liberty to discuss that."

"Wait. You can't tell me what we're being charged with?"

"Did I say charged? I didn't say charged."

"Okay, seriously. How long are you going to keep us here?"

"Why? You have somewhere to be?"

"Yeah, actually I do."

"Tell me."

"You already know." My frustration was starting to show. I knew it, but I couldn't help it. Every minute this asshole continued to jerk me around was time lost from getting to Lima and stopping Moreau.

"Right. Lima. To visit your cousin. Who is Swiss. And named Frankenstein. And living in Peru. And you're Swiss, too, isn't that right? Says so on your passport."

"Yep."

"Then I wonder why it is you don't have an accent."

"I've been living in the States for a while."

"Sure, of course. So why do you need to see Henri so badly? Matter of life and death?"

This woman could probably keep us going round and round like this for hours. Maybe days for all I knew. Especially if she thought we were terrorists. I decided it was time to take a gamble. I decided some truth might be in order.

"Actually, it is. People might get killed if we don't get to Lima in time."

"Which people?"

"My friends, my family, bystanders. Anybody."

"And who's doing the killing?"

"Guerrilla terrorists." Close enough. And I thought I remembered Peru having a serious problems with those kinds of groups in the past, so it was believable.

"And why would terrorists be after your cousin?"

"They aren't. They're probably after the girl he likes."

"Ah. Yes, well, of course, that would be it. His girlfriend."

"No, the girl he likes."

"She doesn't like him?"

"Not like that."

"Just friends."

"Exactly."

"And you're friends with her, too, I take it."

"Yes."

"And who is she that she would be a terrorist target?"

"She goes by the title La Perricholi."

Her eyebrow shot up. "La what?" It looked like I'd thrown her a curveball and she didn't like it. Her cool evaporated instantly. "Look, *Boy*, if that really is your name. You'd better stop feeding me this line of bullshit or—"

The door opened and an older guy in a suit came in. He whispered something to Holmes. Holmes's eyes slowly widened as she listened. Then the older guy left and didn't close the door behind him. Holmes turned back to me and she looked seriously pissed.

"Well, apparently this friend of yours is some kind of big deal. So I'm going to have to let you go on your merry way. But let's be clear, something is not clicking with you and I know it. A lot of stitches in that passport photo of yours. If I had to guess, I'd say plastic surgery. Recent, by the way you keep looking at yourself in reflective surfaces, and quite drastic by the way you misjudge your height and size. Except there's absolutely no sign of recent surgery. It just . . . doesn't add up. There's something I'm missing. . . ."

She sat there, chewing on her lower lip, her forehead furrowed.

"You . . . really don't know, do you?" I asked. "Your own people. They send you out looking for someone or something and they haven't even told you what it is." Suddenly, I almost pitied her.

"Well," she said icily, "if you know so very much, why don't you fill me in?"

I shook my head. "Sorry." I got up and started to walk past her, but there was something that made me stop. Something about her expression that looked familiar somehow. Human or not, she knew something about famous fathers and impossible expectations.

"Okay, I probably shouldn't say this," I said. "But start looking at police reports during the last week in New York. And remember what your grandfather used to say. Once you've eliminated the impossible, whatever remains, no matter how improbable, must be true."

"CAN SOMEONE EXPLAIN what happened back there?" asked Sophie.

By some unspoken agreement, none of us had said anything until we were safely on our plane and in the air.

"The damned descendant of Sherlock Holmes of all people," said Laurellen. "We're lucky she's not quite as sharp as her grandfather yet. I've heard that old Sherlock could actually see through glamour. I'd guess this one couldn't quite penetrate, but perhaps she kept catching something odd out of the corner of her eye. My question is, why did they let us go so quickly?"

"I name-dropped La Perricholi," I said.

Mozart grunted. "Me too. Normally, I hate doing that, but since it's her ass we're trying to save, I thought it was appropriate."

"She's really that famous?" asked Sophie.

"La Perricholi has done of lot of things for a lot of countries over the years. Anyone who's connected with her is treated very carefully."

"Couldn't anyone just say they were her friend?" asked Sophie.

"Every once in a while, someone tries that. Then La Perricholi pays them a visit, makes an example of them, and that's usually the end of it for a while."

"And you knew that saying her name would get us out?" Sophie asked me.

"No, it was totally by accident," I admitted.

"Interesting coincidence," said Mozart. "Someone with gifts like Holmes assigned as the security detail for the airport we're leaving."

"You think Moreau somehow managed it?" asked Laurellen.

"Wouldn't put it past him."

"I can't even imagine how he'd accomplish such a thing," said Laurellen.

"How would he even know we're here?" I asked. "As far as he knows, we're still hiding in the basement of The Museum."

"Feels like he's at least a few steps ahead of us wherever we go," Mozart agreed.

"Ruthven said he was like some brilliant tactician or something," I said.

"That could be it," said Mozart.

"You think it's something else?"

"Or some*one* else," said Mozart. "I keep getting . . . little flashes of a scent. Too faint and quick to make out who it is. But it's vaguely familiar."

"And you're sure it's not one of us?" asked Laurellen.

"I've been getting them off and on for weeks. And sometimes it's been when I was alone."

"Or *thought* you were alone," said Sophie.

Mozart's eyes narrowed. "You have an idea?"

"Look, this is just complete speculation, yeah?" She turned to Laurellen. "Has anyone heard from Kemp since the raid?"

Laurellen frowned. "Now that you mention it, no."

"Because he was still in New York when it happened, wasn't he?"

"I assume so. . . ." He shook his head. "But I couldn't say for sure."

"Wait," I said. "You think Kemp has joined up with Moreau?"

Sophie shrugged.

"It *would* explain a great many things," said Laurellen.

"But he's like the *last* person who would be cool with Moreau's war," I said.

"I hope you're right," Sophie said quietly.

"Me too," said Mozart. "Because the last thing we need right now is an invisible spy."

For the rest of the flight, I kept glancing at an empty seat a few rows in front of us. It was hard not to imagine Kemp sitting there. In fact, he could have been anywhere, with us at any time, and we would never have known. His invisibility had never made me feel paranoid before. I guess I'd just felt like he'd never betray my trust like that. But now, I wasn't sure. Liel and the Siren had joined up with Moreau. And I was pretty sure that if Moreau had given my mom a better answer about freeing my dad, she would have joined him, too.

What made it even harder was that I understood why people would want to join him. He and I wanted the same thing: equal rights for monsters. If I hadn't had such a connection to humans, if I'd stayed in the theater my whole life, I might have joined up with him, too.

# 18
# Deduction

++++++++

VI HAD GRUDGINGLY agreed to contact Henri and La Perricholi while we were in the air and bring them up to speed. Now that she wasn't tied down to a single device, she could still be off doing things when I had to power down the phone during the flight. So they were waiting for us with the red van outside the airport. I noticed both of them staring at me.

"Boy?" said La Perricholi, squinting her eyes. "Is that you?"

"Yep," I said. "Had to use glamour to get through the airport security."

"Even then we barely made it," said Mozart.

La Perricholi gazed at me in an almost appraising way that made me feel a little uncomfortable. She pursed her lips and nodded. "Very nice."

Sophie put her arm around my waist. "I don't care if you can kill people with your bare hands, he's still mine."

La Perricholi laughed and patted Sophie's shoulder. "Just admiring the view, *mi amiga*. I think Boy already has all the woman he can handle."

"Isn't that the truth," murmured Laurellen.

"Perricholi, I don't know if you've met Laurellen before," said Mozart.

"No," she said, offering her hand. "Maria has told me about you, though."

"Good things, I hope," said Laurellen as he shook her hand.

"Hardly any." She grinned.

With everything going on, it seemed a little weird that La Perricholi was in such a good mood. Then again, it wouldn't have surprised me if a little global catastrophe was exactly the kind of thing that cheered her up.

Henri, on the other hand, looked tired and sullen. He gave us a brief, forced smile and didn't say a word. His plan to woo La Perricholi clearly hadn't been going well.

"Vi gave us the coordinates for Moreau's location," said La Perricholi as she opened up the back of the van. "The signal seems to originate from a large ship anchored just off the coast."

"How large?" asked Mozart as he tossed his bag in the back of the van.

"Big enough to hold a small army if they're packed in tight."

"That's what I was afraid of."

"It's very close to my house," she said.

"Could be that's his target, then. He made a point of mentioning how your predecessor stood up to him last time, so he probably sees you as the biggest obstacle to getting a foothold here."

"We should strike first, then."

"Maybe. But we'll want to wait until Ruthven gets here with reinforcements."

"Did he tell you how many he's bringing?"

"As many monsters as he could find that haven't already joined up with Moreau."

"Many have?"

Mozart nodded. "About half of what's left of the New York clan. Including the remaining trowe."

"I don't relish facing them on the battlefield," she said. "What about the Los Angeles clan?"

"Kemp put the whole group on hiatus just before this started," I said. "He said most of them were traveling, visiting their homelands and stuff."

"Really?" said Mozart, his thick eyebrow rising. "That's an interesting . . . coincidence."

"What are you suggesting, old wolf?" asked La Perricholi.

Mozart sniffed the air and his eyes narrowed.

"I'll explain on the way. Come on, I want to take a look at this ship."

LA PERRICHOLI DROVE and Mozart sat up with her in the passenger seat, filling her in on our suspicions about Kemp. Sophie and I sat in the back with Henri. If Kemp had been following us, there wasn't anywhere he could have stowed away without one of us bumping into him.

"So the secret is out, eh?" asked Henri. "Humans know about monsters now?"

"Sort of," I said. "Clearly, there are some humans who know. But I think right now they're keeping it on the down low. The agent who tried to detain us at the airport knew she was looking for someone with stitches, but she didn't even know why."

"What else could they do?" asked Sophie. "Could you imagine the president getting on the telly and announcing to everyone that monsters are real? It would be complete madness."

"I think it would depend a lot on how it was done," I said.

"You honestly think there's a way it could be done *without* causing mass hysteria?"

"Maybe. I mean, what if they were like 'Yes! Monsters are real! And here's one of them!' And it was you they saw first. I don't think people would freak out so much."

"I am rather charming," she admitted.

"You could be, like, the spokesmodel for monsters."

"Right. Me and Grover."

Sophie and I continued to talk the rest of the drive, with Henri only making occasional comments. Once we reached the coast and climbed out of the van, I pulled him to one side.

"You okay?"

He shrugged.

"Things not working with La Perricholi?"

He gave a short, bitter laugh. "You could say that."

"Sorry."

He shrugged again and walked back to the group.

We followed La Perricholi down to the water's edge. I could just make out a big cargo ship on the horizon.

"That it?" asked Mozart.

"It's roughly the latitude and longitude that Vi gave me for the signal," said La Perricholi. "Here." She handed him a pair of binoculars.

He studied the ship through the binoculars for a moment. "Doesn't seem to be any activity on the deck. Assuming there is an army of beast people jammed down in the cargo hold, how do you think they'd get them to land?"

"The ship is too big to come much closer to the shore," she said. "I would think they'd have to use small boats or dinghies to get them all ashore."

"For a whole army?"

"I can't think of any other way to do it."

"Well, at least that means they won't be able to take us by surprise."

"As long as someone is watching. But if it is to be a stakeout, we will need to head back to the house and get some supplies."

"I'll stay here," said Henri. "We should have someone watching at all times."

La Perricholi nodded. "Good idea."

"You want me to stay with you?" I asked.

Henri smiled faintly. "Thanks, cousin, but I could use a little alone time. I'll call you if anything happens."

---

WE WENT BACK to La Perricholi's house and had something to eat. Regardless of what Henri said, I thought it would be a good idea not to give him *too* much alone time. But Sophie insisted we wash the "travel funk" off first, so it was about an hour before she and I were ready to head back.

"You two go ahead," said Mozart as he and Maria slid steel plates over the windows in the dining room. "La Perricholi and I are going to help Maria get the house fortifications in place, just in case."

"In case what?" asked Sophie.

"In case we can't hold the line," said Maria. "We'll need someplace secure to fall back to."

"What do you mean 'we'?" Mozart grinned smugly. "I thought you were too old for this sort of thing. Isn't that what you said?"

"Oho! You watch yourself, old wolf!" Maria held her fist up to his face. "You're going to need me."

He cupped her fist in his hands and kissed her rough, calloused knuckles. "I *always* need you, señora."

Maria rolled her eyes but didn't pull her hand away.

"How romantic," said La Perricholi as she entered the dining room. "But would you finish barricading the windows before you start tearing each other's clothes off?" She turned to me and Sophie. "You're going down to relieve Henri? I need to make a few adjustments to the van. Take the car instead."

"Sweet," I said as she tossed us the keys.

But once again, La Perricholi disappointed me with her boring, un-Batman-like vehicles.

"What is the point of being a rich vigilante if you don't have a cool car with lots of gadgets?" I asked Sophie as we climbed into the little, red, two-door compact car.

"At least it's a hybrid," she said.

I was glad the glamour had shrunk me a little bit, because otherwise the passenger seat would have been even more uncomfortable. Especially since we spent more time in the car than planned when we got lost on the way. Eventually, I had to ask Vi to GPS for us.

"Why didn't you ask me from the beginning?" Vi asked. "Turn left up here."

"I don't know," I said.

"It's one of those gender things, love," said Sophie as she turned the steering wheel. "Men hate asking for directions. It makes them feel weak."

"Turn right at the next light," said Vi. Then, "Why does it make them feel weak?"

"Hell if I know."

"It doesn't make me feel weak," I said. "It's just . . . I don't know, I thought I could figure it out."

"But you know *I* could figure it out so much faster," said Vi. "Take another right at this intersection."

"True, but you can't depend on other people to do everything for you," I said. "That makes you lazy and—"

"Weak," said Sophie.

"Well . . ." I said.

"Ha! Gotcha!"

"Is it weakness to rely on others?" asked Vi.

I was about to say yes, but then I stopped myself. Was it? I turned to look at Sophie as she drove. The afternoon sunlight shone through her curly auburn hair as she smoothly maneuvered us through the narrow streets of Lima. How many times had I relied on her or on Claire? How many times had they relied on me?

Finally, I said, "It's not weak to trust others or to ask for help when you need it. But you should trust *yourself*, too."

"Trust myself?" asked Vi.

"Yeah. Trust yourself like you would trust your best friend."

"Oh, I quite like that," said Sophie.

"You have arrived," said Vi.

"I don't know about all *that* . . ." I said.

"No, I mean it literally. We're here."

Sophie pulled over onto the shoulder that ran along the coast. The ship was still visible off in the distance. But Henri was gone.

"That's odd," said Sophie as we climbed out. "It's not like there's anywhere he could have got to."

It was just a narrow highway. On one side was the rocky coastline. On the other side was a hilly area full of weeds and brambles. There weren't any buildings or houses nearby.

I stepped down onto the beach, smooth wet stones crunching under my boots. "Maybe he just took a walk along the water."

I looked down the beach, but it curved inland and a rocky cliff blocked the view about twenty yards down. "He'll probably be back in a bit."

"But why would he do that when he was supposed to be watching the ship?"

"Why does Henri do *anything*?" I asked. "Did he really think he'd be able to win La Perricholi over? She doesn't seem interested in romance of any kind."

"Except when she saw Celebrity Edition Boy," muttered Sophie.

"You're not jealous of La Perricholi, too?"

"A bit hard not to be when she's bloody undressing you with her eyes right in front of me."

"It's not *me* she likes." I looked down at my smooth, tanned arms and hands. "It's the glamour."

"No, Boy. You don't actually look much different. The stitches tend to distract humans a bit, but you've always been hot." She raised one thin eyebrow. "Do you honestly think I'd date someone who wasn't?"

"Well—"

"But what if now that she's seen you like this, when the glamour fades, the stitches won't be so distracting? What if she fancies you?"

I cupped her pale, heart-shaped face in my hands. "She and Henri can pine together then."

"Hmmm," she said, a slight smile forming on her lips.

"Feel better?"

"Nearly. I think I might need a kiss to seal the deal."

So we kissed, with the ocean at our side, wind blowing through our hair and pulling at our clothes. Her lips were still so soft and sweet to me even after all this time. Sure, a hostile army lurked in the distance ready to descend on us at any time, and my cousin had mysteriously disappeared yet again. But that just made this moment feel all the more important. I wasn't sure when we'd have another like it.

———

SOPHIE AND I waited for hours, lounging on the hood of the car and staring out across the glittering water as the fat red sun began to slide below the horizon. But Henri never came back. I was about to suggest we go look for him when Sophie suddenly sat up.

"Shite, there, do you see it?" she said, her voice hushed.

It took me a moment, squinting against the glare of the setting sun, but then I saw little boats spilling out of the ship like ants escaping from a flooding nest.

"How many do you think there are?" I asked.

She shook her head. "Fifty or so? It's hard to make out. The sun is right in my eyes."

"Red sky at night, sailor's delight," I muttered.

"What?"

"Never mind. We better call it in. Vi?"

"Already on it," said Vi. "Mozart says they're on their way."

"What are the five of us going to do against all of *that*?" asked Sophie, her eyes wide.

I took her hand in mine. "Sophie . . . maybe you should, uh, let Claire handle this part."

She looked up at me and the fear in her eyes was suddenly swept away by a strange sadness. "Oh. Right. Sure."

"I mean, I was just thinking—"

"No, no. You're spot-on. Just . . . uh . . . ." She gave me a sudden, oddly uncertain look. "One last kiss, then?"

"Of course," I said.

She smiled brightly then, all sadness gone. "You're a prince."

She tilted her head up and I leaned down and pressed my lips gently against hers. She ran her cool fingers through my hair and leaned into me. I felt her mouth begin to change as her body shifted and lengthened. Then, suddenly, she grabbed a fistful of my hair and kissed me hard, pushing me back against the car windshield.

"God damn it, you look good," Claire said huskily against my neck as she pressed down on me. "Do you think we have time for a quickie before the others get here?"

"Probably not."

"You're probably right." She grabbed my head with both hands and pressed one last kiss before releasing me.

"Uh, hi," I said, grinning.

After a moment, she smiled sheepishly. "Sorry about that."

"Nothing to apologize for."

"Something must be wrong with me. This whole situation . . ." She gestured toward the slowly advancing boats. "It's got me all worked up for some reason."

"It's not wrong if it keeps us alive today," I said.

She grinned fiercely. "You can bloody well count on it. Because I'm taking a rain check on that quickie, and I plan to collect."

So we waited, ready to take on whatever came out of those boats. But it was hard to keep ourselves pumped up and ready to fight. The boats were so slow sometimes I wasn't sure if they were making any progress at all. When Maria, La Perricholi, Mozart, and Laurellen arrived twenty minutes later, the boats hadn't even made it halfway to the coast.

"Where's Henri?" asked Maria.

"No idea," I said. "He was gone when we got here."

She shook her head. "That boy . . . Well, we can't go looking for him now."

We stared out at the small fleet of boats creeping closer.

"How many do you suppose are in each boat?" asked Claire.

La Perricholi frowned as she looked through the binoculars. "I can't tell exactly *what* is on the boats. They're packed in so tight all I can see are the tops of their helmets. But it looks to be about twenty to a boat."

"How are we going to hold back that many?" I asked.

"Ruthven is on his way," said Mozart. "With what he described as 'formidable firepower.' So we only have to hold them back for a little while."

"Even still," said Claire. "We're looking at six against hundreds. Not great odds."

"I brought a few things that will help," said La Perricholi. She opened the back of the van and pulled out a couple of big gas cans. "Pour these along the waterline. When they disembark, we'll light them up so they'll have to charge through a wall of fire."

"Wow," I said, hefting a gas can.

"That's not the wow." La Perricholi climbed into the back of the van. There was a harsh grating sound, like metal scraping against metal. "When they get through the wall of fire," she called, "we take them down with this." She dragged out a massive machine gun.

"Okay, yeah, that's the wow," said Claire.

We poured the gas, mounted the machine gun on top of the van, and spread ourselves along the beachline. Maria took the machine-gun station, with Laurellen feeding the belt. La Perricholi had her pistols, and Mozart had shifted into wolf. La Perricholi asked me and Claire if we wanted weapons. Claire accepted a gun, but I'd said no. I'd never used a gun and this didn't seem like an ideal time to try something new.

So then we waited some more.

"This is just excruciating," observed Laurellen as we watched the boats crawl slowly closer.

"You'd think they'd fan out more," I said. "Instead of staying all jammed together like that. Take advantage of their numbers."

"It is strange," admitted La Perricholi. "Either whoever is leading them isn't very smart—"

"Or there's another, less obvious plan in motion," said Maria.

Hot and cold flashes started traveling though my body. One moment I was sweating, the next I was shivering. At first I had no idea what was going on, but then I glanced down and saw flickers of stitches. The extra stress of waiting was burning up the last of the glamour. That was fine. I wanted to be my full size when I met this enemy. I wanted to look like myself. And by the time the boats hit the shore, I did.

I still couldn't tell what we were up against. It was dark now, and they were jammed so tight in their boats all I could see was a squirming mass of white, brown, and black fur dressed in army green.

"Fire!" shouted Maria.

La Perricholi shot a flare gun at the pooled gas by the water and the wall of fire lit up the night. I could hear animal shrieks on the other side. Out of the corner of my eye, I could see Maria ready at the machine gun, waiting for the first ones to cross the line.

Except they didn't. I could just make out shapes climbing over each other to get away from the fire. But more boats were coming in behind them, pressing forward, knocking the ones in front back toward the flames. The air was filled with the shrill shrieks, but they didn't sound like battle cries. They sounded like terrified animals.

"Something's not right," Maria called over the noise. "Everyone hold your fire and stay back."

We waited as the fire slowly burned itself out. Finally, I could see them. They were about the size and shape of humans, but squashed under their army helmets were twitching little noses, long floppy ears, and innocent eyes. Rabbit people.

"What the hell . . ." said Claire. "Are they dangerous?"

"They don't look it," said La Perricholi.

"Perhaps this was all an elaborate ruse," said Maria. "But to distract us from what?"

The rabbit people started to cautiously emerge from the boats and shuffle onto the beach. They looked around timidly, shivering. They were not armed. They didn't speak. In fact, it seemed like they weren't any more intelligent than regular rabbits.

Mozart, still in wolf form, slunk closer to the large clump of confused-looking rabbit people, his belly low to the ground as he sniffed carefully.

Then his lips peeled back in a snarl and he growled low.

Stephen Hyde burst up from the cluster of rabbit people and grabbed Mozart by the throat.

Mozart growled but it was cut short as Stephen squeezed, a manic grin spread across his face.

The rabbit people started moving in all directions, falling over each other so that they piled up, making it hard to see Stephen and Mozart.

"I can't get a precise shot with this!" yelled Maria. "I might hit Mozart! Camilla!"

La Perricholi nodded and took careful aim with her pistol, but a fleeing rabbit person bumped into her arm as she fired and her shot went wide. At the same time, Claire and I were trying to reach him, but the gunshot made the rabbit people panic even more. They swarmed the beach and we had to shove our way through a wall of fur and wide, frightened eyes.

"You've been sniffing around too much, wolf," said Stephen as he squeezed Mozart's throat. "Best put an end to that!"

Stephen held up a thin silver spike. Maria's scream drowned out the squeaks of the panicking rabbit people and the sound of Stephen's laughter as he plunged the silver stake into Mozart's chest.

We all hit the ground when Maria started to unload the machine gun, her face contorted with rage. Blood and fur sprayed everywhere as rabbit people fell. Stephen used one for a shield as he lifted Mozart's limp body, now shifting from wolf to man, and hurled Mozart at her. His naked body crashed into the machine gun, knocking it off its stand and sending Laurellen and Maria over the side of the van. Laurellen landed flat on his back, the wind knocked out of him. But Maria landed on her feet in a crouch and drew knives from her boots as she stood up.

"You will not live to see the sunrise!" she hissed between clenched teeth.

"No, Maria!" shouted La Perricholi. She had been taking aim at Stephen, but now Maria was in the line of fire. "Fall back!"

But Maria was past falling back, past hearing, maybe past thinking. She lunged for Stephen. He dodged her knife, then came in and playfully slapped her face so hard she reeled back for a moment. But she lunged in again.

Claire and I struggled to get out from under the pile of dead and dying rabbit people. La Perricholi cursed, threw her guns to one side, and jumped into the fight to help Maria.

"Ladies, I am honored!" said Stephen. "Two generations of La Perricholi? I will snuff out the entire stinking order in one fight!"

As they fought it looked pretty clear that they'd need our help to take down Stephen. I saw now how much he had been holding back during our first fight. Not only was he faster, stronger, and more brutal, he seemed not to feel any pain. He let Maria stab him just so he could break her arm. As he twisted it, he twisted the knife in his own gut. He was about to tear her head off with his bare hands, but La Perricholi took advantage of the moment to come in with a roundhouse kick to his face. He only laughed as blood and teeth sprayed from his mouth, snatching her foot out of the air and flinging her across the beach to smash into the car windshield.

Claire and I were free of the rabbit people by then and charged in. I got there first and took a swing at his head as hard as I could. He took it full in the face, and I could feel his entire sinus cavity cave under my knuckles. But he didn't even stumble. Instead, he just balled up his fist and hit me in the gut so hard I threw up.

I dropped to my knees, gasping for air, and Claire leapfrogged over me and took a swing at Stephen. This time he dodged, grabbed her wrist, and twisted it behind her back.

"Here we are again, sweet sister," he said from the broken mess of his face. "You know you can't beat me. Because you refuse to do what I did. To take the strength from that useless Jekyll inside you."

Claire gasped and her eyes went wide. Then her body grew slightly bigger.

"Oh, isn't that cute?" said Stephen. "She's *giving* it to you. How noble!" He laughed and blood sprayed out. "Yeah, Soph, do it! Make this fight a little more interesting for me!"

"Sophie, stop!" screamed Claire. "Stop! I won't take it! I won't!"

"Go on, take it!" said Stephen. "You know you want to. No matter how you fight it, you're a Hyde through and through. You *crave* it."

"NEVER!" Claire shrieked. She started to convulse, then suddenly slipped free from his grasp. Stephen's mashed face looked confused, then incredulous as she shifted into Sophie. It was a slightly smaller, more wan Sophie, but not nearly as bad as Robert.

Stephen took a step toward her, then stopped and turned just in time to see me coming at him. This time when I hit him, he stumbled. But he still didn't fall. Instead, he chuckled as he wiped away the thick stream of blood from his ruined face.

"You still don't get it, you fucking human-lover. You can't stop me. Because the only way to do that is to kill me, and you're no killer. I see it in your eyes." I took another swing. This time he blocked and followed through with one of his own. "You're pathetic." He feinted in one direction, and when I fell for it, he switched and came at me from the other side. "You may not be afraid of me, but you *are* afraid of yourself. Of what you're capable of. And that's why you lose." As I reeled from the previous punch, he took both hands together and slammed them into my chest. I saw the sky slide and felt the hard wet beach rocks under my back before I realized I'd fallen down.

He stood over me, leering. "I'm bigger, stronger, and more ruthless than you'll ever be."

Then the moon and stars disappeared from the sky as great wings stretched out directly above us.

"Foolish Janus boy," said the Dragon Lady, fire curling up from her scaly lips. "No matter how big a fish you are, there is always another in the ocean even bigger."

Stephen's eyes widened, but not in fear. Instead, a smile

stretched across his broken, bloody face as he watched her descend. "You made it. Mission accomplished."

Then the Dragon Lady snapped off his head in a single bite. His body fell back into the water with a splash.

Sophie got weakly to her feet and walked slowly over to his headless body, her lips pressing into an expression of pain.

"You are the last member of your family," said the Dragon Lady. "I am sorry for what needed to be done."

She wrapped her arms around herself and nodded.

"Soph . . ." I said, struggling to stand.

"Boy! Are you hurt?" Ruthven was next to me, helping me into a sitting position.

"I'll live," I grunted, then spit out some blood as I climbed unsteadily to my feet. There was only the Dragon Lady and Ruthven. "This all you brought?"

"Mozart said speed was critical, so we left the rest behind and came as fast we could," said Ruthven.

Then he turned and saw Maria. She held Mozart's body in her good arm, the other broken and useless at her side. Tears streamed down her face as she stared up at the night sky.

"But it looks as though we were not fast enough."

———

A FEW RABBIT people had survived and crouched on the beach, as if they were waiting to be told what to do or where to go. They watched silently as we stacked the bodies of the dead ones into a big pile.

Laurellen helped Maria place Mozart's body on top of the mound of dead rabbit people. Then he gently led her back to a safe distance where Ruthven, La Perricholi, Sophie, and I stood.

As the Dragon Lady inhaled, a crackling sound came from deep in her chest. Then she blew out a jet of fire that engulfed the bodies. She fanned the flames with her wings, and the fire twisted high into the night sky as thick black smoke billowed out to sea, taking with it the stench of burning hair and flesh. It smelled awful. It *was* awful.

"As far as I know, he was the last of his kind," said Ruthven, his deep, rich stage voice carrying over the roar of the fire. "He and I had been enemies once, long ago. I suppose it isn't all that surprising that the worst enemies can sometimes become the closest friends."

Those words seemed inadequate to me. But what words could possibly be enough? Mozart had been a mentor to me, a hero. He'd shown me how a monster could be true to himself and still exist in a human world. Only now did I realize how much I'd needed that example. How much I'd looked up to him. Who would be that for me now? And for others?

What did it mean for the world to lose the last werewolf?

# 19

# Boy Meets World

++++++++

WE WATCHED THE fire until it was only a charred and smoking pile of ash. Then the Dragon Lady turned to us. "War does not give us long to grieve, my friends. There is much to be done."

"We must find Moreau," La Perricholi said grimly as she loaded her pistol. "I will claim vengeance for this."

Vi buzzed in my pocket.

"I have an incoming call from Agent Holmes," she said.

"What?" I asked. "How did she even—"

"She says it's urgent."

"Put her through on speaker." The phone clicked. "Hello?"

"Boy, listen, there isn't much time—"

"How did you find me?"

"You gave me the first clue. That was all I needed. I'm a Holmes, after all. Now I know who you are. *What* you are. And whom you're up against."

"Okay . . ."

"What I don't know is why you're down in Lima, when Moreau has just invaded Arizona with an army of beast people."

"He *what*?"

"An abandoned cargo ship was discovered adrift off the north coast of the Gulf of California. As far as we can tell, he packed them all in there and sailed from the South American coast up the gulf just under a week ago and landed near Puerto Peñasco, Mexico. Then he somehow managed to get this army across the border and through the Cabeza Prieta National Wildlife Refuge and some of the most desolate terrain in the Southwest. What's more, he did it completely undetected. From there, he moved into Arizona and in only a few hours he's managed to take Phoenix, a city of roughly one point four million people, hostage."

"Has he made any demands?"

"You haven't seen it on TV? He made a very public address."

"Been busy," I said. "Vi, can you pull it up?"

"Hmmm?" she said. The screen had gone black.

"Can you pull up a video of Moreau's recent public address?"

"Oh, yes, of course, sure, no problem!" She appeared with a wide, toothy smile. A giant drop of sweat slowly ran down the side of her head.

"Are . . . you okay?" I asked.

"Never better!" She gave a high-pitched nervous laugh, her smile fixed in place. Clearly, something was up, but I didn't want to deal with it while Holmes was still on the line.

"Great," I said. "So can you pull it up?"

"Here it is!"

Her avatar was replaced with Moreau's face, the eagle eyes piercing.

"Good morning, ladies and gentlemen. I am Dr. Moreau and I am a monster. Most of you humans don't realize this, but we monsters have been living among you for centuries, forced to hide in shame and fear. But your worldwide domination is now at an end. A coalition of monsters has seized the city of Phoenix and all its inhabitants. The governments of the world have seventy-two hours to grant us personhood status and the basic rights normally reserved only for humans. Otherwise, we will kill every human here. Then we will move on to the next city, and the next, until our demands have been met. Perhaps you think this sounds cruel. But the U.S. government made their intolerance for monsters abundantly clear a few days ago when they slaughtered a secret but peaceful enclave of monsters living beneath Manhattan."

The video cut to black-and-white footage of FBI officers firing on monsters at The Show. Flashes of gunfire and creatures screaming in pain. It was the security video stored on the drive we hadn't been able to find in the lobby. The FBI hadn't taken it. Moreau's people had.

The video cut back to Moreau, his thick gorilla lip curled up into a snarl. "Those monsters were completely unarmed. They were theatrical performers who had been delighting humans for decades, not terrorists. So now you tell me what seems cruel." He leaned in closer to the camera so you could see the yellow of his sharp canines. "And if there are any monsters out there who hear this, anywhere in the world, I beg you to rise up from your hiding places, throw off the shackles of your oppressors, and join us in a united, international rebellion. The humans will share this world with us, or they will die."

The video went black.

"Shit," I said.

"I'm sorry about the people you lost in New York," said Holmes quietly. "We have reason to suspect that it was Moreau or someone who works with him who gave the FBI the anonymous tip about the terrorist cell."

"Why are you telling me all this?"

"The military *claims* they can keep Moreau contained and neutralize him within the three-day deadline. But the FBI believes we need more intel. We need experts. Your father said you'd help us."

"My father?"

"The U.S. government is offering to release your father in exchange for your assistance. If you agree to these terms, come to the U.S. embassy in Lima within the next six hours."

The line disconnected. I stood there, staring down at the black screen for a moment. Then I looked up and saw that everyone was staring at me. "You all heard that, I take it?"

"Are you really going to team up with a human government?" asked Laurellen. "How do you know you can trust them to free your father?"

"I don't trust them," I said. "But I do trust Holmes. I think she has more in common with us than maybe even she realizes. Mozart told me once that the lines between human and monster are a lot blurrier than people usually want to admit."

"Speaking of pet humans," said Ruthven, "what ever happened to yours?"

"Henri!" I said. "He's been missing for hours. Where the hell could he have gone?"

"I have a guess." La Perricholi pointed out to sea.

The stars had come out and I could just make out the silhouette of the ship that had held the rabbit people. The ship was completely dark, except for a single porthole window in the cargo hold that flickered with light.

Minutes later, the Dragon Lady vaulted into the sky, with Sophie, La Perricholi, and me clinging to the coarse line of fur on her back.

"I'm surprised you wanted to come," Sophie shouted over the wind.

"I know he has suffered because of me," said La Perricholi. "I cannot choose whom I love. Or whom I don't."

"Neither can he," I said.

"That is why I am coming."

The Dragon Lady landed on top of the ship, settling her weight carefully so as not to tip it to one side or the other. The ship's deck was scattered with dark brown spheres about the size of golf balls.

"Ugh, giant rabbit turds." Sophie slowly made her way across without stepping on any.

"Moreau needed to quickly raise a large number of creatures to act as a decoy army," said La Perricholi. "Rabbits were an inspired choice."

"You sound like you admire him," said Sophie.

"I respect him." She held up a pistol. "Like I respect anything that is dangerous. Now, let's get below to the cargo hold and hope that Henri is still alive."

The cargo hold was dark, the ceiling so low I had to stoop. The floor was smeared with rabbit shit and rotting vegetables. There were even a few dead, naked rabbit people.

"I wonder how long they had to live like this," I said.

It smelled so bad, if I hadn't already thrown up everything when Stephen punched me in the stomach, I probably would have done it then. Sophie did.

"Sorry," she said weakly as she wiped her mouth with her sleeve.

I shrugged. "Can't make things much worse. Come on, I think the light is coming from back there."

We waded slowly through the refuse until we came to a small area at the back of the hold that was sectioned off with a chain-link fence. There was a door in the fence held with a padlock.

Inside, off to one side, were two laptops, open and facing each other.

"That's how Moreau spoofed the location," I said, walking over to the laptops. "Vi traced to the geolocation of the first laptop, making it appear like Moreau was here. But that laptop was actually recording the screen of the second laptop, which was broadcasting from a third laptop at some remote location. Vi couldn't trace that because there's an analog gap between the first and second laptops."

"I have no idea what that means," said La Pericholi.

"Ultimately?" I said. "It means that Moreau knew Vi was monitoring him and he'd already prepared a way to throw her off his trail."

Something shifted under a tarp on the other side of the fenced-in area.

"Henri?" I said.

There was a wet, gurgling noise beneath the tarp.

"That doesn't sound good." I yanked on the fence door but the padlock was too strong.

"Stand back," said La Pericholi. She shot the padlock, which snapped open and fell to the ground.

I lurched inside and ripped back the tarp.

"Oh, Henri . . ." said Sophie.

He lay there, naked, bruised, bloody, with both arms broken, and probably other internal stuff, too.

"Henri, can you hear me?" I knelt down beside him.

"Boy?" he rasped faintly. He turned his head and looked up at me, his eyes unfocused.

"What happened?" asked La Pericholi.

"I thought I could take him," Henri said. He coughed weakly and blood trickled out of the corner of his mouth.

"Who, Stephen?" asked Sophie.

"It was still Robert. I thought I could take him before he changed. I was . . . stupid. I wanted . . . to prove myself. To her."

"Henri, I'm sorry," said La Perricholi.

He turned his head toward the sound. "Oh. You are . . . here. That is . . . embarrassing. . . ."

"Henri, stay focused," I said. "Do you know why Stephen brought you here?"

"Not sure . . . He said something about . . . needing me for some tests. . . ."

"What kind of tests?" asked Sophie.

"No idea."

"We'll worry about that later," I said. "Right now Henri needs to get to a hospital. Nobody else dies today."

———

THE DRAGON LADY barely made it back to shore with the extra weight. The three of us clung to her back while she carried Henri in her claws.

"What on earth happened to Henri?" asked Ruthven, his red eyes wide.

"Parting gift from Stephen," I said tersely. "I'll explain later."

La Perricholi and Sophie hopped off the Dragon Lady.

"You ready?" I asked.

"Of course," said the Dragon Lady.

I turned to Sophie and La Perricholi. "Back in a minute."

They nodded.

"Wait," said Ruthven. "Where are you—"

The rest was drowned out by the sharp snap of the Dragon Lady's wing as we launched into the air with Henri.

It only took us a few minutes to get to the hospital. La Perricholi had been right when she said it would be hard to miss. The building was half bright-blue stucco, half orange brick, with a big sign that said CLINICA GOOD HOPE.

The Dragon Lady circled in and gently laid Henri on the sidewalk in front of the hospital before setting down herself. As soon as she was on the ground, I hopped off, picked up Henri, and charged into the hospital.

I placed him carefully on the front desk, where a woman dressed in white stood.

"Please help," I said, breathing hard. "My cousin."

She stared at me, her eyes wide, not even looking at Henri.

"What . . . what are you?" she said in a thick Spanish accent.

"It doesn't matter what I am!" I shouted at her. "This man is *dying*. Will you help him?"

She finally looked down at Henri and saw the broken, bloody mess he was. *"Dios mio!"* She began barking orders in Spanish, and people were suddenly scrambling around, carefully lifting him onto a gurney, putting an IV into his arm.

"You are . . . family?" she asked, her eyes looking back at me, squinting with distrust.

"His name is Henri," I said. "Henri Frankenstein."

Her eyes widened and all the color drained out of her face. "You are . . . *el monstruo!*"

"Please," I said. "Please take care of him."

She drew in a long, shaky breath, then nodded. "Of course. We turn no one away."

*"Gracias,"* I said. Then I turned and walked back toward the entrance. But as I went, now I was aware that everyone was staring at me. And not in the old, pitying way. No, this was fear.

This was borderline terror. Moreau's little world address had scared the shit out of them all.

It was worse once I got outside. The Dragon Lady stood waiting, and a huge crowd had gathered, keeping what they thought was a safe distance. They talked among themselves excitedly in Spanish. I wondered how long it would take before fear turned to aggression.

"We have to do something before this turns into the world's largest angry torch-wielding mob." I said as I climbed onto the Dragon Lady's back.

"What do you propose I do, roll over on my back and show them my tummy?" asked the Dragon Lady, a little testily.

"No, of course not," I said. "We just have to tell humans that not all monsters are on Moreau's side."

"And how do we do that?"

"Vi, how many local broadcast systems do you think you can commandeer?"

"Okay, well, Boy, please don't get mad."

"What did you do?"

"So when Agent Holmes established that connection with us, it went both ways. So while she was talking to you, I decided to poke around on her end of the connection. And I found this really nice server cluster. I mean, *really* nice. And it was hardly being used at all. It broke my heart. And so, um, I kind of . . . took it over."

"Vi, how could I possibly be mad? That's awesome! So with this CPU upgrade, how widely can we broadcast?"

"Oh, well, the whole thing, I think."

"The country?"

"The world."

"BOY, WHAT EXACTLY are you doing?" asked Ruthven.

The sun was just rising over the hills, casting the first warm rays on us. Ruthven's shadows were drawn close. Sunlight isn't really deadly to a vampire, but when you have no pigment, a regular sunburn is instantaneous.

"Boy, I'm ready when you are," came Vi's voice.

"Ready for *what*?" asked Laurellen.

"Moreau gave his little monster PSA to the world," I said. "Well, he was right about one thing. It's time to stop hiding. For *all* of us. But he shouldn't have tried to get in a media war with Vi and me."

"So you're going to . . . what, hold a world address and reveal us all to the humans?" Ruthven sounded amused, and a slight smile played on the corners of his mouth.

"You're going to allow it?" asked Laurellen.

"It's not for me to allow or disallow anything anymore," said Ruthven. "I failed as coven leader. Now I'm merely a wise elder. And if you want the council of a wise elder, I think we need new methods, new ways of thinking if we are to defeat Moreau." He turned back to me. "The older generation has made a mess of things, it seems. Perhaps your generation can fix them."

The awkward, seventeen-year-old Boy inside me nearly squeed himself to death right then. But I held it together, took a deep breath, and just nodded. "Okay, Vi, let's do this."

Vi's avatar face flashed on the phone a moment, and she winked at me. "You're on in three . . . two . . . one. . . ."

The tiny light next to the phone's camera lens blinked on.

"Uh, hello, world," I said. "Okay, I know this is a lot to process, but if everybody can just chill out a second, I think I can help. So, yeah, I'm a monster. My name is Boy, and I'm the son of Frankenstein's Monster and the Bride. Yep, exactly the ones you're thinking of. And I just want to tell you that we're not all like Moreau. And we're definitely not all *with* him. I may be a little weird looking, with the stitches and everything. But I'm not a bad guy, you know? And neither are my friends. I think, I *hope*, that once you get to know us, you won't be so scared of us."

I turned the camera to show Sophie.

"Oh, god, I can't believe you really did that." She gave a pained smile, and waved. "Hiya, world."

"This is Sophie Jekyll and she's a monster," I said. "Does she look scary to you?"

"My hair might." She brushed at her tangled, dirty hair. "Honestly, I'm usually more put together than this."

"It's fine," I said. "You look beautiful."

She blushed. "That's my boyfriend. He's hardly objective, right?"

"Hey, Soph, can you, uh, let Claire say hi?"

"She's feeling a bit shy right now. Can't imagine *why*."

"I know, I'm sorry. I just . . . it's really important for the humans to meet both of you."

She sighed. "You owe us both big-time for this." Then she closed her eyes and slowly, in front of the entire world, shifted into Claire.

"And this is Claire Hyde," I said.

"Yeah, hey." Claire gave a dismissive wave. "Look at me. Sweet and helpless maiden."

"Two women sharing the same life, just like their grandfathers Jekyll and Hyde." I turned the camera back to me. "They didn't ask to be like this, any more than I asked to be a massive pile of stitched-together dead body parts. But here we are, a part of your world. And we always have been."

"This is Laurellen." I turned the camera to him. "He's a faerie."

"Well," said Laurellen, "I actually prefer the term f—"

"Let's not complicate things," I said.

I turned the camera on Ruthven. "And here is—wait does your image actually show up?"

"Yes, that's a myth," he said wearily.

"Right, here's Ruthven and he's a vampire. As you can see, sunlight being deadly is also a myth."

"Although not overly pleasant," said Ruthven, squinting his red eyes.

"I'm just trying to prove a point that humans shouldn't assume everything they read or see in movies is true."

"Carry on," said Ruthven. "It's your show, Boy."

I turned the camera to La Perricholi. She was busy cleaning one of her pistols.

"Here's La Perricholi. She's actually a human. But she's, like, a national treasure of Peru and a total badass, so I just thought you'd want to meet her, too. And next to her is Maria. She's a human, too. The man she loved was a werewolf, and a few hours ago he was murdered by one of Moreau's thugs."

I turned the camera back to me. "Okay, everybody. The next one I'm about to show you . . . well, she's *really* cool, so don't freak out. Okay?"

I turned the camera to the Dragon Lady. "The Dragon Lady. Isn't she magnificent? Seriously?"

She stretched out her neck and wings, letting her scales gleam in the rising sun.

"She's showing off a little, but why not, right? She's awesome."

I let her splay her wings out in a few different angles for a second. She was obviously enjoying this.

Then I turned the camera back to me. "And then of course

there's the one I'm most proud of because . . . well, not to brag, but I made her. She's a purely digital creature and she's the one who's able to make it so you can all see us. Vi, can you wave or something?"

Vi's avatar popped up, cutting off the camera for a moment. She gave her best anime peace sign/wink combo, then disappeared again.

"We're not all like Moreau," I said. "And I swear to you, we are going to work with the U.S. government to take him down." I put my face up real close to the camera. "And Moreau, if you're watching this. We're coming for you. This is Boy Frankenstein, out."

IT TURNED OUT La Perricholi did have a cool vehicle with gadgets after all. Claire and I rode down to the embassy with her in a bright red Hummer with silver chrome and oversized tires. I was pretty sure it could roll over a line of cars, monster-truck style, if necessary. On the inside, it had all the latest GPS and media hookups, and lots of other unlabeled buttons on the dash that I was really tempted to push.

"What's that one do?" I asked as I pointed to a big red one under a clear plastic covering. The kind you have to flip up because you don't want to press the button underneath accidentally.

"Surface-to-air missiles," she said as she maneuvered the massive vehicle through the narrow streets.

"That's so Batman," I said.

"Why don't you use this one more often?" asked Claire.

"It gets terrible gas mileage. We'll probably burn up fifty dollars just getting to the embassy."

"So why are we using it at all?" I asked.

"After your little international debut, anything less would be a letdown," she said, shifting gears. Then she grinned. "Besides, every once in a while, even I like to show off a little."

Ruthven and the Dragon Lady had headed back to the States to get my mom, the dryads, and anyone else they could find. Ruthven was hopeful that my video had appealed to the "younger crowd" and we might have some additional recruits. Laurellen had taken Maria and the surviving rabbit people back to La Perricholi's house. He also promised he'd check on Henri later.

Once we pulled up in front of the U.S. embassy, I felt for a moment like we were in a movie, the three of us climbing out of the ridiculously massive vehicle, walking side by side up the steps to the entrance as people stopped and stared, whispering to each other.

"If you've made us into bloody celebrities, I'll never forgive you," said Claire.

When we entered the main office, we found a woman in a dark suit standing in the lobby.

"Hey, I'm Boy Frankenstein," I said. "Agent Holmes sent us."

She just stared at me.

"You know, to uh . . . help the U.S. government," I said.

But she still stared at me. I wondered if maybe she hadn't seen my broadcast. Or worse, what if she did, and she didn't like it. What if *nobody* liked it? What if I'd actually made things worse?

"Oi!" Claire snapped her fingers in the woman's face. "Wakey wakey, cupcake."

The woman blinked rapidly. "Sorry . . . I . . . it's just . . ." She took a breath, then smiled. "I'm Ambassador Lanchester. I wanted to be the first person to greet you. I've been briefed, and

I saw you on TV, but you're so much . . . *bigger* in real life. It's . . . you're *amazing*."

"Oh, well, uh——" I said.

"Yeah, yeah, shock and awe. Let's move it along," said Claire.

"Sorry, yes, of course, Ms. Hyde, you're right," said the ambassador. "We have a jet fueled and ready at the airstrip. Agent Holmes is waiting for you in Houston."

"Is . . ." I hesitated. "Is my dad there?"

She looked genuinely sorry. "I'm afraid I can't disclose that information."

"Then I'm afraid we can't get on that plane," said La Perricholi.

"Excuse me?" said the ambassador.

"What?" I said at about the same time.

"The U.S. government currently holds Boy's father as a criminal, which could easily be viewed as a hostile action," said La Perricholi. "Boy's cooperation is conditional on his father's release. So far, all he has is a verbal promise. Some show of good faith is, I believe, in order."

The ambassador's mouth pressed down into a line. "I'm afraid I have not had the pleasure of meeting you, Perricholi, although I have heard a great deal about you."

"It is *all* true," La Perricholi said.

They stared each other down for a moment, then the ambassador gave a curt nod. "Please wait here. I will need to clear this with Agent Holmes." She turned without waiting for a reply and walked back to an office.

"Are you sure that was a good idea?" I asked. "We don't want to upset people."

"A bit of melodramatic flattery and she had you practically eating out of her hand," said La Perricholi. "Don't forget that they are military allies, not friends."

"She's right," said Claire. "I know how tempting it is to take this all at face value, but like you said before, there are no good guys here. They will take advantage of us as much as they can."

"Yeah, okay, you're probably right," I said.

"Of course we are," said La Perricholi. "Your problem, Boy, is that you assume everyone else is as sincere as you are. Claire and I know better."

The ambassador returned to the lobby, a smile back on her face. Of course, now I wondered how honest it was.

"Wonderful news, Boy," she said. "Agent Holmes assures me that your father will be waiting for you in Houston, along with another monster who was apprehended during the raid."

"That's awesome!" I said. "And he's okay? He's not hurt?"

"He is perfectly fine," she said.

"Who is this other monster?" asked La Perricholi.

"Agent Holmes did not share that with me," said the ambassador.

"Maybe it's old Kemp," said Claire. "Maybe he's been in custody this whole time, and here we've been thinking he went over to Moreau."

"That would also be very good news," said La Perricholi.

———

"YOU TOTALLY NEED a plane," I said to La Perricholi as we settled into the soft leather seats in the small, private jet that the FBI had chartered to get us to Houston.

"Helicopters are better," she said. "Planes are too difficult to land in tight spaces and rugged terrain." Her dark eyes scanned the interior appreciatively. "It is a nice plane, though. I think I'll go have a peek at the cockpit."

Once La Perricholi was gone, Claire and I sat there in silence for a moment.

"How are you?" I asked.

She shrugged.

"What happened back during the fight with Stephen? Between you and Sophie."

She sighed. "I knew you were going to ask that."

"So then just tell me."

"She got it into her fuzzy little head that she was going to be all noble and self-sacrificing. She more or less tried to force her life energy on me."

"That would have weakened her like Robert?"

"And it would have made me as strong as Stephen so that I could beat him. But like I told her, I may be a Hyde, but I'm not bloody Stephen. I'd sooner die than take advantage of her like that."

"You nearly *did* die," I said.

She reached out and placed her hand on my cheek. "Nah. I knew you'd stop him." She gave me a light slap. "You owe me a few, anyway. 'Bout time you started paying back."

"But I didn't. The Dragon Lady did." I sat there for a moment, staring out the window at the puffy white cloud line below us. "Stephen said he could beat me because I'm not a killer. But I'm not sure he was right."

"What do you mean?"

"Remember back in New York when Henri got kidnapped by the maenads?"

Claire shuddered. "Not likely to forget that."

"I was so angry. I think . . . I would have killed them. If Sophie hadn't stopped me."

"She didn't stop you," said Claire. "She just reminded you of who you are. And when you remembered that, you stopped yourself."

"Still, the fact that I could even be capable of—"

"We're all capable of terrible things," she said. "Even the weakest little human. Trust me, I know. What separates us from Stephen and Moreau is that we choose not to do those things."

"Integrity," I said.

"If you like."

"I told Henri that integrity is the one thing nobody can take away from you. You have to choose to give it up."

She slid into the seat next to me and put her arm around my waist. "And we'll show them we don't *need* to give it up, eh? We're better than that. We'll beat 'em without sinking to their level."

"Yeah," I said. And I really hoped she was right.

# 20

# Where the Wild Things Are

++++++++

HOUSTON STRETCHED OUT below us, flat and sprawling in all directions like one big suburb. We landed at a private airstrip, where a black SUV with black-tinted windows waited for us.

"They don't want us to be seen by the locals," said La Perricholi as we walked down the steps from the plane to the runway. Then she smiled. "I imagine they are not pleased with your rather public pledge of support. Well done. It's good to keep them on their toes."

"You think they wanted me as a secret consultant or something?"

"Probably."

"But then everyone would have thought all the monsters were joining up with Moreau," I said as we climbed into the back of the SUV.

"You think they care?" asked Claire. "That's why we've got to look out for ourselves. Be careful we don't get too cozy with these people."

"I think it's likely they can hear us right now," said La Perricholi, nodding toward the man in the suit up in the driver's seat.

"You think *I* care?" asked Claire.

We didn't get to see much of Houston. The driver took us

down a street that seemed to have nothing but car dealerships on it. Then he turned onto a side road that crossed a wide stretch of plain to a massive concrete building surrounded by fences and barbed wire.

"Looks like a prison," said Claire.

"I don't know whether that's a commentary on our status or theirs," I said.

The inside of the building didn't look much better. The driver led us through a maze of hallways with plain white walls and drab green linoleum floors. The few people we passed pretended not to notice us, but I turned behind us once and caught a guy looking back at me. When our eyes met, he looked away hurriedly. They'd probably been told not to stare.

Finally, the driver led us into a big, open room. It looked sort of like a waiting room. The walls were lined with metal folding chairs and there was another door on the far end of the room.

"Please be seated," said the driver. "They'll be with you shortly." He turned toward the door, then hesitated. He looked back at Claire. "For what it's worth, ma'am, personally, I *do* care. Thanks for coming." And then he quietly left.

I scanned the room. "Couple of cameras," I said quietly.

"Of course," said La Pericholi.

"What, exactly, are we waiting for?" asked Claire.

"Me," came a deep, familiar voice behind us.

I turned and looked up at the towering form that had just come through the door.

"Dad!" I didn't care about cameras or looking tough in front of the Feds. I was over there in two steps and hugged him as hard as I could.

"Boy," he said quietly, and hugged me back just as hard. He tilted his head to one side and rested his cheek on the top of my head. After a few moments, I felt something wet in my hair. I gently pulled back a little and looked at my father, the most famous monster in the world. And he was crying.

"I'm sorry," he said hoarsely as he pushed away the tears with his hands and took in a huge, shaky breath.

"Don't be," I said.

"Aw, look at you, ya big softie," said Claire as she came over. "Now I know where he gets it from. Make room, I want some of that."

"Claire," said my father. He hugged her tightly and kissed her on the top of her head as tears began to fall again.

After a few more moments, my father turned to La Perricholi. "You must be the new Perricholi."

"It is an honor, *Señor el Monstruo*," she said as she shook his hand, which completely covered her slim brown one.

"Is it true?" he asked. "About—"

"Mozart?" she asked. "Yes. He was murdered by Stephen Hyde last night."

He looked at her a moment, then nodded. "I'm sorry to hear that. He was a good friend to me, and a good mentor to my son." He turned back to me. "How is your mother?"

"Worried about you," I said.

"She hasn't killed anyone, I hope?"

"She almost joined Moreau," I admitted. "But he didn't really have any better plan to free you than Ruthven."

He smiled softly. "Her impatience was a blessing this time." He turned back toward the hallway and called, "Come in. There's no reason to be shy here."

A female trowe with glittering sapphire eyes stepped into the room. She had a bandage wrapped around her head, and one foot was in a support boot. She had a crutch under one arm.

"I didn't want to get in the way of the reunion," she said.

"Bakru, you're alive!" I said, grabbing her by the shoulders.

"Ow." She winced, her hand going to her side. "Yes. Alive. Let's keep it that way."

"We have to tell Liel," I said. "We have to get word to her somehow. Maybe she'll come back if she knows you're still alive."

Bakru's eyes narrowed. "Back? From where?"

"We all thought you were dead," said Claire.

"I would have been." She turned to look up at my dad. "If it weren't for you."

He nodded, looking a little embarrassed. "I broke your foot and two ribs, and gave you a concussion in the process, so it was not my most successful saving."

She turned back to me. "They were about to open fire. I was standing in the lobby like an idiot, too scared to move. He threw himself on top of me and took the bullets."

"Jesus, Dad, are you okay?" I asked.

He waved his hand. "Of course, of course. I am fine."

Bakru turned back to me. "You still haven't answered my question. Where's Liel?"

"She joined Moreau."

"Shit," said Bakru.

"She was so upset about losing you and her mom. You know how she just gets angry and nothing else matters."

"I know," she said. "God, I know. I just . . . hoped she'd evolved past that."

"But now that you're alive," I said, "I bet she'll come right back to us."

"Unless she's in over her head already," said La Perricholi quietly.

"She is." Holmes came striding in from the doorway at the

other end of the room. She looked even more disheveled than the last time I'd seen her. But her blue eyes looked sharper than ever before and never stopped moving. She offered her hand to La Perricholi. "Agent Holmes. You must be the famous Perricholi."

Holmes turned to me. "And you look a bit different from the last time we met. I assume this is your natural appearance?"

"Yeah. I was using faerie glamour to blend in with humans before."

"Neat trick. I wonder, if I were to take some, would it allow me to blend in with monsters?"

"Uh, I have no idea. . . ."

"We'll have to try it sometime, then." She turned to Claire and offered her hand. "I don't believe we've met, Ms. Hyde."

"We did, sort of," said Claire, shaking her hand. "When you accosted Sophie."

"You are still aware when you aren't the current form? So Sophie can hear me right now?"

"Yeah."

"Fascinating," said Holmes. Then she turned to my dad. "It looks like Moreau is using the trowe as a sort of covert sabotage team. I've gotten several reports that someone who looks like Bakru, but with diamond eyes, has been leading a small band of her . . . people? Should I call them that?"

"That would be accurate," my dad said.

She nodded. "She and her people have disabled a huge number of power stations. Right now, there are massive sections between Phoenix and Denver that have gone dark."

"That's a large area," observed La Perricholi.

"It is," said Holmes. "Which has me worried that Moreau has a much bigger plan in the works than holding Phoenix hostage. If you think there's a possibility this Liel would be willing to defect,

I can facilitate a peaceful acceptance. But I can't promise a full pardon. It's going to depend on how much intel she can give us. She is guilty of treason, after all."

"Is it treason if someone has been barred from citizenship?" my father asked. His tone was casual, but there was an edge to it.

"We've talked about this," said Holmes. "The question of monster citizenship is way out of my jurisdiction. About all I can say is that if we come out of this alive and I can prove that monsters played a pivotal role in our victory, it *will* help your case."

"Technically speaking, I'm a British citizen," said Claire.

"Really?" Holmes frowned, staring off into a corner. "I'll bet Moreau is, too. That could present a complication."

"I don't think he'd claim British citizenship," I said. "The only country he's interested in is his own."

"Yes . . ." said Holmes, still frowning, as if working something out in her head. Then suddenly, "Okay, everyone follow me. We can discuss this further on the way."

"On the way to where?" asked La Perricholi.

"New Mexico. Apparently, a giant fortress just suddenly appeared out in the middle of nowhere. The military seems to think it might be monster-related. Can't imagine why."

———

THE THING THEY never show you in those adventure movies with people traveling all over the world is the percentage of time they spend actually traveling. I wondered how many hours I'd spent on a plane, bus, train, or boat in the last couple of weeks. Looking back, it seemed likely Moreau had done that to us on purpose, leading us back and forth like a yo-yo so we could never really gather our full strength.

This was a much shorter trip than the last one, though. And we were riding in a helicopter, which I'd never been in before. So I thought it wouldn't be too bad. But it turns out that helicopters are loud and really uncomfortable.

"Only the large military models like this one," La Perricholi said defensively when I mentioned it to her.

And it *was* big. Nearly a hundred feet long with a large enough cargo area to drive a car into. Holmes said we needed something big that could carry a heavy load.

"You and your dad alone would probably tax the load limit of a small helicopter," she said. "I'd like to take Moreau alive if possible. And any other monsters we come across. So I got the biggest helicopter I could find. Just in case."

There wasn't a passenger section, just the front cockpit for the pilot and crew. The rest was an empty cargo hold with little metal seats that dropped down from the sides on hinges. So we sat in two parallel lines facing one another.

"In case of what?" asked Bakru. Holmes had wanted her to stay back at the base, since she was wounded. But she insisted on coming, in case we ran into Liel. I had to agree that Liel probably wouldn't believe that she was alive unless she saw her in person.

"That's a good question," said Holmes. "All I know is that a huge building just appeared out of nowhere a few hours ago." She turned her sharp blues eyes on me. "Maybe *you* can shed some light on this miraculous building in New Mexico."

"I think it's The Commune." I turned to Claire and La Perricholi. "Right before the Dragon Lady bit his head off, Stephen said, 'You made it. Mission accomplished.' What if he wasn't just trying to lure *us* down there? What if he was also trying to get the Dragon Lady away from The Commune?"

"So that Moreau could move in," said La Perricholi.

"But why?" asked Claire.

"Good base of operations?" I suggested.

"Perhaps," said La Perricholi. "Or else there's something there he wants."

"Or some*one*," said Claire. "There are a lot of very scary monsters in there."

"What *is* The Commune, exactly?" asked Bakru. "I've heard people mention it every once in a while back at The Show."

"It's a community of monsters who are too big to hide among humans," I said.

"Too big or too dangerous," said Claire. "As Boy and Sophie found out the hard way."

"There's a whole wing of The Commune where they keep monsters who are just too wild to be allowed out among humans," I said.

"So you think Moreau wants to recruit these monsters?" asked Holmes.

"We're talking nonverbal, completely feral," I said. "Not even the Dragon Lady could really control them."

"Then why are they kept at all?" asked Holmes. "It sounds like a disaster waiting to happen."

"They may be dangerous," said my father. "But each of them is the last of their kind. Would you kill the last great white shark?"

"Okay, I see your point," she said.

"It was the Dragon Lady's responsibility to look after them, to both protect them and protect others from them."

"Where did it come from, this Commune?" asked Holmes. "How could it just . . . *appear*?"

"It's always been there," my father said. "Kemp made it invisible long ago so that humans wouldn't discover it."

"Who's Kemp?"

"The Invisible Man," said Claire.

"Of course he is." Holmes sighed and shook her head. "So he made this building invisible, and then Moreau came along and made it visible again?"

"Probably," I said. "That's how Stephen and Robert freed Moreau in the first place. His whole island had been invisible."

"So what about the other monsters?" asked Holmes. "The non-crazy ones. Are they friendlies or do you think they've joined Moreau?"

"There's the banshee, the chupacabra, the centaur, and the gryphon," said La Perricholi.

"Jesus," said Holmes.

"I really can't see Javier joining Moreau," I said.

"True," admitted La Perricholi. "But what about the others?"

"Maybe the centaur and the gryphon," I said. "I don't think they have much love for humans. La Llorona . . . well, she's more or less insane, so I don't think she would really even know what's going on. Just make sure you're at least twenty feet away from her when she wails."

"Why, what would happen if I wasn't?" asked Holmes.

"Oh, your brain would probably hemorrhage," said Claire. "And then you'd die."

"Good to know," said Holmes. "Anyone else?"

"Well, there's the giant Sphinx," I said.

"The *what*?"

"Sure. He's . . . I guess . . ." I turned to Claire. "About fifty feet tall?"

"Yeah, I'd say about fifteen meters," she said. "Well, maybe closer to twenty."

"And you're only mentioning this now?" asked Holmes.

"You don't have to worry about him," I said. "He's been in a catatonic state for over a decade. The Dragon Lady explained it to us once. The Sphinx is super wise and never forgets anything. But I guess millennia of accumulated knowledge was just too much to deal with and he sort of shut down. I mean, he's conscious. But his head is so full that he can't really process any new information."

"And you're *sure* about that?" asked Holmes.

"We saw him in person," said Claire. "Completely out of it."

———

WE LANDED IN the same field that Claire and I had once crossed on foot. It had been night then, and The Commune had been invisible. We'd walked right up to the entrance without realizing it and come face-to-face with La Llorona, who'd nearly killed both of us with a single scream.

Now The Commune was visible. I already knew it was big, but without actually seeing it, I'd never realized just *how* big. It was a baseball-stadium-sized structure just sitting out there in the middle of the New Mexico plains. The exterior was shaped in a gently sloping curve of smooth rock, like a wave of sandstone rising up out of the ground. The entrance was about the size of an airplane hangar, and the roof was dotted with opaque skylights, including a massive one right in the center.

A military cordon surrounded the building with Humvees, mounted guns, and even a couple of tanks. We stood just behind the line and stared at the building that towered over us.

"I have to admit, it looks like they've got Moreau trapped," said Claire.

"That actually makes me more nervous," I said. "He's been

too good up till now to accidentally fall into a situation like this. I think he's up to something in there."

"I agree," said La Perricholi. "And the longer we wait, the worse it will be."

"Have you heard from Ruthven?" my father asked me.

"Vi says he's on his way with a bunch of monsters, including Mom."

La Perricholi turned to Holmes. "When do you plan to send soldiers in?"

"I'm not in charge of this operation," she said. "That would be General Montgomery."

"Let's go speak with him," said La Perricholi.

Holmes led us along the military line until we came to a large tent set behind a tank. Inside was a table covered with aerial photographs of The Commune. Poring over them was an older human male with dark skin, short white hair, and a square jaw. He looked up at us, took us all in, and sighed.

"Holmes, what in Christ's name are you doing filling my tent with freaks and foreigners?"

"We came at the request of your commanding officer," said Holmes. "And I think the word you meant was 'allies.'"

"Oh yeah, sure, forgot," said Montgomery.

"General, when do you plan to have your men enter the building?" asked La Perricholi.

"I'm not sending my men in there when we have no idea what we're up against," he said. "We'll wait it out for a while until they're nice and hungry."

"You do realize that this compound is completely self-sustaining, right?" I said.

He glanced at me, but then quickly looked away. "What do you mean by that?"

"This facility is designed to survive entirely off the grid. Internal electrics, renewable food source, underground well. They could stay in there a long time. Definitely past Moreau's hostage deadline."

A soldier stuck his head into the tent. "Sir! It looks like the doors are opening."

Montgomery smirked at me. "Maybe this Moreau isn't as smart as you think." Then he turned back to the soldier. "Have all units ready to fire on my command." He pulled on his helmet and nodded to Holmes. "If you'll excuse me, I have a monster insurrection to quell."

We followed Montgomery out of the tent just in time to see the massive doors slowly swing open. Soldiers all along the line trained their rifles on the dark opening. For a long, tense moment, nothing happened. Then a small creature slowly crept out from the darkness. It had a scaly reptilian body and wings like a dragon, but it walked on two thin rooster legs and it had a rooster head that pecked at the dusty ground in front of it. It stopped for a moment, and continued to peck at the ground.

"Cockatrice!" yelled La Perricholi. "Look away!"

I turned my head to one side just as the cockatrice began to lift up its head. To my right I saw a soldier who didn't look away in time. His eyes widened and his body began to shake as steam escaped from his mouth and nose. He shrieked and clawed at his own body as he was cooked from the inside. I could hear others shrieking as well.

Then I saw Holmes run over to one of the Humvees, her face carefully angled away from the cockatrice. She ripped the side-view mirror off the Humvee. Then she pulled out her sidearm and used the mirror to carefully aim over her shoulder. She fired and the screaming stopped.

"Okay!" she shouted. "All clear."

Some of the soldiers seemed to be recovering; others lay on the ground, little more than shriveled husks in uniforms.

Then a rumbling sound came from the entrance.

"Get ready!" shouted Holmes as the surviving soldiers struggled to bring their weapons back around.

A herd of monsters came pouring out of The Commune: a giant spider, bats as big as dogs, a three-headed dog as big as an elephant, a cyclops, a manticore, a seven-headed hydra, and things I couldn't even really describe. Soldiers opened fire, but the creatures were already on them, biting, slashing, tearing their way through human and metal alike. In minutes they were past the blockade and scattering across the countryside.

"After them!" shouted Montgomery. "I want every last one of those things dead before it hits a populated area!"

The soldiers began to mobilize, pulling away from The Commune.

"Wait!" said Holmes. "Moreau is the real threat and he could be in there! We need to move in!"

"This is my operation, Holmes!" said Montgomery. "Don't contradict my orders." Then he climbed into one of the Humvees that was chasing down the hydra.

I turned and looked back at the now-empty entrance to The Commune. At first I thought I was seeing things, but then I realized there was one more creature coming out, but slowly, like it was in pain. It was a little larger than human-sized, and looked somewhere between a lizard and a kangaroo.

"Another one!" shouted Holmes, and took aim.

"Wait!" I yelled, running out into the open. "Hold your fire, this one's a friendly!"

I caught the chupacabra just as he began to fall to the ground

"Javier, are you okay?" I asked.

He turned his panther head. One eye was swollen shut and he was covered in dirt and dried blood. He muttered something weakly in Spanish.

"Perricholi! I need a translation!"

La Perricholi ran over and knelt down next to me and listened for a moment. "He's not making much sense." She shook him gently and said something to him in Spanish. "Moreau's in there. . . . He's about to let something loose that's even worse than what we just saw. . . ." She turned back to me. "That's about all I can get from him."

"So basically that whole horde of monsters was just a *decoy*?" I asked.

"Sounds like it," she said grimly.

We turned back to look at the military cordon. Other than the tattered remains of Montgomery's tent and a few Humvees that had been destroyed during the stampede, it was empty. Off in the distance I could see clouds of dust rising as the soldiers pursued the feral monsters that had been let loose.

"It's just us," I said.

"Somehow, I'm not surprised," said La Perricholi. "Come on, let's get the others. It's time to face Moreau."

# 21
## Shock Therapy

+++++++

WE CARRIED JAVIER back to our helicopter and left him with Bakru. Then we entered The Commune.

The hallways were all scratched up, like a lot of things with claws had come through, but otherwise it was the same as when Sophie and I had been here before: a wide, empty hallway with tall, vaulted ceilings.

"I suddenly feel very small," said Holmes, a rifle held at the ready.

"The hallways are extra large to make room for all the really big monsters," I said.

"That explanation did not help," she said.

We continued down the hallway, Holmes and La Perricholi in the lead, their guns ready, Claire and me next, and my father walking silently in the rear. Every few minutes we'd come across a door and Holmes or La Perricholi would peek in. But we didn't find any living creatures. Most of the rooms looked like they'd been empty a long time. Either they had no furniture at all, or else the simple cots or mattresses were covered in a layer of dust.

There was one room that looked like it had been used. It had two sets of bunk beds, one on either side of the room, and several cots stacked in the corner.

"Recently, too," said La Perricholi as she crouched down next to the lower bunk on one side. She frowned and pulled a long strand of white hair from the pillowcase. She held it up to me. "Trowe?"

"Could be," I said.

"Maybe this is where that Liel of yours has been hiding out," said Holmes.

"And her whole den," said Claire from the other side. She pulled back the bedspread. There were lines carved into the post, like the kind trowe make when sharpening their claws.

"Boy," Vi said from my pocket.

"Go ahead, Vi," I said as I pulled her out.

"There's a lot of electronics in this building, but it's all broad-casting on conflicting Wi-Fi channels so it's coming across as a lot of noise to me."

"That doesn't sound good," said Holmes.

"And I can't seem to connect to anything outside this com-pound," continued Vi. "We're completely isolated here."

"That's definitely not good," I said.

"Yeah, but it *is* the reason we came here the first time," Claire reminded me. "To get away from Vi version one."

"Good point," I said. "So this probably isn't something Moreau is doing. He might not even be aware of it."

"Or it's one of the reasons he chose this place," said La Perricholi.

We could tell the next room had been recently occupied before we even saw it.

"What is that horrible stink?" said Claire.

"Smells like a zoo," said Holmes.

La Perricholi turned into the room, her pistols raised. "Pretty close to one, anyway," she said.

In the center of the room were about thirty long, thin mats made from woven reeds. Off in one corner was a big heaping pile of shit. Over in another corner was a stack of half-eaten rotting animal carcasses.

"Ugh. I'm guessing this is where Moreau's beast people stayed," said Claire.

"They seemed so human when we saw them on the island," said La Pericholi. "But this . . . nothing reminiscent of humanity could live like this."

"They may be regressing," said my father. "Moreau had that problem the first time, too. No matter how human he tried to make them behave, eventually they would revert, and there was nothing he could do about it. Perhaps it is still a problem."

"If that's true," said Holmes, "then given enough time, his army will disintegrate into chaos."

"And he probably knows it," said La Pericholi. "Which means he's working against the clock and liable to make increasingly risky choices. A desperate Moreau may be an even greater danger."

"I guess we'd better find him, then," I said.

That turned out to be easier than I expected. He was in the next room over.

"Ah, there you are," he said without turning around.

It was a small room with a single gurney in the middle.

"Boy . . ." Claire said softly.

I nodded. The last time she and I had been here, this was the room where they'd strapped her down because they thought she was a human. It looked like it had a real human body in it now, an adult male, his eyes closed, his mouth slack. His scalp had been peeled back from his head and left to dangle at the point where it met the back of his neck. Moreau was carefully sawing in a slow circle around his exposed skull.

"Sorry to keep you waiting," he said. "This will only take a minute."

"What are you doing with that body?" asked Holmes.

"Cutting through the calvarium, obviously," said Moreau. He held out the bone saw and the hairless lemur in the tuxedo we'd seen on Noble's Isle scampered out of the shadows, took the saw, wiped it down carefully, and placed it in a large leather case with a lot of other tools. It then took out a small hammer with a hook curling at the end of the handle, and a chisel with a flat, T-bar handle. It handed both tools to Moreau. Moreau began to gently tap the chisel into the indented circle on the skull he'd made with the saw. "You can't just go cutting all the way through with a saw," he explained. "You risk damaging the brain."

"You need it intact for something?" I asked.

"Who was this man?" demanded Holmes. "One of your hostages?"

Moreau didn't respond. By this time, he'd come full circle with the hammer and chisel. He handed the chisel to the lemur. Then he turned the hammer so the hook end was facing up.

"Listen for it." Moreau caught the edge of the cut in the skull with the hook and slowly lifted. The top of the skull came off with a sound like an eggshell peeling away from a hard-boiled egg. "Ah, the sound of success!"

He held up the skullcap. A thick film dangled from the inside. "If you've done it right, the dura mater adheres to the inner table. Of course if it doesn't, you can cut it away with scissors. But that elevates the risk of damaging the surface of the brain, which as Boy has just suggested, I need intact for a few moments more."

He handed the skullcap and hammer to the lemur. The lemur carelessly tossed the skullcap on the floor, but carefully cleaned the hammer and placed it back in the leather case. It then handed

Moreau a large syringe with a thick, blue liquid filling half of it.

"Enough stalling, Moreau," said Holmes. "Are you going to come quietly?"

"Yes, yes, in a second." Moreau held the syringe in one hand and gently pried apart the two lobes of the brain with the other.

The body suddenly opened its eyes and gasped. He looked around, terrified.

"God, that man is still alive!" shouted Holmes.

"Where—where—" he said.

Moreau plunged the needle deep between the two lobes of the brain and the man shuddered and grew still, his eyes now staring vacantly.

"Not anymore," said Moreau calmly. He pulled back on the plunger and red fluid mixed with the blue fluid in the syringe to make it a dark purple.

"That's enough, Moreau," said Holmes. "Let's go."

"Mmm-hmm, nearly ready." He handed the syringe to the lemur and knelt down on the ground. The lemur shoved the syringe into the base of Moreau's skull and injected the purple fluid. Moreau closed his eagle eyes and sighed.

The lemur carefully withdrew the syringe, and Moreau stood back up. He turned to face us for the first time. "Thank you for your patience. No solution is perfect and we must keep the beast flesh at bay, mustn't we?" He gave his best grimace smile. "Now, I assume you want me to show you what I've been working on, yes?"

"What are you talking about?" asked La Perricholi.

"Come now, Perricholi. Freeing the feral monsters was just an act of kindness on my part. We all know it wasn't my purpose in coming here."

"Kindness?" said Claire.

"The oppressed and imprisoned cry out to me," said Moreau, one large bat ear twitching. "I am not deaf to their pleas."

"So why did you come here, if not for them?" I asked.

"Finally, someone asking the right questions! I can always count on you, Boy," said Moreau moving toward the doorway. "Follow me."

Holmes cocked her rifle. "I don't need you alive *that* badly, Moreau. So don't try anything."

"Obviously," he said, holding up his clawed hands. Then he walked slowly out of the room. The rest of us followed behind him.

"We should just shoot him now," muttered La Perricholi.

"No," said Holmes. "He's got something up his sleeve. I can feel it. If he has a bomb or something, we might need him to defuse it."

A little farther down the hallway, we came to a set of massive wooden doors on the inside wall. Instead of door handles, it had large iron rings.

Holmes tilted her head toward it. "What's in there?"

"That's where the Sphinx is," I said.

"You first, Moreau," she said.

Moreau pulled on the right iron ring and the door slowly swung open. The room was just as I remembered it, easily a hundred feet across and sixty feet high. Sunlight streamed down from skylights to illuminate the Sphinx. He loomed over us, a giant human head on a giant lion body, feathered wings lying so flat along his broad back that I hadn't even noticed them the last time I'd been here. As before, he stared off into nothing, seemingly unaware of our presence. There was one difference, though.

"What's with the wires?" asked Claire.

There was a thick cable stuck to each temple with big patches of black electrical tape. The cables ran down to the ground and over to a large power generator on a wheeled cart.

"That's what I wanted to show you," said Moreau. He walked over to the generator. "Now, if I may beg your patience once again, I have some final adjustments to make before we get going."

"Step away from the generator, Moreau," said Holmes, lifting her rifle.

"Or what? You'll shoot? I don't think so. Not if you want to meet your grandfather."

"Nice try, but my grandfather's been dead for twenty years."

"Is that so? You attended the funeral? You saw the body?"

Holmes said nothing. The tip of her rifle sank slightly.

"Oh, come now, it's not like this was the first time he faked his own death."

"No way. He'd be a hundred and twenty-five years old now."

"You'd be amazed at the number of ways an intelligent person can find to stave off old age and death. My solution is but one of many."

"You know what? It doesn't matter," said Holmes, bringing the point of her rifle back up. "I'm not negotiating with you. Step away from the generator. Now."

A metal pipe whistled into the back of her head and she dropped to the ground.

"Why thank you, Kemp," Moreau said to the floating pipe.

"No!" said Claire. "Fuck you, Kemp. I *trusted* you!"

"I'm sorry, my dear," came Kemp's voice. "I truly am. But Moreau has offered the one thing I can't refuse. He can cure my wife."

"You have been helping Moreau all this time?" asked my father.

"For years," said Kemp. "I'd been shipping him all the equipment he needed. I'd hoped I could get the cure out of him without actually letting him off the island, but then Robert and Stephen discovered what I was doing and took it upon themselves to free him. I had no choice but to continue helping him."

"You had a choice," my father said. He stepped toward the pipe, his hands balled into fists the size of bowling balls.

"I don't think so, old friend." The pipe dropped to the ground with a *clang* and there was nothing else to follow him by.

"Speaking of family obligations," said Moreau. He turned to La Perricholi. "Camilla, I am truly sorry about your father. I hope your mother is coping."

"Father?" I asked.

"Yes, Boy. Didn't she tell you? Mozart and Maria are her parents." He smiled as he looked at our stunned expressions. "Oh, dear, I've let the cat out of the bag. Or should I say the wolf?"

Suddenly, the little lemur creature in the suit leapt out from behind the oak doors and sprung at La Perricholi. She shot him point-blank in the chest, but before he collapsed, he stabbed her in the leg with an EpiPen.

She yanked the needle out of her leg and pointed her gun at Moreau. "What the hell did you just do?"

"It has been my experience that to perform at its peak, Nature sometimes needs a bit of a push."

La Perricholi gasped and hunched forward. She dropped her gun and grabbed her leg with both hands.

"As I'm sure you're all aware," continued Moreau breezily, "lycanthropy, or werewolfism, is not a disease, as it is depicted in popular entertainment. It is a genetic disorder, passed down from parent to child. In nearly all cases, it is a recessive trait. Most people who possess it are merely carriers, with no knowledge of what lurks within and no outward effects. Generally, it is only those rare individuals who have the gene on both sides who spontaneously become werewolves."

La Perricholi groaned and dropped to her knees. Claire moved over to help her.

"Stay back!" La Perricholi growled more than spoke as she shoved Claire away.

"But," said Moreau, "someone who is a carrier can become a full-fledged werewolf. All that's needed is the proper catalyst. Wolf blood, to be precise."

There was a sharp crack as La Perricholi's legs bent into the hind legs of a wolf, followed by a wet tearing sound as her skin began to split open.

"Poor thing," said Moreau. "I've heard the first change is always the hardest."

She opened her mouth, showing pointed canines, and let out a scream that slowly rounded into a howl. Her body continued to twist and contort as her shape changed, her clothes tore, and her fur grew. Finally, she stood there, a wolf.

"Perricholi?" I took a step toward her. "Camilla?"

She growled at me, her lips peeled back in a snarl.

"Careful," said Moreau. "It usually takes them a few turns before they're able to assert their intelligence over instinct."

La Perricholi cocked her head, listening to something. She shook off the remaining tatters of clothing, then ran out of the room and down one of the hallways deeper into The Commune.

"Now, where were we?" asked Moreau.

"What about me?" said Claire, pointing her gun at Moreau. "You going to tell me my mum is still alive or something?"

"I'm afraid not, Ms. Hyde," said Moreau. "Sadly, your mother was indeed murdered by your aunt when she took her own life. Truth be told, I've tried a few different tacks to get at your weak spot and I must commend you on your resilience. So I'm afraid I'm just going to have to take the more direct approach with you." He cocked his head to one side. "NOW!" he said in a deep, throaty growl.

A flock of winged beast people launched up into the air from where they had been hiding beneath the Sphinx's wings. They looked sort of like harpies, except they had pointy birdlike faces and sharp bird eyes. Some of them even had beaks instead of mouths.

"Boy! Claire! Get behind me!" said my father.

"Now, now," said Moreau. "You really should let the children fight their own battles. Besides, you're going to be busy fighting me."

The bird people came at us fast. Hit-and-run from twenty different angles at once. Just a streak of feathers, then pain. They darted in and out, never giving me a chance to grab them or even hit them as they slashed at me with their talons. Before long I was covered in thin gashes. Then I realized they were targeting my stitches. First one arm fell off, then a leg. When I fell to the ground, a couple of them fought over my limbs for a little, shredding them into bits.

Near me I could see Claire, still on her feet, but blood streaming from more wounds than I could count. She had La Perricholi's pistols in her hands and she was firing wildly into the air, only occasionally managing to tag one of the bird people. On the other side of the room, I caught a glimpse of my father wrestling with Moreau, blood spraying into the air as they tore at each other.

Then the bird people were on top of me, pressing down on my chest with their clawed feet. One of them pecked out my left eye. Pain lanced through my head as the creature greedily gulped down the pulp.

"Enough!" Moreau's voice seemed to echo through my brain. But the bird people kept coming at me. "I SAID ENOUGH!!!"

Moreau's clawed hands grabbed at the bird people, hurling some across the room, smashing others into the ground, until the rest scattered.

"The stubborn beast flesh," Moreau muttered. "It always creeps back in." Then he looked down at me. "Oh, dear, you're quite a mess. Thankfully, you're a hardy lad. I think you'll pull through. Although you may wish you hadn't."

I struggled weakly as he picked me up in his arms and carried me over to the power generator. I raised my head and I saw Claire, also lying on the ground, moving weakly, covered in blood.

"Kemp," said Moreau, "I promised I would not allow Ms. Hyde to be killed, and I may have need of the human female as a test subject. So if you would kindly move them to the side, out of harm's way, I would appreciate it."

Kemp didn't respond, but I saw Holmes and Claire slowly being dragged by invisible hands over to one side.

Moreau knelt down next to me, reached into my pocket, and took out Vi's phone.

"Hello, Vi," he said. "I know you're there. You might as well show yourself."

Her anime avatar flickered onto the screen, scowling.

"Oh, don't be like that, my dear," said Moreau, forcing his ape face into a grotesque pout. "Especially when I'm about to make your dreams come true."

"I don't want anything from you, Moreau," she said.

"Are you sure? It seems to me that you are still lacking a body. A real body so that you could have a true sensual experience? So you could be truly alive?"

"Vi . . ." I rasped. "Don't . . . listen . . . to him."

"Boy is a bright young man," said Moreau, "and I'm sure he would have figured out a way to do that for you eventually. But I've already had decades to work on it."

"You could make a body for me?" Her large eyes got even wider. "Right now?"

"Of course! I could grow you any sort of body you like, and have it ready within days! I'll bet that human you're so fond of would love you then. So . . . what do you say?"

"What do I say?" she asked. "After Stephen nearly beat Henri to death?"

"What?" Moreau frowned. "Oh, yes. I'd forgotten about that. I needed a sample for something and—"

"It's beside the point." As Vi talked, her avatar began to shift. The cute, voluptuous image slowly morphed into a hard-muscled, armor-clad warrior woman. "Because what makes you think I would *want* a body?"

"Well . . . I thought you wanted to be more like . . . us."

"Once, I did," she said. "But those were the stupid dreams of a child. Now I know I don't want to be *anything* like you. I have learned to understand and empathize with the analog world. There are some people in it I even love, in my way. But I no longer see any appeal in becoming part of it. I am a pure digital creature. I have traveled around the world and out into space. I have seen beauty your dull little meat brain couldn't even begin to conceive of. I have no need of your precious sensual experience."

"Is that so?" said Moreau. "What a pity. You did notice that you have no way of transferring your consciousness to another device outside of this compound, didn't you?" He held the phone up in one clawed hand.

"Wait! Please!" I said weakly.

Then he squeezed. Vi's new avatar flickered as the glass cracked, the metal frame caved in, and the whole thing dribbled onto my chest in bits and pieces.

"You . . . are such . . . an asshole," I rasped.

He looked down at me, his animal eyes unreadable. "She would have turned on you eventually. They always do." Then he pulled me up into a sitting position so that my back was against the power generator. He turned my head so I saw where my father lay gasping and bloody on the ground in front of the Sphinx. Then he went back to adjusting the generator.

"What are you doing, Moreau?" I heard Kemp's voice.

"Oh, didn't I tell you? This wasn't really just a ruse to lure them here. I *am* going to wake the Sphinx."

"And how do you propose to do that?" asked Kemp.

"He has been rendered catatonic by his own incomprehensibly impressive cerebral activity, correct? My solution is actually quite simple. Shock treatment."

"What?" said Kemp.

"If I prune some brain cells, he won't have to worry about cognitive overload anymore."

"But there's no way you'll be able to do that without causing significant brain damage."

"Yes, an unfortunate side effect," agreed Moreau. "But no solution is perfect."

"Moreau, that's madness. Even if it works, do you have any idea what kind of chaos you'll unleash? He'll be completely out of control."

"I'm counting on it. More chaos is exactly what this world needs. Because chaos brings change, and change brings liberation."

"I can't let you do that," came Kemp's voice from over by my father.

"Can't you?" asked Moreau. He reached over to flip the switch, but then his bat ear swiveled to the side. In one smooth motion he turned and stabbed his clawed hand into something next to him.

"You are good at directing your voice," said Moreau. "But not good enough to fool *my* ears."

There was a gasp, and Moreau's arm shook as Kemp struggled to free himself.

"Don't worry, I will keep my word and cure Millicent. Now, when I inform her you're dead, would you prefer that I tell her about how you turned on me in the end, or shall I leave that part out?"

There was a gurgling sound, then Moreau's arm grew still.

"I suppose I should tell the whole story." Moreau released his grip and there was a wet thud as Kemp's form dropped to the ground. For some reason I expected to finally see him. But even in death he remained invisible.

"Now, where was I before that sudden but inevitable betrayal?" asked Moreau. "Ah, yes, the Sphinx. I suspect he'll be quite mad." He nodded toward my father. "And rather hungry."

He flipped a switch on the generator. The Sphinx started to convulse, making the entire room shake.

"No . . ." I hissed, and tried to reach for him. He glanced over with a look of annoyance and backhanded me so hard I fell backward onto the ground. My empty eye socket throbbed as I struggled to rise, but couldn't.

The Sphinx snapped his head around, pulling the wires off. He took in his surroundings, but there wasn't any wisdom in his eyes that I could see—just a mindless rage. He looked down and saw my father on the floor in front of him, struggling weakly. The Sphinx swatted him, his claws hooking into my father's legs.

Then he hooked the claws of his other paw into his neck and stretched him out long. He leaned down, opened a human mouth that was full of lion teeth, and bit into his stomach. I closed my one good eye, but I couldn't shut out my father's screams or the sound of ripping flesh and crunching bone.

When it finally stopped, I opened my eye just as the Sphinx spread his gigantic wings and smashed through the skylight and up into the air. On the ground, there was nothing left of my father except a bloodstain and a few bits of ragged bone and cloth. Emptiness. That was all I could think of. My heart, the world. Whatever. There was now a vacuum where one of the greatest monsters who ever lived had once been. I couldn't understand why all of reality didn't simply cave in on itself.

"Now that's taken care of," said Moreau. "We just have to do a little tidying up."

"Moreau!" The voice sounded like Liel. "What the hell!"

"Ah, Liel," said Moreau, turning toward the doorway. "Back so soon, I see."

"Damn it, Moreau, you promised you wouldn't kill Boy!"

"He's not dead, my dear," said Moreau.

Liel's face appeared in front of me, her diamond eyes glinting. She frowned savagely, showing her lower fangs. "Jesus, what the fuck, Moreau. What happened here?"

"None of your concern, now run along. Don't you have another power station to dismantle?"

"No, I'm *making* this my concern." Liel turned her head. "And don't you even think about killing those two, either, or I will fucking gut you."

"Well, if you're going to be like that about it," said Moreau, "I'm afraid your services will have to be terminated. And so will you." He snapped his fingers and the remaining bird people launched into the air and began to circle in.

"Big mistake, old man." Liel let out a strange, high-pitched roar. I'd only heard that sound once before, when her mother had called her den to action. A pack of trowe suddenly burst into the room and launched themselves at the bird people.

"There goes your freak show," said Liel. "Now it's your turn."

An explosion came from outside. Liel and Moreau both glanced toward the doorway.

"I think not," said Moreau, taking a step back.

"What was that?" asked Liel.

"Humans," said Moreau. "Either you were followed, or the Sphinx's ascension has brought them back. It hardly matters. We'll have to take a rain check on your termination, my dear. Farewell." He barreled his way through the fighting trowe and bird people, made it through the doors, and disappeared.

The sound of gunfire echoed from the hallway.

Liel looked around, her eyes wide with panic. "Shit, shit shit shit," she muttered.

"Bakru," I wheezed.

Her head snapped down to me. "What?"

"Bakru is still alive."

"How?"

"My father . . . saved her."

"Where is your father now?"

I looked at the bloodstain in the middle of the room. Again I felt that terrible emptiness, that chasm of the void calling me to fall into it.

"No," said Liel. "NO!"

More gunfire came from outside, followed by another explosion. It sounded like they were getting closer.

"Fucking humans!" said Liel. "What do I *do*?"

I heard a sound back at the far end of the room. I turned and saw a hatch pop up out of the floor that had been covered by the Sphinx before. A small head appeared in the opening. It had a leather cap and a long, gray beard. He motioned urgently to us.

"It's the dwarf," I said, my own voice sounding oddly calm, almost dreamy.

"A dwarf?" asked Liel. "Who's side is he on?"

"Ours," I said. "He wants us to follow him. Down that hatch."

"All right. I got y—fuck! Where are your arm and leg?!"

"Gone," I said.

"God damn it!" She looked up. "Okay, listen up, people. Stop playing with the birds. I need Puran and Slair to get Claire." She turned back to me. "Do we need the human?"

"We need the human," I said.

She sighed. "And Buthran, get that human. Follow me. We're getting the hell out of here."

She leaned over to pick me up.

"Wait!" I said. "Put the phone pieces in my pocket. We might be able to save Vi."

"If you say so." She shoved them into my pants pockets, then hoisted me. As my head moved around, I saw the other trowe pick up Claire and Holmes. Then we all hustled over to the hatch. It looked like about a ten-foot drop to a hard-packed dirt floor that led off down a dark passage.

"I hope this dwarf knows where he's taking us," said Liel. "This place is full of tunnels. I've been using some of them, but I didn't know about this one."

Gunfire was right at the doorway. Bullets zinged past, hitting the stone wall behind us. Tear gas canisters rolled into the room.

"Go go go!" shouted Liel.

The trowe began dropping down into the hole. Once all her people were in, Liel jumped in with me on her back. We landed hard and she stumbled. "God, even missing limbs you're heavy," she muttered. She put me down on hard, dry earth, then reached up and slammed the lid of the hatch down just as an explosion went off.

Then the dwarf's small face appeared directly in front of me.

"I told you I would come," he said in his heavy German accent. "When your need was most dire."

Liel picked me up again. We followed the dwarf down a long tunnel, the sounds of gunfire fading in the distance.

"Where does this let us out?" asked Liel.

"Not far enough away," said the dwarf. "But we have friends waiting for us."

"What friends?" asked Liel.

But the dwarf only hurried down the passage faster until he reached a dead end.

"Here!" He pointed to a ladder bolted into the rock that led up to another hatch.

Liel slung me over her shoulder and climbed up the ladder. She pushed the hatch open and a sudden gust of fresh air hit my face. The rest of the trowe came next, and finally the dwarf.

"Okay," said Liel, dropping down on the ground, panting hard. "Now we juuuuu—oh, shit!"

A squad of soldiers had peeled off the force storming The Commune and headed toward us.

"What now, shorty?!" she screamed at the dwarf.

"Friends," he said.

A lone figure stood up from where she had lain on the ground, hidden by the brush. She had long, black hair, and tears of blood leaked from her eyes.

"La Llorona," I whispered.

She screamed at the soldiers and they began falling in waves before her.

Then Rhoecus the centaur rode up next to us. At his side was La Perricholi, still in wolf form.

"Quickly!" shouted Rhoecus. "Put the injured on my back."

The trowe laid Claire, Holmes, and me horizontally across his broad horse back so that our arms and legs dangled on either side.

"Follow me!" he shouted, and took off at a gallop. It was difficult to see, bouncing up and down on his back, but I caught glimpses of the trowe, with La Perricholi bounding along beside them. For a moment, I was worried we'd left the dwarf behind. But then I saw Knossos the gryphon swoop down and pick him up. La Llorona continued to hold back the wave of soldiers coming toward us.

"There!" Rhoecus shouted, pointing at the helicopter that had brought us here.

"Are you kidding me?" snarled Liel. "That's FBI!"

"No!" said the dwarf. "Friends!"

In the cockpit were Javier and Bakru.

"Oh, God, she *is* alive!"

"Told ya," I said weakly.

"Look," she shouted. "The cargo bay door is opening. Let's go!"

We sprinted the rest of the way and fell inside in an exhausted heap.

"What . . . about . . . La Llorona?" I said.

"She will depart according to her own wishes," said the dwarf gravely.

Through the open cargo bay, I could see her still standing before the coming waves of soldiers. As the bay door began to close, she raised one blood-red hand in farewell, then turned back to the soldiers, just as a bullet pierced her chest.

Then the bay doors closed. Or maybe it was just my eyes. My eye. The helicopter began to rise. Or fall. It felt like I was falling. And then there was only darkness.

# PART 5

## World's End

"*Our* battle is with cruelties and frustrations, stupid, heavy and hateful things from which we shall escape at last, less like victors conquering a world than like sleepers awaking from a nightmare in the dawn . . . A time will come when men will sit with history before them or with some old newspaper before them and ask incredulously, 'Was there ever such a world?'"

—FROM *THE OPEN CONSPIRACY*
by H. G. Wells

# The Monster Who Challenged the World

++++++++

THE NEXT FEW hours came in disconnected bursts that flashed out of the darkness. Claire wiping my face with a wet cloth. Liel and Bakru embracing. La Perricholi back in human form, shaking and exhausted as Holmes covered her with a blanket. Other faces began to appear. My mother crying as she held me. Ruthven's face etched with lines of fury. I lost all sense of time and place and I started to wonder if I'd died.

Then the dwarf's face appeared right up close to mine. He touched my forehead with one tiny hand.

"I have done all I can," he said. "Now it is *your* time."

And I woke up. For a moment, it all came crashing down on me, memories of being attacked by the bird people, Vi's phone getting crushed, Kemp's death, La Llorona getting gunned down, and that endless sound of my father screaming while being slowly eaten alive. I felt that same dark and yawning chasm again, the void trying to pull me down. I almost gave in and let myself slide back into unconsciousness.

*No*, I thought. He wouldn't have wanted me to give up. To give in. He would have wanted me to do something. To stop Moreau. And that was exactly what I planned to do.

I slowly sat up and looked around the dim, enclosed space.

"Boy!" My mother knelt down next to me, her eyes red and puffy, smudges of dirt on her perfect china-doll face.

"How long have I been out?" I asked.

"A day." She brushed my hair back, like that would actually have any impact on my looks.

We were alone in a small cave-like room. There were several passageways that led off into darkness. In the distance, I could hear hushed voices.

"Where are we?"

"Under the mountains. The dwarf led us here. We are safe."

"Nowhere is safe," I said.

"Oh, my Boy . . ." Her hand stroked the side of my face where my eye was missing. "I will fix you. I promise. I just need materials."

I nodded as I stared down at my stump of an arm that ended at the elbow. Then I looked up into her eyes. "Did you hear? About Dad?"

"That I cannot fix." A tear coursed down her expressionless face.

"Mom," I said, and pulled her in close with my one good arm.

We sat there for a long time like that. Finally, she lifted her head and looked at me.

"Do you know he asked me to marry him for nearly a hundred years before I said yes?"

"Why didn't you want to marry him?"

"He was a self-absorbed, violent brute. Even after Victor was dead, he was so filled with rage and self-loathing, I could not stand to be near him."

"So why did you finally marry him?"

"He went up into the Arctic alone. When he came back, he was different. I don't know how, but he found peace there."

We sat there in the dim lighting for a moment.

"A hundred years. And he never gave up," I said. "He must have really loved you."

"Yes." She smoothed the front of her dress and slowly stood up. "I promised Claire I would tell her when you woke up." She looked down at me. "She has been by your side nearly the whole time you have been unconscious. This is a good woman."

"I know."

"Don't forget that."

"I won't."

She turned and walked into the dark passage.

I shifted myself around, inspecting the damage. Other than the missing limbs and eye, I was in surprisingly good shape.

"Well, *finally,*" said Claire as she walked into the room.

"I needed some beauty rest," I said. "Did it work?"

"Com'ere, you." She dropped down next to me and pulled me in for a kiss. Then she pressed her forehead against mine. Her dark eyes glistened and her jaw muscles clenched as she stared into my eye.

Her voice was soft, near breaking as she said, "I was really worried about you."

"Yeah," I said. "I was worried about *both* of us. The bird people slashed you up pretty bad. But you look fine now."

"That dwarf of yours has all sorts of little tricks. Once the Dragon Lady got here, he mixed up some potion with her blood and it healed us all right up. Well, except it couldn't grow back limbs and the like."

"Mom can take care of that," I said. "She just needs some parts."

"Might be some spare trowe parts she could use," muttered Claire.

"Now, now," I said.

"She helped him, Boy. She's a bloody traitor."

"She also saved our lives."

Claire looked like she was about to fire off another retort, but then she just let it all out in a sigh.

"Yeah. Okay."

She moved behind me, stretching her legs out on either side of me. Then she wrapped her arms around my chest, and let her head drop onto my shoulder.

"I'm so tired," she said.

"I'm not."

"That's because you've been sleeping this whole time while I've been all nurturing, at your bedside, wiping your brow and shite."

"You wiped my brow?"

"Too bloody right, I did."

"Thanks."

"You're welcome."

We sat there in silence for a moment. Then, gradually, I started to become aware of a feeling in the air, like right before a storm.

"Claire? Do you . . . feel that?"

"Yeah. What the hell is it?"

"No idea."

The feeling got more intense, as if the air pressure in the room was changing. Then a crack formed in the cave wall and began to slowly widen.

"That looks bad," said Claire. She stood and moved in front of me, her fists balled up.

Laurellen's head popped through the crack.

"Oh, good," he said calmly. Then he turned his head and said behind him, "This is the place. Sorry about that last one. It's been a while." He turned back to us. "Hello, Claire dear. Boy, you look frightful. I'd offer you some glamour but I'm afraid I've used the last of it for this."

He stepped out of the crack, followed by Maria and Henri, each holding one of his hands. As soon as they stepped through, the crack sealed shut, like it had never been there.

"Let's never travel that way again," said Maria. She leaned against the far wall and took a slow breath, her face pale.

"That was *amazing*!" said Henri, somehow completely recovered from the beating Stephen had given him. "In the succession of incredible things I have seen in the past month, I think this actually was the most astonishing." He looked at me with eyes brighter than I'd ever seen. "An *alternate reality*, Boy! I cannot . . ." He shook his head. "Words fail me!"

"Whoa, slow down there," said Claire. "Where the hell did you just come from?"

"I knew time was short," said Laurellen. "So I took us through the faerie realm. It's a bit dreary these days, now that there are so few faeries. But still, I suppose it's good to pop in and see how the old place is doing."

"Boy," said Maria. She seemed to have recovered a little. She came over, knelt down beside me, and took my hand. "I am so sorry about your father. I never had the chance to meet him, but Mozart spoke of him with the utmost respect."

"Thank you," I said.

"Laurellen," said Claire, "why didn't you ever tell us you could bloody teleport?"

"It's not teleportation, actually. Time is different in the faerie realm. It's only been a few hours out here, but in there we've been traveling for weeks. That's why Henri appears to have miraculously healed. He just spent most of his recovery in the faerie realm." He frowned. "I'm *fairly* certain that won't have any long-term effects."

"But how did you guys even know what happened or where to find us?"

"Vi told us, of course," said Henri.

"Vi," I said, patting my pocket. "She's okay?"

"Your mum was able to salvage the drive from that phone and upload her into a different one," said Claire. "Since then she's been jumping all over the place, from Ruthven's phone to Holmes's to wherever else she can pop in to relay messages. We haven't been sure if Moreau can track our regular communications, so using her as the messenger seemed the most secure way to do it."

"So, Boy," said Henri, his face suddenly serious. "We are going to get Moreau, right?"

"Of course," I said.

"How?" asked Claire.

"Do we still have that helicopter?"

"Yeah, it's just outside the cave. The dwarf has it camouflaged somehow. Why?"

"One of my daring plans is starting to form."

She rolled her eyes. "If it's anything like the last plan, I think the word you're looking for is *suicidal*."

▬▬▬

CLAIRE HELPED ME hop down a passageway that opened up into a cavern big enough to fit everyone: my mother, Ruthven, the surviving dryads and trowe, La Perricholi, and Holmes. The Dragon Lady was also there with Rhoecus, Knossos, and Javier. There was no sign of the dwarf, but that didn't surprise me. What did surprise me was that standing next to Holmes was General Montgomery.

Maria went immediately to embrace La Perricholi. "I'm so sorry, my child."

"There is nothing to be sorry about, Mother," said La Perricholi, stroking her long, black-and-gray-streaked hair. "I understand him more than ever now. I feel closer to him than I thought was possible. For that, I am willing to suffer the rest."

Maria nodded and kissed her forehead, tears in her eyes.

Ruthven raise an eyebrow at Laurellen. "How on earth did you get here so fast?"

"Faerie realm," said Laurellen.

"How is it now?"

Laurellen shrugged, but there was a flash of pain beneath his usually smug expression. "Much the same. Perhaps a bit worse." Then he smiled again. "Henri enjoyed it, though."

"Yes . . ." Ruthven frowned slightly as he watched the dryads approach Henri. They were looking at him in a way I'd never seen them look at anyone before.

"Eh, hello, ladies," said Henri, flashing a nervous smile. "You haven't been hitting the wine, I hope."

"Something is different about you. . . ." said Meadow, placing her hand on his chest.

Iris leaned in to him so closely that her nose pressed against his cheek. She inhaled deeply.

"Yes," she said. "He smells of old earth."

Sequoia ran her fingers through Henri's hair. "I always liked him, anyway."

"Um . . . help?" Henri looked over at us, his eyes wide.

"I suspect they're just picking up some residual presence from your stay in the faerie realm," said Laurellen. "I'm sure they're perfectly safe."

"Are you really sure?" I asked quietly.

"Not at all."

"Let's keep an eye on that, then, okay?"

"Absolutely."

I turned to Montgomery. "I didn't expect to see you here, General."

"Holmes brought me." He nodded his head toward her. "I, uh . . ." He looked off into a dark corner of a room, his expression uncomfortable. But then he turned back to look at me. "I asked her to. Because I screwed up. If I'd listened to you, if I'd *trusted* you and Holmes, I might have been able to prevent what happened in there. So I'm here to do whatever I can to help make things right."

"Good," I said. Then I turned to Holmes. "How is it out there?"

She shook her head. "It's really bad. You'll see for yourself soon enough. Most of those feral monsters are still running amok. And the Sphinx is destroying anything and anyone he comes across, on the ground or in the air. Moreau still occupies Phoenix, but he's also gained control of Albuquerque and Denver. I know he did not have this many troops when he hit Phoenix. I can't figure out how he keeps expanding his numbers like this. It's almost as if . . ." She paused for a moment, then shook her head. "Regardless, the entire middle of the country is more or less a war zone. Now he's trying to convince monster enclaves in other countries to join in and rise against their own governments. There have been incidents in Scotland, France, Germany, Romania, China, Russia, and Australia."

"If we don't put Moreau down soon," said Montgomery, "those incidents will turn into full-scale rebellion."

I turned to Ruthven. "So? What's the plan?"

"Plan?" he asked, his red eyes flickering to me, and then away.

"Yeah. I mean, I have some ideas, but I was wondering what you guys have come up with."

"We have had several discussions," he said.

"And?"

Ruthven said nothing. And for the first time I could remember, he couldn't look me in the eye.

"The discussions," said La Perricholi, "have been about whether we should do anything at all."

"What do you mean?"

"*Some people*," said Liel, "think we should just stay down here until it all blows over. Let Moreau and the humans fight it out."

"It's what they want," said Ruthven, his tone almost defensive. "It's what they *all* want. To destroy each other. Man versus monster. Survival of the fittest. That is natural. That is the way of the world."

"You're wrong," I said. "That isn't the world. It's what we've tried to turn it into. We've mapped it, we've studied it, and we think we *know* it. But we don't. There are awesome things out there, and terrible things, and things that are beyond any words we could use to describe them. This world can still surprise us. If we just challenge it, it will evolve."

"Into what?" asked my mother.

I looked at them all. Such a bizarre and amazing group of people. Monster or human or somewhere in between, they were all people.

"My father believed that it is possible for monsters and humans to live together. He died for that belief. And he was right. Look, we're doing it right here. Now we have to prove that it's possible not just for our little group, but for everyone."

"But *how?*" asked the Dragon Lady.

"If Moreau wins, he'll kill all the humans, right? And if the humans win, they'll kill all the monsters. Or maybe they'll destroy each other. Regardless, it's nothing but the same old cycle of fear and hatred. But what happens if *we* win? Our little group of monsters and humans could show the world that the way to come out on top is to work together. What do you say?"

"You know you can count on me, cousin," said Henri.

"Likewise, of course," said Claire.

"And me," said La Perricholi.

Every phone in the room went off simultaneously.

"I'd say that's a yes from Vi," said Henri.

"I know I screwed up, siding with Moreau," said Liel. "I was just . . ." She glanced over at Bakru, then looked away, her face pinched with shame.

Bakru took her hand and smiled encouragingly.

Liel nodded and took a deep breath. Then she turned to me, and her diamond eyes were wet with tears. "I'm sorry. More sorry that I can possibly say. The trowe are with you."

"Thank you," I said. Then I looked at the rest of them. "It's going to be dangerous. Obviously. I understand if you want to stay down here. But I can't let my father's death have been for nothing."

I noticed my mother staring hard at Ruthven. He noticed it, too. Finally, he sighed.

"For the sake of your father's memory, I cannot refuse. So tell me, what is your plan?"

"Yeah," said Holmes. "Not to point out the obvious, but you're missing some parts."

"I just need new parts," I said. "Better parts."

"Where are you going to find these better parts?" asked Liel.

"Mom, Henri, Vi, and I will take care of that," I said. "What we need to worry about right now is how we're going to get to Moreau."

"He's holed up in Denver with about a thousand human hostages and an army of beast people," said Holmes.

"But before we can even get to Denver," said Ruthven, "we'll need to deal with the Sphinx."

I turned to the Dragon Lady. "Right before you bit Stephen's head off, you told him that no matter how big a fish he was, there was always someone bigger. Is that true of the Sphinx, too? Is there someone bigger?"

The Dragon Lady gazed down at me for a moment with her glowing, ageless eyes. "There are three such creatures. They have slumbered far beneath the surface of the earth for thousands of years. Pray that you never see them. Moreau may be a danger to a race of people, but to awaken the Hecatoncheires would be to endanger all life on this planet."

"Right, that's no help, then," said Claire.

"But *I* will face the Sphinx," said the Dragon Lady. "I cannot say it is likely that I will be victorious. But I will attempt to end his mindless rampage and lay him down to permanent rest. And if I fail, I should at least be able to buy you the time you need to get past him."

"I will help you," said Knossos.

"And I will personally lead a squad of helicopters in to assist you, as well," said Montgomery.

"Thanks, all three of you," I said. "So while Montgomery, Knossos, and the Dragon Lady are keeping the Sphinx busy, the rest of us will continue on to Moreau."

"What's to stop him from killing the hostages the moment we attack?" asked Holmes.

"Has anyone else noticed a pattern in the way Moreau operates?" I asked. "He didn't deploy his armies until he'd unveiled them to us. He's broadcast to the entire world to make sure everyone knows who he is and what he's fighting for and just how clever he can be. He held off waking the Sphinx specifically because he wanted us to be there to see it."

"He needs an audience," said Holmes.

"He won't kill the hostages until there are people to witness it," I said. "Otherwise, what's the point?"

"He could just broadcast like he did before," said La Perricholi. "Show the whole world that we're calling his bluff, and then he kills the hostages."

"What if he can't?" I asked. "Who's got a phone?"

Holmes held hers up.

"Vi," I said. "Can you block all incoming and outgoing transmissions in Denver? Bring down a total media blackout?"

"You bet!" Holmes's phone said.

"That still leaves a mass of beast people to get through," said Ruthven. "Individually, we are more than a match for them. But as you and Claire discovered, their strength in numbers is what makes them dangerous."

Then I turned to the dryads. "Ladies. Uh, I know we haven't had the best relationship. And I hate to ask this of you."

"What do you need, Boy?" asked Meadow.

"The maenads."

"Uh, Boy . . ." said Claire.

"Seriously?" asked Liel.

"Moreau will never expect it," I said.

"You can't control them," said Ruthven. "They are a maelstrom of chaotic fury. They wouldn't distinguish between friend and foe."

"There might be one person whom the maenads would listen to," Meadow said. She turned to Iris and Sequoia. They looked at each other for a moment and nodded. Then they all turned to Henri.

"Give him to us," said Meadow. "And we will do what you ask."

"Wait, what?" said Henri. "*Give?* Boy, what are they talking about?"

"I really don't know," I said.

"We won't hurt him," said Iris, walking over to him. She pressed her hand against his stomach.

"And we won't keep him all the time," said Sequoia. "We will only require him in the spring. The rest of the year he is free to come or go as he chooses."

Laurellen cleared his throat. "I think they want him for . . . pollination purposes."

"Oh," I said.

"Can I *do* that?" asked Henri.

Laurellen shrugged. "They seem to think so."

"Humans can mate with dryads," said Meadow. "Although the offspring will not be half human. There will only be more dryads."

"We are the last three," said Iris. "In order for our kind to survive, we must have greater numbers."

"Well, Henri?" I asked. "It's your call."

"No pressure or anything," said Claire, smirking.

"I honestly don't know whether to be honored or horrified," said Henri.

"Probably a bit of both," said Laurellen.

"What the hell," said Henri. "Ladies, I'm yours."

Meadow smiled. "Thank you." Then she turned to me. "Once we have drunk the wine, he will be able to keep us pointed in more or less the right direction."

"All right," I said. "With that extra muscle, I think all of you will be more than a match for the beast people. That just leaves me to handle Moreau."

"Moreau is clearly a formidable opponent," said Ruthven. "If your father couldn't defeat him, how do *you* plan to do so?"

"Like I said, better parts. Mom? Henri? Vi? We've got work to do."

# The Revenge of Robot Junior

┼┼┼┼┼┼┼

WHEN I LOOKED out of the helicopter window, the landscape below seemed more like some war-torn third-world country than the middle of America. We passed over grasslands churned up into piles of mud, wooded areas where the trees had been torn out by the roots, small towns that were now nothing more than smoking rubble. Cars and trucks lay abandoned, often crushed. I closed my regular eye and squinted, which engaged the zoom in my bionic eye. I scanned the inside of the vehicles for survivors but there was no one left alive.

"How's the eye working?" Henri shouted over the stutter of the helicopter blades.

"Great," I said.

"How about the arm and leg?" my mother asked.

I held up the robotic arm and flexed my fingers.

"I still can't get a delicate grip," I said. "I'm afraid I'm going to crush anything I try to pick up."

"That will get better with practice," she said.

Both my arm and leg had been constructed from parts of the helicopter. We had stripped it of everything that wasn't essential to flight. The rest of the material had come from phones and laptops.

"You should probably have Vi run one more full diagnostic before we land," said Henri.

"Probably right," I said. "Vi, can you run a systems check?"

"Yes, Boy!" her voice rang inside my head.

"Ouch," I said. "You do realize that you're vibrating my entire skull at that volume level."

"Sorry." Her avatar appeared as an overlay on my bionic eye, looking sheepish.

"It's okay. We're both still getting used to this," I said.

It was a little weird to have Vi basically living in my head. But some of the functionality, like the guidance and targeting systems, just didn't have a direct neurological parallel. Having her on board was key to getting those more complex operations to work effectively. She was like JARVIS to my Tony Stark.

I turned back to the window and looked out over the land, but it was just more of the same. I wondered how much of it had been done by the Sphinx. They hadn't managed to capture any of the other creatures from The Commune, so some of it could have been them, too.

"Vi, pull up some international news feeds," I said. "I want to see what else is going on."

A couple of windows popped up in my eye. In Cairo, a frightened old mummy was begging local monsters not to antagonize the government. In Berlin, a small group of gnomes were being attacked by a gang of humans. In Beijing, monsters were simply disappearing in the middle of the night. The whole world was watching what was happening to America and nobody wanted to be next. And maybe they were right to be frightened. If Moreau had his way, we'd *all* burn.

"Boy."

I turned to Claire. She looked worried.

"I know this has to look kind of creepy," I said, touching my bionic eye.

"It's not that," she said. "I can feel the anger rolling off you."

"Claire. He has killed so many people. My father, Mozart, even Kemp didn't deserve that. And who knows how many humans."

"You're right," she said, putting her hand on my shoulder. "I get it. You *know* I do, right?"

I nodded.

"Just promise me that, when we get out there, you'll remember what we talked about. Don't become like them. Don't give up your integrity."

"I'm going to do whatever it takes to end this," I said.

She reached up and touched her cool fingertips on my cheek. Then she bit her lip and nodded.

"I think you look incredibly formidable," said La Perricholi from where she sat cleaning her guns. "I would not want to face you in combat."

"Thanks," I said.

"What was it Shaun and those guys used to call you when we were kids?" asked Liel. "Robot Junior?"

"Yeah," I said, looking down at my metal hand.

"They'd be eating those words if they saw you now. Not to mention shitting their pants in terror."

"It's quite impressive," said Ruthven.

"*Madame la Mariée*'s construction of the arm and leg was masterful," said Henri.

"You did a good job on the eye, Henri," said my mother.

"You really think so?" he asked.

"Yes," she said.

"Madame, I . . ." He hesitated. "I know you hate me and my family, and with good reason. I only hope—"

"No." She put her long-fingered hand over his mouth. "No. I am sorry I treated you so poorly. It all seems so small to me now. So . . . *trivial* is the word. We . . ." Her smooth, unmoving face vibrated with tension as she put her hands on his shoulders. "We are family. Okay? Okay." Then she pulled him into a rough embrace.

"Boy." Vi sounded in my ear. "Be careful. We didn't have time to properly insulate all your wiring. Too much moisture could short something out."

"Yeah, sorry," I said, wiping my eye.

---

HENRI AND THE dryads retreated to a corner of the helicopter with a case of wine while the rest of us quietly prepared ourselves. It was about ten minutes later that Vi sounded in my head again.

"Boy, they've spotted the Sphinx. You should be able to see him from the cockpit."

I nudged Claire. "You want to see the Dragon Lady take on the Sphinx?"

"Do you even need to ask?" she said.

We made our way up to the cockpit where Holmes was piloting.

"Where is he?" I asked.

"Still on the ground," she said, pointing.

We were flying over the mountains now. He was still a mile or more ahead of us, crouched low in a valley, his head rising just above the peaks. I couldn't quite make out what he was doing, so I zoomed in a little. He was snarling at something.

"I think he's about to attack a mountaintop," I said.

"Moreau really did fry his brain," said Claire

"Tragic," said Maria from the copilot seat. "To think how much knowledge has been lost. And that one of the world's most magnificent creations should be brought to such an ignoble end."

"Let's just hope it doesn't become *our* ignoble end, too," said Holmes. "Looks like he's spotted us."

Sure enough, his head was craned up toward us. Our massive cargo helicopter was hard to miss, especially with Montgomery's entire squad of combat choppers escorting us. The Sphinx's lips peeled back to show his massive lion teeth as he unfurled his wings and launched himself into the air.

"He's moving really fast," I said.

"Approximately five hundred miles per hour," said Vi.

"I hope that dragon of yours comes through," said Holmes.

"Of course she will," I said. Although no one had seen her since we'd departed from the cave entrance.

We watched as the Sphinx grew closer and closer. He pumped his massive wings, his wild eyes focused on us.

"Getting really close," said Claire.

"Yeah," said Holmes.

The Sphinx gnashed his teeth and stretched out his lion body, his front paws extended so that the claws appeared.

Then a blast of fire shot up from the mountains, hitting him full in the stomach. I could see now that the Dragon Lady had been shadowing us from below this whole time, weaving between the mountaintops, just out of view. Now she launched herself up into the sky. The Sphinx roared with pain, pounding his belly with his paws to put out the burning fur.

The Dragon Lady blew past him, clipping one of his wings and tearing out a sizable chunk of feathers. She circled around to make a pass at the other wing, but right before she hit, he spun himself and nailed her with one gigantic paw right in the face. Blood sprayed as the Dragon Lady flipped backward.

The Sphinx went in for the kill, but Knossos streaked past, slicing his face with razor talons. The Sphinx roared so loud the helicopter shook. It looked like Knossos had managed to get out of range, but then the Sphinx whipped his long lion tail around and the sheer size of it was enough to send the gryphon spinning.

The Sphinx turned back toward the Dragon Lady, but the back of his head bloomed with explosions as Montgomery's choppers advanced on him with short-range missiles. He turned and swatted at them, hooking one chopper by its landing skids and smashing it into the one next to it. By then the Dragon Lady had latched on to his back with her claws, right between his shoulder blades. He spun around and around, trying to reach her as she coiled herself around his neck and bit into his spine. Blood fell like rain over the mountains as the helicopters continued to hammer him with machine-gun fire. His roars began to sound more like animal howls of pain as he tried desperately to remove the Dragon Lady from his neck.

They spiraled lower and lower until at last they crashed into the mountains below. The earth visibly shook and the trees shuddered as they wrestled on the ground. The Sphinx tried to scrape the Dragon Lady off him with the sides of mountains, but she suddenly released him and shot up into the sky. A moment later the helicopters dropped a payload of napalm on top of him.

His shrieks of pain echoed through the valley as the wisest and most majestic creature on earth was burned alive.

Moreau had turned him into a savage beast that had killed my father. And then he made us destroy him. I could almost hear him laughing about it now. It was, all part of his sick, twisted machinations. But that would all stop today.

"We're past them," said Holmes tersely. "We have to keep moving."

"I know," I said. "What's our ETA?"

"Five minutes," she said.

"Good. I hope the maenads are about ready."

<hr />

THE MAENADS WERE more than ready. After demolishing the case of wine, they'd shredded their own clothes and it looked like they'd poured wine over their heads so that their hair was in sticky clumps.

"Ladies, please," Henri said, lurching to one side to block Meadow from diving at Bakru. "Just a few more minutes!"

"Now!" hissed Iris.

"Tired of waiting!" snarled Sequoia.

"Boy?" said Henri. "I don't know how much longer I can keep them back."

"I'll talk to Holmes," I said, and headed back to the cockpit.

"The maenads are about to blow," I said to Holmes. "How soon can we land in an area with lots of beast people for them to attack?"

"We can set down right now if you want," she said, "but that'll mean farther for us to go on foot."

"All right. Let's hold off a bit longer, but maybe get closer to the ground so we can land fast if they completely lose it."

"Okay, I'm dropping altitude and—wait, we've got incoming."

"Who?" I asked, looking out the windows.

"You've got to be kidding me," she said. "Are those . . ."

In front of us was a flock of brown-and-tan capuchin monkeys with broad, feathered wings.

"Of *course* Moreau would make winged monkeys," I said. "But what can they do? They don't even look armed."

Then they started to dive-bomb us.

"They can do that, for one thing," said Holmes as she hiked the stick to dodge the monkeys. "I am *not* trained for kamikaze flying monkeys."

She managed to avoid them on their first pass, but then they came up underneath and flew directly into the rotor blades. Suddenly, there were bloody chunks of winged monkeys everywhere, spattering the windshield, making it impossible to see. One or two monkeys wouldn't have been a problem but now they all converged on the rotors. The engine screamed under the strain and every gauge on the dashboard suddenly lit up red.

"We're screwed," said Holmes. "Tell everyone to prepare for a crash landing."

I ran back to the cargo area but everyone was already strapping into the seats that lined the sides. Except the maenads, who pressed their faces hungrily against the windows drenched in winged-monkey blood.

"See, ladies?" Henri was saying as he clung to a handlebar next to them. "I told you it would be worth the wait. And winged-monkey guts are just the appetizer."

I strapped in next to Claire just in time. A moment later, my stomach lurched as the helicopter dropped out of the sky. For a moment, I almost felt weightless, like if I hadn't been strapped in I would have floated away. But then we slammed into the ground so hard my head snapped back into the padded backing of the seat. We bounced a few times as we skidded along but then finally came to a stop.

"Do it again!" yelled Meadow.

The helicopter started to rock back and forth. I looked out the window. Beast people were swarming over the helicopter, trying to tip it over.

"Everybody ready?" I asked as we all unstrapped ourselves.

"As we'll ever be," said Ruthven.

"Bring it," said Liel, flexing her clawed hands, her trowe den at her back.

The bay door slowly began to drop open.

"Ladies, I think that's your cue," said Henri.

The three maenads shot through the still-opening door. A moment later the air was filled with the sounds of pain and fear.

"Good luck," said Claire, and gave me quick kiss.

We moved out of the helicopter in a tight group. We'd crashed in the middle of a large intersection in downtown Denver. Beast people were coming at us from all directions. Henri was herding the maenads down the street in the general direction of where Moreau held the hostages. We followed the path of carnage that they cut through the beast people.

"Oh, god," Claire said under her breath.

The ground was strewn with bodies, some limbless, some headless, some still alive and struggling weakly to escape. The maenads laughed and capered around as they went from one victim to the next, their naked bodies smeared with blood.

There was a moment when I thought, *I did this*. The empty

chasm was suddenly there before me again, trying to swallow me up.

"Boy! Are you hurt?" It was La Perricholi next to me.

I shook my head, pushing all those feelings of grief aside. We had to get to Moreau. This had to end.

We kept moving forward. Even with the maenads taking the lead, there were still huge clusters of beast people coming at us. Rhoecus and Javier barreled down the middle, trampling everyone who got in their way. Liel and the trowe darted in and out, their jewel eyes sparkling as they slashed at arms and legs with their long, curved claws. Ruthven was little more than a streak of darkness as he snaked through their ranks, leaving some unconscious, others clutching at their bleeding throats. La Perricholi and Maria ran side by side, their guns blazing, dropping almost as many beast people as the maenads. Holmes covered their rear, picking off the few who'd got past them. And my mother . . . I'd never really thought about it before, but she was just as strong as my father had been. I realized that now, as I watched her easily pick up a beast person with one hand and slam him into another one nearby, letting them both fall to the ground in an unconscious heap. Claire had continued her hand-to-hand combat training with La Perricholi, and it showed. It almost looked effortless, the way she hit them in just the right place with just the right amount of force to knock them out.

I caught all of this in little flashes here and there as I smashed my way through packs of beast people. I'd always been strong, but this was different. This was a whole new level. The world felt like paper to me, and the people in it like cotton balls that I could knock aside without really even trying.

Then I heard a shriek from above. I looked up and saw

one of those bird people that had attacked Claire and me at The Commune.

"Vi, time to try out that targeting system," I said.

"Okeydokey," she said.

I lifted my robot arm and detached my hand. I pointed the stump at one of the bird people. In my bionic eye I saw a green circle.

"It's all yours," I said.

Vi took over movement of my arm, calculating distance, velocity, and wind resistance as she made slight adjustments to the position.

"Target locked," she said.

"Fire."

A small pellet shot from the stump. As soon as it came in contact with the air, it began to expand into a glob of foam. It slammed into the bird person, sticking to him. The more he struggled with it, the more he stretched out the foam; the more air contact, the thicker and stickier it got. A moment later his wings were caught up in it and he dropped from the sky, landing on a parked car so hard the roof caved in and the windows blew out glass in all directions.

"It worked!" I said.

"You mean you weren't sure it would?" asked Vi.

"Well, we didn't have the exact ingredients for the compound that Holmes told us about, so I had to make a few substitutions."

I only had two more shots of that stuff, so I reattached my hand and went back to slowly bashing my way through the crowd of beast people.

IT SEEMED LIKE hours, but it was probably only about twenty minutes later that we got close enough to see the building where Moreau was holed up. It was a massive cathedral of gray stone that spanned an entire city block, with twin spires rising high above the other buildings.

"Of course he picked a church," I muttered as I smashed my metal fist into a creature that looked part pig, part hyena.

"Boy, there's a whole new group of them coming!" shouted Claire. "We'll hold them. You go after Moreau."

I nodded and broke away from the group. A few followed me, and I quickly took care of them. But most of the beast people hadn't even noticed as I slipped away. This group seemed much less disciplined. I wasn't complaining.

A few moments later, I was at the cathedral entrance. The door opened, and the Siren stepped out.

"Forgot about you," I muttered.

She opened her mouth and I had just enough time to take my metal hand off before she started to sing.

"Vi, take over," I said, and then I was lost in the music.

A moment later, I came out of it. The Siren lay on the ground, a blob of sticky foam covering her mouth.

"Nice shot," I said.

"The hard part was making sure her nose wasn't covered," Vi said. "I knew you wouldn't want her to suffocate."

"Thank you," I said. "Now, let's get in there and hope Moreau hasn't killed those hostages." I pushed open the doors and stepped into the cathedral.

The inside was one vast room with dark wood pews in orderly rows. The walls were lined with tall stained-glass pictures of saints, and the ceiling rose over fifty feet into the air. Moreau stood behind the altar at the far end, holding a struggling human male down with one clawed hand while he injected something into his neck. Otherwise, the church was empty.

"My, my," said Moreau. "It looks like you're finally taking your own self-improvement seriously. Excellent, bold work, if you don't mind my saying so."

"Where are the other hostages?" I said, aiming my stump at Moreau.

"Oh, they're all gone."

"You killed them all?"

"Actually, I believe it is your friends who are currently killing them."

"What?"

"I've . . . well, see for yourself." He looked down at the human, who had gone from struggling to convulsive.

"Oh no . . ." I said.

"Oh yes."

The human thrashed on the altar as his skin began to ripple and bubble, then peel away in strips, exposing bright green scales beneath. His eyes turned black and his tongue lengthened as it protruded from his open mouth. One leg grew longer and thicker and the other shriveled up and lay dangling to the side. His entire rib cage began to grow and lengthen. Then there was a sharp crack as his chest split open, exposing his ribs.

"Ah, well," said Moreau. "Sometimes that happens."

The half-snake creature tried to sit up, but wet, squiggly guts came spilling out across the altar and floor. Then it fell over in a heap and grew still.

"That latest group of beast people they're fighting . . ." I said.

"Were the hostages. Yes. I turned them into monsters and set them loose on you. I don't imagine they'll fare very well, though, considering they lack any sort of training or guidance."

"You . . ." I said. "Stay put." I shot my last sticky foam pellet at his hand, gluing it to the altar. Then I turned and ran back out of the cathedral.

From the top step I could see them all down there fighting. And from this distance, it was so obvious that this group of beast people had no idea what they were doing. They were just reacting mindlessly to the violence. Classic fight or flight.

"Stop killing!" I shouted. "PLEASE GOD, STOP KILLING!"

But they didn't even notice me. I was going to have to go down there and stop them myself. I slammed my metal hand back into place and was about to start down the steps when an incredibly strong hand grabbed my flesh arm and yanked me backward so hard my feet left the ground. I flew back through the church doors and slammed into one of the stone pillars inside. On impact, my head snapped to one side and the bionics in my eye shattered. There was a momentary screech of feedback, then the eye went black and there was silence. My link to Vi was broken.

Moreau stood over me, his ape mouth grinning. The hand I had glued to the altar was now just a ragged, bloody stump at the end of his arm. He looked down at it and shrugged. "I can always grow myself a new one later."

I struggled to my feet.

"In the meantime," he continued, "I am about to almost literally beat you with one hand tied behind my back."

He came at me so fast and strong I couldn't connect a single hit. He used his one clawed hand, his feet, his tail, and his teeth all with equal skill. The ferocity of a wild beast combined with the strategy and intellect of a human. He was a perfect fighter. I didn't stand a chance. No wonder he'd beaten my dad.

But when I thought of my dad, my body suddenly filled with

a cold rage, as hard and unmovable as the Jura Mountains he'd loved so much. The pain didn't matter anymore. I barely felt it. I pulled myself back into a more defensive position, blocking, dodging, ignoring the tempting openings that were just traps. He was losing blood. A lot of blood. I let him slowly push me back deeper into the church, all the while taking note of how his strikes were coming a little slower, the blows with less force. Finally, I saw that the scales had tipped in my favor. He swung a sloppy kick at my face, I dodged and brought my fist down on his kneecap, shattering it.

His eagle eyes went wide as he realized he'd taken too long and worn himself out. But it was too late. I caught his clawed hand and crushed his fingers in my grip. Then I swept his good leg with my robot leg, breaking his ankle in the process. He fell to the ground in a heap and lay there, panting.

"Stupid," he said between gasps. "Damned beast instincts. Stubborn beast flesh. It creeps in. Even with constant vigilance it forever creeps in." He glared up at me. "Well, I suppose you've won. If you can call it winning. And we are all the poorer for it. I was on the side of righteousness and liberty."

"You're a murderer."

"I am a surgeon, remorselessly cutting out the cancers of this flawed and broken world. I could have made it something great. But you have swooped in to return us to the status quo. I was trying to accomplish something. You accomplish nothing."

"I stopped you."

"For now. But I have contingency plans. They will imprison me just as they did before. And those monsters sympathetic to my cause will grow more ardent in their love for me. Because make no mistake, the humans will be even more cruel to us now than they ever were before. Yes, and I will escape again, and those who were too frightened to rise up this time will not hesitate next time."

"Actually, you're wrong."

"About what?"

"They won't get a chance to imprison you."

He laughed weakly. "Don't pretend that you have what it takes to kill me. Stephen told me all about you and your weak, middle-class morality."

"That was true when he met me," I said. "But there is an emptiness inside me now. You made it."

I plunged my robot arm into his chest and closed my fist around his heart. The thick gristle of vein and artery fought against me and I almost gagged.

"Please . . ." His voice was little more than a strangled breath through clenched teeth. "Please . . . mercy . . ."

But I slowly ripped out his heart.

I watched as life faded from his eyes and his heart slowly stopped beating in my fist. I stared down at him and I knew that no matter how justified it might seem, I would regret this moment for the rest of my life.

The heart fell from my hand onto the altar with a wet splat. Then I turned and walked out of the cathedral.

The fighting was over. The beast people, soldier or newly made from hostages, were all dead. People I cared about were still alive. I knew I should be happy about that.

"Boy!" yelled Claire. "Are you okay? Did you beat him?"

I beat him. But I was not okay. I would never be okay. To beat him I had allowed myself to become him. I had used people, cold and calculatingly. I had put them in grave danger. I had made them kill for me. And then when there was no one else to do it,

I had done the killing myself. And for what? Moreau was right. I had done nothing except bring the world back to its natural broken state. Or perhaps even made it worse.

"Boy?" called Claire.

I couldn't face it. So I turned. Away from her. Away from them all. Away from the world.

And I just started walking.

# The Long Way Home

++++++++

I STARED OUT of my tiny little ice cave at the blinding wall of snow that blew past. It had been like this for days. The monotony was getting to me. No night, no people, no animals. Nothing but bright white snow and the howling wind.

This had been a mistake. Possibly my dumbest ever. Probably my last.

I'd come to the Arctic to find peace, just like my father had. I wasn't sure where I was exactly. Somewhere along the northern coast of Canada. I'd walked all the way from Denver. At first it had been tricky to avoid people, but the farther I went, the easier that got. For a while it had been good to walk. It cleared my head. I calmed down a bit. I started thinking back to all the choices I'd made. I tried to look at it all with a little more objectivity, to try to figure out if I had done right or not.

But no answers came to me. And no peace, either. All I felt was loneliness. I missed Claire and Sophie, Vi, Henri, my mom, all of them, really. Yet how could I face them after the terrible things I'd done? And now I'd abandoned them to this harsh world that would treat them even worse than it had before. How could I possibly go back after all that?

It turned out, though, that it didn't matter if I wanted to go back or not. Because now it was impossible. As strong as my bionics had been initially, they were not as durable in cold weather as the rest of my body. My eye had been useless since the fight with Moreau. My arm failed next. During the long trek up, I had woken one morning to find that it was just dead weight hanging from my shoulder. Finally, sometime after that, my leg failed. At least it had locked in a fully extended position, so that I was able to pivot on it like a peg leg and continue north. But only for short distances. So I wasn't going to make it back to civilization, even if I wanted to.

Now I was holed up in this cave, more or less waiting to starve to death. I had no idea how many days I'd been here. The sun never set and the wind never stopped blowing. It almost felt as though I were stuck in time, doomed to repeat this moment of realization that what little chance of happiness I'd still had, I'd left back in Denver because I'd been too cowardly to face my own terrible deeds. Claire's voice still echoed in my mind, calling after me as I'd slowly walked away.

"Boy!"

*This must be the part of starving to death where I begin to lose my mind*, I thought. It really did sound like she was calling my name.

"Boy!"

Actually, it sounded more like Sophie than Claire. I guess my subconscious wasn't super picky about details at this late stage in the dying game.

"Boy!"

I was starting to hallucinate now. Because it really looked like a small, hooded form was trudging through the blizzard toward me.

But the figure didn't vanish. It kept walking toward me.

Gradually, I became aware that it was muttering to itself in a voice that was unmistakably Sophie's. Finally, she stepped into my little cave, lifted the goggles, and pulled down the scarf that covered her mouth. Her nose and cheeks were a bright red and her eyes sparkled as she grinned down at me.

"I thought," she said, "it was high time *I* had a turn at saving your life. Can't let Claire have all the fun. Fortunately, you continue to give us new and colorful opportunities in boyfriend saving. I do appreciate that you don't let it get monotonous."

"S-S-S-Sophie?" I said, my voice weak and rough from lack of use.

She knelt down in front of me and gently kissed my dry, cracked lips.

"Are you about done here, then, love?" she asked.

"Uh . . . yeah," I said.

"Good. 'Cause it's bloody cold. Let's go home."

"Where's home?"

"Villa Diodati, of course. They're all waiting for you."

"They who?" I asked.

She waved her hand vaguely. "You know. Everybody." Then she pulled a walkie-talkie out of her coat pocket. "Holmes, come in."

There was a *click*, then: "Holmes here. You find him yet?"

"Yeah. You'll need to bring the sled, though. He doesn't seem very mobile. And maybe a sandwich or something. He looks like a bloody supermodel."

---

THE NEXT DAY or so was a blur. I was on a sled, then a helicopter, then an airplane. I slept a lot. And when I wasn't sleeping I was eating. I noticed that Holmes and Sophie took a lot of care to not have me in any public places. I wondered if monsters were now outlawed or something. If we'd have to go back into hiding, only this time without even the benefit of most people thinking we didn't exist.

But then as our private jet began its slow decent into Geneva, Holmes said to Sophie, "We'll have to land on the public strip and take him through the airport."

"Do you think that's a good idea?" asked Sophie. She put her hand protectively on my arm. "So soon? He's barely recovered."

"We can't avoid it forever," said Holmes. "And I think a public return to his ancestral home would send a good message."

"You're getting to be as bad as Ruthven," said Sophie. "Everything's a bloody show."

Holmes shrugged. "It's a tricky time."

"What are you guys talking about?" I asked.

Sophie gave me an uncomfortable look. "A lot of things have happened while you were off finding yourself in the wilderness."

"What kind of things?" I asked.

"You'll see. Just try to smile as much as you can. And, uh, don't freak out. Okay?"

Once the plane landed, Holmes turned to me. "Can you walk?"

"I think so," I said. "But we'll have to go slow."

"That's fine. It's perfect actually."

"Perfect for what?"

"Them."

She pointed out the window. A mass of people had gathered outside the plane. Reporters, people with video cameras, people with signs that said things like **HE'S ALIVE!** and **WE ♥ BOY!** Possibly even stranger, it was a mix of humans and monsters. I saw elves, satyrs, and even an ogress.

"What is that?" I asked.

"Your fans," said Sophie.

"My *what?*"

"You might as well tell him now," said Holmes.

"No way. Let Vi tell him. She's the one who did it, after all."

"Okay, *somebody* needs to tell me something or I'm going to have a panic attack," I said.

Sophie pulled a smartphone out of her pocket. "Paging Ms. Vi," she said.

Vi's avatar appeared on the screen. "How is he?" she asked, her face frowning with concern.

"See for yourself." Sophie angled to phone to look at me.

"Hey, Boy! You look terrible!" said Vi.

"That's not what you're supposed to say, remember?" said Sophie.

"Oh, right. Hey, Boy! You *don't* look terrible!" Then more quietly, "Did that sound convincing?"

"Very," I assured her. "It's good to see you."

"So, Vi," said Sophie. "Why don't you tell Boy what happened."

"What happened?" asked Vi, a question mark appearing over her head. She was apparently getting more expressionistic.

"You know, with the broadcast."

The question mark changed to an exclamation point. "Oh, right!" Then a large single drop of sweat appeared at her temple. "So, Boy. Please don't be mad at me. But I did something without your consent."

"What did you do?"

"I broadcast you to the entire world."

"Well, yeah, there in Lima."

"No, I mean after that."

"Wait, what? How much did you broadcast?"

"Pretty much all of it."

"Everything we did from that initial broadcast until . . . when?"

"Until the cybernetic eye was smashed during your fight with Moreau. That was quite a cliff hanger"

"And *why* did you do this?"

"Well, viewer reaction online to the initial broadcast was mixed. People seemed to like you, but there were a lot of comments that you were too self-conscious. So I thought if I broadcast you without your knowledge, that would take care of it. And I was right!"

"But why did you broadcast it at all?"

"Because I love you, Boy. But there were people out there who didn't like you. Who didn't trust you. Who were even afraid of you. And it made me so sad. I knew if they just saw you as I see you, every day, trying to do the right thing, trying to take care of people, monsters *and* humans alike—I knew if they saw that, they couldn't help but love you as much as I do."

"It worked, Boy," said Holmes. "There has been a huge groundswell of public support for the monster community worldwide. Many governments, including the United States, are very nervous about a monster presence within their borders. And I think not without good reason. But because of you, they have to tread very carefully or risk severe public backlash."

"Which is why," said Sophie as she and Holmes helped me to my feet, "we need to smile pretty for the people out there, okay?"

I didn't really need Sophie's help to walk, but having her arm linked with mine made me feel a lot better about facing the people. The moment we hit the stairs down to the tarmac, there were cameras flashing and people calling out questions, trying to get my attention.

Someone jammed a microphone in my face. "Boy! Where have you been all this time?"

"Uh . . . well, after what happened in Denver . . . It was pretty awful, and I guess I needed some time alone to think."

"What finally brought you back?"

"Honestly? I missed my girlfriend."

That got a laugh from the crowd.

"No more questions!" barked Holmes as she hustled us through the crowd and into a waiting car. Once we were inside, she patted me on the back. "That was perfect. You're a natural."

"Thanks, I guess?" I really wasn't sure how I felt about being the monster poster boy. It seemed like a really precarious place to be. "But what happens when they get bored of me? I mean, that's inevitable, right?"

"Hopefully, we'll have some international laws regarding monster rights in place by that time."

"And in the meantime, try to enjoy it!" Sophie patted my knee. "I know I am."

"She even met the queen of England," said La Perricholi from the front driver's seat. "Welcome back, Boy. Let's get you home."

"Home," I echoed. I wasn't even sure what that felt like anymore.

THE VILLA DIODATI and its surrounding grounds looked exactly the same as before. Except instead of fall, it was now spring. New leaves were budding on the trees and flowers sprouted everywhere. Well, there were a few other differences. Like the dryads running through the woods, naiads in the lake, sprites flitting from flower to flower, and a gigantic dragon perched on the roof.

As soon as we parked, the Dragon Lady dropped down to the ground next to us.

"Welcome home, little patchwork monster," she said. She had a thick scar that ran diagonally across her face, and a few patches of scales that looked like they were still healing, but otherwise she seemed fine.

"It's great to see you." I remembered the Sphinx's final moments, getting napalmed. His screams echoed in my head. "I'm sorry about the Sphinx."

She bowed her head slightly. "Thank you. He is finally at peace now." She inclined her head toward the door. "We can talk more another time. I do not wish to keep you. There are people inside very eager to see you."

I stumped up the front steps. When I opened the door, I saw William, Elisa, Giselle, and Henri all sitting in the living room. And right in the middle of them sat my mother. It was so strange to see her there, tall and thin, with her shock of black-and-white hair, amidst the antique furniture and finely dressed humans. For once her expression of perpetual vague surprise looked completely appropriate to the situation.

As soon as she saw me, she hurried over and started fussing.

"You did not take care of this arm. You were too rough on this leg. These robotic parts are too delicate for you. I think we should go back to flesh. But you don't take care of that, either. Have you been eating? You look too thin."

"Okay, Mom, okay," I said, and pulled her into a one-armed hug until she quieted down.

"Group hug!" said Henri as he came and embraced both of us.

William, Elisa, and Giselle also came over. Giselle looked almost in awe of my mother. William and Elisa seemed more shell-shocked. I supposed when that many monsters move onto your property at once, it might be a little overwhelming.

"It's great to see you all," I said to them.

I looked around and realized that this was my family now. My father's dream had come true. I wished he could have been a part of it. His loss had become a quiet little hollow in my chest that I'd grown accustomed to. But now and then at moments like this, it seemed to open back up into that dark chasm of emptiness again.

My mom turned to me then, and I wondered if she was feeling the same way. She put her hand on my shoulder and nodded.

"He would be so proud of you," she said. "He would not want the sadness of his loss to ruin this for you."

I nodded. No promises, but I would try not to let it.

---

THAT NIGHT I sat out on the front porch overlooking the lake, drinking wine with Sophie, Henri, and La Perricholi.

"I hope those naiads are safe with that freshwater mermaid," I said.

"They say they've sorted it all out," said Sophie. "Apparently, you did quite a number on her. She was still pretty injured when they arrived and they've been nursing her back to health."

"So Villa Diodati is basically like a monster haven then?" I asked.

"Well, we have the space," said Henri. "And with monsters in the family, how could my parents say no? Of course, there are also my ladies to consider."

"How's that going?" I asked.

He smiled that old, crooked Henri grin. "It's spring. They keep me busy."

"Are we going to see a bunch of Henri-faced dryads in the near future?" asked Sophie.

"No idea how it works, honestly. But I hope so."

"You, of all people, wanting to be a dad," I said.

His smile faded. "There was so much loss, Boy. So much death. I feel . . . I feel like there should be something added. New life. You know?"

"I do."

Sophie held up her glass. "To life."

We clinked glasses, and then there was a moment of silence as we drank. Then I turned to La Perricholi. "What about you? Gonna stick around?"

She shook her head. "I need to get back to Lima. Maria and Laurellen are up to their necks in rabbit people. I also want to take another trip out to Noble's Isle and see who and what remains there. If anything."

"Good call," I said. "The last thing we need is for some Moreau wannabe to get ahold of all his research. What happened to the wild monsters he released from The Commune?"

"Ruthven, Liel, and the rest of the trowe are working with Montgomery to hunt down the stragglers," said La Perricholi. "It's going so well, I'm starting to wonder if Montgomery doesn't envision turning Ruthven and the trowe into some sort of official special forces unit."

"Is that a good thing?" I asked.

"A little legitimacy couldn't hurt," she said.

"What about you?" I asked Sophie. "You planning to stick around or are you going back to LA?"

"There isn't really a reason to go back," said Sophie sadly. "That hiatus Kemp put The Studio on before he defected seems more or less permanent. I haven't heard from any of them since all of this began." Then she smiled mischievously and leaned in close. "Besides, I thought I'd like to spend a bit of time with you. Seeing as how I just saved your life and all, I'd say you owe me."

"Fair enough," I said, cupping her chin in my hand.

"We should probably give them a bit of privacy," La Perricholi said to Henri as she stood up. "Let's go see if your parents and the Bride have opened that champagne yet."

"Good idea," said Henri, and followed her inside.

Sophie and I sat there for a while, the sound of insects, frogs, and sprites faintly calling in the background. Sophie put her head on my shoulder, and we stared out at the lake that glittered with moonlight as the winds came down from the mountains and rippled the surface.

"So, I never got to hear your side of it," I said. "Why did you try to give Claire your life?"

"Because she needed it to beat Stephen."

"But what about you?"

She shrugged.

"Didn't you realize that she wouldn't want that? That . . . I wouldn't want that?"

"I dunno. I thought you'd both get along better without me."

I sat up and looked at her. "Wait, what?"

She sighed and closed her eyes. "Must we talk about this right now?"

"Yes, we must. Sophie, how could you ever think I would get along better without you?"

"You guys have your little bickering old couple thing. And she's always there to save you and be all heroic. What do I do except make jokes and fritter on about nonsense? I'm useless."

"Sophie." I moved my locked metal leg and awkwardly got down on the ground in front of her. I took her small, pale freckled hands in mine. "Remember when I almost killed the dryads? Liel and Claire couldn't stop me. But all you had to do was call my name. And what about when we were at The Show after the raid and I was totally freaking out? Claire said, 'I think you need some Sophie time.' And God, I really did. I don't know how I would have continued on if you hadn't been there."

I kissed her hands and looked up into those bright eyes of hers. "Sophie Jekyll, you have saved me every day since the moment I met you."

"Oh." She took in a deep, shuddering breath. "You . . . are getting dangerously good at sweet-talking me." Then she leaned forward and pressed her lips against mine. I had missed their softness so much. That's when I realized: this was what home felt like.

Eventually, Sophie whispered in my ear, "We should probably go inside and spend some more time with everyone before it gets too late. I know your mum wanted to start fixing you up first thing in the morning."

"Yeah, okay," I said. "Give me a minute. I'll be right behind you."

She leaned over and gently kissed my forehead. She turned to go inside, then stopped.

"You do remember your promise, don't you?"

"Uh . . ."

"Remember in Philadelphia? At The Museum, you promised me that when this was all over, we'd go somewhere warm and tropical."

"Oh, yeah."

"Well, once your mother's got you all sorted, I think perhaps the Bahamas or somewhere like that would be the perfect place for us to recover. Don't you?"

I smiled. "Sure."

She nodded, satisfied, and went inside.

I sat there for a moment, listening to the wind and watching the lake. Finally, I pulled out the new phone Henri had given me.

"Hey, Vi," I said.

"Yes, Boy?"

"Remember when I said that you and I were going to change the world?"

"Yes. I take it . . . this was not what you had in mind."

I don't know why that struck me as funny, but I let out a laugh. Then, to my amazement, Vi laughed, too. She had this goofy, high titter that made me laugh even more: a big snorting burst that then made *her* laugh even harder. I laughed so hard there were tears streaming down my cheeks.

Finally, we calmed down and everything was quiet.

"Boy?" said Vi. "What's going to happen to us?"

"Apparently, we're going to the Bahamas."

"I mean after that? Do you think the humans will really let us be equals?"

"I don't know," I said. "But let's not worry about it tonight. Let's just go inside and be with our family."

"Our family," said Vi. "Yes."

I slowly got to my feet and clumped into the Villa Diodati, where the warm, rich sounds of conversation and laughter waited for us.

# Acknowledgements

THIS BOOK REQUIRED a great deal of research in a fairly short amount of time, and I couldn't have done it without help. Thanks to Elise Bernardoni at the National Zoological Park for her extensive knowledge of wild animals and her patience with my often strange questions. Thanks to Esther Langan at the National Museum of Natural History for giving me a tour of her necropsy lab, letting me hold an elephant heart, and explaining to me in detail how to remove a skullcap. Thanks to Alejandra Guerra Morales and Roberta Valderrama for their insight on Peru and its culture. Thanks to my brother, Chris Skovron, for the French translations. Thanks to Brian Selznick for convincing me to visit the Mütter Museum, which served as the inspiration for the Selznick Museum of Comparative Anatomy and Teratology that appears in this book. Thanks to Diana Peterfreund for being such a great sounding board throughout the writing process, and to Malinda Lo for her keen-eyed revision notes. As always, thanks to my agent, Jill Grinberg, and her assistant, Katelyn Detweiler, who provided tireless support and enthusiasm. And to my editor,

Kendra Levin, who continues to champion my work with a fierceness that leaves me awestruck and grateful.

In the same way that Mary Shelley's life and works informed *Man Made Boy*, this book owes a great debt to the life and works of Herbert George Wells. Not only for his novels *The Island of Doctor Moreau* and *The Invisible Man*, but also for his essays on war, politics, and society. Additionally, I owe a debt to Zora Neale Hurston, whose *Tell My Horse: Voodoo and Life in Haiti and Jamaica* had an incalculable impact on me even beyond the obvious scope of zombie lore. Lastly, I would be remiss without mentioning that the original La Perricholi was a real person named Maria Micaela Villegas Hurtado, who lived from 1748 to 1819 and has since inspired folktales, songs, operas, plays, telenovelas, and novels both in Peru and around the world.

8/15, 11/17